I0615820

CARL KYLER

THE WAY TO
FREEDOM
PART I
GOLDEN CRISIS

Whatever their future, at the dawn of their lives, men seek a noble vision of man's nature and of life's potential.
Ayn Rand

Only puny secrets need protection. Big discoveries are protected by public incredulity.
Marshall McLuhan

A Golden Vision Media LLC book

Copyright © Carl Kyler 2011

Publisher:
Golden Vision Media LLC
Route des Arsenaux 41
1705 – FRIBOURG
SWITZERLAND

ISBN: 2970072300
ISBN-13: 9782970072300

To Maya,
who made it to the world just before this book did

Acknowledgements

I am indebted to the following persons who provided precious help.
I thank each of you sincerely:

- **Ola,** for your help in challenging and refining the overall plot and the characters, and for reading the very first manuscript, and then reading again later versions. For the priceless gift of free and unlimited advice from a former McKinsey consultant, offered to me even though you are a CEO and father of four, with very little time to waste.
- **Martin,** for your many creative, far-reaching and sometimes challenging suggestions, and for a precious point of view from Asia. For comforting me in the conviction that this novel series is important, and that it must be made as good as is humanly possible.
- **Daniel,** for your valuable comments on early versions, and for liking the manuscript enough to read it with a flashlight while catering to baby twins.
- **Anders,** for helping me to make the complex easy and clear. Something you wouldn't understand, no one else would understand either.
- **Christer,** for your two rounds of both attentive and creative copy editing which transformed the text and the plot details into something I couldn't further improve.
- **Wendy Jo**, for your valuable final round of copy editing.
- **Erik**, for your crucial edits to the very last version.
- **Astrid**, for your kind understanding and support of this project which I undertook at a time when we had so many other important things to do.

I am also grateful to a few leading figures in the history of social sciences, whose work I consider of great importance and value, and without which this novel series would have been impossible to write. Knowing I omit others who deserve mention, I thank those who provided me with the most inspiration: philosophers Aristotle and Ayn Rand, and economists Adam Smith, Ludwig von Mises, Murray Rothbard and George Reisman.

/Carl Kyler

CONTENTS

CHAPTER 1:
Lesson not Learned

"Professor, you know what I sometimes dream about?" Mark Lomack said from behind his long and curly hair that covered much of his face. The words echoed across the classroom, which was almost empty.

"No, what?" Professor Montgomery Benson replied with a curious smile.

"That everybody in the world could learn the lessons about economics you teach us!"

Skeptical but interested, Benson remarked, "How?"

"Until last year's stock market crash, we have seen so many Internet ventures of all sorts. People think that they must be about commerce, about content, or about community. I would like to create one that combines all three. And it would be about the link between individual freedom and the kind of money we use in our society!"

Benson smiled with admiration at his pupil, but as other students were filling the classroom for his lecture to start, he just patted Mark on the back. "If I was a venture capitalist with enough money, I would finance you on the spot. But I'm not, so for now, please learn this course well. It will help you in the future if you ever set out to do what you just said!"

Professor Benson closed the door of the classroom and turned to address his students, appearing not as a teacher but as an inspiring storyteller.

"In nineteen fourteen, many of the world's major countries were preparing to go to war. As most wars in human history, this war was not launched by the will of the different populations to annihilate each other. It was launched by rulers and governments wishing to extend their spheres of influence. However, to launch a war requires enormous materials means: weapons, food, vehicles, buildings, communication infrastructure, to name just a few items. So how did these rulers go about to raise the money needed to start and run their war? The basic option, which had been used for smaller war campaigns during the previous century, was to increase taxes in order to raise the needed money. But in this war, that would prove not to be enough.

"So in what other way could governments get hold on the wealth of their own population, in order to spend it in the war effort? To rob their population was not an option. It would have meant waging a war inside the country just to be able to finance and prepare an external war. Instead, governments in most of the warring countries did something much easier. They printed money bills to roughly double the quantity of paper-money bills in the economy. And they kept all this new money to be used for war spending!

"Technically, this had the exact same effect as if governments had robbed each household of half of all its wealth! It also meant that they left the gold standard. To do that, their governments or central banks ceased redeeming money bills against gold at previous rates. This in turn was a form of implicit bankruptcy for these governments. If you hear people say today that governments can never go bankrupt, I underscore that the World War One period was not the first, and probably will not be the last, occasion of government bankruptcy."

Professor Benson put away the piece of chalk he had been holding in his hand. He glanced out over the classroom where the twenty-five college students of his Economic History course were sitting spellbound, having listened in total silence to this introduction to the Monetary History class.

Professor Benson was fifty-six-years old, and only recently had he been losing some of his dark brown hair, and it was still combed backward across his head. His haircut made him look younger than he was, all the more since he was tall and held his head straight at all times above an agile and fit body. His eyes were dark green and captivated the person he talked to during a whole conversation.

Professor Benson had spent his life learning and teaching economics. It was his major passion in life, along with hiking in the mountains close to the university in San Francisco where he worked. In the academic profession of economists, he was considered an outcast. That status came from his disagreement with many of the economic theories that generally were used by politicians, central bank people, and by the economists who wished to be useful to these two groups. He had accepted this situation and brushed away remarks on his outcast status, "Well, it's not my fault that today's economists and Nobel Prize laureates have missed out on a lot of essential insights from the Scottish and English thinkers who developed our profession in the eighteenth and nineteenth centuries. Let them believe that consumption can precede production or that true lending doesn't require prior savings. I prefer to have my most intelligent students tell me that my teachings make sense. That means a lot more than any official recognition or prize I could have achieved by repeating such nonsense about economics as we unfortunately hear way too often, and from people who should know better."

When Benson was young, he had an economics teacher who had immigrated to the United States from the Soviet Union, thus escaping to find a safe haven in the free world. When he arrived in the Unites States, he had not expected to live all his life there as an outcast. He had become an outcast because he was an uncompromising defender of the American, and universal, value of individual freedom. That belief had not been popular at a time when the trend in society was toward ever more government intervention. But Benson's teacher had been untouched by the loneliness coming from this status. He had gone on with his scholarly work, which had resulted in one of the most impressive set of publications ever produced by any economist. Instead of turning inward on himself in this situation, he had done as Benson now did: he had looked for the brightest and most motivated among his students to take under his wings. Beyond formal courses, Benson's teacher had invited a group of students every week to his own home. They spent evenings and nights on additional courses and discussions on economics. In those late-night sessions, the young Montgomery Benson had learned the most, and had decided that economics would be his life from then on.

The Economic History course he now was delivering was one he always much enjoyed since it allowed for the sharing of vastly important insights about recent history with the students. Such insights were often absent in or contradicted by mainstream history and economic history classes. Now, at the start of the first lecture of the course, Benson was quite satisfied with the level of attention he had captured from his young audience.

Addressing his students, he said, "Now let's imagine for a second that the world's main countries had remained on an unchanged gold standard monetary system up to our days, without a government-backed central bank. Could you please name at least four disastrous events of the twentieth century which may not have occurred, or at the worst, would have taken place on a much smaller scale?"

The tall and thin Mark Lomack raised his hand, and after receiving a nod of approval from Benson, answered. "World War One, World War Two, the Great Depression, and the more recent Internet bubble, or so-called dot-com, crash of last year."

"Excellent, Mark," Benson said. "So you understand why I urge you to reserve some suspicion for the numerous people who claim that the disappearance of gold money and of unregulated commercial banks was a good thing. Or that their replacement by government controlled paper bills and a central banking cartel system has represented a rational progress of our civilization!

"This Economic History course will show that the opposite of these statements is true. We will see how the interdiction and suppression of commodity money and the government controlled monetary system that replaced it made possible and contributed to some of the worst disasters of the twentieth century! And we will also see that it's quite possible that it may provoke even worse disasters during the century which is now starting. Seen another way, we can judge the importance of economics by the issues at stake. And we can judge the importance of money in particular, to our whole civilization, and to how this civilization will develop or regress.

"Is there anyone among you who feels like changing the world in order to make it a better place? Then I urge you to put all other things aside and focus on sound economics! It's as rare today in society as is gold in the current financial system! And money is one of the topics most desperately in need of new ideas, or of reestablishing true old ideas!"

"Professor, you may be right about all that," said Jessica Frostby, a tall blond girl, known for straight talking and sharp thinking. "But as you often remind us, we should start by stating the definitions of the concepts we talk about. So could you please define precisely what we should understand by 'money' and how it developed in human society?"

"Good remark, Jessica. I will obviously state all the required definitions," Benson said with amusement and without any hint of irony or anger. "I will even take the opportunity to teach this last course before your graduation in a new and different manner. This course has two objectives. The first is to learn a number of historical facts about money, banking, and business cycles. That is something *I* will present to you. The second objective is to use all your basic knowledge in economics to analyze and make sense of these historical facts. That is something *you* should achieve by your own thinking!

"In order to combine these two approaches, this course will proceed in what I call the Q-and-A mode. I will advance the course by providing some background, and then I will ask you questions. Your answers to these questions will then help push the lecture forward. And if you think that the information I provide is insufficient for you to answer, which I will sometimes let it be on purpose, then *you* can ask *me* questions, and then *my* answers will take us forward. Are you ready?" he said, glancing around the room and receiving in return a mix of hesitant acceptance and enthusiastic approval.

Quite content with this response, Benson continued after a brief pause, exclaiming as he walked around the room holding a marker in his right hand, "So let's dive into it!"

He went on, sitting on the corner of a table, "It is often believed that the end of the twentieth century and the start of the twenty-first century was the first period when international economic exchange was important. Supposedly, it didn't appear on a large scale before rapid and cheap international travel and transportation were available in our modern times. But that's not true! In fact, international trade, measured as the share of economic transactions made with foreigners, was as high, or higher, during the second half of the nineteenth century, and during the first decade of the twentieth century. What made that possible?

"The short answer is money, more specifically the existence of a single monetary unit used and accepted across the whole civilized world. That money was gold. It had established itself over several centuries, by the free decisions of individual people and traders, as the best money possible.

"What, really, is money? Money is a medium of exchange, something that, first of all, is desirable and valuable for its own sake. But it becomes a medium of exchange when people feel sure they can sell it to other people, and this enables them to use it to get any other goods they may want and can pay for. The 'marketability' of goods depends on several criteria. Can someone imagine what they would be?" Benson asked.

After some reflection, Mark Lomack answered. "Well, I guess it has to be widely demanded by many people. And it's good if it's durable over time and

4

can be carried around easily—small weights but high value. We need to be able to divide it into small units."

"Not a bad answer," Benson said. "So what corresponds to this description?"

"Precious metals, like gold and silver!" Mark answered.

Benson replied, "Exactly! So you see why gold, and often silver for smaller amounts, have been established over several centuries as money on the free market. So that's what money *is*. But even more important is what money *makes possible*. That's what we call indirect exchange or more simply: an advanced economy where people specialize in what they do best. They sell their products or services for money and then buy everything else they need for that money. Let's stop for ten seconds to imagine what life would be like in a world without money. How would you go about to get a piece of bread, a piece of meat, and a bottle of milk, if you couldn't buy them for money in a retail store? Jessica?"

Jessica answered, "Well, I guess I would have to trade things directly with each of the people who supply those things. So I would need to have something for the butcher, to get meat, and for the baker, to get bread. And something for the farmer, to get the milk."

"Right, that's it," Benson commented. "This is what we call bartering. That's how trade worked in the world before there was money. You see that such an economy could only remain on a primitive level, with trade done in a small scale and in small geographic areas. Since nobody could specialize in anything in particular, that kind of economy would hardly go above a stage where every family is working as self-sufficient farmers and hunters. *That* is how important money is to human civilization!"

After pausing to let his audience absorb his previous words, Benson continued. "At the point, when everybody in society needed money, the banking business was born. Initially, two types of banking emerged independently. The first was deposit banking, storing money safely on behalf of its owners. The second was loan banking, lending money to people who promised to pay it back later with interest. Over time, these two activities often were combined, so that banks would both receive deposits and savings and lend money.

"This mix was, and is, a dangerous thing. Why? Because demand deposits, or money on a transactional account, if you prefer, are supposed to be available to the owner on demand for withdrawal or for making payments. But when money on a transactional account isn't being used by its owner, it's tempting for banks to lend it out. If they do, we call that *fractional reserve banking*. Can someone tell me what kind of problem this practice could lead to?"

Mark bent forward and answered when Benson nodded in his direction. "I guess if the money is spent at the same time by the person who borrowed it and by the owner, then the bank won't be able to honor both transactions. Except of course if it uses someone else's money to do that."

"That's a good answer, Mark. If such lending is done on a large scale and the clients of a bank find out about it and come to take their money out of a bank all at the same time, we call it a *bank run*. That has happened in history as a consequence of fractional reserve lending. A bank that was the target of a run would of course go bankrupt."

A boy next to Mark looked confused and asked, "But you're saying banks are not allowed to lend out deposited money? I thought that was the basis of the banking business: to lend out money against interest."

Benson nodded with understanding. "You're right, if we talk about so-called savings deposits, or time deposits. Here, banks lend out money that the owner has accepted *not* to use for a period. So during that period, the person who borrows it is the only one who can use the money. So, yes, you're right; banks can lend out virtually one hundred percent of savings or time deposits. But demand deposits, money on a transactional account, are given to the bank just for safekeeping. The owner can use it for payments anytime, on demand! So the money must always be available. If such money is lent out, then it means several people may want to use it at the same time. And the lending itself would lead to creating more money, which actually doesn't exist! So properly, that should not be allowed, and banks should have one hundred percent reserves against demand deposits."

The boy nodded in understanding. Then Benson went on. "Now, as banking emerged on the market, banks were at first like any other business enterprise on the free market. The monetary and banking system we have today is radically different from that. The easiest way to grasp how money and banking ceased to be normal private businesses is to look at the creation of central banks, such as the Federal Reserve Bank in the United States. What is a central bank? In most countries, it's essentially a government-backed cartel of private banks, with a monopoly to create money and to regulate the whole banking industry. Does anybody know how and why it was created? If we take the case of the Federal Reserve in the United States?"

A girl on the second row answered. "If I remember correctly, I heard in high school that the Fed was created to put an end to crises in the private banking system and to smooth business cycles by lending to banks when they were squeezed."

Benson looked at her gently, shaking his head. "Yes, I think you remember it correctly, because that is the fairytale version of the origin of the Fed, which is taught to the children of our country. The tale lets people sleep well at night, thinking that the Fed is there to protect our financial system from any trouble!

"Now, the truth of the matter is that the Fed, like most foreign central banks, is a cartel of private banks that was actually forced upon the country by the banks themselves. They claimed that they and their customers needed protection against bank bankruptcy. What they really wanted was the ability to lend more money and faster, without the risk of going bankrupt.

But the government also had a strong interest in the creation of the Fed. It was the perfect opportunity to replace gold money with simple paper bills. From then on, the crucial control over the monetary unit went from the free market into the hands of government. This was done through so-called Legal Tender Laws, stipulating that paper bills are money and that gold money is forbidden. Money creation could then be done at any pace the government and the central bank wanted. But a second layer of money inflation comes from what I mentioned just before, so-called fractional reserve lending. It was legalized by central banks and governments, although it can be considered fraudulent to let several people use or borrow the same money. Properly, banks should hold one hundred percent of reserves against demand deposits, but from this point on, they would never do that again.

"Legalizing this activity enabled banks to give out much more credit and make much faster profits. But such a bank is inherently insolvent and may go bust as soon as depositors come to claim their money in some numbers. So this increased the number of bank runs and bank bankruptcies, instead of reducing them. Then, instead of forbidding fractional reserve banking, the central banks and bank interest groups pushed through additional safety nets for banks. Has anyone heard of the features that were introduced in the United States in the beginning of the twentieth century?"

When no one volunteered to answer, Benson picked up a marker to note the name of the features on a whiteboard, as he spoke. "One example is the role of the central bank as *lender of last resort* to any bank in trouble. If that was not enough to save a bank then the central bank could authorize a bank to *suspend specie payments*. That means refusing to pay out money to depositors but still continue in business! The final invention was so called *deposit insurance*. It means that if a bank goes bankrupt in spite of the features I just mentioned, then government will print enough new money to refund depositors! Today, people never question whether central banks should exist, or ask what the consequences of their actions really are. Let's stop for a moment to challenge the generally accepted idea that central banking provides for a rational and fair financial system. We will do it by imagining the consequences if similar features were applied in another line of business. Let's pick the example of real estate management. It will work as follows: I'll distribute seven cards among you. One person will read the text on each card that describes an imaginary situation in real estate management. And the rest of you will tell us what feature of modern central banking this corresponds to. The answer is written on the back of each card. So, here we go!"

Benson distributed the cards. Upon a sign from him, a person on the front row read the first card. "The country was built by free men and women who came here to live their lives. Most of them also built their own houses. But then it was decided that only one firm in the country was allowed to build houses."

"I guess that's the so-called minting monopoly, saying that only government is allowed to create money," a girl answered.

"Good," Benson said. "Next!"

Mark read the second card. "The firm with a national monopoly to build real estate sells an apartment with a surface of one thousand square feet. But when the owner moves in, the surface is only nine hundred square feet."

The class remained silent for a while, so Benson said, "All right, I'll help you with this one. The answer is legalization of debasement, or of the right to arbitrarily change the basic unit of counting. This is legalization of fraud, if you prefer. That situation is comparable to printing paper money: when government increases the money quantity by ten percent, then ten dollars will only purchase what nine dollars did just before that. Of course, the difference is that in central banking, it is allowed while, in our real estate example, the builder would go to jail already at this point. But let's assume he doesn't and stays in business. Next card!"

Jessica read the third card. "An owner of a one-thousand-square-foot flat gives his second set of keys to a real estate agent just to safeguard them, but the owner warns the real estate agent that he may pop in to sleep there any time. In spite of this, the real estate agent rents ninety percent of the apartment to someone else, who rents ninety percent of his part to someone else, and so on, and so on. After a large number of additional rentals, we end up with a situation where there is still just one one-thousand-square-foot apartment, but ten thousand square feet have been rented. What would this be called?"

"Fractional reserve rental," Mark said with a grin.

As the class burst out laughing, Benson commented, "That's a good one Mark, and you're quite correct. This is what the fractional reserve principle would look like in real estate. And as soon as more than one person at a time would want to use the flat, there would be a serious problem. Just as if two people wish to withdraw or pay with the same amount of money lent out several times through fractional reserve lending. The fact that people use their flats more often than the money in their deposit account doesn't take away the fact that we have an absurd and dangerous situation here in the banking system. Fractional reserve lending artificially creates new money, and penalizes people who save, as their money loses in purchasing power. The real estate example would have the same effect on apartment owners, as the market price for rental would fall, due to an artificial supply of rental surface, which actually does not exist. Next card!"

A short girl with short, dark hair and pale skin named Laura Dalaghan read the fourth card. "The real estate agent goes bust after his risky rental setup. He is bailed out by government."

"Lender of last resort!" Jessica said.

"Correct!" said Benson. "Next card."

A short boy with his hair combed back and a strong tan, named Pete Bagnelli, read the fifth card. "The maverick real estate agent refuses to give the keys back to the owner, who has lost the other set of keys. Unable to come into his flat, he sues the real estate agent. But the court confirms the right of the real estate agent not to give those keys back, but to still stay in business. What is this called?"

"Legalizing stealing," Laura Dalaghan said. "Or, more prosaically, Suspension of Specie Payment."

"Two out of two points, Laura," Benson said with a suppressed laughter. "Next card!"

Bobby Cheston, a tall, impressive boy with a crew cut read the sixth card. "In the court of appeals, the defrauded apartment owner obtains the right to a new apartment. Since the one he used to own can't be redeemed, the government expropriates another apartment to give to him."

"Deposit insurance," Pete Bagnelli answered casually. "Although the example is a bit skewed, since deposit insurance implies diluting the purchasing power of existing money by creating new money."

"Really good point, Pete," Benson said. "If I take your remark one step further, the true equivalent of deposit insurance in our real estate story would be for government to remove a very small fraction of all apartments in the country and to assemble them to a new apartment for the defrauded man. This, of course, wouldn't be perceptible to the owners of those apartments each time it occurred. But after a large number of such imperceptible reductions of their living spaces, they might end up with half of their initial living space! *That* is the way piecemeal expansion of the money supply dilutes the purchasing power of people's money, without anyone recognizing what's going on. But let's now hear the last card, which talks about the most unbelievable feature of modern banking."

Pete read the last card. "After some time of government monopoly on building and selling real estate, the government decides it doesn't actually need to deliver a real house to a buyer. The only thing the buyer is sure to get is a prospectus with the photo of the house."

The group again looked confused, and Benson gave them the answer. "Don't you see? *This* is what happened when the link to gold was taken away, when paper money came to be considered as money itself and not only as a warehouse receipt to gold. Imagine what such a rule would do in the real estate market if people were forced to value pieces of paper as if they were real houses! Now you may understand why it's impossible for central banks to refuse the temptation to do something as easy as print paper bills when people are forced to accept it as valuable money, even though it's just paper!"

Benson walked around the room and collected the cards. "If people realized that the actual consequences of central banks and of our current monetary system are just as absurd as our imaginary real estate example, one would expect public outcry putting an end to it all quickly. This is probably why the introduction of these measures and the creation of central banks as such were done gradually, over an extended period in the late nineteenth century and early twentieth century. In order to push it through, the banks and the government needed unprecedented efforts of propaganda to conceal the actual meaning of what was being done! Unfortunately, many large groups in our society are liable to suffer strongly from this system, be they savers, investors, or regular wage earners. This is because it leads to dilution of the value of savings, and also generates business cycles."

"All this seems clear," Laura remarked. "You've explained how money and banks emerged in society, and how bank cartels and government started meddling seriously with the free market. But historically, what really happened to make you claim that changing the monetary system facilitated war or provoked the Great Depression, or the dot-com crash?"

"This brings me back to my introduction," Benson answered. "Early in the twentieth century, government-backed central banks, money creation monopoly, and a few other features had existed for some time in Europe and were about to be introduced in the United States. But a crucial change appeared in the situation I mentioned during World War One. That was when governments broke the link between the underlying value, gold, and the bills used for monetary transactions. What those warring governments did, and what Germany and others kept on doing during the nineteen twenties, was in fact counterfeiting the monetary base. They did it by printing paper-money bills beyond the quantity of gold that backed it.

"And from nineteen thirty-four on, the U.S. government logically forbade private individuals from owning gold and stopped redeeming bills against gold. They then declared dollar paper bills to be the sole money. They made an exception for foreign central banks that could still redeem dollars in gold. When paper money replaced gold as the base of the monetary system, it became possible to easily inflate the supply of money. It became easy because they no longer had the obligation of supplying the corresponding amount of gold. *This* is mainly how governments financed World War Two.

"After World War Two, a limited link to gold was reintroduced, under the so-called Bretton Woods system, which was maintained until nineteen seventy-three. That link, even though limited, was important. It actually constrained the possibility for the central bank to print dollar bills above the rate of production of gold. Notably, from nineteen thirty-three to nineteen seventy-three, the dollar price of an ounce of gold remained at thirty-five dollars.

"From nineteen seventy-three to the end of the twentieth century, that price skyrocketed up to almost one thousand dollars! This indicates that the quantity of money in the economy has roughly been multiplied by thirty, in less than thirty years. Now, printing of dollar bills by the Federal Reserve isn't the only cause of the increase of the quantity of money. As I explained, commercial banks can extend credit with a multiplier of around fifteen on the increase of the base money they hold as reserves, by fractional reserve lending."

"OK, I see that cutting the link with gold has made it possible to increase the quantity of money much faster than before, but what's the actual damage from that?" asked Bobby Cheston.

"In the example of World War One," Benson replied, "the inflation meant a transfer of wealth from the population to the government. The government then used it to finance war. The Second World War was financed in a quite similar fashion. The general issue is that when money is created artificially, whether by printing bills or by fractional reserve lending, this always reduces the purchasing power of the existing money, thereby the value of what people had saved also falls. So the first major problem with monetary inflation is that it penalizes people who save and it favors people who borrow and get the new money cheaply."

Benson paused, then turned back to his students and exclaimed, as if to imprint forever his next phrase in his students' memory, "The second major problem is that monetary inflation generates business cycles. Look closer at any boom-and-bust cycle, be it the Great Depression or the recent Internet bubble and crash. You will always find the combination of the following features, in the boom part of the cycle: low interest rates, rapid creation of money, and a lot of lending. This fuels an increase in debt and creates spirals of increase in asset and stock prices. This is because corporate profits increase at the same time as people have more money to buy stocks. Now, can anyone say what usually puts an end to an economic boom? Just think of the recent Internet Bubble, and you'll have the answer."

"Well," Laura said, "at some point, the Central Bank must start to increase interest rates. That probably happens when price increases in stocks start to spill over on consumer products. I guess that it also happens when people believe they're getting rich from gains on the stock market and want to spend some of that money on consumption. Also, I guess it comes to a point when many ventures people have put money into turn out to make losses. At least that was what we saw recently for many of those dot-com ventures."

When she stopped, Benson took over. "Quite correct. And we could add a couple of steps after that of loss-making ventures. The next step would be that more and more people default on their loans. Then they have to sell off assets to pay back debt. And if they had bought assets with almost only borrowed money, they may go bankrupt. And if too many people go bankrupt, then their *banks* may do that too!

"But now, let's assume the Central Bank doesn't accept to slow down the economy to stop the boom. So it would keep lowering the interest rate still further or making it even easier to borrow in other ways. Then the quantity of money would increase faster and faster. In such a situation, if the public comes to expect prices to rise faster and faster, then this expectation can have a self-reinforcing effect on prices. People will try to get rid of their money as fast as they can to buy goods before prices increase even more. As I told you, a bank run is when large numbers of people draw their cash out of banks. This only leads to bidding up the prices even faster!

"As people draw their cash out of banks to spend it, the Central Bank will have to keep printing more and more money to avoid the collapse of the banking system. This makes prices increase even more and even faster. At this point, things can go out of control, resulting in what we call *hyperinflation*. That has happened for example in Germany during the nineteen twenties. It leads to the breakdown of the monetary unit and to the bankruptcy of all commercial banks. In such as situation, whatever quantity of paper money is printed, everybody just wants to get rid of it. They buy any durable goods they can find, and no one puts any money in a bank anymore."

The next question came from Pete. He was leaning back, weighing on his chair and looking quite nonchalant, dressed in white chinos and a white summer shirt. However, he had listened carefully all along, and now remarked, "Professor, this discussion took less than thirty minutes. And without having gone into the details of monetary theory and the theory of business cycles, I think it makes a lot of sense. My only question at this point is about your suggestion that today's decision makers don't recognize these ideas. If we could understand and learn our lesson in one hour, how come the supposedly smartest people in the country, the political and central banking decision makers ignore much of these basic ideas?"

Benson looked at Pete, and then around the classroom, and thought a moment before saying, "I won't be able to answer your question fully, because it touches on a lot of aspects of politics, human psychology, and even fundamental philosophy and ethics. So I'll avoid the *why* behind your question and focus on the *how*.

"For example, take the chairman of the Federal Reserve Bank, the person I consider most directly responsible for the process of inflation I just described. This process was behind the recent dot-com boom and bust. It enabled vast amounts of credit to projects many of which recently proved to have been loss-making ventures. Over a five- to six-year period, rapid inflows of money to the stock market made for the bidding up of stock prices. That speculation was actually fueled by the Central Bank chief himself, who claimed in the middle of the boom that the dot-com era was a 'new economy' era. He claimed that we could expect uninterrupted growth combined high profits with little price inflation, thanks to permanent high productivity gains enabled by new technology. In this way, he shut out the alarms so that observers didn't question the sustainability of rapid credit expansion.

"Not much later, he claimed that to the extent that there were excessive rallies on the stock market, they were to be attributed to the 'irrational exuberance' of investors. Worse, after the bubble burst, he recently went a step further, attributing the collapse of the bubble to 'infectious greed' of business-men and investors. If you look at the mass media analysis of the stock market crash, they explained it mainly by the existence of stock options.

"Now, it's true that stock options can yield undeserved revenues to their holders in a context of rapid credit expansion where profits boom artificially. It's true about all profits on the market at such a time, not just those related to stock options! However, contrary to the 'new economy' suggestion of the Fed chairman, it's impossible for such a situation to last. As I explained before, the end of the boom had to come when the access to easy credit slowed down, to avoid hyperinflation. I even heard another so called explanation to the Internet crash from the Fed chairman. He claimed that *too much savings* flowing into the United States from abroad had caused it.

"I won't go into details, but I leave you to reflect on the absurdity of claim-ing that a crisis of *too much debt* was caused by *too much savings*. The truth is that the overall ratio of debt to savings increased a lot, largely due to fractional reserve lending, which consists in lending money which didn't exist before."

Benson took a breath before he continued. "So that was a recent example of a powerful person denying basic truths about economics. A more widespread and even more serious issue is the way the Great Depression is explained in history textbooks and in many economics courses. Let's look at what hap-pened back then, when the access to credit was restrained, just as it was at the end of the Internet bubble. From then on, we see the reverse of the 'bull market' process. Instead of increasing profits compounded with increasing demand for stocks accelerating the rally, we see falling profits compounded with decreasing demand for stocks driving down stock prices just as fast. Back in the early thirties, the fall was steeper than during the Internet bubble, so we had widespread bankruptcies and *insolvency of banks*. That can happen when many of their clients default. As I said, bank defaults create a strong deflation-ary spiral as the money previously lent out by banks cease to exist when those banks disappear.

"*That* is what happened in the Great Depression of nineteen twenty-nine. And the reason why it generated mass unemployment in the following years was quite simple, although you've probably heard a lot of other flawed expla-nations of this. Unemployment didn't appear because there no longer was any useful work to do—there *always is* as long as people are alive! It appeared because prices, notably wage rates, weren't allowed to fall as much as the fall in the quantity of money would have made them fall, in the absence of price and wage regulations. You are certainly aware that the vast majority of commentators, as most history textbooks in our country, attribute the Great Depression to some vague combination of capitalist greed, evil, and specu-lation. You would rarely hear that it was caused by government-sponsored inflation and subsequent obstruction of the 'cleanup' process after the crash.

Nevertheless, that's the truth. So I think it's fair to say that a vast majority of people in positions of power and a lot of other people ignore much of the economic facts I have told you in the last hour."

Benson watched his still very attentive audience. "I believe this is enough for the introductory lecture of this course. You know this is the last course I will teach to you before you graduate. In the remaining lectures, we will look in more detail on the historical evolution of money, banking, and the related phenomena of inflation, deflation, and business cycles. Thank you for your attention," Benson said with an appreciative glance at his class.

The students slowly prepared to leave the room, some discussing with each other about what they had heard. No one was left indifferent. Some were skeptical, such as the boy sitting next to Pete. When putting on his jacket to leave, he said, "I think that sounds a bit too fantastic. I fear our professor takes himself for a superhero who is so sure he's right, even though a lot of people don't agree with him."

"Do you have any factual or logical objection to what you just heard?" Pete asked.

"Well, no, I don't know, but I just feel that if a majority believes something, then it's likely to be right, even if I don't understand why."

"If that's your approach to knowledge, then I wonder what you do in a college," Pete said calmly but with a weary look. "Or seen differently, maybe you should remain a student or social science bureaucrat forever. Because with that kind of attitude, I fear you'll have a hard time taking any decisions for yourself out in the real world." Pete turned his back on his classmate and walked out of the room, which now was almost empty.

CHAPTER 2:
Desire to Know and Purposeful Ignorance

One evening a month later, with graduation approaching, Professor Benson was making some coffee in his large kitchen. This was the central room of his house, which was located on the top of a hill. The room provided a view both of the Jefferson-Jackson Private University where he worked, on one side, and the Pacific Ocean far away on the horizon, on the other side. He had just had dinner with his wife Angela. Their son Stephen, now thirty years old, lived in New York and had called them just before dinner to talk about his next trip to visit his parents, planned for early June.

The large pot of coffee Professor Benson was preparing was not intended for his family, but for a group of students. Since the start of this academic year last September, the students had the habit to gather in Benson's living room on Thursday evenings. This provided them the opportunity to talk about economics and to ask questions they rarely had the time to ask during classes. The number of persons in this group had varied, with at most ten people. Only five had been there every time, and they were also the only ones climbing his driveway this night, to ring on the door bell at 8:15 p.m. They were Mark, Jessica, Laura, Pete, and Bobby, five devoted students who had enrolled in all his courses in economics over the last two years. They had started with his basic course and had gone through specialized courses, including his last course on economic and monetary history, which they were now completing.

Benson opened and let the group into the living room. As they silently sat down in the three large couches in Bensons' living room, they had the chance to admire the sunset in the horizon. They saw an orange-pink light where the sky met the Pacific Ocean. The light reflected to where they were sitting, through the vast windows covering most of the wall facing the Pacific, and it lit up the black leather of the couches with orange sparkles.

Professor Benson soon entered the room with a tray of cups, some cookies, a large pot of coffee, and a cup of milk. He looked pleasantly at the group spread out in the couches and said, "I'm happy and flattered that you all made it without exception to what might be our last discussion evening together before graduation. And since this is your last year in college, who knows when we will meet next time?"

Mark Lomack was the tallest of the group, and the slimmest of the three boys. He had blond curly hair, going well down to his shoulders, which made his head look quite big on top of a thin chest. He had long arms and large hands. He usually busied himself with some object, such as a pencil, which he would excel in spinning with his right hand. He spun it when he thought hard, which he often did. Mark had been brought up by his parents in Maine, where he had found time both to practice many outdoor sports and to earn and save money to go to college by doing odd jobs. Mark now was majoring in both computer science and economics, which was an unusual combination. Having done a lot of mathematics, he had found economics a pleasantly logical topic, at least in the classes taught by Professor Benson. Mark had spent some of his high school and college years helping friends launch Internet start-ups, as the dot-com frenzy grew stronger and stronger. But he never went fully into that activity. He had some opportunities to drop out of college and join dot-com firms with impressive funding and growth prospects. But he had concluded that making Internet sites was quite easy. "I can do that later if I still want to. However, I may never again have the opportunity to study under teachers such as Professor Benson, or my computer science teacher Doctor Xianchou."

Next to Mark sat Pete Bagnelli, his roommate for three years. They had met in the beginning of their freshman year and soon had found out that they shared a strong interest in three such different topics as windsurfing, mountain hiking, and financial market products and trading. Since they both had come alone from the East Coast to California with hopes of improving in all those three areas, they quickly decided to share a room at the campus. Just like Mark, Pete came from a middle-class family that had not been able to provide much pocket money for his college years. While Mark worked late evenings at the bar near campus to earn some extra money, Pete tried to make his savings grow by playing the stock market. Since he was cautious and followed his investments on a daily basis, he was quite successful. As graduation approached, his portfolio had grown to a net worth close to two hundred thousand dollars. He had even been able to avoid losing money during the recent fall of the stock market, thanks to advice from Professor Benson. The professor had suggested two years earlier, just before the start of the dot-com crash that he should start betting on the fall of stocks prices. This had helped him earn money when stocks went down instead of up.

As a son of third-generation Italian immigrants, Pete had grown up in Miami in the eighties. This background may have influenced his way of dressing, which was highly causal but at a same time careful and tasteful. He often wore wide, white or light beige linen shirts and slacks, which contrasted starkly with his dark skin, and he carried black sunglasses on most occasions. Pete was one of those people who regularly observe significant quotations in motion pictures. As when he said, "Watching a movie classic about gambling, I observed the complete truth of the statement workers never hustle, and hustlers never work. However, I intend to succeed in life by being a hustler, but a hard working one." Pete had majored in financial markets and products, and intended to make playing the financial markets his full-time job after graduation.

To the left of Pete sat Jessica Frostby, who was only slightly shorter than the towering Mark, with similar blonde hair and deep blue eyes that had the gift of capturing attention. Jessica's mother was an executive in the fashion business, and she had been very proud when people said that her daughter was beautiful. However, Jessica herself mostly dismissed such compliments, as when she said, "Of course I take care of my look, that's a question of self-respect. But I believe that the real beauty of a person is inside his or her head. Unfortunately, such beauty is much rarer."

Jessica, whose great grandparents had come to live in the United States from Sweden, had gotten from her ancestors a keen interest for the world beyond America's borders. She had traveled abroad quite a lot with her parents and with friends, both in Europe and in Asia. She figured international finance and monetary issues would be areas worthy of her future commitment.

Nevertheless, during the different economics courses given by Professor Benson, she had acquired a conviction that things were not as they should be in this area. She had recently stated to a friend, "I'm more and more convinced that as Professor Benson has taught us, there are major deficiencies in the current monetary and banking systems. I think it's clear that these issues have caused multiple economic crises, including the recent dot-com bubble. In spite of this, or rather because of this, I see it as a formidable challenge to change that aspect of the world to the better. This is why I'll do a postgraduate year of economic studies before applying for a position at the International Monetary Fund."

To some people's surprise, Jessica had had only one or two love affairs during college, and she had been without a boyfriend during her final year of college. But to those who pointed it out, she answered, "I guess I'm more romantic and demanding than people would expect, and I just haven't found a great love yet. And I'm flattered that people worry about my supposed loneliness, although that has never been a concern of mine."

Next to Jessica sat Laura Dalaghan, a short girl with pale skin; dark, straight short hair; and brown eyes. Laura was often said to be born a fighter, something she took as a compliment and attributed to her parents and to her Irish grandparents who had come to live in New York and work as shopkeepers. Laura had a consistently high energy level always at her service to move around any obstacle. Her brain reacted just as fast as her small, compact body, and she was someone who was known for always winning an argument. She and Jessica had been inseparable friends during most of college. Among other things, they shared an interest for monetary affairs and banking. Laura had written her thesis on a future vision of retail banking, and she had a strong desire to create an Internet retail bank. More and more people made fun of her for this ambition because the Internet bubble had burst last year and the vast majority of the dot-com start-ups were now bankrupt or in dire need of refinancing. Laura was unimpressed by that context. "I always thought most of those business plans looked quite thin. First, I thought I had missed something but now I see I was right in most cases.

"Anyway, if I start a business it will earn money from the beginning, or else we will stay in whatever garage we have until that situation changes.

The true revolution Internet has created is the ability to start a company with national or international scope using an initial investment of just a few tens of thousands of dollars. *That* is the main difference versus so-called brick-and-mortar, or old economy, start-up investments!

"Therefore I'm surprised that so many start-ups have wasted this advantage by burning loads of money on marketing with the most unlikely payback. And I'm even more surprised that venture capitalists have accepted to finance so many goofy ventures! These observations have convinced me about the rightness of Professor Benson's teachings on savings and investment. He considers that the reason so many bad investments have been done is the abundant supply of easy credit. For sure, if start-ups had needed to obtain the savings which someone had earned though hard work before putting those savings at stake in a new investment, then many of these ventures wouldn't have obtain any money at all. Or if they had, they would have had to prove that their business model worked before getting any larger sums. Are you among those who think that would be a loss to society? That people need to get a chance to experiment in order to find out what business models work and which don't? Then you can give them your money for such experiments, but not mine!"

However, Laura herself had managed to raise money for the Internet retail bank start-up she wished to launch after graduation. She had obtained it from an investor who was known to be the most selective among all the venture capitalists in Silicon Valley: Cornelius Hazelton of Hazelton Growth Capital. He was a friend of Professor Benson and had said about Laura's business, "When judging an investment object the only thing that interests me except projected profits is if it may contribute to the much needed defense of private property and the freedom of enterprise in our society. Luckily, Laura's vision of sound retail banking, with a low-cost Internet model replacing marble office buildings paid for with despoiled depositors' money, fulfills both my pet criteria. And her idea of a future gold-money bank, once that again becomes possible, is definitely something I want to be in on before anybody else!"

The last person sitting around the low coffee table was Bobby Cheston, who took up as much space on a sofa as the two girls together. Bobby had grown up in Seattle, where his father was the successful owner of a consumer goods business. As money had not been an issue for Bobby in his youth, he had used most of his energy in sports and leisure activities. He was a tall, muscular boy, with his brown hair cut short, and a pair of bruises was apparent on his large cheekbones. Bobby was a running back in the university football team and often went with friends, including Pete and Mark, on mountain hiking trips.

He was a gentle person, in spite of his street fighter looks. Even though his youth contained little hardship, he had been taught the importance of respecting other people. He was someone who always kept his word, and he considered this an important quality for the future activity he envisioned as a businessman. He had once said, "The stereotype of a trader or a business- man in today's society is someone who cheats people to get their money by any means. Not only do I consider this caricature quite unjust; I also believe reality is the total opposite. A successful businessman and trader is a man to whom nothing is more holy than his word. And no ingredient in his work comes above doing it the best way possible and respecting the commitment taken towards his customers." Bobby had majored in business administration and was currently applying for positions as product manager in some con- sumer products companies. He figured that it would be a good experience to start his career before, at some point, launching his own international trading business.

Professor Benson let the group help themselves to the coffee and cookies he had brought in. He sat down in his leather armchair in a corner of the room facing both the Pacific Bay window screens and the coffee table around which his five guests were sitting. He said, "This may be our last encounter before you graduate and I think I've had the opportunity to tell you and teach you the key things I wanted. So I suggest for tonight that you pick yourselves the topics you want to discuss or some specific questions you may want to ask."

Pete was the first to seize the opportunity after a brief moment of silence. "Well, I would like to come back to the question you avoided during the recent Monetary History lecture. You remember I asked you why our current political and central bank decision makers don't recognize, accept and apply the kind of basic economics knowledge you have taught us. From their frequent state- ments in the press or on TV, I can conclude for myself that they don't, but why?

"It seems impossible to me that smart people believe for example that in order to restart the economy, it's enough to 'stimulate consumption.' Any child would understand that the hard thing in business and economics is to pro- duce wealth, not to consume it. Another example is what you call the quantity theory of money. How is it possible that people may not accept the idea that the average price level in society will usually evolve in proportion to the quan- tity of money? I mean, it's exactly as if you lock four people inside a room with some objects to exchange—if they each have twenty dollars, you can be sure they will be prepared to pay roughly twice as much for any item as if they had ten dollars, and the total wealth will be unchanged! The only way to double the wealth is for the people to produce twice what they produced before.

"Why and how can people pretend to disagree with something so obvious? Because they *do* disagree with that when they pretend they can create wealth by just printing paper money or when they claim that money creation doesn't destroy purchasing power!"

"Well," Professor Benson said, "first of all, those who want to get away with contesting the obvious wouldn't state clearly any position about such top- ics. They would tend to make things look more complex than they are so that most people will get lost and think economics is some meaningless topic for specialists only. They would say for example that the quantity theory of money is 'subject to varying degrees of approval and ongoing debate within the scientific community.' This is a way to kill a theory without providing any argument whatsoever.

"Now, anyone who bothers to look at actual numbers, which I did in this case, can see that this 'theory' holds perfectly true in the U.S. for the last thirty years. But let's come back to the possible motivations for such dishonest behavior. We need to go back to the period I talked about in my lecture, between the two world wars and after the second one.

"This was the time when society was moving fast to establish some mix between a free society and a totalitarian one that was labeled 'The Third Way.' This happened in all Western societies during that time. The basic principle was that constitutional rights more and more disappeared, removing the protection of private property. This was necessary in order for democratic elections to be able to decide about anything, and to be able to levy any kind of tax on any kind of property.

"A lot of people were, and still are, very proud of this constitutional democracy with elections of a president and/or a parliament. They consider it as a foolproof guarantee against dictatorship. But, beyond the fact that several dictators were elected democratically, we need to understand what an *unlimited* democracy leads to, where safeguards protecting private property and individual rights from abuse by a majority have been removed. It means that anything is possible and that in order to be elected, a politician needs to promise more and better things than his competitors, to as many people as possible.

"This soon created what we still see today, more than ever: pork-barrel politics where candidates bid over each other to implement new taxes, regulations, or bureaucracies in order to provide some form of alleged benefits to some part of the public. The greatest trick they use is to say that whatever is proposed is aimed to improve life of 'the public.' But there's no such thing as 'the public.' There are just a lot of individuals, who, according to different contexts, can be seen as belonging to this or that group. This creates a situation of legalized civil war, where all types of groups try to take it out on each other, using the power to create laws as a weapon. And we start to see the emergence of a lot of conflicts that didn't actually exist in a free market where governments only prevented the use of violence.

"The Third Way generated conflicts such as farmers versus industrial workers, employers versus employees, customers versus shopkeepers, students versus teachers, patients versus doctors, rich versus poor, etc. And in any business, the less able and less moral businessmen and companies started to realize that they could use laws to destroy their competitors. That appeared easier to them than producing better products than their competitors. *That* is how antitrust laws were created and sustained!"

Benson drank some coffee and took a bite of a cookie before continuing. "So, let me come back to the role of economics in all this. Basically, we have politicians, who have an incentive to flatter the largest possible majority of people. At the same time, they want to give the impression that the activity they propose to do if elected is useful to 'society.' Since economics touches on a large number of topics people care about, politicians therefore need to convince people that there is need for government intervention in the economy. The bogus belief about increasing growth by stimulating consumption is tailor-made for this purpose. It pretends that the country as a whole will be richer if money is given to consumers for them to consume. This idea pretends that government intervention is necessary, since it would make the country as a whole better off. And at the same time, it flatters the consumers, who feel that they are important and that it's for the good of society that they are entitled to get 'something for nothing' to consume.

"This tenet has been upheld by politicians of all parties for almost a century. And they have gone to election with all kinds of proposals about what money should be spent on and whether the money should be raised by taxes, by government debt or by just printing new money. Whatever the political color, virtually all politicians of the last century have shared and used these false ideas about economics.

"I know you know it, but let me briefly remind you why they're false. First, taking money from someone without his consent isn't only wrong; in addition, it doesn't create any new wealth. And if these interventions actually led to increased consumption, then it would mean that less money is spent on production. This in turn means that a little later there will be less to consume for everybody and the country will be poorer than it was before!"

He paused for an instant. "So much for politicians—let's now take a look at the role and motives of central bank leaders. They come into the picture regarding two of the three means I mentioned which the government has in order to raise money for spending: creating government debt and inflating the money supply. Obviously, it has been recognized that this will put central banks under a lot of pressure from politicians. Therefore, the *independency* of central banks has been offered to the public as a solution and guarantee. Basically central banks have had, at least in the last decades, as objective to avoid that consumer prices rise too fast. As long as that objective is respected, nobody cares to look too closely at central banks' activity. This sure puts some limits on the pace at which they can dilute people's savings and property by inflating the money supply. But we should never forget that as representatives of a cartel of commercial banks, the central bank leaders will always try to inflate as much as they can within their given constraints. This is because it enables their member banks to extend more credit, which is profitable for them.

"As we saw in the recent dot-com crash, the boom part of a business cycle may well combine slow consumer price increases with rapid increase in the quantity of money. This can only work for a limited time, as long as the new money goes largely into other things than consumer goods, such as stocks. Nevertheless, if the Central Bank makes some statements to pretend that this can go on forever, as recently when the Fed chairman talked about a 'new economy,' then many people will believe that.

"Apparently, many people seem to think that the exceptional power a central bank has implies that its leaders also have exceptional knowledge or intelligence. Unfortunately they are just normal people and they're under a lot of pressure not only from politicians but also from all interest groups in society that can reap benefits from a bull-market period where it appears that everybody is getting richer. And of course, a central bank leader wouldn't dream of defending ideas which would imply that central banks and monetary policy were no longer needed. Just like we seldom hear politicians who are running for an election say that government intervention in the economy is ineffective or harmful. So don't count on any central bank leader to promote a gold-based monetary system with banks functioning as any other private enterprise, and where the central bank could be closed down."

"So in short," Pete said, trying to summarize, "we have a political system where anything goes, and all these politicians and central bank people are just acting to maximize their own importance to defend the partisan interests of the welfare recipients, government employees and member banks they represent. They sort of evade knowledge and common sense. Purposeful ignorance is the label that comes to my mind! But what about the economics professors who endorse all this by fabricating ridiculous theories; what's in it for them?"

Benson answered, "Well, I have to admit that this is what disappoints me the most. It has led me to have fewer friends in my own profession than I would have had, if more economics professors had stood up for basic truths along with me. They have become, as many other social scientists have, completely absorbed by the Third Way bogus. They now regard their own science as simply a question about how to make government intervention most effective. The only explanation I can find is that they consider their only way to make a living is to please government officials while hoping they will use tax payer money to pay for the wages of social scientists. I can't quite believe this explanation, as I myself could never accept selling my soul like that. It would mean to live in a perpetual lie of promoting nonsense as science!

"Now, let's not stick to this slightly negative topic, you might get the impression that I'm whining about it, and that's something I never want to allow myself to do. Do you have any positive thoughts or questions, about the future maybe?"

Laura leaned over the coffee table toward Professor Benson. "What's your outlook for the future of the world? In spite of the unhealthy system you just described, don't you still think some people, including those in power, will have learned a lesson from the recent dot-com crisis? I think the crisis was quite instructive, even though the lessons I learned mostly are things I think I knew already before."

"It's hard to judge from looking at someone's head whether he doesn't understand, or if he does but refuses to apply that knowledge," Benson said, "and then whether he's trying or also succeeding to hide from himself the knowledge he has. This may sound complex, but we should realize we have an awful lot of pretense involved in politics, mass media, and public affairs. As to what we call *political correctness*, there are people who actually believe what they hear and others who don't but pretend to believe. And there are still others who don't believe it but are able to cheat themselves to actually think it's right.

"So the short answer to your question is no. I'm afraid we won't see a lot of effective action taking into account the lessons that could have been learned. While central bank leaders now blame infectious greed of businessmen and investors for the dot-com debacle and stock market crash, politicians and journalists want to ban stock options. The ridicule of these responses shows that they are just finding scapegoats and diverting the public's attention from their own role in the crash. In the meantime, politicians are about to prepare for the next election with new pork barrel suggestions.

"Regarding central banks, they're eager to restart or accelerate money creation, in order not to be accused of preventing the economy to come out of the crisis. So, basically, we face a crash which was caused by too much money in the stock market, too much debt and too much consumption spending using borrowed money. In order to come out of it, what we will get is renewed money creation leading to more debt and more price increase spirals, maybe this time on something other than stocks.

"I hear a lot of talk from politicians these days about the idea that the United States should be a country of homeowners. That would supposedly honor the history of our ancestors who built their own homes after coming here. So maybe the next crisis will be in the real estate market? What if government tries to push people, who can't afford it, to buy houses using money borrowed easily during a boom period with low interest rates? Your guess is as good as mine."

Jessica seized the chance to rebound on this forward-looking conversation. "OK, so much for the country at large, but you have also taught us that one should above all focus on one's own business. Let's come back to just that. We are now going out to find a job. What's your advice to us in order to be both successful and happy? Typically people would think that doing what is right makes you happy. But if the right isn't recognized in society, then doing right might stop us from being successful. And beyond the intentions we may have at the outset, I guess we must expect to be influenced also by the world we live in so that we might, over time, forget things we learned earlier."

Professor Benson looked gently at Jessica. "I don't like to avoid answering a question, but those are tough and important judgments to make, and everyone must make them for him- or herself. I can only give you some general advice: whenever possible, try to do what is both right and feasible. If you see a clash between the two, don't try to be a lone crusader wanting to change the whole world at any price. You will not succeed, and you will only end up frustrated. Focus on your own affairs, and try to do the best you can about what's within your power and your responsibility. Whenever you have the chance to speak up for what's right, do it. But don't become a preacher and don't expect that anyone may want to listen to whatever you have to say, even if it's right."

Pete leaned forward. "Yes, Professor, I like your last remark. I mean, I'm planning to go into financial investments management, trying to grow my wealth, and I wish to set up mutual funds for investors. While I approve of your teachings about what would be an appropriate financial system, at some point, I still need to play the game according to the rules which exist. The fact that I think central bank–driven money inflation isn't a good thing doesn't mean I can allow myself not to use it to take cheap credits. If I want to survive against competitors who are riding a bull market by borrowing as much as they can, to finance investments in order to make the fastest possible profits, I have to do what they do. I mean, my high principles wouldn't be worth much on the day when I'd lose all my customers to a competing mutual fund that has higher returns thanks to using leveraged investments!"

Bobby added, "I agree with Pete. If I look at my personal life, I'm deeply in love with Barbara, and she and I may soon want to get married and buy a house. While I've heard the professor's view on the risks of high leverage, I still need to take a large mortgage if we want to buy a house. Others will bid for the same house I may want to buy. And I bet they will use those adjustable-rate zero-amortization mortgages which government-backed credit institutions are proposing, Funny J and Freddy K or whatever they're called. Those may sound like names out of a cartoon. But the fact remains that these mortgage lenders enable people to bid over me when buying a house. I'm afraid that if I want to be prudent and save until I can pay forty percent of my house from my own pocket, I will then regret having lived in a small flat for years. In the meantime, people who don't bother about the fine economic principles I defend would sit on the terrace of that house I could have bought, sipping on cocktails at sunset with their children all having their own bedrooms!"

Mark took the chance to continue on the same theme. "I see similar issues for me as for Bobby and Pete. I want to go to work with financial products pricing analysis software. I have a lot of ideas about how that could be done according to sound principles of investment analysis. But at some point, I need, before anything else, to try to understand how people today in fact go about to evaluate investments and to try to model *that*, even if their thinking is wrong or irrational.

"And even if I may find some good ideas which can both be good from my point of view and help investors pick the right objects successfully, then it may well be that my boss won't let me do it in that new way. I, for sure, would have wanted to start my own business in this area, but I don't have enough money to get started, and I haven't yet been able to devise a business plan that I could go out and sell to some venture capitalist. So I'll start out as a wage earner in this business and see where that takes me. The other thing I want to do, as you know, is to create an Internet-based network to promote the link between sound money and individual freedom. But for now, that will remain a hobby activity, as I have no business plan enabling me to raise money for it."

Laura shook her head. "I'm not sure I agree with you about all this. I think doing what is right should make us succeed, at least in the long run. If I manage to start an Internet retail bank, then I for sure will apply my principles about prudent credit policy when selecting my clients. And I would also limit the usage of the fractional reserve principle. I do recognize it as a kind of fraud that also could make my bank insolvent on the day when a lot of people come to claim their money.

"You boys might say I will lose the race against competitors on the upside of economic cycles if the central bank once again starts to create an easy money environment? Well, maybe, but when my banking competitors become insolvent because the boom is ending, I'll be the one to survive and stay in business after the next crash. And while I can't, under current laws in the United States, apply my convictions about proposing gold money to customers, I for sure will do that at the first opportunity, be it in the United States or in some foreign country."

Jessica, with a sad but dreamy look on her face, then added, "When I listen to you, I realize that you all are lucky. You at least have a shot to combine what is right and what can work. As far as I'm concerned, I want to work in national and international monetary affairs, to see that our country and others have the best possible monetary system and politics. The problem is that this line of work is currently a government monopoly with the central banks and all these laws Professor Benson has taught us about.

"While I agree with the professor that institutions like the IMF and the Federal Reserve Bank should not exist in a free society, I still have to resign myself to work for these institutions. If I didn't, I would just sit on the side line making bitter comments about the world not being what it should be. But I think that would be the most frustrating and the weakest thing to do. I mean, we all think people who are whiny are boring and annoying and that they should stand up and roll their sleeves up. Well, that's what I intend to do, and who knows, I may even be able to change these institutions from the inside."

Professor Benson took the opportunity to summarize the accounts from the group. "You see what I mean when I say that these are tough judgments that one must make for oneself? I could say that I agree with all I've just heard.

But at the same time, I honestly have to say I'm not sure it will work out well for you all, or as you plan. The world out there is tough and can be strange and disappointing. But, on the other hand, I know that if there are some people who are able to succeed in spite of the obstacles we have discussed, well, then *you* are those people! So I'll just wish you all good luck, and I'll try to keep an eye on each of you. I'm sure that you will be recognized soon, each one within his or her line of activity."

The conversation kept going until 4:00 a.m. At that point, the students were all so exhausted that they stayed where they were and slept sitting on Professor Benson's couches until 7:00 a.m. His wife Angela had a good laugh when she discovered this surprising view in the morning. "Well, it may be a good thing you young heroes are now graduating to go out into the real world. However interesting your future activities will be, I do hope, for your sake, that your employers won't have you come to their homes and make you stay until your crumble into sleep in their living rooms!"

As the team slowly emerged from the living room to leave, Mark turned to her and said with a sleepy but firm voice: "Mrs. Benson, with all due respect, I would give anything in the world to live through a few more such nights. And something tells me we may even come back soon to see you, if you accept it. Because your husband is the best teacher we ever had and whatever we become from now on, he will have had a major part in making that possible. Also, thank you once more for your hospitality and for letting us use your husband's time during all these evenings and nights. Goodbye and have a good day, and I hope we will meet soon again!" Angela smiled back and knew she would see them again.

✵ ✵ ✵

Graduation day at the Jefferson-Jackson Private University this year took place on one of those perfect early summer days. The cloud-free sky was pale blue, and the sun was high up and strong with a dazzling white light. The temperature was not hot; it rarely is in the San Francisco Bay area. But the sun rays beaming down uninterrupted on the large campus lawn where the graduation ceremony was taking place were hot enough for the numerous women wearing summer dresses and skirts to avoid any feeling of coldness.

The spirit among the graduates was also a bit more positive that the year before. The memory of the previous year's dot-com crash and the worsening labor market and business perspectives it had led to was still fresh. The memory was also still fresh with the horror of the most lethal terrorist attacks in the history of the country the year before. The economy was now slowly improving, and more and more people were finding openings for interesting jobs. This cautiously renewed optimism also was heard in most of the speeches during the graduation ceremony.

The five friends had received their diplomas, which contained top grades in all courses given by Professor Benson, and in the case of Mark Lomack, also for all the computer science and mathematics courses he had followed. However, some of them had voluntarily neglected other social science courses such as in philosophy, psychology, and sociology. Pete had commented on this. "Well, that may not look good on paper, but we all know how much nonsense those courses contain. So I'm actually proud of *not* having learned to repeat their teachings as some form of conditioned reflex. In the end, the only thing that was declared to be certain in those courses was that we don't have the capacity to think independently. Luckily, while Professor Benson was supposed to only teach us economics, he also indirectly gave us the keys to philosophy and psychology. In that way, he stood in for the teachers of those topics, who were just fakes."

After the graduation ceremony, they had gathered for a last get-together at the sports bar, the place where Bobby and his team mates used to celebrate their frequent football victories, just off campus. Each of the friends now had checked out of their dormitories and had sent their belongings to the place they would go next.

At Mark's initiative, they had asked Professor Benson to be present at this last opportunity of seeing each other. He had happily accepted. Their outdoor table, fully exposed to the sun, was protected against the light breeze coming in from the Pacific thanks to a windshield. When Benson arrived, the three boys had already finished a first round of beer. They were thirsty from having sweated inside their formal suits bought for the occasion and worn for the first time this day.

The professor greeted each of them and said merrily, "If the ladies don't mind, allow me to buy you a round of beer." Without waiting for a reaction from the group, he waved to the waiter and swiftly held up six fingers, and he lifted Bobby's empty beer mug up to show what he was ordering. He turned to the group. "So, why don't you tell me what you're going to do now? I know you've been doing job interviews, working on business plans, and maybe preparing some more personal projects?"

Jessica was the first to answer. "I'm going over to Europe for a one-month railway trip. I will travel alone through France, Italy, and Spain. I hope to run into some interesting people and places and to find some time to just rest by the Mediterranean Sea. I'll spend the rest of the summer back in Virginia with my parents, and then in early September, I'll take off to London. I will do a postgraduate year to get a Master of Science, specializing on monetary affairs. With this degree in my pocket, I hope to be able to get a job at the International Monetary Fund next year."

Laura spoke next. "I will be spending most of the summer improving on the business plan for my Internet retail bank start-up. It will be the first bank in our time not doing fractional reserve lending of demand deposits!

While Hazelton Growth Capital has given me a basic approval to cofinance the project, they have asked for additional details in order to sign the check. Among other things, I need to make sure I get my banking license. That may seem like a detail, but it's really one of the key issues in this project, as the bank business is heavily regulated. I do plan to take a couple of weeks off, even though that will also contribute to the purpose of my start-up project. Since an Internet business is quite flexible regarding the physical installation, I haven't yet decided where to register the company. So I'll go to a couple of places to check whether I would like to live there. I will also check whether my business would be well received by local authorities and if the labor market looks good in order to find personnel. Nothing is decided yet, but my current bet goes toward Colorado. I'll keep you all informed."

"I'm doing final interviews and expect job proposals from two consumer goods majors," Bobby said. "I'm looking for a position as product manager in charge of marketing strategy and business development for new products. Because I'm interested in all kinds of sports and outdoor activities, those are the kind of products I hope to work with. My job would be in the Los Angeles area, and Barbara is currently looking for jobs over there too. Yes, we're moving in together in an apartment, although we haven't selected one yet. We'll wait until the job search process is over. For the rest, we will do some travelling this summer. The details are secret. I haven't yet shared them even with my parents, since we want to do something just the two of us. So regarding that trip, I'll tell you more afterward."

Pete smiled and gave Bobby a friendly pat on the back. "Man, you know we wouldn't dare to ask what you and Barbara do all alone in nice hotel rooms. But if I close my eyes, I can see it in front of me!"

He and the others chuckled loudly. When Pete opened his eyes, he spoke more seriously. "As far as I'm concerned, I'm studying where and how to register my investment management company. I'll probably do it in New York close to Wall Street, but at some less expensive address. I will start slowly using my own money, instead of aiming for fast growth, which would force me to take in external capital. I'll try to go as far as I can alone, and we'll see at what point I'll hire some people or look for external capital. All this should get started before the fall, but before that, I'll go for some mountain hiking in the Rocky Mountains. With whom? Yes, as you might have guessed, with my favorite ex-roommate, Mark. We will need some time to get used to not seeing each other every day, so this summer trip should serve that purpose. I'll let Mark tell you about his own projects, but unfortunately we will soon have a whole continent between us."

"Yes," Mark said. "You know that I wasn't spoiled during my adolescence by having a beach around the corner. So I've been less inclined than Pete to compromise with my passion for windsurfing and mountain life in order to go into business. I think I've found a decent compromise to safeguard both my leisure passions and my professional development. I will join the Golden Touch Software Company of San Diego, where I'll be product development manager for financial analysis software. Down there, I also stand a chance of being able to keep my haircut, at least judging from the people I met during job interviews!"

While listening to these brief accounts, their beer had been served and Professor Benson now took over. "Thank you for letting me in on your personal projects. I sincerely hope you will be successful and happy. You deserve it. But be damn careful! If the current trends in society continue, we may soon again live through economic crises. And they might be much more violent and devastating than the dot-com meltdown of last year. You are part of an infinitely small minority who have learned the lesson that paper money, government budget deficits, and ever-increasing taxes represent the most terrible threat to our civilization that exists today. If I could ask you just one thing, then that would be to use that knowledge and act upon it! If you do, you stand a chance to reach happiness in life. I don't think that's possible if you end up doing anything less than what you're able to. And, incidentally, you might help to create a better world.

"Look at those feeble people in news media setting the public agenda in our days. I would like *you* to take their place and become the opinion shapers of the future! As to myself, I *will* try to change the world from now on. I believe I've done a lot of teaching about sound monetary systems based on gold and without central banks. In the coming years, I wish to put that knowledge to practice. Just don't go around talking about that, because I don't like to make fuzz about something which is still only an idea. But I promise you; as soon as I come close to succeeding, I'll tell you about it. Now, here's to your future!" Benson said loudly with a hard but gentle smile as he raised his beer mug and smacked it against the other mugs. Then they all drank in solemn silence their last beer before leaving the campus for the last time.

CHAPTER 3:
The Immaculate and the Cynical

On a dark December morning, Laura Dalaghan sat in the waiting room of the Colorado Commission of Banks, the public authority regulating bank activity and especially the assignment of bank licenses. She had been forced to wait two months to obtain this meeting. It was a necessary step to remove the last obstacle in order to launch her start-up bank: to obtain a banking license. The rest of her business plan was all set, and she had even started the search for office space and personnel in the Denver area, where she planned to locate the company. It was now twenty minutes beyond the time for her appointment. As she glanced at her watch, she tried to calm herself by not overestimating the importance of this additional delay. *If I have waited two months to have this meeting, then I can wait a few more minutes. But I wish that bureaucrat would come out to receive me, or I will soon dash into his office and make myself comfortable!*

"Miss Dalaghan?" someone with a sleepy but loud voice said from behind her.

She turned around. "Yes, that's me."

"My name is Mr. Radcliff. I'm the superintendent of the Colorado Commission of Banks. Please, follow me; my office is this way."

Carrying the two things she had with her, a brilliantly red handbag and her laptop computer, she followed Mr. Radcliff. She was asked to sit on one of two chairs placed around a small square table. Mr. Radcliff sat down on the other chair facing her, after closing the door to his office.

He studied her across the table for a few seconds. "So, you want to start a bank and locate it here in Colorado. So you come to see me to obtain your banking license."

He paused, as if giving her a chance to provide some unsolicited response. After a few seconds of awkward silence she did. "Yes, I know that I need to obtain a license to open a bank. Still, I don't quite understand why it's necessary when it isn't needed to open, for example, a grocery store or a warehouse. Newspapers and other media keep complaining that there aren't enough regulations for banks. They even use that to explain how the dot-com bubble could happen. But they seem to forget that a bank can't even be created without a formal approval of government and the Fed."

He looked attentively at her. "Before this conversation takes an unpleasant direction, which certainly wouldn't benefit the goal you came here to reach, let me tell you a few things about the monetary and banking systems in this country which you need to keep in mind at all times."

He looked at Laura with a strange expression conveying a combination of secrecy, evilness, and comradeship. Then Radcliff spoke for almost ten minutes, delivering what, to Laura's great surprise, was the exact same story of the creation of the Federal Reserve System she had learned in Professor Benson's courses. He then concluded with, "So, now you know the truth: the Fed is not some kind of guardian to protect the general public from financial crises. It's a collaborative setup where big banks can make large profits during booms and can be bailed out during busts. And the government is happy to sponsor this system as it holds, through the Fed, the extraordinary monopoly power of creating money at will, by just starting a printing press or by signing checks in the name of the Fed. Of course, this truth should be kept a secret, and I ask you never to repeat it after having left this room."

Laura studied the face of the man in front of her, as if looking for the answer to some riddle that tortured her. "You may not believe it, but I'm one of the few persons in this country who learned in college exactly what you just told me. The way these features have been dressed up to be accepted by the public can rightly be considered as one of the biggest and best concealed lies of our time. This being said, my only question is, why do you take the risk of telling it all to me? I might just run away to call a large newspaper or write a book on the topic."

With cunning, Mr. Radcliff looked at Laura, and after a few moments of thought, he looked beyond her, out through the window, at the snow-covered mountain peaks with a serene expression on his face. "If you did, they wouldn't listen to you or they would think you're crazy. While I can admit that this whole system is absurd and abuses the public, I know for sure that none of those modern, superficial journalists would make a story of it. And if they did, the public would find it too complex to care about. But, in any case, I know you would never reveal this to anyone in the first place."

"What makes you so sure I wouldn't?" Laura said, having some difficulty to hide that her temper was rising, which made her pale cheeks feel hot.

"Well, you came here in order to obtain the permission to create a commercial bank, didn't you? I have studied your business plan in detail, and I see how badly you want to go through with your project to create this Internet start-up bank you have envisioned. As your business plan is quite mature, with a detailed forecast of costs and revenues, and as you have a strong backing from Hazelton Growth Capital, I will approve your license request. From the moment you're a bank owner, you will have switched sides: you will be one of us and will share our common interest. What do I mean by 'us'? Government? The Fed? Banks? Actually, as I explained, all three. So I know that if there is anyone in the world with whom those secrets are safe, it's with the holder of a bank license. Your livelihood and wealth will depend exclusively on defending that very system."

Mr. Radcliff grinned at her as he signed the application form for her banking license and checked the box labeled "Application approved," and then he slowly pushed it across the table. He rose from his chair and gave her a sign that she could leave.

"Good luck with your banking venture, Miss Dalaghan. I'm happy to be able to count you as one of *us* from now on."

Laura, whose temper had continued rising for the last few minutes, closed her eyes and held her breath for a long moment. Then she slowly turned her head to look at Mr. Radcliff, and produced a polite smile.

"Thank you very much, sir. I'll try to live up to the confidence which this license represents, by turning my business into the most successful bank in Colorado."

She slipped the form into her briefcase and headed out of the building, walking faster and faster. She felt the need to get outside and breathe some pure mountain air in order to cut the link with the room she just had left and to try to forget the evil nature of the conversation she had just lived through.

✧ ✧ ✧

Early the next morning, Laura called the to-be majority shareholder of her banking venture, Cornelius Hazelton of Hazelton Growth Capital. He barely had the time to pick up his phone, before she shouted, "Mr. Hazelton, I've got the banking license. We're ready to launch!"

"Well, my congratulations," he answered. "I'm very happy to hear that. As soon as I receive a copy of that document, you will get my formal approval to start your business. From then on, and I expect you to remember this, you'll be your own boss, and I will just be your largest and most demanding shareholder. And next time I talk to Professor Benson, I'll inform him about the birth of the Dalaghan Prudential Internet Bank. Go for it, Laura. Make me proud, and make me richer than I already am!"

As often, Hazelton finished the conversation after this short interjection and hung up. Laura felt a few tears falling down her cheeks, as she picked up her phone and sent a brief text message to her four closest friends from college. She had not seen any of them since graduation day, six months earlier. The message said:

> DPIB up and running! Expect to hear more soon. But don't come for some easy credit. Policy will be as solid as gold, even if not allowed to use such noble material as money. For now. Love/L.

✧ ✧ ✧

Laura spent a few days of paperwork with landlords, with Hazelton Growth Capital, and with the bank of HGC, which was to provide the funds to launch DPIB. She also had to make a few trips to suppliers of office furniture.

On a cold but beautiful January morning, Laura stood in front of the door to her new business office, which was ready to be opened. The metal plate saying "DPIB—Dalaghan Prudential Internet Bank" was already up, placed on the wall next to the glass door on the third floor of this start-up 'incubator' building where Mr. Hazelton had helped her rent a cheap three-room office. That would be enough, at least for a few months, for her and her two employees, who would join her from day one.

She turned the door key and walked in. Her personal office was in a corner with glass walls and a clear view of the Rocky Mountains. Her two employees, Sandra, in charge of credit sales, and Paul, in charge of credit payments collection and deposits management, would sit together in the room next to Laura's office. Both offices were already equipped with laptop PCs and phones, installed the day before. The only additional room inside their space was a small conference room equipped with a telephone, a whiteboard, a video projector, and a flip chart paper board. One of the side walls of the conference room was made of glass with the same panoramic mountain view as could be seen from Laura's office. Bathrooms and kitchen areas were shared with the other tenants of the incubator building's third floor, just as they shared the reception desk and maintenance services. To add a personal touch to this streamlined office, Laura had brought in her private coffee machine and a few of her most used college textbooks, including Professor Benson's treatise and various course materials in economics.

Shortly after Laura arrived, Sandra and Paul turned up. The three of them helped themselves to a cup of coffee and sat down in the conference room to hold the first meeting in the history of DPIB.

"Sandra, Paul, I wish you sincerely welcome to the Dalaghan Prudential Internet Bank, and we start operations today! You know the positions I hired each of you for. You also know, as we're a start-up company, that there are many things to do for which we have no dedicated personnel. This will be particularly true during our first period of activity, when we need to prepare the operational launch of the services we want to propose to our future customers. We must create our Web site, build back-office information systems, design our product and services catalogue, and prepare an operational marketing strategy to reach out to our targeted customers. Of course, all these activities will be guided by our overall strategy, which I have defined upfront in collaboration with our majority shareholder, Hazelton Growth Capital. We will focus on the core business of so-called commercial, or retail, banking, which is managing deposits and providing credits. As you know, my plan to make our business competitive is to accept credits with a prudent risk position. We will focus on customers with a strong credit rating, meaning a low-risk profile. And above all, we will not engage in so-called fractional reserve lending on demand deposits, as all other banks do. We will only lend money we get as savings deposits, which the owner accepts not to use for a time."

"But," Paul asked, "how will we remain profitable if we don't lend the demand deposits, since all other banks do that? They will be able to earn more money than we do, won't they?"

Laura looked both confident and triumphant as she answered. "We will have lower costs than all those brick-and-mortar banks, which have branch offices all over the country. We are an Internet bank, so our cost structure is limited to the persons and physical items present in this small office and some marketing spending. So I'm confident that we will be able to provide competitive interest rates to our loan customers, even though we don't lend demand deposits. And the best thing about not doing fractional reserve lending is that we, and our clients, will be safe once the next crisis arrives. Because even if some customers default or bring their money out of our bank, we won't have any issues with our reserve ratio—it will always be one hundred percent."

She paused to drink some coffee, and looked at her two team members. She invited them, with a nod of her head, to ask questions or to comment on what she just had said.

"I understand we're owned by Hazelton Growth Capital," Sandra asked. "I heard Hazelton is a demanding shareholder. What does he expect from us?"

"You're right he is. I only obtained the funding after having committed to a business plan. He put two million dollars into the bank, and he expects to get it back, with a return. Today we are three. Within two years, we need to be fifteen people and to be managing around forty million dollars of assets in the form of deposits and credits. Our result is expected to be positive from year one, and reach five hundred thousand dollars within two years. Our profits should top a million dollars before year four."

"Boss, do you think we'll make it?" Sandra asked hesitantly.

"Of course I do," Laura said loudly. "Otherwise, I wouldn't be sitting here."

Paul then asked, "Could you tell us more about the work we need to do right now, in the start-up phase?"

"Sure! For example, Sandra will be working to design our specific service offering: what type of credits do we sell and what account types and credit cards do we propose to our customers? Paul, you will work with consultants I hired to set up our Internet site and all the information systems we need behind that to manage accounts and payments. Sandra, you will also have to work out our operational marketing strategy and set up the relation with our Mexican call center which will handle customer sales and support over phone. We really need to go as fast as possible with all these actions—every day before our operational launch is a day when we're not earning any money. In two months from now, I expect all this to be ready and for us to have our first real client. So, let's go to work!"

✲ ✲ ✲

It was a Monday in early fall, and the Washington, D.C., sky was deep gray and misty, with little sunlight coming through the heavy clouds in this late-morning hour. Leaves on the numerous trees surrounding the International Convention Center had started to fall off. The remaining leaves were becoming yellow, orange, or dark red, providing the only colors that gave the scenery some sense of life and energy.

The weather helped the people inside the convention center forget their recent summer vacation. Many of them had spent it traveling around the world in exciting and more colorful places. The group of people sitting in the largest auditorium room of the building was composed almost exclusively of new hires to the International Monetary Fund, the IMF. This group of around three hundred people, all between twenty-five and thirty-five years old, represented most of the 186 member countries of the organization. The new hires had chosen jobs in order to be part of what was widely considered as the most important international organization in the area of money and financial systems. Among the younger was Jessica Frostby, who had succeeded in getting a job at the IMF without a PhD, thanks to top grades achieved in her master's degree at Oxford and thanks to some support from her Oxford professor, who was well known by the IMF leadership.

The speaker standing on the stage in front of this large audience was one of the top managers of the IMF. He was a citizen of a small African country, and he had climbed the career ladder fast. He had done that by being neutral toward all the main Western countries. He also was a major spokesman for the recent, but politically correct, objective of "reducing poverty in the world." This had been added to the IMF-founding objectives, which were previously confined only to the international monetary system.

At the end of his introductory speech, he concluded by going back to the origin of the IMF and said, with a preacher's intonation, "So, always keep in mind why the IMF was created, and how important our role is in the world. After the Great Depression, most major countries followed a policy of strong inflation of their currency. The aim was to finance government spending but also to make domestic businesses more competitive in international trade. The major exchange rate fluctuations this caused made international trade very difficult.

"Also, nationalist sentiments in most countries contributed to reduce trade. This increased poverty, and thereby hostility among countries that saw each other as responsible for their loss of wealth. We all know the disastrous result—this contributed to trigger World War Two and the most terrible destruction of lives and wealth in human history.

"Therefore, when the IMF was created at the end of the war at the Bretton Woods conference, our challenges and responsibilities were immense. It was to design and oversee the international monetary system so that it would favor trade, stability, and prosperity instead of contributing to war, crisis, and destruction of wealth. It worked quite well for a couple of decades, with a system where the paper currencies of our member countries respected stable exchange rates agreed within the IMF. And behind these paper currencies was a base in gold, since U.S. dollars were redeemable in gold, by central banks of all IMF member countries.

"In the late sixties, the quantity of paper money in all countries, including the United States, increased much faster than gold reserves. It was becoming evident that the dollar was overvalued with respect to the actual gold reserves. Therefore, in ninety seventy-three, the last link to gold was removed. Since then the international monetary system has been mainly based on freely fluctuating exchange rates between national paper currencies. There are just some exceptions where national governments stipulate fixed exchange rates for their currency, such as for the Chinese yuan.

"From our initial role of coordinating this system, the IMF progressively moved toward a role as a global central bank. The IMF has become a lender of last resort, to the extent that we started to extend credits to countries suffering from a heavy debt burden. Some of our critics consider this to be support for unsound policies and help for dictators to stay in power and that it is a contradiction in terms to try to cure excessive debt by additional credit. But we believe it's our most noble assignment to help poor countries avoid bankruptcy. After all, each country and each man is his brother's keeper, in monetary affairs as in all other affairs!"

He paused to let this last statement sink into the audience, which remained quiet and attentive. "That's all for my introductory speech. You can now go for a lunch break before we start this afternoon's breakout sessions. There you'll get to know some of your international colleagues, and you'll meet our faculty members who will give you lectures during the coming days and weeks. The faculty includes IMF managers, national central bank personnel, and representatives of government finance departments of member countries. Thank you very much for your attention, and I wish you a lot of success in your new job at the IMF. The world today needs us as much as ever, in order to help the world economy bounce back after the dot-com crash two years ago!"

Jessica Frostby had been listening attentively to this inaugural speech, and now that it was finished, she turned to the boy sitting on her right side. "Hello, my name is Jessica Frostby. I'm from the United States and will be part of the G-20 monetary policy coordination group. Who are you?"

With a gentle smile, she scanned the young man's face and his flawless suit and tie. His short dark hair was combed on the side, and small square glasses helped to make him look like a young statesman. He flashed back an equally friendly and comforting smile.

"Pleased to meet you, I'm François Leclerc. As you may guess, I am French and am a recent graduate of our school aimed at training top-level public servants. I will also be part of the monetary policy coordination group, so I believe we will meet during this boot camp and also later on."

"Pleased to meet you, François!" Jessica replied happily. "I traveled in France this summer. I was looking for some new impressions and some rest, and I found both. May I ask what you expect in joining the IMF?"

"I wish to serve my country and the international community by ensuring that our respective governments and central banks establish the best possible monetary system. That should help avoid that private greed and speculation create financial crises and hurt poor countries as it has done in the past."

"Funny," Jessica said. "That sounds like an extract from my high school history textbook. Later I had an economics teacher who reminded me that money originated on the free market between traders. They used gold to make large-scale exchange possible, beyond barter of goods against goods. And I think that central banks and government intervention into monetary affairs is part of the problem, not of the solution."

"Dear Jessica, luckily we live in highly democratic countries, where all points of view are allowed. But I assume you realize how unusual and provocative your statement is, all the more if we consider where we are. I mean, you sound like a mailman who would tell his colleagues that he thinks the postal system should be closed down!"

"Well, not exactly," Jessica replied, "but if you wish, I would be like a mailman who suggests that maybe the postal service, just like manufacturing of cars or TV sets, could be a private business activity as all others, and not a government-backed monopoly or cartel. That is indeed my idea about money and banking. But I do know and accept that this point of view is uncommon and that it could even be seen as provocative inside the IMF. Then again, I guess you also have some dirty secret, dear François. But I will give you some more time before revealing it to me."

"Dear Jessica, I don't think I have any secrets. I'm just here to serve the public good. But let me tell you that I appreciate your sharp and independent manner. I'm sure we will have a good time together as colleagues. By the way, among the important things I have learned is to never let opinions or convictions hinder pragmatic collaboration with others. I mean, at the national level as in international monetary policy, I think the most important thing is to work together as a team, not to argue about who's right. And I'm sure you and I will make up a great team."

"Maybe so, but you can count on me to try to win you over to my ideas. Because as far as I'm concerned I think knowing what is right, and acting on that knowledge, is the only thing that matters, whether you do that in agreement with the whole world or alone. Now, please, excuse me, François, I need to meet up with the group of Americans for lunch. See you around!" Jessica said as she turned away from her new French acquaintance to dash off to the lunchroom.

✵ ✵ ✵

After three days spent with a lot of plenary lectures and in breakout session groups, the fourth day of the IMF boot camp convention was aimed at letting the new hires meet with the colleagues they would be mostly working with. While the IMF had regional office locations at a number of places across the world, it also had several transnational work groups with people from many different countries. The G20 group for coordinating international monetary policy was one such group, and by many considered as the most important one with respect to the aim of the IMF. Its task was to coordinate the monetary policy of the main member countries in order to ensure stability of exchange rates and to control global price inflation. This was meant to provide the best possible conditions for international trade. While this group was composed of some sixty members, roughly three per country, only ten were new hires, including Jessica and François. These ten new hires were now gathered in a meeting room, along with ten other people already employed in that group since a few years.

The teacher of the class stood in front of the group. He looked quietly around the room and scrutinized each person as they entered and sat down at one of the five round tables spread out evenly over the room. Each person wore a name tag, which their new teacher watched and tried to memorize. The room had large windows with a view of the park that surrounded the convention center. This day was the first day of the week when a few rays of sun had found their way through the thick clouds. It added some natural light to the room, in addition to the indoor neon lights.

The teacher, Steve Harper, was thirty years old but already held a top job at the United States Treasury. He was in charge of coordination between the U.S. government and the Federal Reserve Bank regarding monetary policy in general and regarding needs for financing of U.S. public spending in particular. He had achieved this quick career not only thanks to a degree from the Harvard University School of Public Affairs. He also had personal qualities suited to facilitate his career. Steve Harper was tall, with a tense body, a natural smile disclosing white teeth, light brown hair, and deep green eyes.

He was also truly skilled in accurately judging any new person he met. He used a combination of methodical analysis and intuition, abilities which were automatic to him. He could spot traits of character of people at several levels, all down to their core motivations, what "made them tick." He used his skill most discreetly, and adapted his attitude accordingly, in order to get from each person what he wanted. The other person would rarely feel analyzed or manipulated.

On the contrary, most people who met Steve Harper found him extremely pleasant. They would usually simply appreciate the fact that he would say exactly what they wanted to hear in any particular moment, as an exceptional perceptiveness. Steve had learned this from his father, a career politician.

His father had taught him that the purpose of life was to achieve power over people and then to exercise that power. The means of reaching such power and keeping it was to control people by giving them the impression that he would provide them with what they wanted. From that point, the confidence installed in these people could be used for one's own purposes. Consequently, Steve had gone through high school and college with an amused indifference toward knowledge as such. He had focused only on what theories were accepted or could be accepted by the public and how such theories could contribute to reinforce the power of the politician and public servant he planned to become.

After he had observed the young people coming in and filling up his classroom for five minutes, Steve Harper spoke. "Welcome to our first class together, bringing together the new members of the G20 central bank coordination group. This may sound like a cliché said to army recruits to generate maximum motivation and obedience, but I'll say it anyway, since it's true: you're the best of the best, and you've been selected to the most important of jobs within the IMF: to coordinate central bank policies between the major countries of the world. Instead of making a long speech, I would like to get us started with some interactive discussion. To get us all warmed up, who will volunteer to explain just what a central bank is?"

Jessica raised her hand and, as soon as Steve nodded in her direction, spoke. "It is a government-backed organization with a monopoly on creating money in the economy and on regulating the activity of banks and other financial agents. It can also act as a bank lending to regular banks, if these get into trouble."

"Quite correct." Steve said. "And what are the benefits derived from this system, Jessica?" His eyes met hers and stayed a moment longer than their verbal communication would have required.

Jessica looked back into his eyes and said, holding back a smile, "Well, for large commercial banks, it's like a dream come true, since it allows them to lend money which doesn't exist, as long as they keep some fraction of reserves in their central bank account. This makes possible huge profits on the upside of business cycles, when the central bank stimulates lending in the economy. If they push the risk taking too far, they can be bailed out in the bust part of business cycles. This is because the central bank and government then will want to protect depositors and people in dire need of borrowing money.

"As far as government is concerned, the central bank system gives it the most incredible power that could be thought of. This is the power to arbitrarily create the only allowed money in society by just printing paper bills or by writing checks in the name of the central bank. Since this makes it possible to finance new government spending without levying taxes, it's as close as a government can come to the eternal dream of being a Santa Claus, who can provide gifts to people created out of thin air!

"What about the public? Well, contrary to common belief, they are the big losers in this system, especially people who try to be independent and responsible by saving money for their future in some fixed-income savings product such as bonds or, worse, people who leave their money on an interest-free deposit account.

"Those who get the most out of the system are people benefitting from easy credit or people able to play the speculative game on the upside of business cycles, buying and selling assets at the right moments. So, basically, we have a financial system built on the common interest of large banks and of government, designed to control and abuse the public. So I find it quite amusing when government keeps bashing big banks after an economic crash such as the recent dot-com meltdown. That is akin to a situation where a pimp would give moral reproach to prostitutes about the way they earn their living. Unfortunately, few people see this amusing parallel, as they don't understand the basic workings of the system: its complexity hides its absurdity."

There was a humming in the classroom as the members of the group contemplated Jessica's provocative statement. While most of them looked around the room to see what others thought about it, Steve looked back straight into Jessica's eyes and said, with a smile that was patronizing but still gentle, "That is a most unusual and, I would say, quite cynical, way of judging these institutions. As we all know, central banks were created in order to ensure the stability of the overall economy, to be able to pump new fuel into the system, so to say, if some banks would get into trouble. It can also slow down the economy if it becomes overheated."

He looked even more intensely into her eyes when he added, "But I'll grant you that central banks sometimes have misused their power by facilitating too-rapid inflation of money and prices. This is why all major central banks in our modern era have as a formal guideline to keep the price level stable. So I say that your point is, in part, correct while overstating slightly the negative effects the system has had."Now, let's move to another topic. Who can describe the parallel between central banks, on one hand, and the IMF, on the other hand?"

François, who was sitting at the same table as Jessica was the first to respond. "Well, you know, the central bank aims at the security of the national financial system, by pooling some resources and risks among national banks. The IMF has a similar role in the international monetary system: to achieve the security of the whole international system by pooling risks and by coordinating efforts of the different national financial systems and currencies."

"Quite a good answer, François," Steve said pleasantly. "And may I add a significant difference: while national central banks have the right to create money in their respective country, so-called legal tender, there's no such thing as a global currency. So the IMF has no corresponding possibility of creating money. Its role focuses on maintaining the balance and stability of the exchange rates among all the national paper currencies. They are dollars, pounds, yens, and the newcomer of this year, euros, which now at last exists in the form of actual bills and coins. You, of course, understand that there is a temptation in each currency area to create a lot of money because it provides easy credit, high bank profits, and may make the businesses of that country more competitive in international trade through easier access to capital. Here, the role of the IMF comes into play.

"We are the guardians of exchange rate stability, and we can distribute warnings, and sometimes punishments, to national central banks and governments if they go too far. This shows the importance of your future jobs as members of the G20 central bank coordination group. You will ensure, all together, that the international monetary system evolves smoothly. If you do your job well, the common man will be able to sleep safely with the knowledge that there will never again be any major financial crisis."

Jessica seized the opportunity of a moment of silence to weigh in another statement that raised some eyebrows in the classroom. "Well, thank you very much, dear teacher; we're most flattered by the importance of our future jobs! But let me remind everybody that international trade was even easier a hundred years ago, when a global currency existed, namely, gold. At that time, there was no need for any IMF to 'balance the creation of multiple paper-money currencies.' Regarding the appearance of financial crises, I do hope you're right, but let's not forget that there were never so many or so severe business cycles since these central banking and paper-money systems appeared! The crisis that ended in tears two years ago, with the stock market losing more than twenty percent of its value was not the first one. And I fear that it was not the last financial crisis in our modern world caused by central bank backed inflation.

"I do however agree that we have a great challenge and an important job: to try to control national central banks so that they limit money creation and inflation. We should see ourselves as guardians of the public. In that role we need to protect the public against abuse from the combined effort of the government and of banks, embodied by the central banks of each country."

"Once again, Jessica, you're being cynical," Steve said. "But you're totally right to see us as the guardians of the public. That is indeed our mission and reason for being. Let's end this first discussion session on that positive note, and break out into smaller groups to do some teamwork."

The day went by quickly, with the class engaging in multiple team exercises while getting to know each other. It involved amusing and often confusing discoveries of habits and ways of thinking and being that each of them brought with them from their respective backgrounds. Jessica took pleasure from her conversations with her Japanese and Canadian colleagues. They gave her some embarrassed but amused compliments for her bold statements during the morning group discussion.

At the end of the day, the groups dissolved and people went off to their respective rooms to prepare for the dinner and evening activities. Jessica noticed that Steve, who just had said good evening to the whole group, had left the room before most of his students, who were still talking in smaller groups as they slowly left the classroom.

She saw that he had left a small envelope on her desk, on which he had marked "from S to J." It contained a brief letter, which read:

Dear Jessica,

Although we only spent one day together, I'm not afraid to say that you're the most amazing student I ever had, even though this is the fifth year I've taught this class at the IMF boot camp. I ask you to forgive me for contradicting you this morning; what you said is, as you know, true. But you should understand that everybody isn't ready to hear it said so boldly.

I realize that it is I, not you, who am cynical. But it's my role to reassure and motivate the students as they come here to learn their role as eminent public servants. I can only hope that you understand how much I have longed for having a student say what you said this morning and say it the way you said it with such radiant certainty.

I'm now off to Frankfurt for one week; I left the class in a rush in order to catch my intercontinental flight. But I'll be back at the boot camp next week. Although I won't teach any more classes then, I would be delighted to see you again. If you share the same feeling, please meet me next Friday at 8:00 p.m. in the La Dolce Vita Italian restaurant a few miles south of the convention center. A table for two is already reserved in my name, waiting for us to meet again. Until then, take care, and keep being yourself during this boot camp, which, I admit, is a bit sterile and overly politically correct.

Jessica sat looking out through the window and into the far distance with an inward smile, when François patted her on the shoulder. "Hey, Jessica, will you join the rest of our group tonight after dinner to prepare our presentation for tomorrow morning?"

After a moment of silence, in which she was still mentally in the classroom feeling lonely after Steve had left, she answered. "Sure, I'll have dinner with the Japanese group, we like the same food, and then I'll catch up with you guys."

She carefully slipped the letter from Steve into her handbag and looked around to make sure that none of the people around her had seen her read the letter or fold it away. She slowly gathered her books and stationery and left the room with a faint smile on her lips. She tried to hold her smile back, as if not to reveal that she and their teacher of the day had shared some intimate secret understanding—and that she was already impatient to discover the next steps.

✳ ✳ ✳

The following week went on quickly, as Jessica and her colleagues worked through extensive training classes and team exercises, and started to prepare to go to work for real the week after that. The Friday of the second week came, and after a day full of activities, Jessica was in her room dressing for the evening. She had not tried to contact Steve since the day of his class, nor had he contacted her. But she had kept his letter well hidden in her suitcase, and she didn't hesitate to honor the date at the restaurant. As she entered and crossed the main hall, she walked by tables, most of which already full with dining guests. Soon she caught sight of Steve at some distance, and she winked her left eye to greet him; he did the same in return. As she came up to the table, he stood up and pulled her chair out, then helped her sit.

"I'm so sorry for having contradicted you in public last week. That's one of the reasons why I felt obliged to invite you to dinner, to ask for your forgiveness."

"So that's not the only reason?" Jessica answered.

"No, as I told you in the letter I left you, meeting someone like you, and at the IMF among all places, was a shockingly pleasant surprise to me. I do share the essence of the beliefs you upheld, although, as you understand, I can't quite let that show."

"How are you able to hide your actual beliefs in front of people? I just can't do that."

"Well, that's neither an easy nor a pleasant thing to do, but I have learned that to get along with people in life, and particularly in politics, one has to be prepared to meet people halfway. Sometimes you have to let them believe you agree with them a bit more than you actually do. That will make them more cooperative, and you will have fewer unpleasant situations of open disagreement."

"So you're the kind of guy who can hide his deepest feelings and convictions, as long as the expediency of the moment tells you to do that. I understand what you say, but if this is supposed to be a date, then you should know that I don't like people who hide anything whatsoever. For someone to earn my respect, and something more than that, the first thing I need is to recognize that I'm in front of someone perfectly honest."

"Jessica, that's something I understood the first time you spoke, and it's the main reason why I felt I had to see you again, as soon as humanly possible. I can tell you I was impressed by the way you spoke up in front of a group of strangers with a controversial but crystal-clear statement. It turned an obscure issue into plain common sense."

She looked at him for a long while and thought that he *did* look honest when saying this. She smiled slowly and gently. "Thank you, Steve. To be honest, I wanted to meet you again, too, even before I read the letter. Something told me I would discover what I now discover. And what I like most is that you knew, and I knew, but nobody else did. So let's try to keep this secret between the two of us—total honesty and openness is good but even better when kept to ourselves."

He looked back at her with an equally gentle smile. "Very well! So let's move on to a more superficial topic. How was your second week here at the boot camp?"

"Quite all right, thank you. But I still haven't found a lot of people who think straight about key issues. Most of them appear to have left their brain back somewhere in high school. I get the impression that since then, they just try to repeat what they hear without thinking much. I find such people terribly boring, even if we can work together decently well. What about you, how was your week in Europe?"

"Quite a lot of things to do; I met the people of the European Central Bank. They are very busy since the launch of euro coins and bills in the beginning of the year. On the other hand, most of the people in the former national central banks in Europe don't have much to do anymore. That makes sense, as most of them will soon work for the ECB, or take other jobs. While I was quite busy, I still had time to be impatient for the week to be over, in order for me to be back here and meet you."

They placed their orders and sat watching each other in silence. She looked at him for a long moment, and then started eating the main course, which had been served without either of them noticing it.

The evening went by quickly as they were intensely focused on each other, whether they were talking or were silent, which left room for nothing else in their consciousness. Therefore, they were startled and surprised, when the waiter called their attention to the fact that they were the last guests remaining in the restaurant. It was closing time, and the clock was approaching midnight.

After coming out of the restaurant into the damp September night, they stopped in the street in front of the restaurant. They were each to take a separate cab: Jessica to go back to the convention center, Steve to go back to a hotel near the airport.

"I have a morning flight to London tomorrow morning. Need to spend a lot of time these days with the people from the Bank of England. They are quite scared that the ECB takes up too much of the attention from us here in the United States. I'll be back in Washington in a week from now; I hope I'll be seeing you again, more and more often, if not every day, then at least as often as possible. No, correction, I don't *hope* that; I feel as if I *know* it."

Jessica, who was standing right in front of him, took one more step toward Steve. She leaned toward him and her face approached his, and they kissed for a long while with a light rain falling on both of their faces. Just before turning to step into her taxi, which had been waiting these few minutes, Jessica took his hand and pressed it hard. "I *know* it, too. Good-bye and good night, and see you soon!"

✿ ✿ ✿

Six months after the end of the IMF boot camp, Jessica was sitting on a plane from Frankfurt, where a meeting of the G20 central bank coordination group had just been held. She was flying back to her home in Washington, D.C. She thought about the last six months, which had been quite intense as most previous periods in her life. The IMF boot camp had been an amazing experience on the professional level and on a personal level, by getting to know so many people from so many other countries. But above all, it remained in her mind as the place and time when she had met Steve, whom she now, for a few months, thought of as the love of her life.

While their first conversation had been hostile, she had soon discovered a man with virtually all of the qualities she admired. Steve was intelligent and highly dedicated to his job. But, at the same time, he kept a sort of detachment from it which made her feel that she was the most important thing in his life, even though he was working with matters of utmost importance to the country. He had quickly understood her character and her convictions about politics and economics, which were far from common. While Steve didn't actually subscribe to those views, he made her feel as if he did, thanks to the moral support he would give her in all situations. She even thought that she had learned a few things from Steve. Above all, she had learned to be smoother with other people, not to always let disagreements show and create unnecessary hard feelings.

Steve had also been very encouraging about Jessica's job, as when he said, "I think you chose this job because you understand that monetary policy is extremely important. People say that I have a gift to see and know what makes other people tick. I'm flattered to hear that, but what I know with certainty is that monetary policy, as controlled by central banks, is what makes the whole world tick."

Whenever they discussed topics where they had differences of opinion, Steve would always stop short of actually saying something that would displease Jessica. He would turn any discussion about the nature of her work into personal compliments to her. And during this first period of her job, she tried hard to learn how the IMF and central banks actually worked. To this end, Steve was a good listener and helped Jessica a lot. He provided insights about the new world she had entered and had a hard time to understand, but which Steve knew well since more than five years.

The G20 central bank coordination group had now met five times since she started, once per month. While she liked the preparation work which consisted in analyzing the state of the economy, she felt quite awkward during those meetings. Although mass media always tried hard to interpret statements of central bank leaders, they would also compliment these leaders more, and the harder it was to interpret their statements. If central bank statements were too direct, it was considered as some form of giant "inside information" given to all the players on the financial markets, enabling them to take undue advantage of that knowledge. It was the only case she knew of where providing something totally impossible to understand was considered as the most enlightened form of communication. The meetings of her coordination group resembled this mode of communication—few ideas or decisions were formulated explicitly, and much meaning was conferred "between the lines" of what was said and written. It took great effort and much time for Jessica to grasp this, which was opposite to her direct manner of thinking and speaking. Steve's help had proved valuable to help her overcome this mental barrier.

As her plane started to descend toward Washington, D.C., she thought about the evening to come. Steve had promised to pick her up at the airport, to celebrate the six-month anniversary of their romance at some secret place. Sensing that this night, too, would be special and memorable, she felt the same kind of expectation as on the day of their first date.

When sitting in Steve's car on the way from the airport to downtown Washington, Jessica said, "So where are we going tonight, dear?"

"Somewhere really, really nice," Steve answered. "If you want it to be a surprise, then I suggest you put this blindfold on. It won't be long, so don't worry. And I'll of course help you out of the car."

She did as he said, and sat silent waiting for the car to arrive at its destination. She did not indulge in small talk as she tried to prepare for what she expected to be a great surprise.

When they had parked the car and taken an elevator up in a building, and had gone through a couple of doors, Steve took her blindfold off. What she saw was a large dining room with a small table for two set in the middle. The floor was covered by red carpets, and the tablecloth was made of thick white tissue. Silver candelabras lit up the room, along with the light of a distinguished lamp crown hanging from the ceiling. A waiter dressed in a black tuxedo stood silently alongside the table where a champagne bottle was waiting to be opened. Behind the table was a large window open to the night lights of Washington. Jessica saw that they were in the heart of the city. She turned back to face Steve. "This is wonderful! This is exactly the place I would have selected for this kind of celebration. And I'm so happy that you felt the same way."

Steve looked at the waiter and made a sign to him to serve the champagne. He took Jessica's hand and made her follow him and slowly across the room all the way to the window. He opened a door giving access to a large corner balcony, and they went out. Standing in the fresh but clear March evening, they received the champagne glasses from the waiter and put the glasses on a stone table standing on the balcony. They stood alone on the balcony from which the Washington Monument, Lincoln Memorial, the White House, and the Capitol could be seen. These monuments were lit up as much by their own white-yellow lights as by the stars and the full moon.

Steve took a step closer to Jessica and looked her straight in the eyes. "Thank you for your compliments; it gives me additional courage for the question I'm about to ask you, and which I've been contemplating since the first time I saw you."

"What's your question?" Jessica said with a curious smile, looking straight back into Steve's eyes.

"Will you marry me?" Steve said slowly, with a cautious smile.

Jessica noticed an unusual uncertainty in Steve's face as he waited for her answer. While smiling gently and radiantly back at him, she said, "You know I'm really starting to think you can read my thoughts, because that was the question I was hoping you would ask me! So the answer is yes! Of course I will marry you!"

Steve closed his eyes for a moment, in relief and to recapture his usual total self-control. He quickly produced a small box from the left pocket of his jacket, and took out a ring. It was a massive gold ring with a large single diamond. He pushed it onto Jessica's finger and took her in his arms, and they kissed passionately.

They opened their eyes at the same time, and their eyes met again. Jessica picked up their champagne glasses from the stone table. She raised her glass. "Here's to us and to our future."

"Here's to the most wonderful woman in the world and to everything that we will be able to achieve together," Steve answered, while making a wide gesture with his arm, pointing to the monuments of America's history and power.

From this view, Jessica recalled the idea of a country built by free and responsible men, with a government whose only role was to protect their life and property and leave them free to pursue their happiness in life. She thought that for the third time this night, the two of them were thinking the exact same thoughts, and this made her smile toward Steve. They both remained silent, and then Steve kissed Jessica again for a long time. He took her hand, and they returned into the dining room. The hors d'oeuvres were served, and a long, romantic dinner was ahead of them.

CHAPTER 4:
Playing Along in Doing Wrong

September in Nevada was as usual very sunny and hot. Only a few months after his graduation, Bobby Cheston and his girlfriend Barbara were sitting in an air-conditioned hotel room dressed in formal clothes. It was their wedding day, and they had just come back to the hotel from the ceremony at a Las Vegas chapel.

The two of them had spent most of the summer securing jobs and finding a place to live in the Los Angeles area. They had decided to move there after their deep romance period, which had started not long before Bobby's graduation. During summer, Bobby had asked Barbara to marry him, and she had happily accepted. However, they both had complex relationships with their families, which also were from quite different social backgrounds. Barbara's parents were a divorced lower-middle-class couple from Salt Lake City, and her mother had serious drug addiction problems. Barbara had been working as a waitress in Salt Lake City for a couple of years. Early this year, she had left everything behind to go to San Francisco to start a new life.

Bobby's father was a successful, rich, third-generation owner of a Seattle-based family business in the consumer goods area. It manufactured and sold tools and equipment for gardening and outdoor maintenance. Bobby had disappointed his father when he had declared that he would not go to work in the family business. He did wish to stay in the same line of business, but he preferred to go to work for a large international company.

Working as a waitress in the sports bar near the Jefferson-Jackson University campus, Barbara had seduced Bobby, a frequent patron of that establishment. He had fallen in love with her beauty and charm and with her lust for life and adventure, which, to his surprise, she had shown by following him on long walks in the mountains near San Francisco.

Because of their family situations, they had decided to keep their marriage secret and to not invite anybody to attend their wedding. They planned to inform families and friends of the happy event by sending out postcards afterward.

Barbara had told Bobby her view on this: "Imagine that we're the only two people in the world who know that we're now married, except of course the priest who married us. I think there is something profoundly right about it. I mean, a marriage is something intimate between two people, and the more intimate we keep it, the more precious and exclusive it is. We will have time to share it with the rest of the world later."

"I agree, honey; I like it this way. You were gorgeous at the ceremony, as you always are! So please wear your wedding dress during dinner tonight. That way, at least some Las Vegas tourists and gamblers will have a chance to see that we have just married," he said with a light chuckle. "By the way, we need to go to the restaurant now; we should not be late."

The restaurant was on the top floor of one of the major casinos of the city. They had a panoramic view of Las Vegas by night, with all the colored and blinking lights it provided. This sight of energy and movement contrasted with the setting of the dining room, which was soundproofed and with few tables, most of them close to the windows with a clear view of the city. The only sounds were a low background sound from the conversations of the other guests and the occasional waiter moving by with dishes on wheeled carts. They had already finished the main course, when Barbara slowly said, with confidence, "Now that we've married and exchanged our rings, I have an additional surprise and gift for you, darling..."

Bobby looked at her, trying to guess what she now would tell him. But he didn't really have any clue, so he remained silent, waiting.

"I'm pregnant," she said, "with twins!" She looked profoundly happy when saying this. And she looked at Bobby to see his reaction with unease. They had never talked about having children.

"Wow!" he said, "That sure is a surprise. When were you told?"

"Two days ago. But I wanted to wait until we were married to tell you. Are you as happy about it as I am?"

"Yes, I'm very happy about it, but surprised. When will they be born?"

"In seven months, mid-April next year."

"Well, I thought we would have children together, but I didn't expect it that soon. Anyway, let's drink a toast to our future children!"

They raised their champagne glasses, which had already been served along with their wedding cake dessert. He thought for a few seconds and then said, "Now, since we soon will be a family of four, that two-room flat we rented down in Los Angeles will not do for long."

"Let's buy a house!" Barbara shouted.

"That would be great, but do you know what a house costs in the north-western area of Los Angeles where we want to live? We would have to get a huge mortgage to cope with that."

"Don't worry about that. I've got a job in the movie business so that's going to be much better than a waitress's salary. And you're soon going to be a big shot in that sportswear manufacturing company. So let's not worry about money. Do I have to remind you that we're at the start of a six-week honeymoon trip across the most astonishing places in the United States: the national parks of the southwest? We can find that house, and the financing we need, when we will be back from our trip."

"Right, honey, let's leave it at that. I do look forward to this trip. But from now on, I'm going to prevent you from doing any dangerous climbing and hiking as you've done before. Mrs. Cheston, and the two babies she's carrying, is up for a safe and comfortable trip which I will ensure!"

"Bobby, stop talking like that; you turn me off," Barbara said with a loud giggle and flashed her most seductive and sexy smile across the table. "I want us to keep having as much fun as we always did. Starting tonight!" As always, Bobby fulfilled her wishes, and they spent a sleepless night in the giant bed of their wedding suite.

✲ ✲ ✲

A few months after his wedding, Bobby called Laura Dalaghan. "Hi Laura, this is Bobby. I got your text message about the launch of your Internet bank. Congratulations! How are you doing?"

"Thank you very much. I'm doing well, although I guess you can imagine how much work it is to launch a new business. What about you? I didn't congratulate you either, but I got your card from Las Vegas last fall, announcing your marriage to Barbara. I see the two of you didn't waste any time after your graduation, having met just a few months before."

"Well, that's for sure, and you're more right than you know, because in addition to getting married, we're also having children—twins, to be born just three months from now."

"That *is* a surprise, Bobby; I never thought you would be the first one in our group to go into full blown family life! I hope you have adjusted your plans for housing accordingly."

"Yes, and that's something I wanted to talk to you about" Bobby said, switching to a more cautious and formal way of speaking. "You see, as we have both found jobs in the northwestern Los Angeles area, we're looking to buy a house there. I'm sure you know that prices are pretty steep there and that none of us has any fortune in our pockets to pay the house with." He paused, as if expecting Laura to pick up on his hint.

"Well, so what?" Laura said after a few seconds of silence.

"I thought I would give a boost to your new start-up bank by asking you to provide me with the mortgage. I figured this would be a good thing for you in this early stage of your company's development. I imagine you must be looking desperately for new customers. So you should understand my surprise when my application, processed by your credit advisor Sandra, was dismissed without any possibility to negotiate about it. So I just wanted to ask you to correct that error, so I can get my mortgage and at the same time help your business to get going."

"Bobby, what were the credit conditions you asked for, and what did you propose to back it with?"

"A loan of eight hundred thousand dollars, corresponding to the full value of the house we want to buy, with a no-amortization adjustable-rate mortgage. That would enable us to honor the monthly interest payments with no more than half of our combined salaries, which amount to six thousand dollars."

"Bobby, you have to understand that the answer you got wasn't an error or an accident—there's no way that we would lend on such conditions.

Not to anyone in the world, even to a close friend of mine! Even if you're able to deduce interest payments from your taxable income, thereby paying lower taxes, those monthly payments would still be huge for you to manage."

"I'm quite disappointed to hear that, Laura, and I ask you to consider this: the people who are bidding against us to buy this house seem to have a quite similar financial situation, and they already got a mortgage."

"But they didn't get it from DPIB, I can assure you!"

"No, that's true; they got it from one of those government backed credit institutions, aiming to extend credit 'democratically,' to all those who need it and want it."

"Then you could do as they did. But, as a friend, I strongly advise you not to. My advice would be to find a smaller house, or a house in a not-so-expensive area. That way, you could have smaller monthly payments and maybe save to pay down the debt a bit. That would be much more prudent, and should save you from financial worries in the future."

"Well, I thought about that, but Barbara won't take any of it. She wants this house at any price, and with a minimum monthly payment, and I'm unable to reason with her about it."

"I'm sorry to hear that. And I should admit it makes me quite worried. I really hope you married the right person and that she won't get you into trouble."

"You have a lot of nerve to talk like that about Barbara," Bobby said with a sting of anger in his voice. "She's much more ambitious and serious than you guys may have understood back in San Francisco. She has even managed to get a job in Hollywood to play minor roles in motion pictures, even though her only previous job was as a waitress! And I have started as product manager of outdoor sports gear at the World Wear and Food Company. So we will go ahead with our project, with or without the backing of your so-called Prudential Bank. It was nice talking to you, Laura, but I think all is said for now. Good luck with your bank, even if I allow myself to think you have chosen a losing strategy, refusing customers like us."

"Thank you, Bobby, I appreciate it, but I'm quite certain I'm right about my banking strategy, even though I hope I'm wrong when worrying about your financial situation. Say hi to Barbara, and keep in touch."

She hung up after these words and turned back to her desk. A financial newspaper was lying there, and she was seized by the headline "A Country of Homeowners—How America Should Rebound after the Dot-Com Crisis." The article referred to a recent speech of the president of the United States, who had reiterated his desire to see as many people as possible become owners of the house or flat they live in. The president had said, "This country was made by people who built and owned their own homes, which was their main safeguard against uncertainty and their main means for saving. Thereby they ensured their future and financial independence. I wish that our banks be benevolent and fulfill their social responsibility to provide mortgage to all people who ask for it, whatever their financial resources. That's how the American dream of individual success and independence will spread more widely during the twenty-first century."

Either I'm going crazy, or else the president is—he's asking banks to lend money to people who have no sure means to ensure payments! And he's asking people to achieve financial independence by indebting themselves beyond the limits of what they can pay back. I'll be damned if one day I accept to apply such a credit policy!

At this point, she also recalled the conversation from the last night she and her friends had spent at Professor Benson's house, just before graduation, when the Professor had said, "So maybe the next crisis will be in the real estate market? What if government tries to push people, who can't afford it, to buy houses using money borrowed easily during a boom period with low interest rates? Your guess is as good as mine."

Laura desperately hoped that the professor's guess would be proved wrong, although she feared that this time too, he would be right.

The day after his disappointing phone conversation with Laura, Bobby obtained his mortgage according to the exact conditions which Laura had refused. He got it from the government-backed lending institution with the weird sounding but homey name Freddy K. They even added in an unlimited credit card to Barbara, usable on credit against steep interest, but with a very low annual fee. The letter of intent guaranteeing the acceptance of this mortgage enabled Bobby and Barbara to conclude their house purchase and to move in one month before the planned birth of their twin children. Barbara had read the same newspaper articles as Laura; however, her reaction to them was the opposite. She figured that if the president of the United States was endorsing what they were doing, then it could not be wrong or unadvisable.

When they signed the contract to purchase their house, Barbara looked at Bobby and said with a smile, "So much for those, including our parents, who said that buying this house was foolish and that we wouldn't be able to do it. We did it!"

As they walked out together, waving her hand in front of Bobby's face holding up the credit card she had got from Freddy K, she said, "And I prefer to listen to the experts who claim that it's the consumers who keep the American economy running. We'll be among the best economy-runners in the coming years!"

In October of that year, Bobby and Barbara held a small party in their West Hollywood house with some friends and colleagues in order to celebrate their twin sons Jeff and Paul being six months old.

None of the members of the group of friends from San Francisco had been able to make it, but at least Mark Lomack had taken the time to browse through the large number of photos of the two babies he had received in an e-mail from Bobby. While he was happy to hear from Bobby, he had not been able to drive up from San Diego to Los Angeles to attend the event. He had to be at the release party of the first software product he had developed since he started working. It was already being hailed in the IT and financial newspapers as one of the most promising financial software products ever.

The software, called QRD, as in Quick, Right Decision, was aimed at financial portfolio managers and traders. It would help them process the vast quantity of information available in the fastest way possible in order to provide recommendations about what financial assets to buy, and what to sell. The marketing release note of QRD had said, among other things,

> The end of fundamental valuation of financial assets, and the beginning of radically increased productivity for your trader teams! With QRD, you'll get the opportunity to judge financial product prices by sophisticated software which integrates, in real time, data about all transactions done on all financial products on all major market places. No more old-school fundamental analysis, requiring you to make cumbersome cash flow and risk analysis on individual companies or financial products.

> Instead, QRD will analyze and predict the actual trend in the market prices of all assets. If they are about to rise, it will advise you to buy. If they are about to fall, it will advise you to sell. So this is really as scientific as financial product valuation will ever become!

> It is widely acknowledged, be it in financial affairs or in politics, that what a majority of people think is by definition what is right. So you'll save time by not trying to go against the odds, staking your judgment against the market. Just go with the flow, but be sure to be quicker than most other people! Both in buying our product, and later when you start to use it!

> As always, timing is everything; on the day which we believe to be not so distant, when virtually the whole market will use QRD, the profits you'll be able to reap from it will obviously be smaller. So go for it now! Ride the renewed bull

market, driven by real estate, to give your investors rates of return unseen earlier, even during the Internet boom!

Mark had not approved the writing of that release note, even if he was the chief programmer of the project and felt rightly proud that the product was now ready to be put on the market. He had disagreed with his boss, Mike Harding, both about the product's final design and about the way it was presented in the marketing material. Mike was the CEO of Golden Touch Software, and at the company's internal release party held this night in their office, he had made a vibrant speech to congratulate the whole team which had worked on QRD and, above all, Mark.

Mike walked up to Mark, who was helping himself to some snacks at the buffet table which had been set up in the main conference room of the small but light office of Golden Touch Software. The office was located in a modern glass-frame building right next to the beach, just south of San Diego.

"Mark, why don't you cheer up a bit? One could believe this is the funeral of some close relative of yours. We are holding a party in the honor of you and your team. You have finished the QRD product ahead of schedule, with more features than initially planned, and while respecting the planned budget! Now *that* is a feat I had never seen before in my twenty-year career as software development manager. In addition, the buzz is already sky high about the product. Virtually the whole financial community is already hailing it as *the* software to help investors and fund managers play the new bull market to make as much money as possible."

"Well, I don't want to repeat a discussion we have had several times, but I'm concerned about having removed the fundamental valuation from the product. This means people will more and more come to buy stock in companies without having a clue about the viability of the company as such. They will only look at what price other people are ready to buy and sell those stocks for. It's the same with more complex financial products, such as mutual funds or those new mortgage-backed securities, which are just a repackaging of the mortgages some banks have sold to their customers. Let's assume we will be successful in selling QRD to a large number of financial market agents. It would mean that none of those agents will take the time to think about the viability of the actual assets that are underlying the financial products they buy and sell!

"This gives me the creeps, because I don't see what would be the safeguard against products which are just dressed up junk bonds. Just look at what happened during the savings-and-loans crisis a few decades ago, or in the recent dot-com bubble crash. And I think you know that the most successful investor in all of financial history, Buffy Warrington, is known for having made most of his money by picking the right stocks based on fundamental valuation!"

"Mark, as you know perfectly well, there is an exception even to the most valid rule. That guy is the exception that confirms the rule. Now, I really don't like to see you in such a negative mind-set, especially not on a day like this.

"You know that few people want to do fundamental valuation anymore—it takes way too much time. And given how much those traders are paid nowadays, they better do as many transactions as possible in a day to make it pay for their employers to hire them. Those who have spent time looking hard into income statements and balance sheets often feel that they have wasted their time. Just take that energy firm or that accounting firm that went broke with a big crash last year. They had jiggled their books for years, with fundamental analysis revealing nothing until it was too late anyway. QRD will help investors take better decisions, earn more money, and spend less time doing it. After all, who wouldn't want to buy such a software product?"

"Let's see about next month's trade show," Mark said wearily. "But let's not argue about fundamental analysis. It has been taken out of the product, right. What disturbs me even more is that you had the marketing guys lie about the actual potential of the product, saying it works as well in a downturn as in a boom. That's just not true, and I can tell because I have built the product!"

"Mark, why should we argue about questions of truth? The product works in a boom period. And we're moving into a boom right now. So why should we, or anyone else, worry about downturns? I'm not so sure there will even be another downturn. Why should there be, if all investors remain faithful and keep buying assets?"

"Damn you!" Mark shouted before turning his back on his boss, rushing out of the office, and driving home to his apartment.

✳ ✳ ✳

Early in the following year, Mark, Mike Harding, and Joey, the company's sales manager, flew across the continent to participate in the annual Financial Markets Trade Show, held in a giant convention center outside Boston. It was one of the largest, if not *the* largest, such trade show in the financial services business anywhere in the world. This year the trade show was back in a positive mood, triggered by the steady rise in financial market indexes compared to the previous year. First real estate, and then the stock market, had picked up in less than two years to erase much of the losses made by investors in the dot-com bubble crash.

In spite of this more and more general euphoria, Mark had not been particularly eager to go, given his moral doubts regarding the software product they were promoting. Mike firmly wanted him to come, since Mark was the only person able to fully understand and explain how the QRD product really worked. But what had made Mark accept going was the prospect of meeting Pete Bagnelli.

They had not seen each other in almost two years, as Pete had moved to the East Coast to start his mutual fund and investment business outside New York City.

When the small delegation from Golden Touch Software had finished preparing their booth in the morning of the first day of the trade show, Mark left Mike and Joey there. He started walking across the enormous trade show floor. It was organized in straight-line corridors with company booths on both sides. They covered the full area of the square building, which was the size of twenty football fields. It took Mark almost ten minutes of uninterrupted walking to reach a small, dark blue booth, almost completely hidden by a large sign post in the same blue color saying "Bagnelli Investment Funds." Pete was not expecting to meet Mark at this event, as he had told him he didn't want to go. A radiant smile exploded on Pete's face when he saw Mark standing with his hands in his pockets in front of him.

"Man, how happy I am to see you!" Pete shouted. Then he squeezed Mark against his chest and punched his back with his left fist. "Great to see you still have that surfer's hair cut, although I have to say that seeing you in a suit feels quite strange."

"And what about you?" Mark answered, "You who used to wear white linen at all occasions. It's really weird to see you in a gray suit and with a dull tie!"

Pete shrugged. "Well, that's the way people look in New York, especially those who wish to build enough trust to sell mutual funds to other people. So I have left my old clothes at my parents' place down in Miami. But they come handy every now and then when I fly down for some rest from the busy life up in New York. Now let's stop talking about clothes. How are you doing in San Diego?"

"Not bad. I've had time to do a lot of surfing, hiking, and skiing. And we recently released the new software I developed, ahead of schedule and on budget. It seems to be a lot of buzz about it here on the trade show. I'm here to answer any tricky questions about the product, which my boss will try to sell to the whole financial community.

"What about you, Pete? The last time I saw you, you were an economics graduate with two hundred thousand dollars in your pockets, talking about becoming the world's richest and most respected investor. How close did you come to that ambitious goal in two years time?"

"Well, things aren't going as fast as I wished, although I have had some success. During my first year up here, I only gambled on the markets with my own money. That was quite hard since we were just coming out of the bust period following the Internet bubble crash. But I still managed to double my capital. That was enough for me to set up a first mutual fund and to hire a person to manage it with me."

"What's the focus of that mutual fund?" Mark asked.

"Commodities: precious metals, raw materials such as oil or coal, and basic agriculture products such as cereals. All these things had ridiculously low valuations during the dot-com frenzy. Back then, people came to think that anything as physical and uncomplicated as commodities was hopelessly outdated next to those zero-capital, unlimited-profit ventures that Internet whiz kids were bragging about.

"Today, most of those guys have gone bust, and commodity prices are soaring as all these emerging economies, such as China, India, Russia, and Brazil, show double-digit growth. They have rapidly growing middle classes starting to demand food, clothing, and housing much like what we have in the Western world. I spotted this trend before most people, so I made a lot of money on it. Now my challenge is to spot other types of products with a huge profit potential. But I don't want to spend years of my time in scrutinizing company balance sheets or hundreds of pages of description text. Such red tape is frequent these days on new, complex financial derivative products. But I don't really care about understanding all that, as long as I can make quick money."

"Then I have the perfect solution for you, Mr. Bagnelli!" someone said from behind Pete and Mark.

They both turned around, and Mark could confirm to himself that it indeed was the voice of Mike Harding he had heard.

"What are you doing here, boss? How did you spot me among these thousands of booths?" Mark said with a hint of irritation.

"Well, I figured I would follow you to say hi to this fancy investor friend of yours, whom you've been talking about so often in San Diego. Mr. Bagnelli, I believe that our QRD product, as for Quick Right Decision, is exactly what you're looking for in order to manage your investment portfolios more efficiently, and making more and faster profits!"

"That's indeed what I wish to do, but how could your product help me to do it?" Pete asked casually.

"Boss, I don't think—" Mark started,

"QRD," Mike said and stepped between Mark and Pete to address the latter looking him straight into the eyes, "is connected to all major financial markets and uses a unique algorithm developed by your genius friend who's just too modest to admit the value of the product he developed. By analyzing all the data, the product forecasts ahead of time which assets will increase in value and which will fall, and it will recommend you to buy the former and sell the latter.

"In our first month of track record, we have seen the relevancy of how our product picks assets, and it hovers at record levels. Those who have made fun of financial markets by saying that we might as well hire monkeys to pick stocks arbitrarily were almost right, as it has been proved that the analysis arms of major financial firms aren't right in much more than half of their recommendations. It's not much better than pure guessing, which is why QRD will take investment picking to a new level."

Pete turned to Mark for some confirmation of what Harding was saying. Mark shrugged. "I did my best to develop a strong product. But keep in mind that error-free investment picking isn't possible, since nobody can really predict the future."

Pete, used to making fast decisions, nodded and then turned back to Harding. "So, we may be able to do business together. But I guess your flagship software must be worth a fortune. Otherwise, if it as good as you say, you would be better off playing the market with your own money and not letting anyone in the world use your software. So what does it sell for?"

Mike produced an enduring and friendly smile and then said lightly, "You sure are a smart guy, as Mark told me. You almost guessed how our business model works, although it's a novelty in the software business. As a matter of fact, we don't sell licenses of our software. We give it to you with no up-front cost, but instead we will take ten percent of all the capital gains you make thanks to our product. How does that work? It's quite simple.

"As a part of its data collection system which tracks transactions, the software will tell us over the Internet what financial products you buy, when and to what price, and whether we had advised you to do so. Then we will look at the market price of that same asset when you sell it, or if you don't, at year-end, and compare to your previous purchase price. It works the same way, in reverse, for products you sell on our advice. In both cases, we take ten percent of the gain you made, which is the only way you will pay us. If you don't earn any money with our product, you don't pay a cent for using it. So, you see, it's totally risk free for you. You can imagine that we wouldn't propose such conditions if we weren't sure to profit from it."

Pete stood and looked at Harding as if judging what he should think of this, but he was interrupted by Harding, who stretched his hand out to Pete.

"Now do we have a deal for the Bagnelli Investment Funds to buy our QRD product?"

"We do, Mr. Harding" Pete said and shook Mike's hand.

Mike produced the same salesman's smile as in the beginning of their conversation. "You won't regret it, Mr. Bagnelli. Now, please, let me go back to our booth to cater to our other, no less worthy prospects."

He produced a one-page letter of intent, which Pete signed. He slipped the second copy of it into a Golden Touch Software promotional leaflet, which he handed over to Pete, before turning around and heading back to the other side of the building.

Watching his boss walk away, Mark stood voiceless, his face red from embarrassment and anger. A third emotion he felt was panic. It came from a vision of the future that popped up in his mind, of his best friend Pete going bust from using the software *he* had developed.

CHAPTER 5:
Living too Fast Will not Last

It was an early morning in March, and Bobby Cheston had already got up from bed. He was not an early riser, but he had made an exception this morning in order to prepare a wake-up surprise for his and Barbara's twin children on their fourth birthday. Two years ago, Bobby and Barbara also got a daughter, Jennifer, whose birth had caused much joy but further increases in their living costs. For this anniversary, Barbara had bought a cake, and Bobby was now putting four small candles on it. He made coffee for Barbara and himself and hot chocolate for the kids. When this was ready, he quietly woke Barbara up.

Barbara had not been in a good mood recently. Her irregular work as an actress with minor roles in Hollywood movies and TV shows had not developed, as she had hoped, toward more prestigious and better-paying roles in better movies and shows. Her situation had remained much the same since four years, and she had only worked a bit more than part-time on average. The rest of her time she spent by either sitting home and feeling bored or doing the only thing which could help her get rid of that boredom: going shopping in nearby Beverly Hills.

Recently she had accepted the need to shop in less expensive areas, as their financial situation was becoming more and more problematic. Two years earlier, they had extended their mortgage to 130 percent of the purchase price of their house, and they had monthly payments which first had required half of their monthly incomes. As market interest rates had started to rise over the last two years, the burden had become harder and harder, since the mortgage rate was adjustable and pegged to market rates. That had meant relatively low interest in the beginning, but now it made it increase by around a third. In addition to the mortgage, they had built up a significant consumption debt, caused by the purchases Barbara made with her credit card. It had come to a point when they were unable to honor monthly payments of both these debts for a few months. Since the rate of interest on the credit card debt was higher, they had chosen to suspend the payment of the mortgage, trying to pay down the credit card debt a little. Bobby had even asked the mortgage institution Freddy K to get a revised payment plan, but this had been refused. The refusal letter recalled that they already were on zero amortization, meaning they were only paying interest. Freddy K would not let them cumulate unpaid interest, which would only make it even harder for them to be able to pay back their debt.

Often, these issues made her itchy and unpleasant both with Bobby and with the kids. However, this morning she managed to produce a smile when emerging from bed and facing Bobby in the kitchen.

"Good morning, honey. The cake is lovely with those candles! Did you also find the birthday presents I hid in the closet?"

"Sure, they're right over there. But can you fetch Jennifer first? I'd like you to carry her when we go into the boys' room," Bobby answered.

Jennifer was a cute child who got along well with her elder twin brothers Jeff and Paul. Bobby loved all his three children. Nevertheless, the birth of Jennifer was, in his mind, linked to a decision he much regretted now. That was to extend the mortgage on their house in order to buy a bigger car and to pay for their swimming pool. It was undeniable that both the car and the swimming pool had brought much comfort and pleasure to the family. But now these items appeared as the major cause for their growing financial difficulties, from which Bobby had not yet found a way out.

He shook those thoughts out of his head as he took the tray with the cake and the hot drinks, and started into his sons' bedroom. Jeff and Paul opened their eyes, woken by a loud version of 'Happy Birthday', sung by Barbara. Jennifer was too young to understand what was going on, but she remained quiet and content and had her own breakfast served by her mother.

It was a Saturday morning, and neither Bobby nor Barbara had to go to work. So the whole family spent some nice moments together having breakfast in the boys' bedroom, with Jeff and Paul opening and discovering their birthday gifts. Their children's happiness made both Barbara and Bobby forget, for a moment, their financial worries and their more and more frequent disputes triggered by that.

This moment of relief came to a brusque end when the doorbell rang around nine o'clock. Bobby went to open, and to his surprise, the man standing in the doorway had a police uniform.

"Good morning," Bobby said after a moment of hesitation.

"Good morning," the man answered. "I'm the sheriff of West Hollywood. I come to deliver a certified mail letter which your wife refused to receive from the mailman earlier this week."

"Did she?" Bobby turned around to see if Barbara had come to join him, but she was not in sight. "I don't know why she refused it, but please let me sign and receive the letter. Do you happen to know what it is?"

"Yes, I do. I was sent here because you're not allowed to refuse to receive this type of correspondence. It's a complaint from your mortgage company, Freddy K."

"What's a complaint?" Bobby said uneasily, as it came to his mind that they had not honored their mortgage payments for the last few months.

"A complaint is the first step taken by your mortgage company in the process of foreclosure of your home."

"You mean they want to take our home and throw us out in the street?" Bobby said, with a touch of panic making his voice edgy.

"Well, that's basically what it means. Unless of course you're able to pay what you owe the mortgage company, and if you do it fast."

Bobby stood speechless for a few seconds, then took the pen extended to him by the sheriff, and signed the sheet acknowledging receipt of the letter.

He said good-bye to the sheriff, slammed the door shut, and ran up to drag Barbara out of their sons' bedroom.

"Why didn't you tell me about this letter you refused to receive?" he shouted at her.

She looked away from him and sighed, and said indifferently, "What difference would it make? We have no way of paying those debts anyway!"

"So you're telling me you realize we're going to get thrown out of our house, and you don't plan to do anything about it?"

"I said we have no way of paying the debts! Now get off my back, will you?" Barbara snapped while turning around to go back to Jeff and Paul.

The boys had heard their parents arguing and were standing watching them at the end of the corridor leading to their bedroom.

Bobby rushed up to his home office room, closed the door, and spread out his pile of unpaid bills on the desk. After going over them for a long moment, and after checking up through his Internet bank interface the amount of their current financial assets, he sat back in a chair and closed his eyes. He felt a cold terror creeping onto him, and he wished it were just the winter morning cold. But he knew his feeling came from what he had just realized: Barbara was right. They had no means of paying their debt back, and consequently, they would soon be thrown out of their house.

A few weeks later, in a late but sunny April evening, Bobby had stayed late in his office, after all his colleagues had gone home. He was to make an important phone call to someone he has not talked to for over three years: his father. Their relationship had gone cold when Bobby refused to stay to work in the family business. His parents had cut off contact with him after learning about his marriage to Barbara, which they disapproved of. They had come once to see his twin sons and their new house in West Hollywood, but that was the only time Bobby had met his parents during the last four years. The visit had been short and unpleasant. It felt all the more unpleasant now since the situation that came to his mind was when his father looked him in the eyes and said, "How can you afford a house like this on the wages of a young product manager and of a waitress who occasionally is an actress?"

Bobby tried to shake off the uneasiness triggered by his recollection, as he dialed the number of his father's cellular phone.

"Martin Cheston speaking," a man with a sharp voice answered.

"Hi, Daddy; this is Bobby."

"Hi son," Martin Cheston answered after a moment of surprise. "What do you want?"

"Well, first of all, we haven't talked to each other for several years, and I think that's a shame, even if you didn't approve of my marriage. But I also have a serious issue I wanted to discuss with you."

"What's your serious issue?""We're threatened by foreclosure on our house, for not honoring mortgage payments."

"I'm sorry to say it, Bobby, but this isn't a surprise to me. Do you remember what I told you last time we met?"

"Yes."

"Then what do you want me do to about it now? I warned you about the risks of excessive debt, but as always you wouldn't take my advice. Don't you think you have a lot of nerve to come back to talk to me about it afterwards?"

"Daddy, I don't want to argue about all that. I just have one question for you, and it's a simple one."

"What is it?"

"Would you accept to lend me fifty thousand dollars, which I would pay back over an extended period? After having looked at all possible solutions, this is the only remaining way out which could save us from being thrown out of our house two weeks from now!"

"Son, let me rephrase what I'm hearing. You are asking someone, whose advice you've never taken, to take a financial bet on you which, by your own admission, no financial institution in the country will accept to take. Why should I do that?"

"I won't bore you with a plea on the basis that you're my father. Well, you *are* my father, and I would like us to get back on normal terms again. But that's not the issue. The reason I ask you to help me out is that I have learned a lesson. I now admit that you were right, that we shouldn't have bought this house and, of course we shouldn't have extended the mortgage. Now knowing this, I wish to start over again, and this loan would give me a chance to bounce back."

"I'm sorry, son, but your financial decisions aren't the only or the worst errors you have made. As long as you stay with that girl, who I consider evil and irresponsible and who drew you into this financial mess, I won't bail you out. I won't, because I'm not confident that you will take sound decisions as long as you're under her influence. I might help you the day you come back to admit that your *marriage* was your main mistake, and that you're no longer married to that waitress and wannabe actress.

"This said, son, I wish you all the best. I sincerely hope you'll get out of this mess. But you must do it on your own strength, assuming responsibility of your own past actions and decisions."

"Damn you, Daddy. Don't you dare talk like that about Barbara! If that's the way you feel, then forget what I just asked you. You can keep your money and go to hell!" Bobby shouted before hanging up, smacking the receiver violently against the telephone set.

Afterward, Bobby remained sitting in his office, looking out the window for a long while. For the first time, he started to realize that they *would* be thrown out of their house. Nevertheless, he had a hard time to accept it, and his mind was racing over any possibility he might find to avoid it. Finally, he stood up, punched his fist against the wall, and swore to himself as he had earlier sworn to his father. Bobby was usually a calm guy, but what he now realized made him furious: there *was* no way out of it.

☆ ☆ ☆

The local newspaper had announced, two weeks before, the sale of their house on behalf of the Freddy K mortgage company, and Bobby and Barbara had received a notice to leave and empty the house within thirty days. Now only one week remained before the end of that notice. Bobby had explained to Barbara that they had no chance to get out of the trap and that the last possible escape, a loan from his parents, wouldn't happen. The only thing that had surprised Bobby was Barbara's reaction when he had announced the inevitability of the foreclosure.

For once, she had not shouted and screamed hysterically, as she did in most difficult situations and when she faced a tough fact. She had just said, "Oh, yes? Well, that was to be expected from a loser like you." She had said it without real emotion, and she had then walked out of the room, dropping the issue. She had not even wanted to talk about solutions for housing after they got out of the house. Therefore, Bobby had himself arranged to rent a small two-room apartment in a much cheaper area about ten miles from where they were currently living.

This night, after work, he drove to the real estate agency that would rent out the flat, to sign the rental contract and to pay a small advance on the rent. When he got out of there and drove back home, it was already 8:00 p.m., and the sun was setting in the beautiful spring evening. When approaching their house, he was surprised to see that no lights were on inside. He shrugged and wondered where Barbara and the kids could be at this hour, and called her on her mobile phone, without getting an answer.

As Bobby came into the kitchen and turned the lights on, he recognized that a few objects were missing, such as the blender and coffee machine. When he walked up into their bedroom to change his clothes, he found something even more surprising: the closet holding Barbara's clothes was open and totally empty. As he slowly started to realize what could have happened, he caught sight of an envelope standing alone on the desk in front of their bedroom mirror. It said "To Bobby," and he opened it and read it.

Bobby, I understand that you will hate me for doing this, but you should understand that I hate you for letting this happen to us. When I came to San Francisco five years ago, I expected to marry a to-be successful businessman, who would take care of me and our family, not someone who would let it all slip to have us thrown out of our house a few years later. You say I spent a lot of money on useless things and pushed you into an untenable situation. Well maybe, but in that case, you should have stopped it earlier, as you were smart and responsible! I was just a former waitress who dreamed about becoming an actress. I knew my looks were the only asset I had, and I expected you to have the brains to make sure we'd stay out of trouble! I now know you failed on that, so I have taken my responsibility to try to give our kids a chance to have a decent living standard and not to go through hardship.

As you read this, I have left you for good, and don't count on seeing me or the kids again for a time. I have met a lovely man who is richer and more responsible than you are. He has accepted that I and our children move in with him. I have already filed for custody of our kids, and he has signed the papers as my fiancé and financial benefactor. I'm certain it will be processed quickly, since you have no financial guarantee to offer our kids.

I have also filed for divorce; you will receive the paperwork in a few days. Even if you're broke today, you can count on me trying to get half of whatever assets you still keep and to make you pay for the living expenses of our kids. This said, I don't intend to let you see them more than the court will force me to.

I now wish you good luck, and I let you sell or keep the remaining furniture in our house. I also leave you free to try to settle the debt on our credit card, which, as far as I understand, will not be covered by the money obtained from selling the house. Now I need to get going. So let me just say that I, too, regret it had to end this way. Bye, bye, Bobby.

Barbara

Bobby closed his eyes and gritted his teeth, and in an unusual loss of self-control he crushed the bed room mirror with a violent punch of his right fist, which started bleeding.

"Goddamn fool!" he screamed, not referring in his mind to Barbara, but to himself. He thought of his recent conversation with his father, who finally had been right, both in judging Barbara's character and about the decisions and actions Bobby had taken under Barbara's influence. He sat down on the bed, let himself fall back, and lay down. He thought again about his father's words, and felt slightly reassured when he realized that he was now totally alone to try to rebuild his life. The only remaining piece of value in it was his job as a sportswear product manager at the World Wear and Food Company. He suddenly felt an eager motivation and sense of adventure in the face of the challenge to turn his life around, starting immediately. He took a first initiative in this direction by calling a lawyer he knew well.

"Jonathan? How are you? ...Good...I'm in deep shit, though. Barbara left. With the kids! And with some rich guy she has started dating. We are getting thrown out of our house. Now, I guess I can live with that, but I can't live with the idea of not seeing my kids. But Barbara took them with her, and she says she won't let me see them much! Damn her, I'll fight her for the custody. Can you help me, man?"

"Of course I will," the lawyer said. "But it won't be easy. You don't even have a place to live from what I hear. And if she's with a rich guy, that will bring a lot of financial guarantees for the kids. But let's try, if you want to and are able to carry the cost of the legal procedure."

"I'm not, but I don't care! I'll find the money needed to defend my right to my kids, even if I'll have to wash dishes for years to pay it back. So please prepare the case, and let's talk within a day or two," Bobby snapped before hanging up after some minimal greetings of politeness.

For the rest of the evening, Bobby remained in a state of shock, and he only managed to eat some warmed up hamburgers and drink a couple of beers. From his mental exhaustion, Bobby fell asleep little after 10 PM. He remained the whole night in the sofa in front of the living room TV, with slacks and a t-shirt still on and wrapped inside a thick woolen blanket.

✲ ✲ ✲

Laura Dalaghan sat in her Colorado office looking thoughtfully out through the window, and felt a strange kind of exhaustion. The exhaustion itself made her profoundly angry: she had always been used to having unlimited energy and enthusiasm for whatever tasks she undertook, and whatever was the effort needed to succeed. Now, in her fifth year as a bank entrepreneur, she felt that she was beginning to lack the motivation to do her job, to do it in the very best way.

The first two years of her bank's operations had been encouraging. They had eaten into the market of local players such as the First Denver Bank and into those of the large national retail banks, thanks to their low-cost model. Being present on the Internet, DPIB had managed to win customers from all across the United States. As deposits flooded in, thanks to the attractive interest rate they offered on savings deposits, the bank was able to grow the teams both for credit sales and for credit collection and deposits management. But at the end of year two of operations, Laura and her shareholder had held a crisis meeting to understand why profits suddenly approached zero and why growth slowed down. They realized that the cause for this was Laura's greatest pride: the rule of holding a hundred percent reserves on demand deposits while competitors lent out up to ninety percent of them.

So while DPIB was still competitive compared to the large, brick-and-mortar retail banks, it was about to start losing money due to competition from other Internet banks. They had just as low costs as DPIB, but in addition, they all did extensive fractional reserve lending and lent money to much riskier clients than did DPIB. Regulatory bodies and politicians encouraged what was often called a 'democratic credit policy', meaning basically that banks should offer credits not based on ability to pay it back, but based on the *need* of the borrower. In this context, Hazelton decided they had to start practicing fractional reserve lending and to loosen the low-risk criteria when selecting clients. Laura accepted this decision, but from that day on, she got the feeling that she and her bank somehow had lost their souls.

Her sadness was limited by the results of year three and four, which were excellent. The fast growth of the bank required her to double the number of credit counselors from seven to fourteen to take care of the increasing number of credits. The profits of the bank were strong in year three and year four, and were back on track with the initial business plan. But now, in year five of their operations, they started to see defaults on credits, notably on credits given in year three in application of the new, looser credit policy. Fearing that this situation might worsen, Laura felt weary and wondered whether her decision to accept to change the credit policy had been right. But as always in the innumerable occasions when this question had tortured her mind, she didn't find any answer. Therefore, she felt relief when she was interrupted by the ringing of her mobile phone. She picked it up and said, "Who is it?" as the display indicated an anonymous caller.

"Laura?"

"Yes. Pete?" she answered.

"Yes, it's me. It's been a long time. How are you doing?"

"Well, I guess I'm alright. I won't bother you with the issues about my banking business, which is still doing all right, after all. What about you? Last time I heard you were making ever more money as one of the most successful mutual investment fund newcomers in the asset management business."

"That's true; I've been riding the wave of the bull market for over three years, especially since I bought the Quick Right Decision software developed by Mark. It helped me not only to pick the right investments but also to maximize the profits of our funds by playing the 'leverage game.'"

"Being a banker, I know that leverage refers to debt-backed investments, but could you tell me how that plays out in your business as an asset manager?"

"Well, leveraging investments means that I borrow money with my owned assets as collateral and then use that money to buy still more assets to make still faster profits as most of all these assets keep rising in value. The QRD software tells me when to sell off assets to reap some capital gains to be reinvested in other products that are about to rise in value and which the program points out. That most, if not all, asset management institutions use this leverage strategy is kind of absurd if you think about it. It means that everybody's assets are used as mortgage for loans, with no one putting away assets safely as savings. Everybody borrows, not from each other, but from banks who lend out money which is being created out of nothing, since you banks too are leveraging, so to speak, by doing fractional reserve lending."

"Yes, I know," Laura said with a sigh. "Even we at DPIB do that now, since two years. We just couldn't compete without doing it. Back to you, Pete. So you're doing great, making still more profits from this game of speculative investments?"

"Well, I have done fine for four years, but this year, it's getting tougher as we start to see a lot of assets losing in value. Real estate is doing badly, but also some stocks and even the raw materials businesses, which I have become deeply exposed in. The result is that when you leverage one hundred percent of your assets, you become vulnerable. A few percent drop in value of your assets is enough for you to end up having more debt than assets, which means you're technically bankrupt. Except if you find cash to pay or renew debt which is coming due. I start to realize that being on one hundred percent leverage is just like someone in a casino who forever keeps playing double or nothing. As long as he wins, he wins more and more, but he's always in a situation when he quickly can lose everything."

"Why do you keep doing that instead of reducing your leverage rate to a more reasonable level?"

"Well, I think it's the same thing as for you with your fractional reserve lending. You know it's not good, but you have to do it to stay competitive. In my business, people buy mutual funds after looking at who made the largest profits over the last quarter. And my competitors play the leverage game to the fullest, so I have to follow if I don't want to lose my customers. As long as the markets keep rising, and as long as the banks provide us with unlimited cheap credit, it's just such an easy way to make fast money! It used to work so well, and only recently, it has started to be difficult, as some of my leveraged assets have lost in value. Now my banks don't like me to have what they call 'uncovered positions,' and they call me to pay off what I owe them, and fast."

"I guess you can just sell off some assets to get liquidity back to pay your due debts?"

"Yes, I started doing that, only it makes me lose a lot of money as the assets I sell are suddenly worth less than what I bought them for. And as many competitors are in similar situations, price falls tend to accelerate."

"So what else can you do? I mean you won't let your multimillion-dollar funds falter just because the market is going down a few percents?"

"You're quite right, Laura, and this is something I wished to discuss with you. As you understand, banks have started to increase interest rates, and often quite steeply, especially when they know what the money is intended for and that the fund that will take the credit is already highly indebted. As we're friends, and even used to be lovers back in college for some time, I figured you might accept to give me a line of credit on decent conditions."

Laura stopped for a while to prepare what she would answer. The turn of the conversation made her see in a flashback the whole history of her bank venture. "Pete, drop that talk about our previous romance. You know I like you very much and have a lot of respect for you, but we're talking business, and I need to look at your request from that point of view only. I think you may know that I refused a mortgage to Bobby Cheston a few years ago. He was angry about it back then, but today I think he regrets not having listened to my advice. I told him not to buy that house in the first place. As you may have heard, his house recently was foreclosed and sold, and Barbara left him and took their kids with her."

"I know," Pete said. "I'm terribly sorry about what happened to Bobby. I must admit that I see some parallels to my own situation. He also played a sort of leverage game, trying to live a bit too fast, and lost. I just want to avoid ending up like him, and I think it's still possible, if you could help me out with some credit."

"Pete, I think you know that I started this bank on the principle of accepting only sound and low-risk credits. But in order not to lose too much ground to competitors, we have loosened our risk analysis of our clients. But your situation doesn't sound good to me. How much money do you need?"

"Two hundred thousand dollars, and my bank won't lend it to me. Can't you help me?" he said, his usually confident voice breaking slightly.

"Pete, this may seem strange to you, and maybe rude. I don't want to give you that credit. But I will."

Pete hesitated before asking, "Why?"

"I know it's a credit that should not be given. But I also know that if I don't grant it to you, then one of my competing Internet banks would. This is the way it has worked for the last year: we have gone into fractional reserve lending and into accepting higher-risk customers because a lot of other banks do and we have to do the same if we want to stay in business."

"It's funny," Pete said thoughtfully.

"What do you mean?" Laura snapped.

"Oh, I don't mean funny like that," Pete said, as if awoken by Laura's reaction. "I just mean it's like you're in the same situation as me. You're playing along in a game you know is crazy because those are the rules of the game today. It makes me think about Bobby when he bought a house he couldn't afford, just because everybody else was taking on crazy mortgages. I just hope we won't end up like him."

Laura answered, uneasily, "Pete, I start to fear we might. But for now on, let's stick to what we're doing. Go ahead and write up an application for a two-hundred-thousand-dollar loan over six months, and send it to my credit department. I'll give instructions for it to be accepted."

"Thank you Laura, I appreciate it," Pete said with a sigh and hung up.

✳ ✳ ✳

Bobby Cheston was in a terrible mood. He had not seen his three children for almost six months, since the day Barbara had left him. During this period, the legal procedure to decide on the custody of their kids had been dragging along slowly. Bobby had lived through it by focusing his attention and energy exclusively on his job at the World Wear and Food Company. It had helped him to stay focused on something that conveyed meaning, since he had slowly started to put away money. He certainly wanted to be able to pay back the remainder of the credit card debt which Barbara had left for him to carry alone.

He was at a low point because the effort of reconstructing his life had been broken by an unexpected calamity: he had just lost his job. His company had announced the day before that they would lay off half of their product managers in an effort to roll back marketing costs. This was judged necessary to survive the more difficult economic period that was looming. The product managers who were to be laid off had all received a phone call from the HR department. Bobby's phone had rung late in the afternoon, giving him the information he had feared more or less ever since the sales of sportswear had started to slow down a few months earlier. Even worse, today he had received the decision in the custody trial: he had lost. It appeared that his recent loss of his job had come to the judge's knowledge, and they had taken their decision claiming that Bobby as a jobless and indebted bachelor was "unable to ensure the livelihood of his children, who need a safe and caring environment."

Now, sitting in his small Los Angeles flat, he felt more alone than ever before in his entire life, and he wondered what to do. The notice period was only two weeks, and then he would be unemployed. This happened at the worst possible time since more and more financial commentators had started to talk about a general economic downturn. Unemployment was expected to increase, making it difficult for people in Bobby's situation to find a new job. At this point, when he would never have expected any human being to think about him or care about what he was becoming, he was proved wrong by the ringing of his telephone. It was his father.

"Bobby? Are you all right?"

"Well, yes, I guess so. No, honestly, not really, Dad. I'm not well at all."

"I read in the news about layoffs at the World Wear and Food Company. I hope you're not affected by that?"

"Sorry, Dad, but I am. I lost my job a few days ago. But that's not the worst. I just learned I lost the trial for the custody of my kids!"

The line remained silent for a long while, as Bobby's father searched for the right words. He then said, "I'm so sorry, Bobby. All this is unfair. I believe you did a great job as a product manager. And even though I haven't seen your kids for a long time, I'm sure you were a great daddy. Certainly a much better parent than Barbara. I did disagree with you about your marriage and about taking on too much debt.

And even if it's hard to say, I do think that what happened to you with the house was deserved. But now, this, while you were trying so hard to start all over again on a sound basis...It's so unfair. By the way, what are you going to do now?"

"I really don't know. I won't be able to keep paying the rent for my flat without a job. And of course I no longer will be able to keep paying down my old credit card debt."

"Why don't you come home to stay with us for some time? I know it may feel humiliating at your age, and after you have lived on your own for almost ten years. But the fact is that you're now no longer independent: you have debt to pay back and you can't afford expensive housing. If you stay with us for a while and get a job up here, you could pay down the debt and remake your life bit by bit. What do you say, son?"

Bobby hesitated for a moment. "Does this mean that you've forgiven me for our old disagreements?"

"Bobby, what is done is done, and I still think you were wrong and did mistakes back then. Maybe you even agree with me about that now. But that's not important. What *is* important is that you're trying to make a new start, and your mother and I sincerely want you to succeed in that effort. So do you accept to move up to Seattle for some time to try to put all those worries behind you?"

"I do, if you swear to me you don't want me on my knees begging for mercy. I do realize I have made some mistakes. But I will make up for them myself, and I don't want to go around apologizing eternally to others. I'll take care of myself; that's it."

"That's perfect, son; that's exactly what I want. So move out of that apartment, and come home. Your mother will be very happy to see you, after all these years."

"So will I. See you soon, Daddy," Bobby said and then hung up a second faster than needed, as he felt his voice was breaking.

When Bobby looked at himself in a mirror, he was surprised to see a combination of hope and happiness in his own face. He smiled at his image. "I'll get out of this. To hell with hardship!"

He felt a violent strength and a desire of revenge bubbling up inside him, but this time he resisted what he had done when Barbara had left him, and after a second's hesitation, he loosened his fist instead of hurting it by breaking yet another mirror.

☆ ☆ ☆

Professor Benson was awoken from an afternoon nap in his second residence during his Christmas vacation by a telephone call.

"Montgomery, things are going out of control! The economy of our country is running completely crazy. As a professor of economics and as your friend, I darn well know your teachings about how central banks can abuse by printing too much money and how commercial banks may engage in fraudulent fractional reserve banking while protected by the law. Well, it appears our country is about to break a record in those areas. I'm afraid! I'm afraid that our whole financial system might go bust. And our government as well."

Benson struggled to recapture his usual presence of mind as he said, "Calm down, what's going on?"

The man who had called him took a few deep breaths and then said with more self-control, "I got hold of the preliminary end-of-year statistics for monetary data. You won't believe me if I tell you that our central bank almost *tripled* the quantity of basic currency, compared to last year. And commercial banks were not much better: they abused the fractional reserve principle, almost *doubling* the amount of demand deposits.

"So you see if I'm scared shitless about what will happen when the financial markets get hold of the statistics in the beginning of next year! The exchange rate between our currency and the main currencies of the world has not moved that much yet. But, logically, its value should be divided by two or by three!

"And what about the solidity of our banks? If their customers understand what's going on, and that bank reserves compared to total deposits have fallen radically, then they might come in hordes to draw their money out. We would see bank runs all over the place, which would hurt our country all the more because many depositors are foreigners! Hell, the size of our banking sector is larger than the GDP of the country. Montgomery, what the hell could we do to get out of this mess?"

Benson's mind was now running in lightning speed as he digested the information he was hearing. Not yet completely awake, he spoke without realizing that his words left his mouth to be heard across the phone. "Wow, this may be the opportunity we have been waiting for."

"What?" the man on the other line shouted. "Why on earth are you talking about opportunities? I think we should rather use words like *crisis, meltdown,* or even *apocalypse!*"

Now fully awake, Benson responded. "Sorry my friend, you're right, of course. This sounds like a terrible squeeze for your country. But if I may try to give you back some hope, could I remind you that a radical crisis may often, as history has proved, be an opportunity for making radical changes to the better? Changes that wouldn't have been accepted in normal times."

"What on earth are you talking about, Montgomery?"

"The situation you're describing is a perfect textbook example of the disastrous results of central banking and government-controlled paper money. But maybe the terrible crisis that seems to be ahead of you can be turned into a fantastic opportunity: the opportunity to shut down your central bank, to scrap your paper currency and to introduce a free-market monetary system based on gold money, where fractional reserve banking would be just as forbidden as any other form of counterfeiting!"

The two men soon hung up, but only a moment later Professor Benson's phone rang again. However, this time, he was fully awake, excited by the thoughts that his previous conversation had left him with. This time too, the speaker on the other side was desperate.

"Professor, I don't know how to get out of this mess, and I never wanted to come into it in the first place!" Laura Dalaghan, with a vanishing self-control, yelled as she spelled out her disarray to Professor Benson. She had called him up for advice on the difficult situation her bank now was facing. The situation had become apparent to her during her end-of-year vacation when she was preparing the so-called flash result that her shareholder expected every year.

Benson quietly said to himself, with wonder, "Definitely, today my phone is an emergency hot line!"

"What?" Laura yelled with a tense voice.

"Sorry, Laura, never mind. Now, please, calm down and tell me what's going on," he said with a low voice, aiming to reassure his former student.

"Right, Professor. Excuse me for being panicky. But we're making a loss this year, which will amount to one-point-nine million dollars, or twenty-five percent of our total revenue! In order to improve our growth and our profits, we decided three years ago to go into fractional reserve banking and to be less demanding about the credits we accept. It worked for two years: our revenue and profits increased, as we got a lot of new credit customers. But this year, the share of clients who defaulted on their debts has increased to eight percent, three times more than before!"

"So if that's the case, both you and I understand that you need to change something. You and Cornelius may have been too ambitious, wanting to grow too fast. But growth based on fractional reserve lending and risky credits won't last. So, in your place, I would now, first, focus on cutting costs in a radical manner, since you probably will see even more of such bad credits defaulting, and, second, stop accepting risky credits. You're better off with a lower growth, but with clients who pay back their loans. If you do these two things, you might be able to ride out the storm."

"What storm are you talking about?" Laura asked hesitantly.

"Oh, I guess you may not be aware of it. But I've been looking more and more closely at data on the banking sector recently. And, as a matter of fact, the situation of your bank isn't an exception. Actually, many much larger banks than yours are in an even worse mess than you are."

"So how do you want me to feel about that?" Laura said again with hesitation in her voice. "Should I feel better from the fact that my competitors are in trouble too?"

"Of course you shouldn't! Their troubles won't make yours disappear," Benson answered slowly. "And I even think it should worry you even more, since we might be up for a general and severe crisis of the whole banking system of the United States, or of the entire world. A kind of financial winter. Or maybe an Ice Age, lasting for a long time. If that happens, banks like yours might just go down the drain, while the largest banks could be bailed out by government."

"All right, Professor, I've got it. So I guess I better start working on a radical costcutting plan. From now on, I'll put my bank in survival mode, even if I have no idea whether it will be enough to save it."

CHAPTER 6:
The Flaw that No One Saw

"Crisis and Recession—Or Radical Cut in Interest Rates?"

The headline in London's largest financial newspaper used strong words. Behind it was a detailed ten-page special report which justified these words. It outlined the background and the decisions at stake for the upcoming G20 central bank coordination meeting. Bad economic news was appearing every other day, in the form of worsening indicators or reports of bankruptcies, and expectations were high on the central bank leaders to respond forcefully. One of the participants of this meeting which would capture the world's spotlights for a day was Jessica Frostby.

Jessica had now spent five and a half years at her job at the IMF. She spent much time preparing and following up on the meetings of the G20 central bank coordination group. The group met every quarter. The preparation of the meetings consisted of analyzing economic indicators in order to prepare decision-support reports for the central bank leaders of the G20 countries. Basically, the analyses were aimed at understanding at what stage of the business cycle the economy currently was. If indicators showed mostly decreasing economic activity, that provided arguments for the central banks to lower interest rates to boost activity. On the other hand, if economic activity, measured by indicators such as the prices of stocks, raw materials, or real estate, had started to increase a bit too fast, then that provided arguments for increasing interest rates.

The March meeting was to be held in London. Jessica had flown in the day before and was now sitting in the hotel restaurant to have dinner. She was in the company of her French colleague François Leclerc. While they had different opinions about many things, they liked each other and had become friends. They often spent some time together in hotels or airports, travelling to and from the meetings. This night, they were talking about the years they had spent together, and the monetary policy that had been decided during those years.

"François, you know, when I look back at these five years, I think that the monetary policy our central banks have decided on didn't work at all."

"Why do you say that?" François answered, frowning.

Jessica looked up from her plate to François' eyes and sighed. "Well, during the first year and a half, our group met five or six times across the world, but the only conclusion of those meetings was that the U.S. interest rate, at one percent, was so low that we couldn't lower it anymore, even if we would have wanted to in order to make bank lending increase more. So we just kept it at one percent for a long time. Then we came into a second period, when we suddenly considered that the economy was becoming overheated due to too much credit. So during a period of two years, every time we met, we just decided that we should increase the interest rate a bit more to slow down bank lending and to avoid economic overheating."

"Well," François said, "I think that's quite all right. I mean, this is what we call the counter-cyclical monetary policy. The economy is heating up, and we try to cool it down a little bit. What's your problem with this?"

"The problem is that we were increasing the interest rate every month during two years in order to slow down the economy. But the economy didn't slow down at all! People were just borrowing more and more money and buying more and more stocks and real estate and getting more and more debt. So the ever-increasing interest rates didn't slow down bank lending. But they *did* increase the cost of capital for people who borrowed, making it harder for them to pay interest on their loans. So the two-year period of increasing interest rates only ended when we realized that the people who had borrowed money were becoming insolvent and that the value of the assets they had been buying was flattening out. From this point on, and for one year, we just kept the U.S. interest rate flat at around five percent. I conclude that at this point, we were confronting an impossible or even absurd choice, and we didn't know what to do."

"What do you mean?" François said, with both tension and curiosity.

"I think that our central bank group was like a cornered rat. We knew we couldn't increase interest rates, because that would result in the bankruptcy of a lot of people and companies. On the other hand, we didn't want to decrease the interest rate, because we knew there was way too much debt in society and we didn't want to increase bank lending. Confronting two impossible choices, we did nothing, and just kept the interest rate where it was, at five percent."

Francois looked a bit frustrated. "Jessica, suppose you're right. What would you have proposed in that situation?"

"I'll come to that in a while," Jessica answered. "Let me just finish my review all the way until today. Six months ago, reality helped us to put an end to our inability to decide about interest rate changes. Last summer, more and more observers started to talk about a subprime mortgage crisis. People with low incomes had taken on mortgages which they were unable to pay back. Of course, it's bad for the people who were affected. But the worst thing for the economic system as a whole was that a lot of banks had repackaged those mortgages and then sold them to investors, including other banks. The mortgage-backed securities were expected to yield a high return based on the assumption that all the subprime people would pay back their mortgages with high interest rates. Now, as many of them are unable to pay back their loans, the value of the securities is falling. Consequently the capital of banks and financial institutions that bought the securities also falls."

"Sure, I know all this," François said. "And in this situation, our central banks decided to decrease interest rates, which is correct. Over the last six months, the U.S. interest rate, the federal funds rate, has been lowered from five to four percent. And tomorrow, dear Jessica, we may vote to decrease rates even more, by one percent, all the way down to three percent! I believe all this is fine, and it's the best we can do to try to save the economy."

"François, I won't argue with you about whether the interest rate should decrease more or less, or faster or slower. That's not my point. But I want to explain my conclusion about these five years. My conclusion is that those changes of the interest rate don't really influence the economy at all. I know it's contrary to what everybody in the world believes, including us in the central banks, but I'm sure it's true."

"How can you say that? Everybody knows that higher interest rates will slow down bank lending and that a lower interest rate will stimulate it."

"No, I really think you're mistaken. But I'll forgive you for that, since the whole world makes the same mistake as you do."

"What mistake are you talking about?" François said, raising his voice and looking into Jessica's eyes with a puzzled expression.

"If you want to understand, allow me to remind you how our banking system works. In our current system, a bank that receives thirteen dollars in deposits reserves can actually keep one single dollar in reserves and lend twelve dollars to its customers, although the depositor expects all of those thirteen dollars to be lying in the bank vault for him to withdraw at any time. This *is* allowed by the current laws of our country, so let's take it as a given. My only point is that as long as the banks have enough reserves, lending out money is profitable for them. This is why banks will always keep lending as much as they can during a boom phase, as long as they have enough reserves and regardless of any increase we may decide in the interest rates. Do you see? We should not believe that increasing the interest rate will stop bank lending as such."

"How can you say that the bank's profits will increase when we increase the interest rate?"

"Because banks are the only institutions allowed to borrow from the central bank at the federal funds rate. They also obtain savings deposits from the public, paying them a rate often *below* the federal funds rate. Since they will keep a steady markup above the federal funds rate in the interest they charge for a loan, they will actually make greater and greater profits the more we increase the interest rate. That is, if they're able to increase the return paid to savers less than the increase in their lending rate. They often are."

"Assuming you're right, what would put an end to the boom? We know that the recent boom is about to end, or has already ended."

"While increasing interest rates won't reduce the willingness of banks to lend money, it will at one point reduce the demand. The interest payments are becoming higher and higher for a given amount of loan. People will be less and less able to borrow money. When people will have less borrowed money, it will put an end to the increase in prices of what they buy with borrowed money, such as real estate or stocks. People who have borrowed a lot will be heavily squeezed. Falls in prices of real estate or stocks, even small falls, will create a need to borrow more money to pay back debts, since the assets they had bought now sell for less. At the same time, the interest rate has increased, making it harder for them to borrow. On the real estate market, this effect is now combined with the additional downward pressure on prices coming from the bankruptcy of many subprime borrowers."

"I know all this," François said. "And that's why we're deciding about a decrease in the interest rate to ease access to credit. Even if we agree that a lot of people have too much debt, we can't let them down now, when they need borrowed money more than ever. What's your idea? That we should *increase* interest rates now?"

"I haven't said that. The point I want to make is that whatever we decide regarding the interest rate, it won't restart bank lending as long as the reserve and capital ratios of banks are below the allowed levels."

"Why not?" François said. He was very attentive now.

"After having extended credit rapidly for many years, many banks now have fewer reserves than what is legally authorized. They will either have to increase their reserves or have to decrease their stock of outstanding credit. Now, if banks need to quickly increase their reserves, they can always borrow at a cheap rate from the central bank. Or, an even easier method is to sell some government bonds to the central bank. If they do, the payment they receive becomes new reserve money. But in addition to reserve requirements, banks also have capital requirements. As you know, this means that the value of the bank's capital must not go below a specific percentage ratio of the value of the total assets managed by the bank.

"Under current regulations, the capital is required to be at least eight percent of managed assets. Now, we must remember that bank capital includes a lot of financial assets which the bank is buying and selling on the market. For many such assets, we see falling market prices today, especially for mortgage-backed securities. We need to look at the average value of a bank's capital. Even if it falls by just one percent, it means that the managed assets of the bank should be reduced by twelve times more in order for the bank to maintain its capital ratio. A bank in such a situation won't offer credit to anyone, whatever the interest rate it could get! It would rather try to get rid of customers to reduce its outstanding asset base in order to conserve its capital ratio!"

"If we assume that you're right, Jessica, it means our currently planned decrease of interest rate won't make bank lending start over again to fuel the economy. Then what do you propose to do to save the economy?"

"The only really satisfying solution would be to scrap the current central banking system and to start considering banks as regular private enterprises. They would have to manage their own risk and would only be able to lend out money which they had received as savings deposits from somebody else.

One hundred percent reserves on demand deposits should be the rule, so fractional reserve lending wouldn't exist. And money should be a valuable commodity such as gold and not some arbitrary paper-bill unit controlled by the government."

"I admit that your arguments are convincing, even though your proposed solution would be considered as unthinkable by most people. But why don't you try to share these ideas with our central bank coordination group?" François said.

"François, since you were trained in one of those French politician schools, I expect you to be a bit less naïve. You do understand that the type of a financial system I talk about would mean the disappearance of all central banks? So don't expect me to try to convince central bank leaders to close down the powerful institutions they are controlling today and then to put themselves on unemployment relief. Obviously, they would never do that. And I would just look ridiculous, since I've worked within one of these institutions for five years."

"So what's your outlook? Let's assume that at our meeting tomorrow, the coordination group decides on a major decrease in interest rates, and that it won't be enough to make banks start lending again, nor will it stop the ongoing spiral of increasing bankruptcies. What will happen?"

"Your guess is as good as mine, but I imagine we'll keep decreasing interest rates all the way down to zero. We may also see banks going bankrupt, since they will be unable to correct their capital ratios. We may also see a spiral of bankruptcy among their credit clients. And their depositor clients will come running to take their money out of the bank before it goes bust."

"And then what?" François said with a trembling voice, and he looked sincerely frightened by this prospect.

Jessica shrugged. "At that point, anything can happen since we would be in a terrible financial crisis. I guess we would see bank bailouts and bank nationalizations in order to boost bank capital. You see, at that point, no shareholder in the world except governments would want to put a cent into banks!

"I suggest we stop thinking about that misery perspective for now. It's almost midnight and we have a whole day of meetings tomorrow starting at eight. Let's finish our desserts and go to bed. All right?"

"Sure," he said without conviction and with a tense look on his face.

Both of them finished their cake and coffee and swiftly took off back to their respective hotel rooms.

✲ ✲ ✲

The meeting was held in an old prestigious mansion in the countryside outside of London. This setting, far from the financial and political community in the city, provided some appreciated discretion and a pleasant environment. An international hotel resort was located next to it; Jessica, François, and most of the other delegates stayed there. The group of almost fifty people representing the central banks of twenty important countries was now gathered in the main conference room of the mansion. This room had been tastefully designed inside a large barn used originally for keeping cattle, back in the time when the mansion belonged to an English lord.

As the delegates sat down around the large, U-shaped table, the chairman of today's conference, who was the head of the Bank of England, prepared to start his introductory speech. He stood in front of the group behind a pulpit with a built-in microphone. On the lectern was written "G20 Central Bank Coordination Group, March Meeting."

As silence settled in the large room, he looked around slowly at his audience and started to speak with a cautious but firm voice. "Dear friends and colleagues of the international central bank community, I wish you sincerely welcome to London and to our quarterly conference. We have crucial matters to discuss and important decisions to make.

"As you all know, we're entering a period of financial turmoil. It might become more devastating than the so-called Internet bubble crash which happened seven years ago. We have recognized over the last three or four years that our policy of increasing interest rates in the economy is largely insufficient. I say this because it didn't prevent a bubble of excessive increase in asset prices combined with excessive levels of credit and indebtedness across most of the economy.

"As during the Internet crash, bankruptcies of both businesses and households are becoming more and more frequent. What makes me say that it might be worse now is that we are also seeing banks having major financial worries, like last summer, when we saw a run on a large English bank. That could have led to a great panic, had we not intervened to deter the depositors from withdrawing their money and by nationalizing the bank and injecting government money to restore its capital and reserve ratios. When that happened, we believed and hoped that it would turn out to be an exceptional event."

He paused to observe the reactions from the audience. They appeared to be captivated and troubled. "Today, I fear we may have been wrong, as we see more and more banks on the market taking serious losses. They do so largely due to the loss in value of mortgage-backed securities, which they have been buying from each other over the last few years. Those securities are now becoming more and more worthless, as it turns out that a lot of people are failing on their mortgages. As a consequence, the capital-to-asset ratios of banks owning such securities are becoming very low. To restore those ratios, they are severely restricting credits, in spite of our repeated decreases in interest rates.

"As you know, in the last six months, most of our member countries have been lowering interest rates by around a quarter of a percent per month. The current state of the economy, where credit is drying up more and more, and where we see an increasing number of bankruptcies, makes me think that we have acted too little and too late. Therefore, I believe that the main objective of our conference today is to consider a much stronger decrease in interest rates. Ideally, such a decrease should be decided and be applied at the same time by most of the major central banks of the world. It would send a powerful signal to the markets showing that we won't accept that the economy goes into a recession or, even worse, a depression."

Jessica, sitting next to François, held back a smile and turned to whisper into François' ear. "Now you see what I mean when I say that central banks have way too much power in the current financial system? Unfortunately, that exorbitant power makes them think they have more influence on events than they actually have. It's truly ridiculous that he thinks that just because he doesn't wish the economy to go into a recession and that him saying so would prevent it from actually happening."

"Jessica, I think this situation is much too serious to joke about," François whispered back to her, before turning back to the speaker.

"I agree the situation is serious," Jessica replied. "But I wish that man and his fellow central bank leaders would understand that their declarations today can do little to control the financial world. They would need to make fundamental reforms if they really want to save the world from a new crisis."

François didn't answer, but kept listening to the speaker, who concluded his speech. "Given the dense agenda of our meeting, I wish that we move immediately to the review of the economic indicators of the last quarter. We should be through with this before lunch and then spend the afternoon discussing the relevant monetary policy to be applied. Thank you very much for your attention."

The agenda of the conference was, as always, respected, even if some items provoked lengthy and intense discussions. However, these discussions always focused on technicalities and never covered fundamental issues as Jessica and François had done in their casual dinner discussion the previous evening. Here, in a prestigious mansion, the fifty most powerful people of the world's financial system spent a full day together. But they would not dream of questioning any of the fundamental principles of that system, even though it now appeared to break apart. They focused all their intelligence and attention on minute details. The morning session was spent on a detailed analysis of some specific economic indicators. The afternoon session was spent on discussing whether the appropriate level of interest rate decrease was 0.75 percent, 1 percent, or 1.25 percent. After two hours of plenary discussion of the issue of the interest rate decrease, the conference ended in a consensus to schedule an immediate 1 percent interest rate decrease across most of the member countries.

Jessica felt a combination of guilt and weariness when she sat alone in a taxi to a London airport: guilt because she had spent a whole day in a room with the only fifty people in the world who could influence monetary policy, without taking the opportunity to speak up to them about what she believed to be the right thing to do. That there was no agenda item where she had a real possibility to do it did not remove the feeling that she might have, even should have, stood up to scream her convictions. She felt weary because she knew that had she spoken up about this, no one would have listened to her. If someone had listened, the person would have dismissed her ideas as totally impractical, even if admitting that they were the right thing to do. *Why do I have this job? If I quit the job, what else could I do, which would better help to prevent the disaster I see unfolding before my eyes?*

At that moment, in the taxi, she found no answer.

✻ ✻ ✻

A few days later, at breakfast, Jessica met her husband for the first time in about ten days. Steve had been traveling to the West Coast for work. A team from the Department of the Treasury had met with California officials to discuss an urgent need of public financing to balance the books of their state. Steve's flight back to Washington had been delayed for a couple of hours, and he had arrived at their apartment in the middle of the night and had managed to get into bed without waking Jessica up. Due to his late-night arrival, and taking advantage of the fact that it was a Saturday morning and he didn't have to go to work, Steve got out of bed one hour later than Jessica. He met her when she was finishing a cup of coffee at the breakfast table. He walked up to her slowly from behind, gently put his arms around her neck, and bent forward to kiss her on the cheek.

"Good morning, honey. You could never imagine how much I've been missing you for the last ten days! Our phone calls never make up for not spending time together. My week in California was quite rough; bankruptcies and unemployment are rising quickly over there. The state government is in immediate need of additional financing to cover handouts to an ever larger number of needy.

"This so-called subprime mess gives me the creeps. We drove through some neighborhoods where every second house was under foreclosure and for sale. Only I'm not sure they're able to sell the houses, even if they lower the prices a lot! Because no one seems to be able to get any mortgages anymore, since banks and lending institutions are approaching insolvency themselves. Coming back from that trip, I realize that seeing you and being with you is the only thing that can make me feel better. So how was your trip to the U.K.?"

"All right, thank you," Jessica said, looking out through the window and contemplating the Washington downtown area a few miles away.

"Hmm, you don't seem to be in great shape, if you allow my saying so. What solutions did you come up with to respond to the economic crisis?

After all, the world is watching you IMF and central bank people and expecting you to find solutions to our economic problems."

Jessica stretched across the table, picked up a Washington newspaper, and put it in front of Steve. The headline on the first page announced the 1 percent decrease of the federal funds interest rate, which had been announced by the Fed spokesman in the previous evening. The subtitle said, "The Fed Fights Back against the Crisis by Bringing the Federal Funds Rate Down from 4% to 3%." In the article, the reporter pointed out that this was the strongest one-shot interest rate decrease ever made by the Fed. The reporter expected the decrease to slow the fall in prices of real estate and many stocks and give a new start to the economy.

"Oh, I see you took your responsibility to act against the economic downturn. That's great," Steve said with a gentle smile.

"I don't know," Jessica said. "I don't think it's great. Most of those banks and lending institutions are in such bad shape that changing the interest rate from four percent to three percent won't enable them to start extending credit again. Hell, most of their capital and reserve ratios are so bad that they wouldn't lend money even if they could access reserve funds from the Fed at a *zero percent* interest rate!

"Today, their only concern is to *sell* assets and *get rid* of credit clients to restore their capital ratio to acceptable levels. So I don't see any of this pulling us out of the mess we're currently in. People and businesses will keep going bankrupt. And this will put banks in a still tougher mess, making them restrict credit even more, making even more people go bankrupt, and so on. It's a vicious spiral, and I don't see the way out of it. Many of the banks themselves may end up going bust! And if their depositors would understand the sorry state of their banks, they may come running in masses to get their money out, while it's still possible."

"Darling, I think your outlook is overly pessimistic. I hope you never talk about it like that with anybody but me. Even if you're right, spreading those kinds of ideas could just accelerate the panic in the country. We need people to conserve hope and an optimistic view of the future. When I was at the airport last night, I listened to the Fed spokesman on the radio. He was much more optimistic than you are, and underlined the major stimulus that the economy should get from the interest rate decrease. He also said he was hoping it would make private consumption pick up by making it easier for people to get consumption credits."

"You mean that the economy would be saved by people who are already drowning in debt borrowing even more money for consumption? Getting it somehow from banks that can't afford to give credit to anyone anymore? That idea is both foolish and unrealistic." Jessica's temper was rising, which showed in her edgy voice.

"Take it easy, honey," Steve said, as he often did when he tried to make Jessica control her temper. "I would just like to understand what *you* propose to do to get out of this mess. After all, you're representing the IMF and the central banks. Hell, that international coordination group you're part of controls the monetary policy of virtually the entire world."

"Funny you would ask me that," Jessica said. "The night before that conference I got the same question from my French colleague François. I told him my deepest conviction, but now I regret I did, as he just dismissed this as something ludicrous."

"Honey, you're never ludicrous. Sometimes you may be a bit radical or, should I say, politically insensitive, but not ludicrous. Now what is this great idea of yours?"

"Shut down the whole central banking system and replace our government-controlled paper money by the only thing that was good enough during history to be considered as money on the free market: gold. That would bring the power back to where it belongs, which is with the working people and businesses of the country. They would thus control their own money. Its value could no longer be inflated away by bureaucrats in a central bank, just by pressing a button on a printing press. We would be done with the economic cycles we have seen in the last decades. We would once again have a banking system based on common sense where banks could only lend money which had been saved by someone else. So it drives me crazy to hear every day that people blame free enterprise for the mess we're currently in. Someone should stand up to tell them the truth, which is that they are being abused by the combined interest of politicians, central bank bureaucrats, and large commercial banks!'"Now, Jessica, I sincerely hope *you* aren't considering speaking up about that, being an indirect employee of the central banking system as you are by working for the IMF. That would be quite inappropriate.

"This conversation reminds me of the first time we met, when you embarrassed me in front of the whole class of the IMF boot camp with a bold statement. So I repeat what I told you then: what you say makes sense, but it's not a proper way of putting things.

"Now I'll add, since you've been working for more than five years inside this system which you're criticizing, the following advice. Don't ever speak like that again, and don't spread those ideas to anyone. Maybe it's true that there is a cartel system uniting the interest of the government with the interests of large banks through the Federal Reserve as the central bank. But then you should remember that we live off that system and that we might go from masters of the world to simple beggars, if that system would disappear. And we're to become parents before the end of this year. We need to be responsible and not jeopardize our way of making a living."

Angry, Jessica frowned and looked at Steve. "I think that's a cheap and easy way to get out of a crucial argument about the world's financial system, to bring it down to a question of our personal, material well-being! Now, if I should link that topic to the perspective of a mother, my first concern would be to aim for the kind of world I would like my child to live in. That world would *not* include government-sponsored central banks which destroy the value of people's savings and generate business cycles, making millions of people poor and unemployed!"

"But, honey, we live off this system, and we could never do without it. And the public needs help and guidance more than it ever did. So we better keep and reinforce all the central structures of power rather than talking about breaking them down. For example, in my job at the Treasury, how on earth would we finance new government deficit spending if we didn't have the Fed to buy our bonds using newly created money?"

"Well, maybe you wouldn't be able to finance deficit spending, but then I think that would be a good thing. I find it deeply immoral that you indebt future generations just to finance the pork-barrel politics you will use to win the next election." Jessica said with a defiant and hard smile.

"Honey, don't provoke me. We are talking about my job and my career!" Steve said tensely in an unusual but brief loss of self-control. "If you understand the amount of responsibility I have in my job, you should show me a little more respect."

Jessica rose from her chair, violently tore apart the newspaper lying on the table, and threw it in the garbage bin. She picked up her car keys, and before leaving for work, she snapped loudly and aggressively. "You know, Steve, what scares me is that the more I understand about the nature of your job, the less respect I have for it. It makes me sick, and I admit that although we haven't met for over a week, I'm already fed up with your cynical, bureaucrat reasoning. Have a good day."

Steve stood as frozen in the corner of the kitchen and looked at her as she turned her back on him and slammed the kitchen door.

✧ ✧ ✧

It was a morning of early May in Denver, and the sun was just about to rise above the mountain peaks in the horizon. The peaks were still covered by a layer of snow, but it grew thinner each week. As the spring sun melted the snow, it pushed the snow limit up the mountain sides.

Coming into her office unusually early at six, Laura Dalaghan should normally have been in a great mood when seeing this view through the large office window. However, on this particular day, she didn't even notice the beautiful panorama. She had come in early simply because she had been unable to sleep the whole night. At five, she had had enough of rolling around on her bed, and she had decided to get up and walk over to her office, which was just a mile from her home.

After two large cups of black coffee, she was quickly emerging from a dizzy state of half-sleep toward full consciousness. At this point, she realized that it felt like her worst day since she started her bank business, even as the worst day of her entire life. She had developed her business for almost six years with a team of coworkers, many of whom had become close friends to her and to each other. Now she faced the awful task of announcing to them that half of the team was to be laid off due to the severe financial problems the bank had run into during the last year. Some of her closest staff members suspected what was about to happen, but Laura had been careful to not leak any rumors or any premature information. She had simply summoned the whole team to what she had called an "emergency staff meeting" at eight this morning.

For regular staff meetings, Laura would always prepare a slideshow, usually accompanied with numbers from a spreadsheet. Today, she was incapable of writing anything down. Her way of preparing the meeting was just to sit in her office with her eyes mostly closed. She let her mind run over the key events she had lived through since the start of the company. She remembered their unbridled optimism at the opening day, when she had met with Sandra, in charge of credit sales, and Paul, in charge of credit payment collection and deposits management. She recalled the many happy moments, when they had celebrated some success when increasing growth and profits had enabled them to expand their team and their customer base. Thinking of those moments made her unconsciously smile, and she shed a tear, both for the past happiness and in revulsion at the disappearance of that happiness.

Sandra brought Laura back to reality when she stepped into Laura's office just before eight. "Boss, the whole team is waiting for you in the conference room. Are you all right?"

Laura shot up from her chair and looked at Sandra, first drowsily and with surprise, but soon with her usual focus and energy. "Well, yes, I mean, not really; I'm a bit tired. But never mind, I'll be there in a second."

She filled up her cup of coffee and walked into the conference room where forty highly worried faces were looking her way as she took place at the end of the room facing them. They were all sitting on plastic chairs, for the occasion placed in the middle of the room with the large meeting table put aside in a corner to free up space.

Laura looked around the room for a moment, drank a big gulp of coffee, then put her cup down on a small table. "I know you know that we have been facing more and more serious difficulties over the last two years. Except for a dip in profits during year two, we have been making money since we started.

"But, in the last year and a half, we have erased the cumulated profits of the four previous years. There are three reasons. The first is that we have seen competitors push down the cost of credit. They have been able to do that by aggressive fractional reserve lending, something we started to do too three years ago. But as we went fast into fractional reserve lending, our reserve ratio fell. It decreased further as we kept losing some of our deposit customers to competitors. It is now close to the lowest allowed value.

"The second reason is a strong increase in the number of credit customers defaulting on the payback of their loans. Even when we can sell the collateral, such as a house or a car which they have to give us when they can't honor payments, we usually lose around thirty percent of the loan amount, plus the interest income we no longer get."

A member of Paul's credit collection team raised his hand, and Laura nodded his way. "How could we end up like that? Our bank was founded on the principle of only extending credit to secure and worthy borrowers, with minimum risk of default, and of not doing fractional reserve lending. I know we abandoned that initial vision, but why did we?"

Laura sighed and looked gently at him. "You're absolutely right. That was how we wanted to run the bank. But three years ago, I and our shareholder realized that we were unable to compete on the market without doing fractional reserve lending and without accepting clients who our competitors were accepting. So we changed our credit policy. That's how Sandra's credit sales team increased the number of credits by a factor of three in just one year. And that's why we were able to grow the credit sales team from seven to fifteen people in just one year, reaching twenty people the year after. Today, in order to contain costs and in order to avoid us going bankrupt next year, I'm terribly sorry to announce to you that we will reduce staff in credit sales, bringing the team down from twenty to five people."

Without waiting for Laura to pause or to continue, Sandra cried out, "But why can't we keep the team and double our efforts to find worthy credit clients? When we lose customers due to them defaulting, we need to find other, safer clients more than ever, don't we?"

"Generally, you would be right Sandra, but this brings me to the third issue I was about to explain when I got a question. We also have seen a bad fall in our bank capital and thereby in our capital to assets ratio. As you may know, the founding shareholders of this bank put two million dollars into it, six years ago. Since then we have had cumulated profits of around three million dollars, which we have placed in financial products selected by our trading desk. Thanks to the general increase in market prices of most assets, including the ones we invested in, those three millions have grown to be four million, and our total bank capital to be six million.

"But you know there is a limit to how much credit a bank can extend with respect to the size of its capital. The ratio is around one to twelve, meaning that a bank can have a credit portfolio twelve times the size of its bank capital. We used to have a large security margin, with a credit portfolio of around five times our capital. But following our rapid increase in credits over the last two years, we have reached the one to twelve ratio.

"That would have been fine, except for two things: we made a huge loss last year, reducing our bank capital, and we have now started to see a fall in the market value of the securities we own; above all, of mortgage-backed securities. As most banks on the market have the same problems as we have, with an increasing number of defaults on mortgages, you see why the market value of those securities is starting to plummet. Other securities we own, such as stocks and mutual funds, are also falling, although less. Overall, our capital has decreased from six million to four million dollars."

"But that's not so much, is it?" a young man of the credit collection team said from the back of the room.

"No, it isn't, if you look at the capital as such. But you should remember that one-to-twelve ratio. Since we were at the limit of our allowed capital-to-assets ratio, it means we now have to reduce our stock of outstanding credits with twelve times that amount, or around twenty-four million dollars. And if our capital keeps falling, we would have to reduce our credits even more.

"So now you understand why our challenge over the coming months isn't to *increase* our number of credit customers. Our objective is to *get rid* of as many customers as we can until we come down to the authorized capital-to-assets ratio. This is why that recent decrease of the Federal Funds interest rate by one whole percentage point, which the mass media considers an enormous boost to the economy, won't change a thing for us. As long as we need to decrease, not increase, our number of outstanding credit customers, no interest rate decrease in the world will make it possible for us to offer new credits.

"I know this may sound crazy, since we know that many people and businesses currently need credit more than ever. But that's the way the current banking system works."

Sandra and most of the members of her credit sales team shared a look of horror on their faces. Sandra still found the strength to ask one more question. "But, boss, it doesn't make sense that we're being sacrificed and will lose our jobs, although we have done exactly what government and regulators asked us to do. We did fractional reserve lending and gave loans to poor and needy families. How come government doesn't help us out? I mean, I have heard about several recent cases of bank bailouts by government, both in the United States, and in the U.K.!"

"Sandra, I know this will sound terribly cynical to you, but I think it's the reality of the situation. We are much too small a bank for the government to care about, so they won't bother to bail us out. They will figure that we can get out of it by firing personnel and slashing costs for some time, and if we don't, the public won't know or care about it anyway. They will focus their bail-out efforts on much larger banks, where tens of thousands of jobs are at stake and where millions of people would risk losing their bank deposits if their banks would fail. The bottom line is that those Wall Street banks are considered 'too big to fail,' but *we* aren't. Sorry, but that's the way it is."

Sandra lowered her eyes and was unable to hold back her tears. She left the room and was followed by two of her credit sales team members.

Paul, the head of credit collection and deposits management, spoke up after a few seconds of uneasy silence. "Then I guess we will spend what remains of marketing and sales efforts on getting in more deposit money? At least that could give us some breathing spell to offer credits to all those people who now need it more than ever. That's what I don't understand: we're a bank and should provide credit to people when they need it. But we provide it only in good times, not when people are starting to get squeezed and need the credit most, as now."

"Paul, you're right we need deposits more than ever, since we need to respect a second essential indicator, the reserve ratio, which measures our reserves against total demand deposits. Our reserve ratio has fallen over the last few months from ten percent, which is the level we're supposed to respect, to seven percent. The fall corresponds to three percent of our depositors taking their money out of our bank, for varying reasons: to pay off some debt, or switch to competing banks. Or maybe, in some cases, they thought it would be safer to keep cash in their homes than in our bank.

"The terrible thing is that they're right; it *is* safer for them! The reason is that if ten percent of our depositors would come to claim their cash, we would be unable to give it to them. So before making campaigns to get new depositors, we need to do a campaign to keep the ones we have. I have decided to provide a fidelity bonus to demand deposits accounts where the balance is above a thousand dollars. I will ask our credit sales team and our call center to make sure we call all our depositors to reassure them and to tell them about this bonus. We don't want to make the headlines as one of the first U.S. banks in the current crisis to be subject to a bank run. If that happens, we would be bankrupt within a few days. And please remember, since we're a small bank, government won't bail us out."

Paul, and all the other team members who remained in the room, looked at Laura with terror in their eyes. After a moment of awkward silence, Paul summarized what they had heard. "So, to make a long story short, our reserve and capital ratios have plunged, due to bad credits and because we started to do fractional reserve lending. We are losing money, and at the same time, we're unable to provide credit to customers who need it more than ever. We are so unable to offer credit that we're laying off seventy-five percent of our credit sales personnel. The only ambition we're able to set is to prevent our current depositors from withdrawing their money, even though in reality, they would be safer withdrawing it and hiding it in their homes. Boss, do you confirm this is the mess we're in?" Paul yelled, losing some of his usual politeness and respect for Laura.

Laura looked him stoically in the eyes. "Yes, that's the mess we're in. I can only say...I'm very sorry, too. More sorry than you can imagine. Now, if there aren't any further questions, I will end the meeting."

No one in the room volunteered further questions. The meeting was over in less than half an hour, but Laura felt as if it had lasted half a day. Coming back into her office, she noticed that her blouse was soaking from sweat. Her next task didn't make her feel any better: she had the feeling that she was committing murder when she sat down with the HR manager to go over the list of employees to check the names of the credit sales clerks to be laid off.

CHAPTER 7:
The Moral and the Practical

Shortly after the layoffs at the Dalaghan Prudential Internet Bank, Laura did something she had wanted to do for a long time: she took a week off to visit her best friend from college, Jessica. They had only kept in touch through e-mail and occasional phone calls, as both their lives had moved on with an unrelenting pace in different locations.

Laura had met her husband Kevin four years earlier, when her banking business in Denver was just starting to grow and was showing some success. Many considered them an unlikely couple, as Kevin was the total opposite of the best-in-class-college-graduate type many would have expected Laura to end up with. However, their marriage reflected a logic few would recognize: Kevin had everything Laura would like to find in a man: simplicity, honesty, strength, courage, and loyalty. He had many fewer qualities which she had in sufficient doses herself, such as career ambitions, intellectual interests, and a tendency to work too much and sleep too little.

Kevin was the owner and manager of a small hunting-and-fishing business outside Denver. He organized outings for groups of tourists and, more often, for small businesses in the area who wished to take their customers or employees out on a pleasant trip in the Rocky Mountains. They had met when Laura had organized a fishing weekend with her management team one summer. She and Kevin had had a hard time hiding their love-at-first-sight romance from Laura's colleagues. They had suspected what happened during that first weekend well before Laura announced her engagement to Kevin a few months later. Since then, they had two children, one boy, Andrew, who was now two years old, and their baby daughter Janet, six months.

This week was the first time since her children's births that Laura went away without her husband and children for more than a day or two. Actually, Kevin had encouraged her to go on this trip. He had recognized the strong distress Laura was feeling from her worries at the bank. He had heard how she talked more and more often about Jessica as the only person she might confide in and express her distress to, because she was her "sister in spirit" and would know what she felt and why. So Kevin had just booked a ticket to Washington, D.C., for her and had handed it to Laura, saying, "You need to go off and spend a week with Jessica."

Surprised but happy, Laura had said, "Wow, that's a good idea; thanks a lot! But what if Jessica isn't available?"

"I talked to her a few days ago. She will be in Washington the whole week, and she has even taken the week off to spend it with you. She seemed to need a vacation as much as you do, so I think I'm doing a good thing for both of you."

"Wonderful! I don't understand how you can know better than me what I need and when."

Kevin had smiled back at her without speaking, and had gone to get the car while Laura went to pack a small suitcase. He drove her to the airport and watched her take off for her flight across the American mainland.

☆ ☆ ☆

Jessica and Laura spent a few days in Washington, D.C., and Laura got to better know Jessica's husband Steve. She had only met him a few times, the first time at Steve and Jessica's wedding party. The two girls soon felt the need to be alone to catch up with all the time they had not spent together for the last six years. They both wanted to get away completely from their daily routines. So they took Jessica's car and drove down south, through the Carolinas to northern Florida. They both felt relieved by the simple fact of moving, although none of them cared much where they went or at what pace. Just being in the car, with Jessica driving and Laura checking the road map, was all they needed to be happy. The longer the drives, the longer and more interesting were the conversations.

The second day of their trip they spent on an uninterrupted four-hour drive in a June sun, which became hotter and hotter. The conversation turned for the first time to look back at the past, which was something exceptional for these two busy and forward-looking girls.

"You know," Laura said, "it feels quite stupid that we have waited six years to spend some time together, and even more stupid that it was my husband's idea, not mine."

"I agree," Jessica answered. "But I accept the fact that I have chosen to live a specific life and that I don't have time to do a lot of other things. I guess I'm fine with spending huge amounts of time on my work, as long as it feels meaningful and interesting. But recently I have come further and further away from that ideal situation. Not only am I getting bored with my work. I also feel I'm doing something which is wrong. I'm sitting in those IMF and central bank global meetings where my colleagues pretend to rule the world. In the meantime, the interest rate decreases we decide about do nothing to stop the developing economic crisis."

"Funny you should say that. I also feel a strong frustration in my work. As a bank entrepreneur, I started out wanting to give only low-risk credits, to hold one hundred percent reserves against demand deposits. But we were almost pushed out of business by competitors lending almost all their demand deposits and offering credits to any risky customer. So in order to stay in business, we had to play along in a game which I always felt was bad, even insane."

"Well, I see you're in a terrible situation, but at least you're living and acting in the real world. The international political meetings where I spend my time are so far away from reality that I wonder why and how anybody cares about them. Steve keeps telling me it's very important and so on, but he is having more and more of a hard time making me swallow that talk."

"Why do you stick around in that job? Why don't you change to something else?"

"As a matter of fact I will, in a few months from now. I have an agreement to leave the IMF and to get a job at the Federal Reserve instead. While that still is a bureaucratic job, it's one step closer to economic reality than my current job at the IMF. And in any case, I'll have some time off. As we will have a baby in three months, I managed to keep a perk which the IMF offers to young mothers, to have one year of maternity leave with full salary. So I'll stop working in a few weeks from now, and then I won't come back until the middle of next year, when my baby will be more than six months old."

"Wow, that's great! I didn't have that luxury when my kids were born. As I am my own boss, I just treated myself to a bit shorter working days, and Kevin helped out a great deal with the kids. The good news for me is that I then managed to find a great nanny in Colorado. And Kevin is still very helpful; he drops off the kids at the babysitter in the morning and often picks them up in the evening."

"You're lucky to have such a caring husband. I don't count on Steve doing the same when we will be parents. He's under such pressure these days in his job at the Treasury. They are the guys who need to find financing to all government programs. Currently, with the economic downturn, the needs are increasing everywhere while they are more and more hard-pressed to find financing. I guess that when I come back to work for the Fed I will hear a lot from Steve in my work, as they appear to be planning to issue more and more government bonds to finance increased public spending. When they do, the Fed comes into the game, in order to buy or sell these bonds."

"I just wonder how you can cope with having to deal with your husband at work. Kevin doesn't give a damn about banking. So I know I won't talk shop when I'm at home. But you and Steve, not only are you in the same line of activity, but you also seem to have quite opposite convictions."

"Yes, that's true," Jessica said thoughtfully. "But I keep the hope that I will manage to turn him around. I mean, my arguments make sense. And one day, I'm sure he will admit that. From then on, there should be less strain in our marriage when we talk business at home."

"I hope so, for your sake," Laura answered. "Now, talking about the Fed, when you start there, don't forget to try to get in touch with the people handling bank regulation issues. I don't know whether my bank will survive the current crisis, but I know for sure the whole system is crazy. I mean, we're pushed into doing what we're told to be right—extending credit blindly and quickly. And then we end up as victims when the policy turns out to have indebted a lot of people who are beyond any hope of paying back. Those debtors end up in a deep mess, and we, their bank, are under threat to go bust. Everybody is losing in this game."

"Not everybody," Jessica answered. "Look at the large Wall Street banks. I bet you that when *they* fall into the same situation, which is bound to happen, they will be bailed out by their friends in the government and at the Federal Reserve! I don't know if you've realized it, but the Federal Reserve System is nothing else than a perfect cartel where government and big banks have a common interest. Government can rule and exercise power by controlling the monetary unit and the financial system, and they can finance public debt by creating money. The banks get a system where they can make quick profits during a boom and get bailed out when they go bust."

Laura looked out through the car window at the horizon and contemplated what her friend had said. After a while, she said, "Funny you should say that. That was, in essence, what the clerk at the Colorado Commission of Banks told me back when I got my banking license. Looking back at these years, and at what's happening right now, it appears to me that what he said is true. I refused to think like that when I started my bank, since it was so far from my vision of making a living from supporting and rewarding productive citizens and businesses in need of credit. You're the first person to talk about it with me since that clerk six years ago.

"I feel there is some giant pretense involved here, with a lot of people closing their eyes not to see what's going on. And those who *do* know and understand don't speak up. And I can't make any sense of it—how can such a system be allowed to go on, and where will it lead us? I should admit that I can't guess or know. But I do know that I'll stick to the advice I got from Professor Benson: from now on, we will stop giving easy credits, and we will slow the fractional reserve lending. That's our only chance of surviving the unfolding bank crisis."

☆ ☆ ☆

Summer was coming to Colorado, and Laura was sitting in her office on a July morning. She liked this period of the year quite a lot, in part because of the frequent mountain trips she made with Kevin and their two small children but also because she had much more time to work without interruption. Her colleagues, customers, partners, or shareholders would usually call her for all types of matters, which they most often considered extremely urgent. Many of these callers were now off on vacation, or at least had slowed down their pace of work over the summer period. This morning, when she had a cup of coffee at eleven, she happily realized that she had not received a single incoming call during the whole morning.

Therefore, she was startled when the phone rang at 11:30. She also recognized the number of someone she had not talked to for a year, when he had called her to ask for a line of credit of two hundred thousand dollars. It was Pete Bagnelli.

"Pete?"

"I see you now have my number in your phone contacts. I guess that makes sense, since I must be one of your larger credit customers."

"Don't start out like that Pete; you'll put me in a bad mood right away. Regarding credit customers, these days I tend to think they are more cumbersome the larger their credit is, since that means a larger risk for me if they default. And the way our capital and reserve ratios are going, we need to get rid of a maximum number of debtors rather than find new ones. So I hope you call me to confirm that you'll pay back, as planned, the remaining hundred thousand dollars of your loan. If my memory is correct, it should be due in a couple of weeks?"

"Well, that credit *is* what I wanted to talk to you about. But not in the way you hope. I would rather like to ask you to extend it for six more months and to give me an additional credit of two hundred thousand dollars. I need that to avoid bankruptcy of my mutual fund within a week or two," Pete said with a cautious voice, having a hard time to conceal that he was much less casual and in control of himself than usually.

Although she could not see him as they were speaking over the phone, she could imagine him looking down at his desk where he was sitting, as if to avoid the scrutinizing eyes of Laura and the harsh answer he expected her to deliver.

"Pete, as I just told you that's purely impossible. And even if I could, I won't lend you more money. I even regret that I gave you that loan a year ago. I guess you just used it to keep playing your so-called one hundred percent leverage game even further. And I can imagine where that has taken you, with more and more assets losing in value!"

"Well, yes, that's the problem. When some of my assets lose a couple of percent in value, I need cash to cover up my positions. To get the additional cash, I need to sell assets, and if I sell assets, I lose money since most of them are worth less now than when I bought them. So the only way out for me is to get a major line of additional credit. Only no bank will give it to me these days. So I figured I would ask you, as you helped me out last time I was in a squeeze."

"But, Pete, don't you see it had to end like this, sooner or later? Even if I and other banks have kept lending money to you over the last few years, you must have recognized that interest rates kept increasing. Since many people use borrowed money to buy financial assets, as you do, you should understand that your purchasing power would start to decrease, as you pay more and more to borrow money. This is why asset prices can't rise forever, even if the banks have kept lending more and more for several years!

"I'll tell you one thing, since I'm living through it myself. When you sneeze from falling asset prices, we banks have a lethal influenza, because we also own financial assets! Hell, most of our bank capital is actually placed in financial assets such as the mortgage-backed securities which are now losing value ever more from one day to another. Our outstanding credit volume is almost fifteen times higher than our capital. We are below the lowest authorized ratio of capital to managed assets. We actually need to reduce our outstanding credits with twenty-four million dollars, almost thirty percent of our credit stock! So you see what I mean when I said I'm not looking for new credit customers, but I'm looking to get rid of those I already have."

"I'll go bust," Pete said wearily, not in order to argue with Laura but as if stating to himself what he now realized for the first time to be inevitable.

"Yes, I guess you will, Pete, and I'm sorry about that. But as you understand, there's nothing I can do about it. Bye now, and I wish you a lot of courage."

"Bye Laura, and sorry for letting you down. I guess my default on that remaining line of one hundred thousand dollars of credit will worsen the mess you're in, too. All I can say is what you also just said: there's nothing I can do about that now."

He hung up before she could reply, which left her sitting with the receiver in her hand. She had thought that she had been right in the decision she had made after talking to Benson, but she had not expected it to be so hard to apply. In spite of the perfect summer scenery outside her window, her professor's words about a financial winter or even financial ice age, came back to her and made her shudder. She reckoned that Pete's previously flourishing mutual fund business now was among the casualties of that ice age. She wondered whether her bank would soon be, too.

✲ ✲ ✲

During the last week of July, Mark Lomack was on vacation but had remained in San Diego to do some windsurfing, and to clear his mind from what was going on in his professional environment. Because of the lively public debate about their role in the financial crisis, the communication department of Golden Touch Software had forbidden employees to talk to journalists. In spite of this, and even though he was on vacation, Mark had accepted to talk to a journalist, who had come to see him, in a bar at the San Diego beach front. Mark had promised to accept that parts of the discussion would be published but that his statement would remain anonymous. The journalist had flown in from New York and looked awkward and uncomfortable in a gray suit under San Diego's burning sun. As the journalist sat down at Mark's table, a waiter had already delivered two large soft drinks to their table.

"Thank you," the journalist said earnestly, as he eagerly drank from his fresh drink.

"Thank *you*," Mark said, "for coming this far to speak to me."

"Well, you're the developer of one of the most famous financial software products. So I think your view on the current situation may be of interest to our readers. Now, a lot of people consider that the financial crisis provides ultimate proof of the failure of the market economy, which seems to be running crazy. What's your view on that?"

"I agree that we today see inappropriate speculation on financial markets. I agree that a lot of people took on way more debt, and accepted way more risk, than they should have. But the first point I would like to make is that the financial market we see today is so far from what 'market economy' or 'capitalism' actually means.

"All the evils that are denounced today such as excessive debt and excessive risk taking wouldn't have been possible if the financial system had been a *real* free market. They are possible only because banks are allowed by law to lend money which doesn't exist and because the central banks provide a set of protections to banks which give them incentives to act as casinos. Correction: not as casinos, but as gamblers who come into a casino to play double or nothing until they lose. Because in the current system, when a bank goes too far and risks going bust, the central bank can bail it out, or allow it to continue while not fulfilling its obligations to customers."

"You may be right about that, even though it's a point of view I haven't heard very often. But still, don't you think that companies like Golden Touch Software, and notably the QRD product which you developed, also have a responsibility in what's happening?"

Mark grinned and consented with a nod before answering. "You're right that QRD has contributed to increase the speed and amplitude of speculation, by making people taking quicker decisions, with less prior analysis. I can tell you that I disapproved about the way the product was designed and even more about the promise with which it was sold. But I know that wouldn't justify the fact that I actually built it."

"No, it wouldn't," the journalist said. "It sure has led a number of investors and financial institutions on a trip, so to say, from heaven to hell. A lot of them made major profits for several years, but it turned out your product couldn't protect them once the markets started to fall. In the last weeks, we have seen a number of bankruptcies that have been related to usage of your product. By the way, I believe the guy who filed for bankruptcy this morning in New York is a friend of yours, isn't he?"

The blood froze in Mark's veins in spite of the excessive summer heat. He tried to speak normally, but his question only came out as a whisper. "Who are you talking about?"

The journalist was surprised that Mark didn't know. "Why, Pete Bagnelli, of the Bagnelli Investment Fund. He has mentioned in several interviews over the last couple of years how the usage of your QRD product had made him stop doing fundamental analysis of investment objects, letting your product tell him what to do. Well, now Bagnelli has gone bust, as he no longer was able to refinance all the debt his company had used for leveraged investments that now have dwindled in value."

Mark closed his eyes, gritted his teeth, and prevented himself from screaming in agony, which took an effort that lasted for many seconds. Once he gained control of himself again, he looked at the journalist with a sad expression. "Thank you for telling me. But now I have to end this interview to take care of some personal matters that are long overdue."

A second later, Mark had already left the table in front of the surprised journalist who just had time to see him jump into his car and drive off in a high speed.

Mark went to the Golden Touch Software office, which was only a five-minute drive from the beach. He walked into the office wearing only his Bermuda shorts and sunglasses and looked furiously around him. Soon he found the person he was looking for, spotting his boss Mike Harding standing in front on the vending machine which delivered free drinks and pastries to employees.

"Damn you, Mike! Do you know what you did to Pete Bagnelli?" he screamed for the whole building to hear.

"Why, yes," Mike answered. "I sold him the best software which exists in the financial world, which made him earn tens of millions of dollars. That also made us earn, more modestly, five to ten percent of what Pete made thanks to our product."

"Well, that was during the first two or three years, when the economy was in a boom period!" Mark yelled back much less smoothly than his boss was speaking.

"But do you realize what has happened now? Pete has gone bankrupt by using our product, and we haven't lost a penny on it. We offered him profit sharing, but he had to keep all the risk!"

"Well, that's tough luck for Pete, but I don't see why *you* should care about that. Or even less why you should come bothering *me* about it. After all, *you* developed that product, including the so-called one hundred percent–leveraged, asset-buying profit-maximizing module. So you better shut up before I fire you for insubordination." Harding said, now with a firmer voice, before turning swiftly to go back to his office.

Mark remained standing in front of the vending machine, and he trembled from a combination of anger and of guilt: anger with his boss but also at himself, for not finding the right words, neither now nor at that trade show when he might have prevented Pete from buying their software, and guilt for knowing that his boss was right, at least in part. It was he, Mark Lomack, who had developed the product and who thereby had made possible the results it had led to.

Mark was a man of ruthless intellectual honesty, so he would not and could not have evaded the knowledge of these facts nor of their relation to the strong guilt he now felt. When all this became clear in his mind, a few seconds after Mike Harding had turned to walk away from him, Mark screamed, even louder than the first time, "Mike! Come back here. I have something for you."

While Harding reluctantly and slowly turned to come back, Mark grabbed a paper and a pen from a nearby meeting table and scribbled down a few sentences on it. "Here! This is my letter of resignation, so you won't have to fire me. I will only say that I admit that you were right. I did develop that product, although I shouldn't have. My error was to accept the idea that something could be practical without being moral. So from now on, I'll switch to only doing things which are good, because *that* is the only practical thing to do!"

✧ ✧ ✧

Early August on a Saturday, Pete Bagnelli was lying in bed late in the morning in his Manhattan apartment. He had rented it during the boom period and now, following the bankruptcy of his investment business, he would have to leave it shortly, since he was unable to pay the rent.

He hadn't been expecting any visitors that morning, so when the doorbell rang, he frowned and wondered who had come to see him.

I hope it's not some lunatic investor who wants to kill me for losing all his money in the bust of the Bagnelli Investment Fund. He chuckled. But he stopped chuckling when he recalled having read several recent stories in the newspapers of assaults of that kind. He walked up to the door and saw that a small envelope had been pushed in under it. Before picking it up, he looked through the peephole in the door, but the person outside had put his hand up there to prevent him from seeing who it was.

"Who are you, and what do you want?" he said tiredly, but without care while he picked up the envelope on the floor.

The person outside didn't answer, but Pete picked up the envelope and opened it. Inside it was an airline ticket from New York to Nepal, leaving in a week, and with a return flight six months later. He realized it was a real flight ticket and that it had his name on it.

"What the hell is this? A flight ticket to Nepal? I'm a financial investor in New York City; I wouldn't spend more than a few days in a place like Nepal, except of course if I was going with my best friend," Pete said addressing the person standing behind the door.

"You are," the person on the other side the door said firmly.

"What?" Pete asked back.

"You *are* going there with your best friend. Or at least with someone who *was* your best friend, before he ruined your life."

"Mark, is that you?" Pete said and opened the door.

"Yes, it's me," Mark answered, and produced a sad smile when the door opened a second later.

"Man, am I happy to see you," Pete shouted. "You still look the same as always! Now what's this thing with Nepal flight tickets? And why do you have such a sad look on your face? I'm awfully excited to see you. It must be something like four years since we last met, at that financial trade show,"

"Yes, I know," Mark said, "and that's what I wanted to tell you. I mean, I'm so sorry that my boss sold you our software product; I know it has contributed to the ruin of your business. And I wanted to come here in person to apologize."

"Well, Mark, I'm very happy you came to see me, but you don't owe me any apologies at all. I bought that product and used it—it was my own decision. I knew what I was doing, and I assume full responsibility for what happened to my business, even though I obviously didn't plan for or expect it to end as it did. Now what is this Nepal trip?"

"I have left my job at Golden Touch Software, and I want to take some time off to think through what I will do later when I come back. You know that mountain trekking is my favorite hobby, along with windsurfing. But I've been surfing almost every day for the last years. So I figured I would go to Nepal for some time. And... and I really would like you to come with me, if you'll accept."

"Of course I will. But I see you didn't wait for my answer before booking the tickets." Pete looked closer at the ticket he was holding in his hands. "I even see that the last date for refund was yesterday. Now *that* was a smart way of convincing me to come, but I assure you it was not needed—I would have gone anyway."

"That's great!" Mark said, starting to feel better. "But what will you do with your flat?"

"Oh, this one? I was planning to leave it in a couple of weeks anyway. As you know, my revenues have dipped slightly lately. So I guess I'll put my stuff into storage somewhere before we leave. By the way, are just the two of us going?"

"Yes, why?"

"I talked to Bobby Cheston recently. He has been going through a rough couple of years since they got thrown out of their house, just before his wife took off with the kids. A few months later he lost his job and couldn't find another one in his line of business."

"Yes, I know," Mark said, "I heard about that. It's terrible. I hear he is now working in a fast-food restaurant and that he has moved back to live with his parents in Seattle."

"So let's ask him to come with us. I think Bobby too, just like the two of us, needs a fresh restart. And I'm sure he will be better off spending some time with us rather than hanging out with his parents."

"Deal."

Mark picked up his mobile phone, and called Bobby Cheston, who was as happy but possibly even more surprised than Pete to hear from his two best friends from college. He accepted their proposal without hesitation.

One week later, the three of them, with a renewed sense of opportunity and adventure in front of them, were off for Nepal, leaving their troubles behind them.

CHAPTER 8:
The Eternal and the Infernal

"Wow, that must be the peak of Mount Everest!" Pete cried. He stopped, threw off his backpack, and picked out his binoculars.

"No, stupid, it's the Nuptse and Lhotse peaks," Bobby replied, shaking his head with his arms crossed over his chest and watching his less athletic friend with a smile. "If I didn't know you're bad at geography, I'd think you're trying to get extra breaks along our walk." Bobby chuckled.

"Well, whatever, but one thing is sure, this is the most beautiful scenery I ever saw. And even if they aren't Everest, those mountain peaks are still damn impressive and beautiful," Pete said, without taking his eyes from his binoculars. "And don't try to make fun of my physique; we have been trekking for two months now, and as you can see, I'm still alive and kicking." Pete put his binoculars down and flashed a confident and happy smile at Bobby.

Mark, who had been walking a bit ahead of the other two, came back down and said with a grin, "Pete, whatever good reason you come up with, it's always you who makes us take breaks. On this trek, just like you did back in college. But never mind. You're right; it's beautiful here. Hand me the binoculars." Mark took them and looked up to the Lhotse summit. "Wow, amazing. This peak looks like a perfect pyramid, with a giant steep snowfield below steep, flat walls. That would be an amazing ski run."

Bobby chuckled and said, as he stood up to prepare to resume walking, "For sure, I'd love to try that too, but I don't know if it's possible. And for now, I would be happy if both of you could keep your focus on our immediate objective. Need I remind you that we're going to see the Everest panorama at lunch? So let's get back on our feet and keep walking!"

Mark and Pete sighed and took the time to shoot a few photographs with their cameras before catching up with Bobby, who had already started along the trail they were following.

Mark wanted to use this trip to forget about his previous job at Golden Touch Software and to find some energy and vision for new projects. So far, he had succeeded with the first part of his challenge. Every day had contained a lot of demanding and interesting events grabbing all of his attention, such as meeting local people, shooting pictures of a staggering mountain landscape, or cooking food for his two friends. Mark was the most skilled cook among the three, and he took a lot of pleasure in preparing meals using products bought along their trek. The tasty and heavy meals had helped him avoid losing weight, something he was happy about since he was already thin enough when starting the trek.

That was less true for his two friends. Pete had lost his physique during the years spent in New York due to long working days. He had mostly eaten junk food, often in front of his computer in the office, be it lunch or dinner. Pete's being overweight had made the first two or three weeks extremely challenging for him. In spite of making strong efforts to keep up with Mark and Bobby, he had often slowed the group's progress. He was nevertheless happy about being able to manage their challenging daily walks of five to six hours, often with some significant vertical slopes, both uphill and downhill. Entering week eight, Pete had lost most of his extra weight, and he was feeling better and better and less worn out in the evenings. This helped him recapture his usual self; in their group, he had always been the funny guy, telling stories and exposing his friends to practical jokes. That he, too, was forgetting about his recent past back in the United States also contributed to make him more lighthearted. The bankruptcy of his mutual investment fund had been a hard blow to Pete, but he had always been uncompromisingly optimistic and sanguine. After a few weeks, he had put those worries behind him, and he figured that he had learned the lessons needed to avoid similar failures in the future.

Bobby had also lost some weight, gained when he was working in a fast food restaurant close to his parents' home. He had taken advantage of the possibility to have free food from his employer, to save more money and accelerate the payback of his debts. So just like Pete, Bobby had suffered during the first weeks of trekking, although less than his shorter and less athletic friend. Bobby had also needed less time to recapture his former stamina, that of a running back of the college football team. Now after eight weeks he had even surpassed Mark in endurance, and Bobby frequently carried a bit of extra weight in order to relieve his friends of some burdens.

In early October in this part of the world, the season was the end of fall preceding the start of winter which was expected in just a few weeks. Leaves were falling off the trees along their trail, and some nights, the temperature approached the freezing point. They were alternating between sleeping in their tent and sleeping in lodges they would find along the road. Some of these were large installations with the capacity for many hikers; others were more private, such as with farming families who would lodge three to four people in their own home and share dinner with their guests. Tips for lodging either came from their well-written guidebooks or, more frequently, from the people they met along the road.

This night, they were aiming to reach a reputed Nepalese farmer's lodge that a couple of German trekkers had told them about with a lot of enthusiasm two days earlier. They were still four hours of walking from that destination, and they had a tough road ahead with a lot of uphill trail, but to be compensated with a view of Everest for their planned lunch break.

About one hour after their previous break, Mark and Pete were lagging behind Bobby, who turned around and shouted, "Hey, what's your problem back there? Don't you want to see Everest before the sun sets?"

Pete looked up from his feet, which he had been staring at for some time while walking, and raised his head up toward the hill where Bobby now stood with his arms crossed looking down at him. After a few deep breaths, Pete managed an answer. "Don't be so smart. You know I'm carrying the tent today. And you can bet I want to see it as much as you do."

"Me too," Mark said. "But we shouldn't fall back to our old bad habits of wanting everything to go fast. That's how we miss out on things. Just look at that!" He pointed at his left where a family of Nepalese reindeers walked by at a short distance, unimpressed by the three noisy humans.

They all kept quiet until the animals had moved out of their sight. Meanwhile, Pete and Mark caught up with Bobby, who said, "I guess you're right. Every time we take the time here to look around, we see something marvelous. I wonder whether it would be the same back home."

"What do you mean?" Pete asked.

"I mean that if we should take the time more often to look around and contemplate what we see, maybe we would see and experience things which we miss since we move too fast all the time."

"Bobby, I appreciate this dose of philosophy, because I think you're right but also because it gives me some needed breathing spell," Pete said, recapturing his breath and managing to produce a smile.

"True," said Mark, "but I still can't wait to see Mount Everest. Let's keep pushing a bit more and then maybe we will get the sight of our lives."

They got back on the trail, climbing higher and higher toward the mountain pass where they would stop for lunch.

✻ ✻ ✻

"Wow!"

It was hard to tell which of the three young men had said it first when they stopped to admire the panorama that opened up before their eyes when reaching the top of their morning climb. They all recognized the characteristic pyramid shape of the Mount Everest, with its steep walls of rock and snow connecting the top of the world to the ground below. They were too far away to identify camps or human beings moving, but they did see some thin clouds moving around the summit. They looked like a mixture of clouds and snowflakes from the mountain, stirred up by the wind, which was always strong up there, and glittering from the reflection of sunlight.

They stood silent for a long while, the only sound coming from the wind striking their faces when they came up to the mountain pass.

"So this is what the top of the world looks like," Mark said, breaking the silence.

"I marvel at the enormous distance between it and us! I mean, we see it as if we were close to it, but it's tens of miles away," Bobby said.

"I'd give anything to go from here to there in a helicopter." Pete said. "That would be the flight of my life!"

"Yeah, maybe, but it would certainly be the last flight of your life. You should know that the air is too thin up there for a helicopter to keep its altitude," Mark answered.

"Sure, I know. But seeing this great void makes me want to fly out there. But now let's keep our feet on the ground and have some well deserved lunch. Mark, what's your suggestion for this special picnic in front of the top of the world?"

"I'll heat up the stew remaining from last night, and we have a lot of bread and sausage to go with it. And, surprise of the day, in the last village we passed through yesterday, I traded one of my T-shirts for a bottle of red wine! I thought we'd need something to toast with on this special occasion."

While Mark prepared the food, Bobby and Pete spread out some blankets on a rock where they would sit down. They took the opportunity to shoot some photographs of this perfect postcard scenery. Then they set the automatic shot function of the camera and got a photo of all three of them with the Mount Everest behind. As they dug into the plates prepared by Mark, Pete showed the photo.

"That's one picture I'd like to send back to the world as a postcard," Bobby said.

"Yeah, me too!" Mark said, picking up his small paper calendar from his pocket. He used it to keep track of the passage of time, be it only to get the right references in the diary notes he wrote every night before going to sleep. "By the way, could you guess what day it is today, and how long we have been cut off from any news from the world? May I remind you that the last time we read the news on Internet was on September first?"

"Not a clue," Pete said.

"Me neither," Bobby said.

"Today is October fifteenth, which means we have been totally cut off from the so-called civilization for six weeks!" Mark said triumphantly.

Pete looked straight at Mark, and said, after some contemplation, "Wow, that's a long time. And I can't say I really have been worrying or caring about whatever happened back there. And when you see a sight as the one in front of us, it makes me feel as if the world has never changed and will never change, and as if nothing could make it fall apart."

"I agree," Bobby said. "I already feel as if my house foreclosure and job loss, and your bankruptcy, Pete, where just minor incidents in our lives."

"I don't know," Mark said. "I think the world was in a bad shape when we left it. Even if we're forgetting our personal worries, I'm not so sure the rest of the world is doing well."

"Well, since we don't know, and since none of us has a sixth sense, let's check it out," Pete said, and turned on his smart phone, which had been off for weeks. He opened the Internet browser application and went to the site of the Global News Network, GNN, to the Monthly Highlights page.

Pete's face changed slowly from his usual casual look, which this day combined with an air of serenity and happiness, to something that looked like horror personified. Mark and Bobby put their plates and glasses down and watched Pete as his face turned white and as his eyes seemed about to pop out of his head.

"What the hell is going on?" Bobby said anxiously.

"I say the sky is about to fall down on people's heads back home. Come and look. There's a video here we can watch."

Pete pushed the button and launched the video, which was a discussion sequence between two of the main stars of the GNN. They were Manuel Jones and Kevin Larrison. Jones was the special reporter of politics and economics. His short fellow news anchor, Larrison, was the most famous face on American television, as the host of the prime-time show *Events That Change the World*. The discussion was properly set up with Larrison asking questions to Manuel Jones. In the shadow of a mountain, Pete, Mark, and Bobby could see Jones' and Larrison's faces as the video started.

"Manuel, why don't you recall the unbelievable events which are changing, pardon me, disrupting the world, since a month or two?"

"Well, one significant aspect of the present situation is that the image of the United States has changed. While we used to be seen as the undisputed economic superpower of the world, today the country is a sort of financial disaster zone."

"Can we say it started with the nationalization and the final federal takeover of those mortgage institutions the government had been backing for a long time, Freddy K and Funny J?"

"Yes, if you wish, but I believe that the bankruptcy of one of the top five Wall Street banks, one week later, was even more spectacular. As that focused attention, the last-minute rescue and takeover of another top Wall Street bank by a competitor almost went unnoticed."

"Yes, just as the one-hundred-billion-dollar loan made from the Federal Reserve to a top insurance company to save it from bankruptcy. But then again, once it became known they were celebrating that rescue in a luxury retreat, those guys got their dose of attention, and of heat," Larrison chuckled.

"True," Jones said. "But let's look at some events which got less air time in mass media, but were all the more remarkable and radical. For example what happened on the U.S. corporate bond market, which was a virtual bank run. During one week, we saw withdrawals of one hundred forty billion dollars. That's *fifty times* more than in a normal week."

"So this must have triggered other major shocks?"

"Yes, it led to the virtual freeze of corporate short-term financing. And this gave the banks the creeps; they even lost confidence in each other, putting a violent stop to the overnight interbank lending. Of course, this made banks themselves freeze lending to their customers. Some banks got into serious trouble, such as that giant retail bank put under Federal Deposit Insurance protection."

"Yes, this brings us to the much talked about emergency bank bailout plan devised by the Fed chairman and the secretary of the Treasury," Larrison whispered.

"Indeed, the voting of a seven-hundred-billion-dollar envelope for bank bailouts was unprecedented in U.S. history. As of today, a few weeks later, two hundred fifty of that seven hundred billion has indeed been used, giving a shot in the arm to virtually all of the remaining major retail and investment banks in the country. On top of that, the tax law was changed in an emergency move to make it easier for banks to buy other banks, which has incited some of them to save their competitors by taking them over."

"True, Manuel, but what gives *me* the creeps is that all these radical measures appear insufficient to recreate confidence on the markets. I mean, we have seen the U.S. stock market lose twenty percent in one week. That's its worst performance in seventy-five years! And, in the meantime, the crisis has spread to Europe, where similar events have been unfolding."

"Yes, Kevin, all this is indeed scary. And don't ask me what the next two months will be like. I wouldn't like to be as terribly wrong as I would have been if I had answered that question two months ago. So let's just keep doing our job and follow events on a daily basis."

Larrison sighed from authentic anxiety, but tried to display a smile as he concluded the short interview. "Right, that's a flash overview of recent events. You can count on me to follow up on all this in my own show, as we are, for sure, seeing events that are changing the world."

Pete, Mark, and Bobby looked at each other, incredulously. What they had heard felt more unbelievable than many disaster movies they had seen and all the more unreal as they were in a place where the world felt so clear, safe, and eternally stable. Pete was the first to speak, with an uncertain smile. "Now, for the first time in my life, I'm happy not to own any financial assets anymore."

Mark didn't listen to Pete's joke. "It's a disaster, worse than any nightmare people may have ever had at Wall Street! And guys, do you realize we contributed to it?"

"What do you mean?" Bobby said with a frown.

Mark looked and them with a sad expression. "Bad mortgages driving down mortgage companies and banks? Bobby is one of the many people who went into that trap. Heavily leveraged financial institutions becoming insolvent after only a minor fall in the value of their assets? Well that's exactly what happened to your mutual fund, Pete, and *I* am strongly responsible for making that happen, since I developed this freak software!"

"Chill out, Mark," Bobby said, shaking his head gently. "Your problem is that you have such a strong conscience that you think you should carry the whole world on your shoulders and such bold confidence that you think you might!"

Mark froze and looked strangely at Bobby for an instant. "Thanks, man. That's a good point. I guess I always accepted what you say regarding other people. But I may have forgotten it regarding myself."

Bobby nodded rapidly, concentrating too hard to reflect on Mark's response, before continuing. "I think the truth is that we were just pawns in a giant, mad scheme leading to disaster. The most powerful people in the world didn't see it coming. They even helped it happen by shutting off the alarms. Hell, how can we accept any form of guilt for a crisis which no one expected, in spite of all the bad economic news of the last two years?"

Pete leaned forward and looked at the devastated faces of his two friends. "I think there are a few people who *did* see it coming. Only they may not be the kind of people who are listened to by the power elite. Take our Professor Benson, for example."

Pete picked up his smart phone again and swiftly looked up the page of Professor Benson's Web site. On Benson's blog, there was just a brief message referring to an article he had written three years earlier. The article included a prediction that the next financial crisis could be centered on the real estate market. It also had the suggestion that it might be more violent than previous crises because the level of debt, and insolvency, would be higher and more widespread this time and might have an impact on banks themselves. Along with the link to that article, there were only a few text sentences:

> *I'm known as an opponent of fractional reserve banking and the underlying monetary system based on government-controlled paper money. However, I'm acutely aware that a significant decrease in the money supply must be avoided at all cost. This is because a deflationary spiral could create mass bankruptcy and an economic crisis of unprecedented scale. That would happen if prices, most notably wages, can't decrease at the same pace as the quantity of money and spending in the economy. Therefore, the immediate priority is to ensure we don't face mass bank failures and bank runs provoking the evaporation of bank deposits. This risk is perfectly real as bank deposits in the current banking system are largely not backed by actual currency bills and coins. While admitting the necessity of some short-term emergency actions, I underscore that this crisis must be used to understand the fundamental causes of what has happened. This includes showing the immense responsibility of governments and central banks which have meddled with money and credit for several decades, indeed, for more than a century.*

As they went over other news commentaries, they saw that the media and public opinion were aware about the need for avoiding mass bankruptcies by preventing bank failures. But they showed no awareness about what a student of Professor Benson would consider as the obvious causes of the crisis. No one looked at why and how the very nature of the banking system had inexorably led to piling up of debt. New commentaries instead cried out, loud, about "excessive greed among bankers," "the final failure of the free economy," and all sorts of variants of those messages.

Mark had been rereading the paperback version of Benson's old textbook in economic history before tucking in to sleep in his tent. When they had stopped reading on Pete's smart phone, Mark summed up what they all felt. "If that's the level of understanding people have who stay all their lives in the middle of the rat race, then we would do well to stay *here* for a long time."

Still in a state of shock and unable to analyze further what they had learned, they finished their lunch and packed their bags to continue their walk. That afternoon, their speed of walking slowed, and the energy and sense of expectation of the morning were replaced by a sense of doom within the group. Mount Everest remained in sight on their left side for the rest of the day, but it no longer appeared like a monument of strength and of stability, more like a giant avenger. As its shadow crept over them in the late afternoon, the three boys felt as if the mountain would engulf them.

✡ ✡ ✡

It was past five when they reached the destination of the day's trip: a modest Nepalese farmer house where they found room and board. Mark, who in addition to being the chief cook of the group also played the role as their cultural ambassador, tried out a few sentences of Nepalese which he had taken the effort to learn.

The farmer was a man around fifty years old, with multiple layers of thick clothes wrapped around a body with leathery skin. He had protruding but attentive eyes. He answered with a smile, first in Nepalese, but then he switched to hesitant English. "Thank you for those words in our language. But I have learned some English. Please you can go to your rooms, and then you can have dinner with our family. I would like to hear about your adventures and to tell you a bit of our life out here as farmers."

"Thank you so much!" said Pete, who was the first of the three to enter the room they had been shown into.

Before washing themselves and preparing for dinner, the three of them dropped onto their beds and almost instantly fell asleep. They were exhausted after a day of strong, physical effort with heavy mental strain under the shadow and protection of the Mount Everest.

After an hour of sleep and having selected the least filthy and least wrinkled clothes they had in their backpacks, Mark, Pete, and Bobby went into the dining room. In the middle of the room, a large and heavy wooden table stood surrounded by eight wooden chairs, equally heavy and worn but steady and decorative. Candles provided a dim light to the room, where smoke from the nearby kitchen combined with the vapor from incense burning in the room's corners.

The table was set with ceramic plates painted with dark green stripes. The two adolescent children, a boy and a girl, sat quietly at the table waiting for their parents, and looked shyly at the guests of the night. The farmer came into the room and asked his guests to sit down. Soon thereafter, the farmer's wife came in from the kitchen and served the first dish before sitting at the end of the table. The farmer was the first to start a conversation, after each of them had tasted the spicy dish they had been served along with some rice.

"We had an American family here last week; they told us there is terrible financial trouble in your country."

"Yes," Mark answered. "I guess you learned about that long before we did. We have actually been cut off from news from the United States for six weeks, and only today did we learn the terrible news. I guess we still don't quite understand what we heard; it all feels unreal. And it's really hard to understand what's actually going on."

The farmer nodded. "Yes, I can imagine. Your world is so complicated. Out here, the economy is very simple. We grow as much crops and vegetables as we can. Then we use some of it ourselves, and some of it we give to other people. I don't mean "give"—how do you say—"trade," I think?"

As Mark nodded, the farmer went on. "Yes, we trade some of the things we have produced against things we don't have ourselves but that we can get from other people. Sometimes we trade things against things directly, but if that doesn't work out, we can also give them some tea or some wheat. Everybody wants that, so it can be used to trade with other people afterward. I guess this seems really primitive to you. But that is what our life is like out here," the farmer concluded, before quietly continuing to eat from his main dish.

Mark, Pete, and Bobby looked at each other with wonder, and Mark said, "That's very interesting, sir."

Not one of them spoke further, which the farmer may have interpreted as a lack of interest. What silenced the three American trekkers was a combination of wonder, physical fatigue, and shame.

They politely pursued the dinner conversation, telling about the splendid sights they had seen for the last few days. Then, after two hours with the farmer family, the three young men returned to their bedroom.

They were all exhausted after a long day, but Mark still had the strength to summarize what was on all of their minds before the three of them crashed into bed. "Do you realize how wrong he was when he said their economy is primitive and ours is advanced? Actually, the opposite is true. They still recognize that the main challenge of economics is to produce, not to consume. In the United States, we hear every day that consumption is the motor of the economy. And here they have money which is a valuable commodity, such as tea or wheat, while we have useless pieces of paper for money. Those are the terrible errors we have accepted in our view of economics and of society. And my feeling is that the current crisis is only the beginning of the price we will have to pay to correct those errors!"

✳ ✳ ✳

As Mark, Bobby, and Pete went to sleep in Nepal, Montgomery Benson's mobile phone rang on the other side of world in San Francisco. The man on the phone had a dark, heavy voice, which indicated that he had a large, strong body, but he sounded like a young child facing his worst nightmare. "Montgomery, the world is falling down on our heads! The stock market has lost ninety percent! Trading is stopped. It has been stopped several times. Nothing seems to help!

"What I feared when we talked ten months ago now is coming true! Our whole banking system is falling to pieces, and speculation is going wild against our currency. I guess we can't blame the speculators either, knowing how much money our central bank printed and the crazy race of fractional reserve banking our commercial banks have been running! What the hell are we going to do?"

"Listen to me," Benson snapped. "You're the size of two regular men, and had you lived a few centuries ago, I am sure you would have been among the first of your countrymen to cross the Atlantic Ocean in a ship. So now is the time not be afraid, but to be bold."

"What are you talking about?" the man answered hesitantly.

"I'm talking about what I told you ten months ago. The time may now be ripe to scrap your paper money and shut down your central bank. Hell, they may even disappear by their own fault before we have the time to move! I say let's give it a shot to convince your president and your government about the virtues of gold money and one hundred percent reserve banking. They should be ready to listen to that now, having lived through history's most violent real-life lesson on the topic!"

The man settled down to think through Benson's words, and said: "Yes, I guess you're right. I'll talk to the president about it. He's a friend of mine. I told you we went to university together and had a lot of fun."

"Great," Benson said. "So it appears that we're approaching the perfect point in time to correct more than a century of errors in monetary policy! Or at least *start* to correct them, because your country is still a small part of the world economy."

"That's for sure." the man said. "But today it doesn't feel like that. We have journalists from all over the world flying in to take a close look at what many of them call the worst disaster zone of the worst economic crisis of the century. So I guess we're up for a period of firefighting, where everybody will be busy to save whatever can be saved. I promise to talk to the president as soon as I can. Hopefully, come spring next year, I'll be able to set up a meeting with him for you. That is, if he's still in power, and we still have any economy left over here."

CHAPTER 9:
Pyromaniac Firemen

On October 16, the phone rang at 10:00 a.m. in the Washington, D.C., apartment of Jessica Frostby and Steve Harper. Steve had already been at work for a few hours, and Jessica had been busy since early in the morning taking care of their baby daughter Lisa, two months old. Jessica picked the phone up with a slight irritation, as she was busy and didn't expect a call at this time.

"Jessica Frostby speaking. Who is it?"

"Good morning, Jessica," a man answered. "This is Jeffery Hastings."

Jeffery Hastings would be Jessica's new boss, when she had finished her maternity leave and went to work for the Federal Reserve. Jeffery was a member of the board of governors of the Federal Reserve, and Jessica was to be his closest aide and associate.

"Hello, Jeffery; how are you doing? Oh, I guess that's a stupid question in the middle of this financial crisis. I can imagine you're doing eighteen-hour days trying to get the financial world back on its feet."

"Yes, as a matter of fact, these are terribly busy days for us at the Federal Reserve. And that's what I wanted to talk to you about."

"What?" Jessica answered. "Well, please go ahead, but you know I still have eight months of maternity leave ahead of me."

"I know, but I would like to ask you, or rather, to beg you on my knees, to consider shortening that maternity leave to come back to work right now. We are in a terrible squeeze, and as you will be my closest associate, it would be such a great help for me to have you here right now."

"You're asking me to turn down the chance to spend eight more months full-time with my baby daughter? How do you expect me to consider the idea of giving that up?"

"Well, of course, I'll make sure you have a strong financial incentive; for this period, I will double your salary. But I don't expect that to make you change your mind. My only hope lies in what I read in your file, and what I hear from people who have worked with you."

"What's that?"

"That you're a very intelligent person who, in addition, has strong convictions and that you want to put your intelligence to the best possible use. I hear you always wanted to be able to change the world to the better. Well, here is the opportunity to be part of a small group of people who will have that chance. Or at least, the opportunity to make sure we still have a world to live in, a few months from now."

"Jeffery, you should also know that I'm sort of an iconoclast. I actually have a doubt about whether the Federal Reserve, and this whole system of government-controlled paper money, should be allowed to remain in existence at all. So don't expect me to be your yes-man, or yes-woman, spending my time cleaning up in front of Fed's door, and to hide our heavy responsibility in this whole mess."

"Jessica, I hope you're not serious about shutting down the Fed, and in any case it is not in your power to do so. But please believe me when I say that we're becoming very open-minded in looking for ways to improve our financial system. Obviously none of us in power wanted this to happen, but we want to do everything possible to make sure it won't happen again. So do you accept to come back to work try to save the financial world together with me and the rest of our team at the Fed?"

"OK. But I count on you to help me find the best babysitter in Washington, D.C. And I will ask to go back to part-time work, for the remainder of my eight months, as soon as the worst crisis period is over. Do we have a deal or not?"

"Deal! Would it be possible for you to come in tomorrow, Friday? And to plan to work this weekend?"

"Why?"

"The interbank lending market is still virtually frozen because the money market mutual funds have ceased lending. They did that in order to compensate for the huge withdrawal of funds they have suffered over the last weeks. So we need to look into radical measures to restore liquidity and confidence. If we don't, banks and businesses all over the country will start going bankrupt early next week, at an accelerated pace."

"OK, I'll see you tomorrow morning in the office," Jessica said with a deep sigh. "Now let me spend the rest of this day trying to find a babysitter for Lisa."

"Thank you so much, Jessica! I will be eternally grateful for your flexibility and your loyalty."

"Thank you for saying that. But I'm not so sure you'll want to repeat it in the future. But never mind; see you tomorrow." She hung up and rushed over to Lisa, who was crying in her bed as if she had understood the meaning of the conversation her mother had just ended.

✼ ✼ ✼

The current crisis was a most unsuitable situation for someone starting a new job at the Federal Reserve, but once Jessica had accepted to start working, she had to deal with learning her new job amid a severe financial crisis. Jeffery Hastings was the Federal Reserve governor in charge of responding to the financial crisis, and Jessica was his closest associate.

In her role, she had to refresh a dashboard of critical situations on a daily basis. This involved tracking not only the large financial institutions that risked bankruptcy but also other issues, such as the credit freeze on the interbank lending market. This freeze had been dealt with, during Jessica's first week at work, through the Fed purchasing more than 500 billion dollars' worth of bad assets from money market mutual funds. The Fed did so simply by writing a check in its own name, which instantly and by the exceptional power the Fed enjoyed according to American law turned into 500 billion dollars of newly created money.

In the week of November 20, Jessica, Jeffery, and their team of five analysts held a one-day workshop to elaborate on proposals for the main crisis response actions that Jeffery would have to present the coming week to the board of governors of the Federal Reserve. This was only a few days after a much-hailed meeting of the presidents and finance ministers of the G20 countries, which had produced little tangible results. The most experienced among the five analysts, a middle-aged man named Bruce Bowler, who had been with the Fed for fifteen years, had prepared and facilitated the team's presentation. Jeffery, who had read and contributed to the material prepared before the workshop, intended to let Bruce introduce and then intervene as needed to make sure the right decisions were made.

After an introductory discussion about the most recent events and some updates to Jessica's "Firefighting Dashboard," Bruce outlined the key issues of the workshop.

"Let's summarize the staggering problems we're facing: banks and credit institutions have suffered strong credit losses. Their asset portfolios, notably mortgage backed securities but also most other types of financial assets have lost a lot of value. This has made the capital-to-asset ratios of banks insufficient. Banks have also suffered major withdrawals, but not yet amounting to bank runs. Still, given that they have been extending very high volumes of credit, their reserve ratios are in most cases below the authorized levels. In addition, we have a lot of financial investors, businesses, and households in a bad situation. Each has lost capital through the massive fall in asset prices, they have more debt than they can handle, and they have insufficient levels of cash."

"At the level of the overall economy," Jessica added, "this means that spending, both from businesses and from consumers, drops due to a combination of two factors. First, both these groups wish to hold on more to the little cash they have, reducing the circulation of money. And, second, the overall quantity of money in the economy decreases.

"When a debtor defaults on a credit, the money borrowed in most cases ceases to exist. This is true for all loans that were fractional reserve loans in the first place: the bank lent out the same money several times, artificially increasing the total quantity of money; much of the loans were not backed by actual currency bills and coins. So when the loan disappears, the artificially created money disappears too. The same thing happens, on a larger scale, when a bank goes bankrupt: all the money it has created through fractional reserve lending ceases to exist. Depositors will get bailed out though, if the Federal Deposit Insurance mechanism is applied, as it should be up to one hundred thousand dollars per deposit account."

"Thank you, Jessica," Jeffery said. "So this boils down to the following: we have banks that will go broke if they keep on lending money, but on the other side, we have businesses, investors, and households who will go broke if they can't access additional credit. Overall spending in the economy is already decreasing, starting a deflationary spiral. The general ability to pay back debt will worsen, as there is less money in the economy. At the same time prices, notably wages, and also debt payment amounts, generally don't fall. A true nightmare situation, but we have to deal with it!"

"Good point, Jeffery. Therefore, we should urge our friends in government to remove as quickly as possible all laws and regulations preventing prices from falling because the only way the economy can go on with a lower quantity of money is that prices and wages must fall. If they don't, we'll see increasing bankruptcies and unemployment, as businesses won't afford to pay workers nor pay other costs."

"Jessica, hold it a moment. That would be deflation! And we definitively don't want to see deflation, and even less to trigger it ourselves."

"Jeffery, I see you make the same mistake as many economists. Falling prices is not a proper definition of deflation, it's only a necessary *consequence* of it. And a very important and virtuous consequence, as it enables the economy to keep functioning with a lower quantity of money, without generating unemployment or excessive business failures. As you pointed out, we have today too much debt and too little cash in the hands of businesses and households. The way out of the crisis is for them to use more of their revenues to pay back debt and to keep some of it to increase their cash balance."

"But that means consumption would fall; and thus, GDP would fall; and we would have a recession, or even a depression. We don't want that!"

"If people pay back debt, Jeffrey, that will give banks a breathing spell and make them able to get back on their feet, eventually being able to extend credit again. And as people and businesses keep some more cash for themselves during some time, they will be able to manage without getting additional credit. In any case, banks aren't able to provide such credit currently."

"Well, Jessica, all this is interesting on a theoretical level, but I don't think that's the way to get out of the crisis. Let's keep it simple: we have people and businesses that need credit and banks that aren't able to provide it. So let's boost the capital and reserve levels of the banks so they can get back to lending the money people need to borrow."

"You mean, since banks have been lending too much, we will intervene to make sure that they can lend even more and so that people who already have too much debt could get even more debt?"

The tension was rising in the room, as Jessica and Jeffery's discussion was turning into a verbal fight. The other people in the room looked uncomfortably at each other and hoped that they would not be asked to take sides in the argument.

Jeffery stood up and said aggressively, "Jessica, we're facing an emergency situation. We should consider ourselves as firefighters trying to extinguish a fire, not as architects trying to devise a perfect financial system! And when you extinguish a fire, you should not keep your eyes on the water meter!"

"Well, in that case, I would say we are firemen acting as pyromaniacs. I don't think it's water you're throwing on the fire, but rather gasoline! How much additional reserves are you planning to inject in the banking system?"

"Around one trillion dollars."

"What is the current level of reserves?" Jessica asked, rhetorically, since she knew the answer.

"Around fifty billion dollars."

"So," Jessica said, "you plan to increase reserves by a factor of twenty, knowing that almost all of that will be so-called excess reserves, enabling the banks to extend new loans. And if you inject additional reserves, do you plan to increase the legal reserve requirements, so that fractional reserve lending won't make the same thing happen again?"

"No, don't be crazy. If we did that, the banks couldn't restart their lending, and some of them might go out of business. Instead of making reserve and capital requirements harder, we will give the banks some breathing room. We'll do that by taking away the requirement to report all assets at market value in their balance sheets."

"But maybe they *need* to clean up their books and build up some authentic capital and reserves before they 'restart their lending', as you put it," Jessica said. "And I think restoring confidence in the financial situation of the banks is essential. Giving them the possibility to declare arbitrary values of their assets is not a step in the right direction!"

"That's just theory again! The reality is that people need to borrow money *now*, so banks need to be able to lend money *now*. And we need to make that possible *now*."

"So that's for *now*, but what will happen *later*, Jeffrey? Will you state to everybody in the room the possible consequence, with our current fractional reserve banking system, of multiplying the bank reserves by twenty?"

"What do you mean?" Jeffery snapped, becoming angry and tired of arguing with Jessica.

"That would make it possible for banks to increase their stock of demand deposits by a factor of twenty. Unless, of course, you increase the minimum reserve requirement significantly, but you just said you don't want to do that. So we could see bank deposits going from around one and half trillion dollars to more than thirty trillion dollars, or if we look at the wider definition of deposits, which is today around eight trillion dollars, they could move to one hundred sixty trillion dollars! Do I need to underscore that this would mean hyperinflation and the possible breakdown of the whole dollar system, thereby the American and the global economy?"

Jeffery went red with anger. "Stop scaring the team with such talk! You should know that banks are much too scared to use the possibility to make such loans!"

"Maybe today, but what about tomorrow? In a year or two, banks will have put this crisis behind them. Then they will, as they have always done, use the fantastic opportunity provided by the fractional reserve system to make profits by lending several times each amount of demand deposits and reserves they have. My concern here isn't about today, but about the long run prospects for our economy."

"In the long run, we'll all be dead! Now, let's come back to the propositions I wanted to share with you," Jeffery yelled impatiently.

Jessica took a deep breath, closed her eyes for a second, and then turned to Jeffery with a cold smile. "Sure, whatever you say, *boss*. Now, what are these propositions of yours?"

"As I already said, we should do a massive injection of additional reserves into the banking system. According to my estimation, around 1 trillion dollars would be appropriate. This should be implemented by a mix of asset purchasing, paid by newly created money, and loans to the banks at an interest close to zero. In addition to this, I will defend the idea that the government should keep its equity positions taken during October in the nine major banks that got a shot in the arm in the form of capital injection. After all, if we use taxpayer money to save them, I don't see why government should step back and let them run their business down again in the future, by taking all kinds of improper risks."

"Jeffery, should I remind you that the Federal Reserve is, at least in theory, a federation of private banks? While it has objectives and prerogatives regarding monetary policy, it's not an arm of the federal government," Jessica remarked with some sarcasm.

Jeffery was concentrating too hard to notice the irony in her voice. "Of course, Jessica. This being said, you know that most of the governors of the Federal Reserve, including myself, have a lot of friends in government. But, of course, that's something which remains quite informal and rather confidential."

"Let me come back to my proposed monetary policy and bank regulation measures. As was already announced more than a week ago, we, the Federal Reserve, will also provide around one-point-three trillion dollars of loans directly to businesses, during the period when it can be expected that banks won't be able to lend sufficiently."

"So instead of being a lender of last resort to banks, we will increase our risk exposure by lending directly to businesses? Sounds to me a bit like a sport referee who decides to jump down in the field to start playing," Jessica remarked.

Hastings this time noticed the sarcasm, but he pretended not to. "During the coming period, and as a short-term measure, we will do both, that is, lend to banks and lend directly to businesses. To conclude, the final major initiative

I propose is to dedicate somewhere between five hundred billion and one trillion dollars to buy mortgage bonds issued or guaranteed by Funny J, Freddy K, or other major mortgage backers."

Jessica stood, holding her arms crossed across her chest. "So, if I summarize, we're talking about around three trillion dollars expended by the Federal Reserve to fight the crisis, or rather more if I include the five hundred billion dollars used last week to buy bad assets from money market mutual funds.

"Let's just stop for a second to realize how much money that is. Three trillion dollars is more than twenty percent of the annual GDP of the United States. It would allow the purchase, at five billion dollars apiece, of around six hundred of the best available aircraft carriers, air craft included, which is about thirty times more than the number of active such ships owned by the U.S. Navy today.

"At five billion dollars apiece, three trillion dollars could also buy six hundred of the world's most advanced nuclear power plants, having a life of over fifty years. Keep in mind that less than half of that number of plants would be enough to supply the total need of electricity for the United States.

"*That* is how much three trillion dollars is! And in order to spend it to bail out banks and other financial institutions, we're just seven people sitting here in a room to work it out over a couple of days. And it will be done, if our board of governors votes yes to our proposal in their next meeting.

"The indifference surrounding our spending of three trillion dollars can be compared with the enormous fuzz about the government bailout plan of seven hundred billion dollars, which was first rejected by Congress and then was finally voted through. In the end, much of the money won't be used because further analysis showed it was wasteful. This fuzz is what's called the democratic process. I think this crisis situation gives a good example of the absence of democratic control over the Federal Reserve!"

Jeffery looked at Jessica with surprise and irritation. "Well, the Federal Reserve has been given the monopoly power to create money in this country, by simply printing or signing checks in the name of the Fed. So why should we not use that power along with our prerogative to perform monetary policy actions such as providing reserve money for banks? I think, contrary to your point, that our independence and freedom of action is a key success factor in this crisis situation, when we must move fast and avoid useless debate or too much political pressure or influence. And I underline that we don't ask the taxpayers to pay a single dollar—we will create these three trillion dollars, out of thin air!"

"Yes, thank you for specifying that point. But I guess everybody understands that creating three trillion dollars will dilute the purchasing power of existing dollars in proportion to the money that is created, or rather even more than proportionally. Since every dollar of new bank reserves can result in up to 20 new dollars of credit, without banks violating their reserve requirements! *That* is what will happen when this money will circulate out in the economy and when banks will provide massive new credits using their new fresh excess reserves.

"So in the end, it's still the taxpayer who will buck up, by a decreased purchasing power. If we consider that these actions by the Fed will double the monetary base of the United States, and that after some time the total quantity of money will increase in the same proportion, then it means a dollar tomorrow will be worth what half a dollar is worth today. This reminds me of a historical fact I learned in college, about how several countries financed World War One. They doubled the quantity of money, which obviously was much easier than travelling around the country and seizing half of people's wealth. So in the end, I understand why the Fed must do this kind of spending away from the spotlight—if it was subject to public attention, there's no way it would be accepted. And the only reason that we don't see speculation against the U.S. dollar is that European and Japanese central banks are doing pretty much the same thing!"

Jeffery looked at Jessica with fury in his eyes. "Enough of this rubbish! Let's stop wasting our time and get back to work. Now, does anybody have any additional suggestions or remarks regarding my proposals?"

The attendees remained silent, and as Jeffery looked around to get their reactions, participants shook their heads slowly to signify that he could move forward.

"Then I'll leave you under Jessica's leadership to iron out the final wrinkles of these propositions. I want fully operational action plans for each of them so that we can move fast once we get the approval of the board of governors. And please abstain from continuing those philosophical discussions about our actions. They *are* needed to save the country from the crisis, and it's our responsibility to safeguard the financial system of the United States. Period!" Jeffery picked up his notepad, put his glasses back on, and walked out of the room.

"Sure, *boss*," Jessica said stoically to his back. "I'll e-mail you the output of our workshop by tomorrow."

She felt a stab of uneasiness about being instrumental in deciding policies she considered to be wrong, not to say completely mad. At the same time, she figured that if she didn't do it, someone else would, and at least this situation let her be where she had wanted to be, when she decided to move from the IMF to the Federal Reserve. That place was in the middle of the action where monetary policy was decided and implemented, and she hoped that some day, she would be able to influence it in a more sensible direction.

✵ ✵ ✵

"Laura, how are you? Can I talk to you?"

"Hi, Jessica! Why, yes, of course, you always can. What's up? Are you still in the office?" Laura asked, as she recognized Jessica's office phone number.

"Yes, I am. You know, we're approaching end of February, and I have now been with the Federal Reserve for four months. And I am beginning to see that all the things decided during those first hectic weeks have now been implemented."

"Well, isn't that a good thing?" Laura remarked.

"Well, I guess a lot of observers consider the economy has been saved by all the measures taken. But, at the same time, we see that the financial crisis has evolved into an economic crisis. Today, we foresee a period of negative growth, and no one knows how long it will last."

"Sure, but that's not *your* fault. I mean, all that has happened was just the result of a long period of crazy credit expansion on behalf of the Fed and the private banks. Including mine."

"Yes, but I still disapprove of the action plan that my bosses decided. I fear that today's radical increase in banking reserves will be the seed to radical debt and inflation bubbles in the future. Basically, what the reserve increase will do is to make it possible for people and businesses to keep piling up debt, before they had time to pay back the previous debts!

"The more I think about it, the more terrible I feel about having been part of those decisions, even if I voted against them. Just look: ten days ago, the government decided on a so-called stimulus plan of additional spending amounting to eight hundred billion dollars. People say that the federal budget deficit will approach one-point-seven trillion dollars this year! And I realize that my main role in the Fed will be to make sure we create the money needed for all the spending. So I'm basically a key player in the largest money counterfeiting scheme the world has ever seen!"

"Hey, I hate to hear you low like this. I think you need to find a way to live with what you're doing, or else get a new job. Now, I was in a similar mood some time ago, and *you* helped me out. You remember what you advised me to do?"

"What?" Jessica said dreamily.

"Call Benson!" Laura answered. "I just talked to him for a few minutes, but after that, I put the past behind me and was able to focus on the present and the future. I suggest you give him a call too. What you feel now is something he must have felt for decades, being an outcast in the economist's profession."

"Yes, that's a great idea! I'll call you back as soon as I've got in touch with Benson," she shouted happily before hanging up.

She felt a sense of urgency, and picked up her telephone and dialed his number. After a few seconds of impatient waiting, she heard a man say, "Montgomery Benson speaking."

"Hello Professor, this is Jessica Frostby. Do you remember me?" she asked tentatively.

"What a question. Of course I do! You know I have stayed in touch with Laura Dalaghan, who runs an Internet bank owned by my friend Cornelius Hazelton. I talked to her not so long ago, and she told me that you had changed jobs from the IMF to the Federal Reserve. I guess you must have been going through hell these last months?"

"Well, it was quite tough in the beginning, as I started during November in the middle of the financial crisis. But now the workload and the overall environment are coming back to normal. But I feel terribly awkward about my work, and especially about my contributions in the last months. I think you remember I was a serious student and a firm believer in what you taught us about economics and monetary affairs?"

"You bet I remember that, and I even heard about the stunt you put up during the boot camp at the IMF. I don't remember who told me, but I'll always remember the story. I'm grateful that you learned my lessons and that you have acted as a spokeswoman of my ideas since you graduated."

"Maybe I have, but I have the impression I'm just talking and whining. At the end of the day, I have spent seven years at the IMF and the Federal Reserve doing things contrary to your teachings and to my personal beliefs."

"Don't worry; you don't have the power to change those institutions all by yourself. I can tell you I feel much better knowing you're in there than if you weren't. This way, we don't just have a bunch of technocrats, brainwashed by mainstream views about economics, able to do what they want. That said, I understand your frustration. It resembles what I have felt myself for the last few years as I've seen that people don't listen to common sense, not even now after the subprime crisis. Actually, what I have felt was not really frustration, but boredom. Luckily, I found a way out of it."

"How?" Jessica said holding her breath.

"You remember when we had our last drink after your graduation? I told you I would try to change the monetary system of the world. Well, I have found a country that might accept to scrap their paper money and central bank to introduce gold money. I'm going to see them in a few weeks."

CHAPTER 10:
A Drop of Sense in a Sea of Confusion

The Reykjavik International Airport was surrounded by a heavy fog. As a taxi moved him slowly towards the city center, Professor Benson felt sincerely relieved that his flight had been able to land without trouble. When he walked across the tarmac ten minutes earlier, the cold wind and the extreme air humidity had crawled inside his clothes and made him freeze. He had swiftly picked out a woolen scarf from his bag, and it was now wrapped around his neck. He would first check in to his hotel, in order to get some sleep after a rather sleepless night flight from San Francisco to London, followed by a short, early-morning connecting flight. After he arrived to the hotel, it only took ten minutes before he was asleep.

Professor Benson was woken up four hours later by the alarm clock. This first evening he would have dinner with his Icelandic friend Ivar Larsen, a professor of economics working at the University of Reykjavik. Benson and Larsen had become friends more than ten years ago at a large international conference of economics. They had found out that they shared a lot of ideas about economics, among a mass of mainstream economists who showed little interest or consideration for their views.

Ivar Larsen was tall, though not much taller than Benson. But his figure was very impressing, with large, towering shoulders; thick, muscular arms; and a dense beard of the same blond color as his thick and curly hair. Because Iceland is a small country of only two hundred fifty thousand inhabitants, a lot of people know each other. Among the people Ivar Larsen had known since his years as a university student was Sigfrid Gudjohnsen, the current president of Iceland. Professor Benson had used his friendship with Ivar Larsen to obtain a meeting with the president in order to advise him on modifications to Iceland's monetary and banking system. The meeting was planned for tomorrow and they had scheduled to have dinner together to catch up with each other and go through the plans for the meeting. Professor Benson was a bit early to the dinner date and was sitting sipping a cold soft drink when Ivar Larsen showed up.

"Hello, Montgomery; how are you doing?" said a man with a dark and firm voice from behind Benson.

Benson turned around. "Quite all right, my friend, thank you! Good to see that you haven't changed. The last couple of times we talked on the phone, you sounded like a frightened child. Although, now that I see you, it's *me* who got scared! I'm relieved when I recall that I'm not living eight hundred years ago, when guys like you sailed over to the United States and wreaked havoc."

"I guess that's a compliment to my unprofessorial looks," Larsen replied. "But you should get those ideas out of your head and accept the fact that the

Vikings were above all tradesmen, even if they looked like they could take and get what they wanted without people's consent. It's the same with me, in spite of what people may believe. I always try to convince people with rational reasoning, which works fine most of the time. And if I sounded scared over the phone lately, then it was for a good reason. My country has been through an incredible mess!"

"That's true, and tomorrow we'll have the chance of our lives to exercise powerful rational persuasion," Benson answered. "I should remind you that what we're about to propose to your president is considered a total anachronism by most contemporary economists."

"Yes, I know. But I also know that a severe crisis opens up people's eyes. And I think Iceland is the country in the world which has suffered the toughest blows from the financial crisis. Hell, our whole country almost went bankrupt, and all the three major banks of the country collapsed before being bailed out by a combined effort of the government and the IMF. As a result of the crisis, our country is in a severe economic recession; the nation's gross domestic product decreased by five percent in real terms in the first months of this year. The full cost of the crisis can't yet be determined, but it already exceeds seventy-five percent of the country's precrisis GDP. Outside of Iceland, half a million depositors found their bank accounts frozen amid a diplomatic argument over deposit insurance!"

"Yes, I know all that, and that's why I think your president should be open to hearing about a monetary system where bank runs would be impossible since deposits would be backed to one hundred percent by real money *and* where no central bank could arbitrarily increase the quantity of money," Benson replied with hope in his voice and a smile on his face. "In addition, the virtuous boom of the financial services sector this would generate would provide a well-needed increase in economic activity and employment over here. In the meantime, at least the major fall of the króna has had one positive consequence: foreigners like me can have a decent dinner at a decent price here, which was not the case before!"

"Yes, that's your angle," Larsen said, "but, on the other hand, I feel like a poor beggar when I go abroad."

"You're just lucky that the central banks of many European countries accepted to make loans to or to bail out the branches of the Icelandic banks. As you know, the Icelandic banks had played a game of very aggressive fractional reserve lending, increasing króna bank deposits by an average of thirty-six percent *per year* in the six years before last year. The peak was at almost one hundred percent the year before the crisis. But those banks were relatively serious compared to your central bank."

"Yes, I know," Larsen answered. "The Central Bank actually expanded the monetary base, consisting of bank reserves and currency in circulation, by a staggering forty-nine percent per year, over the same six years. We saw a compounded increase of eleven times, or eleven hundred percent, of the monetary base, and six times, or six hundred percent, of bank deposits. *That* is how much the króna should and could lose in value, against the euro and the dollar."

"Indeed!" Benson said. "I hope the president doesn't think that what happened to the Icelandic economy was some kind of natural disaster. It was just reality that caught up with a major stunt of inflation launched by your central bank. So I'll have some serious arguments when I advise him to shut that institution down, once and for all."

"Yes, I guess so," Larsen said. "But be careful not to push those arguments too far. There may still be sentiments of national pride over here that you should avoid humiliating too much."

"I won't humiliate anyone; I will just outline a way to avoid that what happened happens again. And I think the president, the prime minister, and the finance minister will listen attentively to what I have to say. After all, if the result is that capital which fled Iceland since nine months back would start coming back, then I guess they would be the three happiest guys on earth."

"You better convince them about that. You know they are currently applying to join the European Union. And if they join the eurozone, I guess our cause may be lost, or it will be more difficult. So not only do you have to convince them, but you also have to convince them fast, so they implement the new money before the EU accepts their application for membership."

"Well, we'll see tomorrow," Benson concluded, before attacking his huge T-bone steak.

✡ ✡ ✡

Professor Benson got up early the next day. During the first part of the morning, he remained in the hotel and prepared for the meeting scheduled at eleven.

Benson and Larsen met in front of the building where the president's office was and presented themselves at the reception desk. Benson had the time to reflect on the simplicity of the place, which didn't look like a presidential office. After a few minutes of waiting, they were brought by a secretary into the president's office.

"Ivar, it's been a long time!" said the president, who was only slightly shorter and less muscular than Larsen. He shook hands with Larsen and patted him on the shoulders. "So this is your American professor acquaintance you brought all the way here to meet me?"

"Yes, may I introduce Professor Montgomery Benson of the Jefferson-Jackson Private University of San Francisco."

"I'm honored to meet you, Professor," the president said.

"It is I who am honored, Mister President." Benson replied.

"If you're a friend of Ivar, you can call me Sigfrid."

Benson hesitated for a brief moment to overcome his surprise, and then said, "Very well. You can call me Montgomery."

The president went on. "Allow me to present to both of you our prime minister and our finance minister."

The two men, who were both smaller and more reserved and formal in their behavior, stepped forward to shake hands with Benson and Larsen. Larsen knew them too, but not on a personal level as with the president.

"So, Montgomery, have I understood Ivar correctly, that you're here to outline a plan for us to create a monetary system based on gold?" the president said.

"Yes," Benson answered, but was interrupted before being able to continue his sentence.

"Why on earth should we do that? Don't you know we're in the process of submitting an application to join the European Union, and thereby establish the euro as our currency?"

"I know. I come all this way to propose an alternative because I'm convinced that it will provide a much better solution to the problems you have encountered within your financial system."

"Please explain."

"Of course. The crisis you have lived through in Iceland had the same cause as the similar crisis in the United States, and which has plagued Europe. That cause is excessive debt and credit supplied by banks, with an often ignored, but nevertheless essential, precondition: rapid money creation by the Central Bank.

"The Central Bank typically also decides the reserve and capital requirements, which control how much risk regular banks can take. This type of crisis is possible, and even inevitable, because of the so-called fractional reserve system of banking. It means that banks can lend out the money that depositors believe is being safeguarded by the bank on their behalf. We end up with a situation where the bank actually keeps only a few percent of deposits as so-called 'reserves.' The rest of the money is no longer there because it has been lent out to somebody else.

"So in such a system, banks are in a permanent potential bankruptcy situation, the only thing preventing them from failure is that depositors don't come to take their money out of the bank. Well, that's what they ended up doing, in several of your banks and their foreign subsidiaries."

"But why is gold necessary when we have modern paper bills?" the prime minister asked. "To secure the system, it would be enough to increase the reserve and capital requirements, so that the risk in the system is under control."

"The basic reason is moral: in human society, wealth is created by private initiative. Government, in its proper role, has the power to regulate, forbid, and destroy, but it cannot create wealth. Gold is wealth, and its production should and must be private. Government-controlled paper money is an illegitimate attempt to move around this and turn government into a creator of wealth.

"In addition, there are several practical problems with the fact that paper bills are the basic money. The first is that anybody who is given the power to create out of thin air what is legally imposed as money will be awfully tempted to use that power as much as possible. Also, a central bank with the power to create money will want to regulate the banking sector. It typically legalizes fractional reserve lending in the false belief that it would create faster growth, creating a safety net to bail out banks that get into trouble. From the point when the idea of one hundred percent reserves has been abandoned, the level of required reserves will tend to be lowered. It is lowered by the combined efforts of bank lobbies and people in government who believe that easy credit is good for their constituents and thereby for their own popularity."

The finance minister said, "I don't see why you incriminate central banks. I'm happy with ours. We just suffered from an evil speculation against our currency, the króna."

Benson was surprised that the finance minister seemed unaware of what he was going to say, and he cleared his throat before cautiously proceeding. "Maybe I can remind you of some basic numbers: in the year before the financial crisis exploded, your central bank increased the monetary base by one hundred eighty-two percent. And commercial banks increased the total money supply by eighty percent. That's in absolute values much more than the increase in the monetary base, due to the fractional-reserve multiplier, which is often between ten and twenty. Basically, in one year, you doubled the quantity of króna in the country. This means that the purchasing power of each króna was roughly divided by two."

"I was not aware of this, Montgomery," the president said. "Please go on, and explain how gold money could prevent this from happening."

"Well, gold has several advantages compared to paper bills as money. It has a usage value. This is why it could become money in the first place, when people started to trade and the need for money appeared. Second, gold production can't be increased arbitrarily, which means that people who hold their savings in gold are quite safe, contrary to holders of government-controlled paper money such as your króna. Or dollars, euros, or pounds, for that matter. And to the extent that some people are able to extract and produce gold, they have earned it and will be able to put it on the market and obtain values in exchange for it."

"OK, I get it," the president said. "But I'm not so sure about forbidding fractional reserve lending. Most advisors, including the finance minister, claim that it contributes to 'economic efficiency' by avoiding that the money 'sleeps' in the bank vaults."

"The first thing to recognize is that fractional reserve banking is actually a fraud, as money in a demand deposit account is supposed to be always available for immediate use by its owner," Benson answered.

The president shrugged. "But what if the depositors agree to take that risk, in order not to pay a fee for the safekeeping of the money? Hell, they may even ask for and get a positive interest?"

"Then it's *they* who are defrauding the people they're paying bills to when writing checks backed by their deposit account. For in reality, the money behind that account doesn't exist anymore. Or more precisely, it's being held and spent by someone else who borrowed it from the bank. What they're doing is similar to rent your flat to someone and getting paid a rent, but still go there to sleep from time to time.

"Regarding the argument about economic efficiency, you should remember that creating money artificially doesn't create any wealth. So the only consequence of the fact that some money 'sleeps' in vaults is that prices in the economy are be at a lower level, due to lower levels of money available to be borrowed and used. But that doesn't change overall economic efficiency in any way whatsoever," Benson concluded.

The president, and the prime minister and the finance minister, looked thoughtfully at Benson for a few moments; then all of them nodded approvingly.

The finance minister, who was the most skeptical, asked, "But how would we be able to integrate into the world's financial system? Our idea behind joining the EU and the euro is mainly to be safe and to not stick out our necks alone with our own currency which doesn't inspire confidence today. In what way would your proposal be better than that?"

"You would be integrated into the world's financial system by the fact that gold is a commodity which is traded at several liquid markets across the world, at steady and rather increasing prices in dollars, euros, pounds, or yen. While I can't guarantee that European politicians would appreciate this initiative of yours, I can assure you that depositors all over the world would come running to enter their money in gold banks. They would because Icelandic banks could offer them payment cards enabling them to convert the money to their own currency, when making purchases or paying bills in their home countries. After having been pointed to as a financial pariah, you would soon become one of the world's most attractive financial centers, with a steady inflow of capital. And a one hundred percent reserve rule would ensure that you would see neither boom-and-bust business cycles nor any spectacular bank failures."

"But banks still would be able to fail?" the finance minister asked.

"Yes, of course, just like any other business. But banks would be evaluated by customers and investors on the size of their own capital versus deposits and loans. And banks would be careful not to take too much risk, since they would know that would be the end for them, when there no longer is a 'lender of last resort.'"

"But could they not be bailed out by the Central Bank?" the finance minister asked.

"In the monetary system I propose, you wouldn't have any central bank. And most notably, you would have no law saying that government-controlled króna are valid money. Just leave the market free, and I bet you anything you want that you'll see gold money appear quickly. But if you're not sure, you can introduce it yourself."

"How?" the president said loudly, totally focused on what Benson would say next.

"By allowing every citizen to cash in their króna bills and coins against gold. And you would provide gold to banks to cover all demand deposit accounts with one hundred percent gold reserves. Most important, at the same time as you do this, you should establish by law that fractional reserve lending is forbidden on demand deposits. In practice, it's quite simple: the banks would have to ask every client who deposits money if he wants to store it in the bank, keeping the ability to spend it, or to lend it to the bank for a time. In the first case, the bank must keep one hundred percent of the deposit in its vaults. In the second case, it can lend all of it during the period the owner accepts to abstain from using it."

The finance minister was looking more and more enthusiastic and asked a more positive question. "From where would we get the gold needed in order to redeem all króna? And how much gold would we need?"

Benson replied slowly, and while glancing across all the people in the room to make sure they were following him: "While your central bank sure has put you in trouble, by expanding the money supply much too fast and by letting banks do the same through fractional reserve banking, your country has one great strength making this new plan possible."

"What?" all three of the Icelandic politicians said with one voice filled of hope and curiosity.

"You have a level of foreign currency reserves which is very high compared to the size of your economy. For example, compared to your country's GDP, your level of reserves is about seventy times higher than the reserves of the United States."

"What does this mean?" the president asked impatiently, trying to have his brain move faster than Benson's explanations.

"It means that your foreign currency reserves of roughly three-point-three billion dollars are enough to buy all the gold needed to redeem one hundred percent of your money supply, which is around five hundred billion króna. With this, you can redeem at a rate of one hundred fifty króna per dollar and at a gold price of one thousand dollars per ounce. This would correspond to around eighty-three tons of gold, which would from then on constitute the only money in Iceland. It is less than one-third of a percent of the world's gold supply, so I don't think the market price would change that much, at least not *before* and *during* your move to gold. What happens *afterward*, we will see."

"Wow, you sure have some interesting ideas!" the president said. "But what more should we do to make gold our money?"

"As I told you, you need to shut down your central bank. The purchase of the gold needed to transform your króna supply to gold would be the last action of your central bank, but its most virtuous action ever. At the same time, you need to scrap the legal tender law stating that paper money is the only accepted currency. You should make it legal to establish contracts in any currency, including gold. And as I said, you should ban fractional reserve lending on demand deposits. Most important, you must scrap any existing laws forbidding private individuals to use gold or other precious metals as money, and you must repeal any undue taxes on owning precious metals."

"Why do you emphasize that last point?" the president said. "I'm not sure we have such laws."

"No country wants to let it be known—it's kind of a dirty secret they all share—but I can tell you that every country in the world has some law aimed to prevent gold from being used as money."

"How can you be so sure about that?"

"Because if there was one country in the world that did not, then we would already have seen private individuals switch to gold for much of their savings. At least instead of leaving money on interest-free accounts where the money loses value every month and year. And you would see savings from much of the rest of the world moving into that country. By the way, that's another beneficial effect you could expect from introducing gold as money."

"Really?" the finance minister said with a smile that was becoming wider and wider and with a curiosity that was growing stronger and stronger. "Please tell us more about how the reputation of our country as a financial market would be improved."

"Well, it's quite simple. On the day when you have banks in Iceland who propose gold deposit accounts associated with international payment cards that people can use in their home country, then Iceland will be the most attractive haven for bank deposits in the whole world. Imagine that the average money supply inflation in the main currencies is around eight percent per year, as it was for the last ten years, and that the gold supply could increase no more than two percent per year. Then your deposits in gold instead of in dollars or euros would earn six percent in purchasing power, every year."

"Wow, I guess as long as we're the only country to have such money we would attract a major share on the world's bank deposits!" the finance minister said. "By the way, how much is there in deposits in the world?"

"Around sixty trillion dollars, or twenty-two thousand times more than the deposits currently existing in Iceland. It would be enough for you to attract one-tenth of a percent of that in order to triple the size on the bank deposits in Iceland, thereby roughly to triple the size and value of your financial sector."

"All these numbers make my head turn around," the president said, smiling. "But in a pleasant manner!"

The finance minister still had questions. "Do you think we would be an attractive destination also for company registration and stock exchanges?"

"Yes, the fact that corporate accounts, and profits, would be labeled in weights of gold, and not in some paper currency, would mean that there would be no artificial profits being taxed away. In a country with monetary inflation, there is."

"I don't understand," the president said with a frown, but the finance minister already looked satisfied by the answer.

Benson looked at the president. "You know, Sigfrid, a company has expenses before they get their sales revenues, often with a time lag of as much as a year. Say you spend ninety dollars, and then a year later, you get a revenue of one hundred dollars. This will generate a corporate profit of ten dollars, being taxed, say, at thirty percent. But actually, in real terms, if the money supply had increased by ten percent, then those sales revenues actually only represented ninety dollars in terms of the value of money of the year before. So that taxed profit was artificial. And the tax took away from the company funds that the company would have needed just to replace worn-down machinery and such.

"Given these artificial profits, the stock of the company may increase in value, creating similarly artificial capital gains for shareholders who sell stock, which also will be taxed. But if the accounting of the company, and the quotation of its shares, were counted in grams of gold, then we wouldn't see these artificial profits leading to more taxes. The company and its owners would instead benefit fully from the increased purchasing power of gold money."

"I see," the president said, now apparently satisfied. "But this just seems too good to be true. All aspects of this project seem favorable: we would remove the risk of ever experiencing a general banking crisis or an economy-wide bust or recession. We would secure the value of the savings of Icelanders and of all other depositors and investors who would place money in our financial market. We would make our country, which has been considered a financial disaster zone, look like the most secure, and one of the most attractive, financial centers of the world! This simply makes me wonder why no other country has gone this way. There must be a catch?"

Benson smiled thoughtfully. "Well, that depends on your viewpoint. The main 'catch,' which explains why no country in the world has gold money today, is what *I* consider as the main moral and practical *advantage* of this kind of system. Namely, that it's impossible for the government to finance public spending by artificially creating money. With gold as money, governments need to obtain all money it spends through taxation, or by obtaining loans that have to be paid back in gold. History has proved that the need to obtain money through taxation sets much tougher limits on public spending. This is because citizens understand how much they pay and when they pay it. That's not the case when government dilutes the value of their money by just printing more of it.

"So, two ideas were behind the destruction of gold as money which took place across the world over an extended period during the nineteenth and early twentieth century. The first was the dishonest desire to dilute the value of people's money and savings. The second was the false idea that increasing the quantity of paper money can somehow stimulate the economy and increase the creation of wealth.

"Large banks were not innocent either, as they came to benefit from the fractional reserve banking system, which essentially is a legal license to produce counterfeit money. Well, you recently lived through a concrete illustration of this, so I guess I need not explain further."

"Thank you, Professor." the president said. "You have indeed convinced me to move forward with this, even though I probably will need a bit of time to realize what we're about to do. It feels like a revolution. Now, assuming we take a step into the unknown, I have an important question: should we push it through parliament, or should we launch a referendum?"

"If I may give you one final advice," Professor Benson said solemnly, "it would be to keep this project extremely secret and then push through a vote and implement it before anybody in the outside world understands what's happening."

"Why? Do you think we should force it onto the people like a blow to their backs? That sounds undemocratic to me."

"Sigfrid, Mister President, if you decide on these changes, it will be the most beautiful gift a government can give to its people. The meaning of introducing gold is that you're giving the freedom back to the people, by rendering them their economic safety and independence! In fact, if you do, you would be the first government in history to do that. On the other hand, what you *should* worry about is what your so-called friends and helpers of the European Union, the IMF, and the United States will think about it. *They* may hate you for it, and might make any conceivable effort to stop you, if they learn what you're about to do. This is why I advise you to keep it secret and to push it through parliament as fast as humanly possible, once you're ready."

"Why would they care about what a small country like Iceland does? Our economy is so small and insignificant in the world economy!" the prime minister said.

"Try to think of the international money market as a competition between different moneys, or currencies, to attract the savings and deposits of the world. To attract investors, a money needs to offer little risk of losing its purchasing power.

"The problem of the world today is that such moneys are becoming rare. Among paper moneys, the German mark used to be quite well managed. Their central bank didn't increase the quantity of money too fast. The same has been true for the Swiss franc. But now the financial world is dominated by the dollar, which suffers from rapid inflation recently compounded by astronomical government budget deficits, and by the euro, which unites a lot of countries, many of which don't have their government deficits and debt under control. Those European countries keep increasing taxes and deficit spending well beyond the rules of the European Union.

"If you introduce gold as money, you'll attract savings from the whole world, and the very existence of your money will put a strong check on how much the EU and the United States can inflate their own paper money. Why is that? The explanation is that if their populations get the slightest hint that their money loses in value compared to gold year after year, then they will rush in large numbers, to transfer their deposits to Iceland."

The president stood up to conclude the meeting. "Thank you very much, Montgomery, and thank you, Ivar, for bringing this extraordinary professor to us. You have given us very good advice. We will mull it over, and if we decide to go ahead, we will push it through parliament during late fall. To simplify bookkeeping issues for businesses and banks, I think we would do the changeover on January first next year. I don't see that we need to cancel our EU application; they should be able to accept us even if we have separate money, like the U.K., for example. And as far as I understand, our money will be much more reliable than the euro itself. So maybe EU would want to adopt our money and not ask us to adopt theirs."

"I wouldn't count on that," Professor Benson said cautiously. "But never mind, once you have gold as a money the only thing Europe can offer you of any value is free trade and free movement of capital and people. And I think you already have such an agreement with the EU. As far as I'm concerned, I will soon travel back to San Francisco, but I can propose to work as your consultant during this crucial phase of preparing your new monetary system."

"Montgomery, name your price. Whatever it is, you're hired!" the president said loudly as he patted Benson on the back with so much force that Benson almost stumbled.

"Fine," Benson said as he left the room with Ivar Larsen. "And I will also introduce you to some bank and investment entrepreneurs who would love to be the first to set up shop here with gold-based retail banking and mutual funds."

He smiled radiantly toward Ivar Larsen, and then he picked up his smart phone and sent two text messages. The first was to Mark Lomack:

> Mark, I remember you said you would transform your social network about freedom and sound money into a business once the world again had one country with gold money. So get going!/Benson.

The second was to Laura Dalaghan:

Laura, I think you always wanted to create a gold-money bank with 100% reserves. It's possible! Tell Hazelton I told you. Tell Pete he can set up a gold-based mutual fund company!/Benson.

CHAPTER 11:
Free Men and Real Money

"Sir! I think you want to hear about this! Please hurry, I have turned on the GNN. Manuel Jones is on the air with breaking news from Iceland."

Joseph Miller, secretary of the U.S. Treasury, grudgingly dropped what he was doing. As he sat down in a leather chair, he heard Jones's excited story.

"I don't know if it's a coincidence, or if the date was selected deliberately by Iceland's leaders. But today is September fifteenth, one year after the sub-prime crisis turned dramatic. A year ago, Iceland was a country hit worse than most others by the crisis; their government almost went bankrupt, and their stock market lost ninety percent of its value. Now they are writing financial history again, but in a quite new way!

"We learned, minutes ago, that the parliament of Iceland this morning passed a top-secret bill to scrap their paper currency, the króna, and to replace it by gold money. The switch is planned for January first, in less than four months. Starting now, the Central Bank of Iceland will buy gold on the market and redeem króna bills and coins against gold. On December thirty-first, Iceland's old currency, and the Central Bank, will cease to exist.

"I've been an economics reporter for two decades, but let me say that this is the most astonishing news I ever had the honor to present. It's the first time since the nineteenth century that a country has taken the step to so-called commodity money. I wish to remind our viewers that the money that emerged on the free market through history always was a valuable commodity. We have seen a lot of things being used as money—tea, cigarettes, flour—and, of course, the most popular choices: gold and silver.

"Commodity money disappeared when governments forbade it and forced people to instead use paper currencies without any real, underlying value, called *fiat money.*

"This decision may prove to be a blessing for Iceland, but we may wonder what it will do to the large paper currencies of the world. They now have a serious challenger in Iceland's gold money. Gold money may attract people who want to secure the value of their bank deposits in these times of ever-increasing government debt and inflation."

Miller picked up the remote control, turned off the television, and snapped at his advisor, "I can't stand that Jones guy! Why doesn't he say what he should have said: that Iceland is a godforsaken island up by the Arctic Circle with three hundred thousand souls? How the hell could that island influence the world economy or endanger our paper currencies?"

Miller's advisor replied cautiously, "Sir, I wouldn't be too sure about that. Judging from your strong reaction, I guess you're not so sure either. We will have to watch closely how this develops."

With unhidden fury, Miller answered, "All I know is that their free-market gold money won't get anywhere. And you can take my word on it!"

✵ ✵ ✵

September days are often misty and gray in Iceland, and this day was no exception. The dull weather contrasted with the mood in the office of Iceland's president, where three people met in an excited atmosphere, and they exchanged warm greetings. On September 16, five months after his first visit to Iceland's president, Montgomery Benson, again accompanied by Ivar Larsen, was again present in the office of Sigfrid Gudjohnsen.

The bill voted on the day before had completely surprised the Icelandic and international mass media. The bill passed had specified that Iceland's central bank would redeem outstanding króna currency and bank deposits against gold until December 31, at a price set at six thousand króna per gram of gold. This was consistent with the current market price of gold, around thirty dollars per gram, and required a total quantity of eighty-three tons of gold. In American newspapers, these prices were displayed using ounces. The gold had been purchased by the Icelandic Central Bank in the highest discretion during the summer on international gold markets. It had supervised the transportation of all the gold to Iceland, for it to be available early September just before the bill was to be voted on. The gold was now stored in secret high security locations. The only known gold storage location was the Central Bank's Reykjavik branch office, where redemption of króna against gold would start the following day, on September 16.

After enthusiastic greetings had been exchanged, President Gudjohnsen showed his two visitors a copy of a leading American financial newspaper. It had given first-page attention to the news from Iceland, along with five pages of details.

"Montgomery, Ivar, I can't believe that we made it. When you guys came here to talk to me about this idea five months ago, it felt totally unbelievable. I mean, in the beginning. Since you had precise answers to all our concerns and questions, it made me realize that the project *was* possible, and highly desirable. I sincerely believe that it will do great good to our country, and who knows, maybe to the whole financial world!"

The president put down the newspaper and waved to a waiter standing in a corner for him to serve them from a champagne bottle, which was waiting in a cooler.

As Larsen and Benson received their glasses, the president raised his and exclaimed with a wide and friendly smile, "Here's to the two of you for having helped us transform Iceland from the sick man of the financial world to a major financial center. That's what I expect! We are now the only country in the world to have scrapped government-controlled paper money in favor of the only thing good enough to be established as money on the free market: gold."

"Thank you very much, and congratulations to you!" Benson said before sipping on his champagne, and looked happily at the others.

"The praise should go to Professor Benson," Larsen said. "He had the vision and the brains to help push this plan through. I just played the role of connecting the two of you."

"Which is also crucial, because had you not, this change would never have happened," Benson said gratefully. "While I'm happy about the bright prospects this opens for the people of Iceland and for the rest of the world, I should admit it's also an enormous personal satisfaction to me. After a lifelong commitment to economics and to defending ideas of sound money and individual freedom, I consider this by far the most important real-life implementation of my ideas."

"Well," the president said, "if no one followed your ideas earlier, I think that shows how stupid people in power can be. I hope that it also shows the opportunities opening up for us, now that we have gone against the flow in the crucial domain of monetary affairs. By the way, I guess you have seen the hostile comments in newspapers from the political leadership of the European Union and from the United States?"

"Yes, I warned you about their reaction, and you now know why they react like that. They correctly identify what Iceland now is doing as a threat to their ability to maintain government-controlled paper currencies. It threatens their ability to continue with rapid inflation of the supply of their paper currencies. If they do, major flows of savings and deposits could be triggered from there to here."

Larsen weighed in: "Yes, and we will probably see, at least initially, more of downplaying the importance of what happens rather than direct criticism. Take that guy from the European Central Bank who was on TV last night. He said that he was surprised that an event in Iceland, which features a population of three hundred thousand people and an economy representing only three-hundredths of a percent of the world's GDP, would get any attention at all in the financial community!"

"I'm fine as long as they talk like that," the president replied. "It will leave us free to continue rebuilding our country and, I hope, contribute to rebuilding the financial world as a whole. Now, let's forget about what people abroad think. What matters is that we get the Icelandic population on board, and I think we're on our way to succeed with that. Take the finance minister, for example. You remember how skeptical he was when you came here the first time? He now explains the virtues of gold money to everybody he meets. By the way, he's supposed to appear on television right now, to answer questions from a group of Icelanders. And he will do it in English, as the show is planned to be broadcasted also outside Iceland's borders. Let's watch it!" the president said and turned on the television.

The finance minister appeared on the screen as he received a first question from a shopkeeper: "What about prices for goods? Today we display them in króna!"

The minister answered with a confident smile: "I suggest you start to display prices in gold right away! If you don't want to change your prices, use a rate of six thousand króna per gram to convert your prices. During some time the gold prices can be displayed along with what the price would have been in króna. Then logically, from January first, you should only show prices in grams of gold."

The shopkeeper asked, "Why can't we keep the name 'króna,' since people are so used to it? And just state that six thousand króna is equal to one gram of gold? That would probably be easier, and in that way, we could keep the existing króna bills in circulation as well."

The minister answered with full concentration on what he considered as a key issue. "There are several important reasons why you must *not* do that, but rather must remove both the name króna and the króna bills as soon as possible. First, people need to understand that gold *is* the money and that króna bills are not. Gold is a universal metal and there is no reason to give a nationalistic name to it, be it dollar, króna, or something else. In order for people to get used to understanding that gold is the actual money, they should get as much opportunity as possible to carry gold coins, and store them where they like, as pocket money or deposit them in a bank for safekeeping.

"May I remind you that the so-called Bretton Woods monetary system had a gold backing of the dollar, with the dollar being set at the rate of thirty-five dollars per ounce of gold, for several decades? The relation of thirty-five dollars per ounce was meant to last forever and to safeguard the value and purchasing power of dollar holdings. Since people were becoming used to only handling dollar bills and token coins, the U.S. government, through the Federal Reserve, soon inflated the supply of dollar bills much faster than their gold holdings grew. This meant they were producing counterfeit money, as long as they maintained the illusion of redeeming an ounce of gold against thirty-five dollars. They were supposed to do that on demand, at least from foreign central banks.

"In nineteen seventy-three, that bluff was called, the U.S. government formally removed the link to gold, and the dollar became a pure fiat money, with no underlying commodity value. All of this wouldn't have been possible if the United States had stayed with gold as money and made transactions quoted in weights of gold. But then again, that was probably not what the people in power in the U.S. government and in the Federal Reserve wanted to do, anyway. They had found the best way for people to get used to *not* using gold as money, and thereby to accept the absurd idea that money could be something else than a valuable commodity. That took a couple of decades, and we can imagine that it made some people in power impatient, when we see how much they have inflated the dollar supply *after* nineteen seventy-three. The fact that the gold price today hovers around one thousand dollars an ounce indicates that the quantity of dollars has increased by around thirty times in just a few decades!"

"OK, I see. So we better make sure we use only gold as money," the shop-keeper said with a thoughtful nod.

Another person in the audience asked, "But we still should be able to use paper bills, and payment cards for that matter, shouldn't we?"

"Yes, if it's clear that the paper bills are considered as the equivalent of the weight of gold written on them and can be redeemed on demand by going to the bank. The bills should be considered as warehouse receipts for the gold held in the bank, if we talk about a demand deposit account.

"For savings deposits, the bill is still a warehouse receipt, only the right to use it is now with the person who borrows the money from the bank, not with the owner of the money. He can't get it back or use it for payments before the agreed duration of savings or loan is over. Regarding payment cards, and other so-called money substitutes such as checkbooks, the principle is similar. Any payment made should be done in grams of gold, and ownership of that weight of gold, then switches to the person who received the payment."

A local bank manager in the audience asked, "Minister, to make all of this work, how should we banks handle the clearing and physical displacing of gold between us? It seems quite complicated, and the risk of theft and robbery raises security issues."

"It's not more complex than the interbank clearing mechanisms that exist today. I'm sure people who are smart enough to successfully start and run a bank should be able to figure that out themselves," the minister said with a friendly but provocative smile. "You're used to monetary affairs being com-pletely regulated by government, by central banks and by other regulatory bodies. So you may need some time to get used to being a business like any other. In any case, there will be different possibilities. If a person deposits his gold in a safekeeping box, he may not be able to write checks against it; doing that should require that his gold is exchangeable against any other similar pieces of gold of the same weight. It means that he accepts not getting the same gold back as he put into the bank when he makes a withdrawal. But he knows he can and will get *as much gold* of the same quality and weight. For exchange-able deposits, clearing will be straightforward, and you should be able to find a smooth and inexpensive procedure. Does this make sense to you?"

"Yes, it does," the bank manager answered with a nod.

An Englishman asked, "I will have gold deposits here, but I want to be able to use my payment card in England. How will that work if I make purchases in pounds?"

The minister answered gently, winking at the bank manager who had spoken just before. "That's something a bank owner should tell you, but they haven't had a lot of time to think about it since our announcement yesterday; therefore I'll suggest to you how it will work. You know that gold is traded on several international marketplaces with good liquidity. Anybody can buy or sell gold at market prices. Banks in Iceland will certainly commit to do that. If you shop in England with an Icelandic debit card, then your bank in Iceland would credit the shop in pounds and debit your gold account according to the pound market price of gold at that time. Banks would need to specify to their customers what marketplace they use as a reference for the gold price, and whether they charge a fee. And if they don't have enough pounds to credit the beneficiary of the payment they would sell some gold against pounds on the market."

The Englishman looked content but had a second question. "What if I have my monthly salary wired to my gold account, how would that work?"

"The same way, in reverse: the bank would buy gold in the open market to be able to credit your account in gold. This shows why a gold deposit account is such a good idea and that it can provide inflation proof deposits for people all around the world. For sure, the gold price has been recently fluctuating, also with downward changes. But it's much less likely the gold price will ever fall again once gold is widely accepted as money.

"On the contrary, the relative value of gold should keep increasing, as the number of people and countries who accept to use it as money increase. In your case as a foreign depositor who has his money in gold in an Icelandic bank, you can still do payments in foreign paper currencies against it, as I just explained. At the same time, you're protected from loss in purchasing power of the paper money your salary is paid in, pound sterling. Just look back: the average annual increase in supply of the pound was twelve percent per year over the last decade. Just try to imagine how much purchasing power you would have saved if you had been able to store away your wage payments on a gold account during this decade."

As the camera showed the baffled but smiling face of the Englishman, the president turned the television set off and turned to Benson. "What do you think? Not bad, right?"

Benson nodded enthusiastically: "Yes, I'm really impressed, I couldn't have answered those questions better myself. Your finance minister has really become a great ambassador of gold money. I see I was right when I asked some friends of mine to come and meet him."

"Who?" the president asked with curiosity.

"Oh, yes, I hadn't told you. One of them is flying in tomorrow along with her main shareholder and investor. Her name is Laura Dalaghan, CEO of the Dalaghan Prudential Internet Bank. DPIB is a successful independent full-Internet bank in the United States. Laura was a student of mine some years ago, one of the best I ever had. Her shareholder's name is Cornelius Hazelton, of Hazelton Growth Capital. He has been waiting all his life for the opportunity to create a gold bank, which is why he won't be wasting his time now. They have asked to meet the finance minister in the coming days, to tell him about their projects."

☆ ☆ ☆

Two days later, Laura Dalaghan and Cornelius Hazelton met with Iceland's finance minister.

After customary introductions, Hazelton was first to speak. "Dear minister, you passed a law this week where the essential novelty is that a bank from now on is considered as any other private enterprise, thereby not requiring any license from the government. So you will appreciate that we came here by simple courtesy in order to share with you our plans for what we hope will be a very successful bank venture."

"Yes, I appreciate that," the finance minister said. "I do wish to hear about your project. I understand your bank in the United States is an Internet-only bank. Is that what you plan to have also here in Iceland?"

Laura glanced at Hazelton, and as he nodded, she spoke. "Yes, to the largest extent possible. We will strive to conserve the cost advantage derived from minimal physical contact with our customers and from letting them do as much of the account management work as possible. We will have two categories of customers, who will require different services. Foreign deposit customers who rarely or never use gold coins for making purchases will do fine with an Internet-only service where they can manage their account, do online payments, and purchase our proposed financial savings products. Along with a debit card usable in their home countries to make payments against their deposit account, these are the key services they will need and get. However, Icelanders who will use gold coins for retail transactions in daily life will naturally need to make withdrawals to obtain coins. For this reason, we will have a few branch offices, with over-the-counter deposit and withdrawal of gold coins. With time, as the number of clients will justify, we will also deploy gold coin automatic teller machines in the major cities of Iceland. Deposits will probably remain managed at branch offices, even though it could be done, under certain conditions, at ATMs also."

"I see. But where will you store the gold, and where will the coins come from?" the finance minister asked.

Hazelton answered. "The gold will be stored in the vaults of our branch offices and of our Reykjavik head office. The coins will be produced by a minting company I created this morning, which starts operation next week. The mint will buy gold, produce coins, and sell them to banks. Their first customer will obviously be DPGB, which is the name we plan for the Dalaghan Prudential *Gold* Bank. I expect other Icelandic banks also to become customers shortly. As a venture capitalist, I usually remain discreet about my own involvement in a business, but this minting company is something I feel strongly about so I decided to make an exception and call it HMM, as in Hazelton Money

Mint. The mint should manufacture all forms of gold needed, from small coins to bullion and bars, which will be convenient for larger transactions and for interbank clearing."

The finance minister looked worried. "But how on earth will we be able to protect people from using false coins, which look like gold but are not?"

Hazelton smiled reassuringly at the minister. "That concern about a free market in coinage is frequently heard, to my surprise. I mean, government itself has turned out to be history's worst and most professional counterfeiter, so if it can be trusted, why shouldn't private enterprise be? Now to answer your question, the responsibility to check the quality of money will be a personal concern for all traders, be they consumers, shopkeepers, or banks.

"The good news is that modern technology has developed something that didn't exist a century ago when gold and silver were used as money: a portable electronic device that can weigh and check the quality of pieces of precious metal. Such devices cost no more than one hundred U.S. dollars, sorry, three grams of gold. And we will obviously distribute such devices along with the money we provide to banks and shopkeepers. That's really no more complicated than the devices existing today to check currency bills. And, of course, such devices combined with the trust a brand like ours should inspire, will make gold transactions safe and simple! And we have people working on some innovations to check paper bills and checks. This has always been an issue in all countries."

The finance minister looked satisfied but still thoughtful. "I see you're all set to produce gold coins and bars, but will that be appropriate for all kinds of trade? I mean the gold price is around or above thirty U.S. dollars a gram, which means that even the smallest possible coins will be very valuable. Will we no longer have small change for small transactions, such as buying a cup of coffee or buying a newspaper in the street?"

"Good point, Minister." Hazelton replied with an excusing smile. "I forgot to tell you about that. The reason I named the minting company Hazelton *Money* Mint, instead of Hazelton Gold Mint, for example, is that it will supply all kinds of money needed for the market to function.

"At this first stage, we will provide silver coins as small change. As silver costs around sixty times less than gold for the same weight, this means one gram of silver is worth half a U.S. dollar. But even silver may not be enough, as the smallest coin we will produce would weigh two grams, and would be worth the equivalent of a U.S. dollar today. The banks will probably also propose token coins of nonprecious metals made to represent gold weights of less than one gram. This will be similar to having paper bills with a gold weight written on them that can serve in transactions, being warehouse receipts against the gold weight written on them.

"Finally, for small retail transactions, we should see the more generalized usage of not only regular debit and credit cards but also so-called cash cards, where the owner 'downloads' an amount of cash in the card which can be withdrawn by a card reader when the transaction is done. All this will take some time to set up, so for the time being, we will at least have gold and silver coins, along with regular debit cards."

The minister nodded. "I understand, but the usage of silver raises an issue about retail prices. I'm advising retailers to display prices in grams of gold. But now you say silver coins may be used for many smaller transactions in shops and cafés. How can we be sure that retailers will accept silver coins? That will create additional work for them, and they must display prices both in gold and silver weight."

"Minister," Hazelton said with an understanding smile, which made what he intended to say sound gentle instead of condescending, "you have been used to considering the monetary system as something controlled and regulated by the government and the Central Bank. And I see you keep the same mind-set, asking how you could force or impel people to do this or that. You should try to keep in mind that from now on Iceland has a free-market-based monetary system, where everybody will act freely according to their own best interest. Retailers will accept silver, simply because they want people to buy their products, and they will make the needed efforts to facilitate payments by their customers.

"As a matter of fact, they can use whatever type of money they want. May I remind you that the fact that the law you voted this week will result in the government replacing the whole króna supply by gold doesn't imply any obligation of whoever to use gold as money? We are just betting on the fact that gold will establish itself as the major money, with silver as a complement for smaller transactions. That's how the free market established money since thousands of years, and there is no reason things would be different now."

"All right, but a lot of people think gold and silver are 'not modern' and that our current age would require some form of computerized, nonmaterial money. How can we best answer this challenge?"

Hazelton gently shook his head. "People who think that make the mistake of mixing up money with money substitutes. It follows from common sense that money on the free market must be something valuable, a value which can be expected to be as stable as possible. Otherwise, people wouldn't accept it as payment.

"The only way governments were able to impose paper money without an underlying commodity value such as gold was by creating two laws: the first to ban people from using precious metals as money and the second to state that only government paper bills were acceptable as money, as so-called legal tender. So the need for money to be a commodity with a real value has not disappeared, as anyone would find out who would try to create a paper-money currency on the free market. No one would accept that as payment, as long as they were not forced by government to do so.

"So what needs to and can be modernized using contemporary technology isn't money itself, but so-called money substitutes. Money substitutes are anything that can facilitate payments by being the equivalent of money: this includes paper bills, which should have a gold weight written on then and be redeemable upon request and without delay. Bank debit and credit cards are also money substitutes, as are checkbooks and any modern computerized payment systems used on Internet or in interbank relations. The key issue about money substitutes is that they must all respect the rule of being backed by one hundred percent reserves in the bank where the person who uses the money substitute to make payments has his demand deposit account. As long as this rule is respected, there will be no undue and fraudulent increase in the money supply. And the money will conserve its full value corresponding to the value of the quantities of gold and silver behind the money substitutes. Does this make sense to you, Minister?"

"Yes, it does, and I see you have clear plans for launching your businesses. But do you have any actual customers yet?" the minister asked with a hint of polite mockery.

Laura answered calmly, "Our Reykjavik branch office is scheduled to open early October, so before that, we won't have any Icelandic deposit customers, or at least they won't be able to deposit any gold before then. We know that the legal tender law says that króna is the only valid money in Iceland and will be valid until December thirty-first. So we don't expect a lot of business before then.

"However, as we had some prior information about the law you were going to pass, we took the opportunity to prepare the Web site of DPGB, which looks much like the site of the mother company, DPIB. The day after the vote of your law, we launched a marketing campaign directed at all our American clients. We are offering them to transfer their deposit account to Iceland and to change its denomination from dollars to grams of gold. The first step of that was just sending an e-mail, and a telephone campaign will follow. Already, after a few days, we have almost a thousand positive answers, corresponding to one percent of DPIB customers. We expect the number to increase above ten thousand in a few weeks."

"I see. But how do you expect to win Icelandic customers? All the major domestic banks will be in competition with you, and all Icelanders already have an account with one of those banks. Those accounts will now be converted into gold accounts, using the gold our central bank has bought."

Laura looked straight at the minister. "We realize it will be tough to win over those customers. We also think that gold deposit banking will soon be a commodity service, although everybody today considers it as something radically new and innovative. We believe the battle for customers will be won in the area of savings products. We are planning a partnership with the Bagnelli Gold Mutual Fund Company, which will propose attractive investment opportunities for long term saving and asset management."

"I think I heard about Mr. Bagnelli. Didn't he go bust in the subprime crisis?" the minister asked.

"Yes, he did," Hazelton said, "which is why he isn't the majority owner of the business this time. Even though the company has his name, this time *I* will be the majority owner. I will, because I believe in this business and I believe in giving a second chance to someone as competent and sharp as Pete Bagnelli. I have become acquainted with him through Laura and through Montgomery Benson, who was their professor of economics. Pete will come here in a couple of weeks to start registration of our first fund. It will include raw material businesses, including gold mining, and other business enterprises that will select to register on Iceland and which we believe will be successful."

"I see you have it all worked out. I just hope the growth of the banking sector won't be too rapid; you know what dire troubles we had during the subprime crisis. The banks in Iceland were managing assets which were much larger than the local economy itself, which made it impossible for our central bank to bail them all out without help from foreign central banks."

"Dear Minister, with all due respect," Hazelton said, "I think you're aware that the problem was not in the size of the assets of the banks. It was in the fact that they were practicing fractional reserve banking with very slim reserves, and the Central Bank was inflating the basic money supply with almost a hundred percent a year!

"Whether you like the idea or not, you should accept that the crisis in Iceland was neither caused by the U.S. subprime crisis nor by the assumed evil of people speculating against the króna. For sure, this happened at the same time as the subprime crisis unfolded, and a lot of people *did* speculate against the króna. But that speculation was really to be expected, when you look at how much your central bank and commercial banks inflated the króna money supply over the last years. What we will see from now on is totally different. Now there will be a steady monetary base consisting of gold, growing in proportion to the inflow of deposits, and the free market will ensure any bank that practices fractional reserve lending will go bust."

"Bank failures..." the minister said with fear in his voice. "I hope we don't have to see any of those. It would be a hard blow for depositors, who from now on won't have any deposit insurance from a central bank.

"You know as well as I," Hazelton said, "that central banks never insured whatsoever. They just pushed a button to dilute the money supply when a bank went bust, diluting the value of everybody else's money. But in the absence of a central bank, I think you'll see that no bank is stupid enough to practice fractional reserve lending, or accepting too risky credits. And I think the feature you put into your new bank law, to make shareholders liable for any losses due to fractional reserve lending, was a nice way to discourage such lending."

"I hope you're right. And I do hope it will be as smooth as you think. I'm just worried that people will not understand all this in the beginning."

"Dear Minister, there is a solution to every problem. Your last remark brings me to think about another venture which I like, even though I haven't put money into it so far. I'm talking about the social network Internet site being launched these days by another of Professor Benson's former students, Mark Lomack. His Web site will be dedicated to the two closely linked topics of individual freedom and commodity money. It should help spread the word and share information and understanding in these areas, across the whole world."

"Really?" the finance minister said with interest. "What's the name of that Web site?"

Hazelton answered, with a mysterious smile, "I believe that is still secret. But you will certainly hear about it very soon."

✡ ✡ ✡

October 1 was a Thursday, and the weather in San Diego, as usual, remained summerlike. A warm breeze came in from the Pacific Ocean onto the long stretches of beach reaching out many miles in both directions. In a small glass building located in a business center area a few miles up the hills behind the city, Mark Lomack had rented a three-room office with a view over the Pacific beach. The beautiful weather reinforced Mark's positive mood this day, as Professor Benson had come to visit him.

Benson had flown from Iceland the day before in order to be present at today's event in San Diego. The event was a press conference announcing the launch of the Web site Mark Lomack had been developing over the last few months. Professor Benson had a major role as an associate.

Ten journalists had gathered for the press conference. They had come because Cornelius Hazelton had used his personal network to promote the event as something "business and political journalists would not want to miss." Hazelton had remained in Iceland and was attending the press conference by Internet connection.

After the press conference, a press release, summing up the question-and-answer session of the conference, would be published. It was intended for some local and national newspapers and, most important, for Internet publishing aiming at reaching millions of people. While an audience of ten people for the press conference might be considered modest, it was enough to fill up the only meeting room of Mark Lomack's office. The sense of expectation that had brought people to come and listen was palpable in the room, and made it feel like a much larger event than it actually was.

At noon, Mark Lomack turned on the microphone. "Thank you very much for coming here today to the press conference for the launch of a Web site called FreeMenRealMoney.org, which I have developed over the last few months. My name is Mark Lomack, owner and developer of this Web site. For those who don't recognize the man sitting next to me, allow me to introduce

Professor Montgomery Benson of the Jefferson-Jackson Private University of San Francisco. I will use the shorthand FMRM to refer to our site and to the human network of people it aims to foster."

Mark paused a few seconds, as a couple of photographers shot pictures of him and Professor Benson. "As most of you may remember from the dawn of the Internet, it was considered that the purpose of Web sites could be described by the 'three Cs': commerce, content, and community. FMRM will provide commerce and content, but will primarily be a community site. Its aim is to create, enlarge, and strengthen the connection among people who care about individual freedom and who recognize that a sound monetary system is an absolute necessity to make individual freedom possible in society.

"We consider that a sound monetary system should be free of government intervention, with money being market determined commodities such as gold. Why is that? Well, you only need to look at what's happening now, and what has happened over the last years, culminating in the subprime crisis. It led to the more general economic crisis that we're currently in the middle of.

"A year ago, in order to counter the subprime crisis, the Federal Reserve spent or lent out around three trillion dollars of newly created money. This year, the U.S. government will run a budget deficit of around eleven percent of the GDP, which means around one-point-seven trillion dollars.

"This new government spending is mainly being financed the usual way, through money creation. The Fed buys a lot of the new bonds with newly created money and then sells some of those bonds on to the market. Living in a society where government can radically and arbitrarily increase the quantity of money is comparable to living in a house with no lock on the door, where at any point in time any stray criminal may drop by to pick some of your wealth. You may be surprised by this analogy, but after my explanation, I trust you will agree it is correct."

Mark drank some soda before continuing. "In the decade preceding the subprime crisis, the quantity of money in the United States increased with an average of around eight percent per year. Regarding the dollar bank deposits, which a lot of people keep in zero interest accounts, this means they lost eight percent of purchasing power every year. This can be compared to a situation where the government takes eight percent of people's cumulated *after-tax* wealth, every year! In the United Kingdom, that same number was *twelve* percent.

"Luckily, in a society where we have rapid economic progress, there are productivity gains which compensate in part for this dilution of the purchasing power, as businesses produce more with the same resources as before. But with annual productivity gains in the U.S. below three percent over this period, we would have expected consumer prices to climb by more than five percent. As a matter of fact, consumer price growth was only half of that: around two point five percent. This was low enough for people not to worry about inflation, even though they should have. The explanation to the slow increase in consumer prices is that most of the newly created money went into financial assets and real estate. *Their* prices grew with an annual seven percent, almost three times more than consumer prices. So we can see the money inflation unjustly creates winners and losers. The winners are people who borrowed money cheaply to buy financial assets or real estate, and who were wise enough to sell them before prices fell in the subprime crisis. The losers are people who kept their money in bank deposits, earning little or no interest. On average, everybody who did not get any of the newly created money, and did not benefit from speculative asset price increases, made a yearly loss in purchasing power equal to the rate of newly created money: eight percent in the United States, and twelve percent in the U.K.

"Also, contrary to common belief, the fact that the dollar is the world's 'reserve currency' doesn't justify this increase in dollar quantity, since the dollar already was the reserve currency ten years ago. Actually, it was even more of a reserve currency before the introduction of the euro, and the geographical area where dollars are used has not changed much recently.

"So, that the government and the Federal Reserve can create money arbitrarily means that peoples' savings aren't safe and can be diluted at will. This is a major attack on their individual freedom, as the absence of protection against theft and financial ruin puts people in a situation of dependency. It puts government in a situation of totalitarian power where public spending can be financed without the need of taxation, thus without the consent of taxpayers, by simply creating money and using it for public spending.

"Luckily, there is one great solution possible to this problem. It is currently being reinstated in the small country of Iceland. This is a free-market monetary system where valuable commodities such as gold and silver are money and where government has no power to create money arbitrarily."

Mark paused and looked around his audience, inviting questions. A representative of a large national weekly magazine on politics and economics asked, "What's the purpose of your Web site? Is it to provoke an overthrow of the current American monetary system and the abolishment of the Federal Reserve? That would amount to a revolution as important as the original American Revolution."

"FMRM is not a network with a political agenda. Our primary purpose is to spread understanding among the public about the intimate relation between sound money and individual freedom. We perceive a complete lack of such information, judging from the debate that has raged in mass media since the subprime crisis, where analysis of possible fundamental changes of the monetary system has been completely absent. Obviously, we hope that an increased awareness among people will lead them to favor ideas and policies that will change society in the right direction. But before an overall change of the monetary system may happen in the United States, people first need to think about their own financial independence and what they could do to safeguard their own savings in a better way."

"Yes, that's a topic everybody will be interested in. But what will FMRM have to say about it?" the journalist asked.

"It's well known that a lot of people lost money on the stock market during the subprime crisis. This pushed many of them to shift their savings to cash holdings or to so-called low-risk monetary placements such as treasury bills or government bonds. This increases the need for these people to understand the risks of such monetary placements denominated in a government paper money, such as the U.S. dollar. This option for saving combines a zero return, for bank deposits, or just a few percents, for government bonds with major risks of dilution of the purchasing power, as explained. There's also the additional risk that banks may fail, putting deposits at risk, or that government may fail on its bonds, turning them into useless pieces of paper."

Another journalist, working for a Washington newspaper reputed for its close connections with the power elite of the country, asked aggressively, "So you will be out there to do propaganda against government bonds, as a filthy speculator who tries to kill the currency or the government of a banana republic? May I remind you we are the United States, the world's foremost economic and military power?"

"We don't have any desire to criticize the U.S. government, or any other specific government. However, we will provide fact based information and advice to people as to the sustainability of government budget deficits and associated debt-backed financing. To this extent, our stance in regard to a specific country will depend completely on how its government and central bank act, not on any specific agenda on our behalf."

Another Washington journalist raised his hand and asked, as soon as Mark nodded in his direction, "So, you're out to change the world by making people think about key issues they never hear about in mainstream media but which are crucial to their financial and personal independence. That sounds like a fine objective. But how are you going to reach out to people, and what financial and intellectual power will you have to do it?"

Mark smiled, as he had waited for the opportunity to answer this question. "As you may know, Internet traffic is increasing quickly, notably for social network sites. Examples are dating, professional careers, or more narrow special interests such as fans of pets, of some TV show, or cooking. FMRM will be a social network for people interested in improving their financial independence and individual freedom. In today's society, government is omnipresent and people are used to consider that their financial future is their government's responsibility, as illustrated by the ongoing trend toward government-controlled social security or retirement pay systems. So you may think we will have a small audience. It will for sure be a challenge for us to cut through the indifference created by this political context, but we're confident about the possibility of reaching out to people thanks to the Internet and by stating our cause clearly and simply. Twenty years ago, when physical mail was the only way to reach out with ideas, I would have considered our project as impossible. Today, I don't."

"But what are your financial means? As far as I understand, FMRM is today a one-man company, founded and run by you alone."

"That's correct, but FMRM will generate several revenue streams. We will soon propose online courses in economics taught by Professor Benson, where people will pay for signing up. The cost per person will be lower than for physical training classes, but on the other hand, we will accept up to a thousand attendees to each Web class. There will be a standard fee, giving the right only to listen, and a premium fee, allowing for up to five questions per session. A second revenue stream that we will have is the subscription to elaborate investment advice analysis reports, which will be sent out through e-mail to subscribers. Here, too, we will have a premium option giving access to an online question-and-answer session with the author."

With a skeptical frown, the second Washington journalist snapped, "And how much will those on-line economics courses cost?"

Mark answered, in a polite matter-of-fact manner. "We are aiming for a simple pricing scheme, where the standard fee is one gram, or thirty-five-thousandths of an ounce of gold per hour of course attended. The premium price will be three grams, or one-tenth of an ounce, of gold. The price of subscription to analysis reports and other services we will sell will be determined later and specifically in each case."

The journalist was baffled. "What do you mean by 'grams of gold'? Will you not accept dollars as money? And how much is a gram of gold?"

"Oh, yes, I forgot to tell you in the introduction" Mark said, "that FMRM is registered in Iceland and that our accounting currency is gold, which is the only currency we will accept to trade in. But since gold is traded in dollars and in other currencies on international markets, we will accept to convert into one of those currencies using the market spot rate, against a little fee, of course.

"Currently one gram of gold, which is slight less than one-third of an ounce, costs around thirty dollars, so a two-hour course would cost around sixty dollars with today's gold price. But if the United States keeps inflating the supply of dollars, the dollar price of our courses will double, if the gold price doubles. That risk will be taken by those who choose to hold their money in dollars, not by us.

"We will keep steady prices in gold, but let those who want to hold paper currencies instead accept the risk that they may in the future pay more for our services. On the other hand, if they accept the teachings of our courses, they will soon have their bank deposits in a gold account. Then they would avoid the issue of exchange rate risk when they deal with us, and they would safeguard the value of their money for all other forms of spending they could want to do in their home country."

The same Washington journalist challenged Mark, as if hoping to find a weak spot in the venture, "So you have some ideas about how to generate revenue, and you have this fancy feature of charging prices set in quantities of gold. But where will you find the people to sign up for it? Those topics you're talking about, such as individual freedom and sound money, don't appear to generate a lot of buzz these days on the Internet. People are content to publish and look at their own video clips or bootlegged copies of music or movies, not to mention adult material. My point is that, although you are proponents of free markets and of a high-standing moral ideal, you may have a content which is way too intellectual for the average member of the general public."

Mark and Benson watched the journalist who had said this, and were both surprised that his response came with a subtle but smug smile. Mark answered more earnestly than the man deserved, in the only way he knew to address a fellow human being: with respect, "Our foremost challenge is to reach out to develop our audience and to make them feel they're part of a network which becomes a key source for both knowledge and more intimate friendshiplike relations. In order to reach this goal, we will combine state-of-the-art Internet marketing techniques and optimization of our visibility on the Internet. Here we will benefit from the huge potential of the so called network effect. It kicks in when people come to think that FMRM is the best and largest network of its type and that it will be more beneficial to them, the more members it has

"From then on, our members and more casual visitors will become our foremost source for spreading the word about FMRM, driving new visitors and members to it. And I should highlight that the concern about one's financial independence and the value of one's money is by no means of interest only to rich or to intellectual people, as you may believe. On the contrary, people with modest savings and income levels should be all the more concerned. They have smaller financial safety margins and typically keep a larger share of their savings in plain bank deposits or in fixed-income products such as government bonds. Once *that* becomes understood by the public, then our potential audience will approximate the whole computer-literate share of the world's population."

"Right, all this is fine, at least in theory, but what real-life topics are you able to talk about that would arouse the interest of the public?"

Mark nodded at Benson to let him respond to this question, which he promptly did. "I can answer that, and I invite you to quote me for the article you may publish after this conference. If I should venture to be a bit less diplomatic than Mark regarding the present situation in the United States, I would compare the government's response to the economic crisis with a drug addiction clinic trying to cure its addict patients by doubling the doses of the drugs those people had abused in the first place.

"The whole idea of government stimulus packages is founded on the false idea that increasing consumption will increase growth and wealth creation in the economy. It furthermore disregards the fact that the recent financial breakdown was caused largely by excessive debt. And that instead of facilitating further debt, households and businesses should *reduce* their debt by paying back a part of their loans. Instead of that, the government and the Fed push harder than ever to make access to credit *easier* than it has ever been, as witnessed by the lowest-ever levels of the federal funds interest rate. It is as close as it can be to zero for almost a year.

"For sure, last year we saw a slight reduction in the quantity of money in the United States, caused by a large number of defaults of debtors and even of a few banks, wiping out the money created when those defaulted loans were initiated. But we're now in a situation where the inflation potential of the banking system is becoming extremely important. This is due to the combination of record-low interest rates with bank reserves that were multiplied by twenty as a consequence of the Fed's and the government's response to the subprime crisis. This inflation potential has not yet materialized, since banks are still pretty scared after the subprime crisis and are only slowly moving to expand credit again. But the coming years could involve a monetary inflation never seen before in the modern world, if we exclude Germany in the nineteen twenties."

Benson looked up at the audience of journalists. They remained silent and waited to hear Benson continue.

"An additional reason to expect an accelerating increase in the supply of dollars is that the government budget deficit, and thereby the cumulated government debt of the United States, is reaching record levels. The only way to keep financing such public deficits, and to make the payback burden a bit lighter, is to keep inflating the money supply.

"Since the stimulus strategy is fundamentally flawed, it will not reach its stated objectives, which is to create growth and employment. It will instead create a combination of lower output, since consumption spending will increase at the expense of productive spending and of lower employment; since productive spending will decrease, so will employment.

"The only thing that will keep increasing is the quantity of money, yielding higher prices on consumer goods. But as long as the government in power is convinced that the idea of economic stimulus by the government is sound, they will keep trying even harder. That's what I referred to as 'curing the addict by doubling the doses' of debt-financed public spending. As long as that policy doesn't change, the race may go on all the way to hyperinflation of the dollar and a default on the government debt of the United States, which our government may become unable to refinance."

The journalist interrupted Benson. "Well, that's *your* point of view of a more or less distant future. But I asked you what real-life topics you could address which are of concern to the common man as of today?"

Benson remained calm and, in contrast to the journalist, waited for his turn to speak. "The accelerating dilution of the value of the U.S. dollar is already happening. Its effect is only being concealed by a similar process of inflation in the other main currencies such as the euro, the pound, or the yen, making exchange rates remain quite stable. We do hope the current policy of the United States will be rapidly reversed. A radical cut in public spending and deficits could slow or stop the dilution of the value of the dollar. But if that doesn't happen, we will advise all holders of dollar-denominated bank deposits to put their money in a safer place."

The journalist once again interrupted Benson, asking with a smart grin, "And what might that safer place be? From what I hear, you wouldn't recommend anyone to purchase government bonds. And we saw last year how unsafe the stock market can be, when it lost more than forty percent in value over only a few weeks. So what's your miracle outlet for safeguarding people's money?"

Benson hesitated for an instant. He was surprised that this sophisticated journalist had not made what he believed to be an obvious connection with something Mark had mentioned. After a short pause, Benson said, "As you may have read in the financial press recently and as Mark mentioned, Iceland is restoring a commodity monetary system. They are in the process of redeeming the whole outstanding stock of their former paper currency, the króna, against gold which they have purchased using their foreign currency reserves. Their central bank will be closed down once this operation is completed. Icelandic banks already propose gold deposit accounts to foreigners, who will be able to use them as transactional accounts. They can have their monthly pay sent there and make their payments against that account. This will indeed be the first inflation-proof monetary savings option in existence since gold money was abandoned at the start of the twentieth century.

"FMRM is preparing a large information campaign on the topic, which is pending the publication next week by the federal government of its final budget for next year. If that budget remains similar to this year's, with a deficit of around or above ten percent of GDP, then we will actively advise all American depositors to put their money away in this new safe haven."

"Do you think people will follow such a fantastic and unpatriotic suggestion?" The journalist frowned with a disdain he no longer tried to hide.

"We will see who does, and who doesn't," Benson said calmly." But I think those who don't, will regret it in the future, whether they are what you would call patriots or not."

This conversation threw everybody in the room, at least the journalists, into a tense mood. As time had run out, Mark wrapped up the conference. "As the professor pointed out, that campaign is pending the final information on next year's budget deficit, which will soon be announced. So, look closely at that, as I guess you would have done anyway. Expect to hear more soon about

FMRM. Our Web site is up as of this morning, and of course, we strongly encourage you to take a look at it."

Mark turned the Webcam equipment off and stood up to signal the end of the conference. As the journalists rose, Mark moved to the exit door and handed a high-quality leaflet to each of them. It was titled "FMRM—the social network no one in the world can afford to ignore!"

CHAPTER 12:
Statesmen's Con Games

The one-year anniversary of the subprime crisis had been on everybody's mind inside the Federal Reserve a few weeks before. But Jessica Frostby had nevertheless been able to settle into a more normal pace of work than during that exceptional period one year earlier.

After the first few months when Jessica had been part of the anticrisis response task-force, she now had two main assignments inside the Fed, as a direct report to one of the Federal Reserve Governors, Jeffery Hastings. First, because she had experience from the IMF and knew all the people in the G20 central bank coordination work group, she had been assigned to remain in that work group. Her second main assignment was domestic: to be in direct contact with the Department of the Treasury, in order to arrange for financing of public spending, especially to cover government budget deficits. Hastings recognized that Jessica was a very competent professional, but he also observed her strong intellectual independence and her hot temper. So he had asked her to be more diplomatic and to refrain from what he had called provocative or aggressive statements.

Although her husband Steve worked for the Treasury, he was not Jessica's contact person. The contact was James Mortimer, a graduate from the Yale University. James was an intelligent career politician who had climbed fast inside the Treasury and held one of its top jobs at the age of thirty-five, in charge of the public debt. Although he wasn't as good-looking, he shared many of the qualities with which Steve had succeeded within the same political environment. This included a polite smoothness when talking to people whom he did not know and a capacity to say what people would want him to say at a given moment. His way of communicating was the opposite of Jessica's direct, matter-of-fact way of speaking and thinking. She did not like James; she considered him annoying and did not appreciate his way of giving half answers or of avoiding a question by answering with a counter-question.

Due to her tense relation with James, the meeting she had scheduled with him in the late morning made her feel strained, almost approaching revulsion. He came to meet her in her office to explain to her the need for new financing to cover the budget deficit of the U.S. government for the coming year. That need was based on the federal budget, which was being formally confirmed in late October, after having been outlined since about six months and reviewed by Congress.

As the time of the meeting approached, Jessica's secretary opened the door to her office. This interrupted an economic analysis task which Jessica by far preferred to the meeting she was about to start, and she looked at her secretary with a pale smile.

"Jessica, Mr. Mortimer of the Treasury is here to see you."

"All right. Show him into the conference room, I'll be there in one minute."

"Will do," her secretary answered before turning around to bring the visitor in. Jessica picked up a pile of documents, containing her personal file on next year's federal budget. She walked reluctantly and slowly to the conference room where James Mortimer was waiting for her.

"Hello, Jessica, how are you?" James said with a wide and shining white smile. As always, he wore a flawless, tailored three-piece suit, which this day was dark gray and complemented with a red tie.

"Fine, thanks, and you?" Jessica said politely but without enthusiasm.

"Very well, thank you. Let's dive into our business. As you know, we need to confirm the bond issue required to finance the federal budget deficit of next year, which will amount to around one-point-two trillion dollars. I know you think that's a lot, but keep in mind it's only eight percent of GDP, down from eleven percent for the current year."

"Well, that's one way to look at it. Another way is to compare the deficit, not to GDP, but to the actual revenue budget of the federal government, which is around two-point-three trillion dollars, from what I know. This means the federal government, at an expense level of three and a half trillion dollars, spends more than one and a half time the money it's able to raise through taxation. Do you think this is either reasonable or sustainable?" Jessica cried.

"Jessica, this is the federal budget, which has been defined by the president and validated by Congress. It's not up to me or to you to question it. Our job is to make sure we raise the money needed to finance the part of that budget which isn't covered by taxation."

"Yes, I know, but it still gives me the creeps. The amounts are huge, and I doubt we'll ever be able to pay this debt back."

"Jessica, you know as well as I do that this spending is crucial to stimulate the economy in order to get out of the financial crisis and in order to finance our new, nobler social security system where government will make sure everybody is covered for the contingencies of life."

"As far as I know, those stimulus packages are just wasting a lot of money which is being drained away from regular business activity that tends to go bust or to move off-shore to get away from ever-increasing taxes. And I frankly don't see they point in enacting a social security system where everybody will be under the illusion that someone else will be paying their bills for health care, unemployment benefits, or retirement savings. If we can't finance it with current government revenue, then it means we're just piling up a mountain of debt, which will end up exploding in our faces one day. Basically, in order to get out of the mess that the subprime crisis created, we're moving toward a situation where the federal government of the United States itself might end up as one of those subprime credit customers: in bankruptcy, unable to pay back its debt, and forced to give away its last assets in order to do some justice to creditors!"

James was intimidated by Jessica's rising temper. "Stop that talk! I hope you realize how ludicrous it is to compare the world's most powerful government to a low-income family who got its private economy messed up. After all, we represent the richest country in the world."

"I can stop it if you want, but you won't stop me from thinking it all the more. Let's get down to our dirty business. How can the Federal Reserve help you to finance this round of, what did you say, one-point-two trillion dollars of pocket money for the U.S. government, which, as a reminder, means borrowing four thousand dollars on behalf of each American citizen, just to cover deficits of the coming year? Or rather five thousand dollars per citizen, if we include the additional money needed to pay interest on these bonds. Assuming you will be able to sell them at the rate of return you expect, below four percent per year?"

"Well, as a matter of fact, we have opened discussions with the usual main subscribers of government bonds, such as the central banks of China and Japan and those of a few oil-producing countries. The thing is that they are becoming a bit hesitant to buy our bonds, and the share each of them asks for is generally smaller than last year. When I add up what they want to buy and what we're able to sell to our domestic social security trust funds, we still lack three hundred billion dollars. So I would kindly ask you to ensure that the Federal Reserve buys the remainder of the issue. After that, you would of course be free to sell those bonds on the open market."

"James, I wouldn't personally approve that, even under torture. But you probably know that my superiors will, as they have often done in the past when called upon."

"Yes, I know," James said pleasantly. "So please take this paper, which confirms that the Federal Reserve will commit to buying the three hundred billion of ten-year treasury bonds remaining for us to sell in order to complete this issue. Have Jeffery Hastings, or, if needed, the chairman of the Fed, sign it before tomorrow evening."

"Sure, give it to me," Jessica said aggressively and browsed the document. "I don't think I can ever get used to signing checks for amounts as large as the annual sales of the world's largest private business enterprise, or as large as the annual GDP of countries such as South Africa or Finland. I mean, this is money which doesn't exist but is being created by our signing that paper!

"What makes me most sick is that the Fed's approval of this bond purchase will imply that the purchasing power of dollars is diluted by that much. Just as if we would have collected the three hundred billion dollars through taxes, taking it out of people's pockets. But people would never accept that, and this is why we're using this undemocratic procedure."

James looked thoughtfully out through the window of Jessica's office, where the White House could be seen in the distance. As he prepared to leave the room, he said, "Yes, why do you think government took control over the monetary unit and created a central bank in the first place, if not in order to be able to do what you and I are currently doing? This is what I like the most about our job: that we have this extraordinary power to decide about the money of the country, how much we should have of it, and how much government should add to it for its own usage."

"James, I guess you know me enough to believe me when I say that that's what I *hate* the most about this job. Now get out of here and go prepare your next press conference. I guess you will triumphantly announce that the government bond issue to cover next year's public deficit has been subscribed up to one hundred percent of the required amount!"

Jessica then stopped, as a more pleasant thought came to her mind. She continued, this time with a cruel and confident smile. "Just enjoy this triumph of yours, because I'm not so sure it will last. You heard that Iceland is moving to introduce gold money? If you ask me, I believe, and I hope, that their move will put an end to the practice of financing public deficits with newly created money. Because when people realize that their bank deposits would be much safer in gold in Iceland than in U.S. dollars, our currency might suffer from the same kind of speculation the Icelandic króna did last year. And you would have to stop doing what you do every year, unless you accept that the dollar would lose its status as the world's reserve currency. I guess you will fight this new gold money harder than you have fought against any savage terrorists. Because you're right if you think it's the most serious danger your big-government scheme has ever encountered! This time, you won't be the good guys. The legalized counterfeiting you push the Fed into doing is morally indefensible, and it's destroying the economy, as the crisis has shown."

She let her words sink in. James was too surprised to answer her. "Now, we're finished. Please get out of here!" she snapped while standing up to leave the room, then showing James to the nearest elevator.

On her way back to her office, she folded away the bond purchase sheet into the binder of documents to be signed by Jeffery Hastings before slamming it closed. She was angry about how the political leadership used the Fed as a tool to finance deficits and dilute the value of people's money. But she was excited by the hope that these methods would soon become impossible to practice.

✲ ✲ ✲

A few days after his meeting with Jessica Frostby, James Mortimer joined Steve Harper to see the secretary of the treasury in order to confirm the tax policy and the public debt financing for the coming year.

Miller received them, but in a tense mood. His first question was, "Are we all right for debt financing?"

"Yes, thanks to the Fed buying a bit more than three hundred billion dollars' worth of bonds with new money."

"Excellent," Miller answered. "So we won't have any worries regarding debt financing next year. That's very good news. Now, we shouldn't exclude that it becomes tougher the year after, the way our public spending is increasing. But, in that case then, I have an idea up my sleeve.

"What's that?" Mortimer asked with curiosity.

"Tax increases," Miller said with calm satisfaction.

"What?" Harper said. "I hope you aren't talking about increasing the income tax for all. If we would like to erase the deficit of this year, for example, we would have had to more than *double* the income tax!"

Miller shook his head as a teacher facing a couple of naïve but well-meaning students would. "Of course not. Don't you think I know the rules of contemporary democracy? I wouldn't be here if I didn't. Of course I know that we must get the most money possible while upsetting the smallest number of people possible."

"So who would foot the bill?" Harper said with a cautious smile, as he began to understand.

"The rich, stupid!" Miller said, and all three of them laughed.

After a moment, Mortimer spoke with an anxious tone. "Sir, I want to report to you an incident that happened when I secured the last three hundred billion of deficit financing. You know the Frostby girl of the Fed, Steve's wife, she told me Iceland's move to gold might put an end to our ability of engaging in what she calls 'legal counterfeiting'!"

Steve shrugged humbly and guiltily in Miller's direction. "Yes, my wife can be quite provocative. But don't worry about that."

"I don't worry, but her talk sure is rubbish." Miller said sharply. "How do you think the actions of a country which has less than half the population of the smallest American state could change anything whatsoever on a global scale?" He paused and then went on, more thoughtfully. "Then again, we can't know for sure, so we'd better take things into our hands. I believe there's a quite easy way to kill this gold-money system before it becomes anything much."

"How?" Mortimer and Harper exclaimed at the same time.

Miller paused to raise their attention even further. "Those free-market gold-money people have the nerve to compare our money creation to counterfeiting. They forget that the risk for counterfeiting is never as big as on a free, uncontrolled market for money. I say we should stage a *real* counterfeiting scandal—this time regarding the gold money those people are so proud of calling inflation proof."

Both of Miller's aides looked awed, and after a moment, Harper reacted. "But how should we do that? We don't want to get our hands dirty by doing things that are illegal."

"Of course not," Miller said reproachfully. "Who said we would? But we can suggest this opportunity to some private counterfeiters. There's a bunch of them on record at the Fed. Most have had some success for a time, before being caught by the long arm of the law. Mortimer, you're close to the people at the Fed, get their list, and find some mavericks who might want to go to Iceland for some business.

"Of course, avoid the Frostby girl. Contact Chairman Clearwater directly on my behalf. Ask the Fed to ensure the counterfeiters we select get compensated. They must understand that this time around, they're doing us an invaluable service by showing to the world that the only safe monetary system is one controlled by a central bank and with paper money that the government has a monopoly on creating. Of course, I don't want to see any e-mails or paperwork about this. It stays between the three of us!"

Both of them nodded approvingly, and then Harper said with a sting of jealousy: "Sir, is there any way *I* could be of help in this matter?"

Miller looked him in the eyes for a long moment and then chuckled. "Yes, maybe we can open a second line of attack here. I believe you're a friend of many of the big shots on Wall Street, Harper? Why don't you talk to the people at the Zach Morgano Bank? Ask them to set up a subsidiary in Iceland. I would be most pleased to see them become the market leader in banking over there. Sure, the Icelanders say they want to ban fractional reserve lending. But Zach Morgano is a champion of that, as they have shown here at home. I'm sure that they'll get away with it if they leverage their strong brand and credibility. From the additional money created by their fractional reserve lending, we will get a double effect in terms of monetary inflation in Iceland. This will prove to those who may have doubted it that gold money is even more risky than any of the paper monies it pretends to challenge!"

CHAPTER 13:
Brave New World

The first business day in Iceland's history after the end of the króna paper money and the closing of the central bank was January 2, a Saturday. Most banks in Reykjavik had planned exceptional opening hours for what was expected to be one of their busiest days ever. Still, few of them had anticipated the magnitude of the event, and the workload that would be required of their personnel to open a large number of new accounts in a very short time. Laura Dalaghan was one of the few bank owners who had planned in detail for the opening day through a project she had called "Inverse Bank Run." In the hope of winning customers from competitors unable to manage the business volume on opening day, she had hired two hundred temporary workers who had been trained in opening deposit accounts. Laura had obtained the right, after a negotiation with the mayor of Reykjavik, to rent most of the square in front of her bank office for the whole week following the switch to gold money.

On January 2, Laura had arrived at her office at 5:00 a.m., along with the team of ten full-time employees and the two hundred temp workers. Some of her managers from the Colorado office had also come with her to Iceland, including Paul and Sandra.

As the clock approached eight, crowds were amassing across all of central Reykjavik in exceptional numbers, and specifically in front of bank offices, where they lined up to wait for the opening hour. As the native Icelandic banks had a bad reputation from the subprime crisis, the Dalaghan Prudential Gold Bank enjoyed a strong position in the minds of potential customers. This was all the more true since virtually all large American and European banks were absent. These banks had followed the recommendation of spokesmen of governments and central banks advising them "not to participate in what should be seen as a ridiculous effort to turn back the clock of monetary evolution more than a century, to the primitive conditions of the era before the invention of paper money and central banks."

At eight, Laura stepped outside of the office, and felt a cold wind at her face. She realized that the crowd was even larger than she had expected. There were not only a lot of local people, but also a large number of Englishmen and other Europeans, who wanted to be present on this historical day. As people were becoming restless in the lines that grew longer by the minute, Laura turned on the sound equipment she had rented. She stepped up on the back of a large billboard with the name of her bank on it and addressed the crowd.

"Hello, everybody! I'm Laura Dalaghan. Thank you for being here with us today to make history." She stopped for an instant to hear the loud cheers from the crowd. "You know we are making history, because all the money you deposit in our bank will be stored as solid gold and with one hundred percent reserves! This means that you can claim your gold or use it for payment whenever you want, without fearing that we have lent it out to someone else. Unless, of course, if you accept to put it on a savings account. If you do, we'll lend it out to someone else, against interest. The best thing for you is that the purchasing power of your money is safe with us. As you can imagine, we haven't yet found the secrets of alchemy. The total quantity of gold in society will only increase slowly, as mining companies dig up more of it. Compare this to paper money, where government can and do increase the money quantity radically fast, which reduced the purchasing power of money with the same speed."

She laughed and so did the crowd. She went on with a more serious tone. "Still, what happens in the paper-money systems in the rest of the world amounts to just that: creating money out of thin air by just printing it. That's fine if you're the government and control the printing presses. But it's much less pleasant if you're a saver who put your hard earned money in a bank, hoping for it not to lose its value. Now, for you, me and the people here in Iceland, paper money is history. I certainly expect that all those of you who have come here with euro or dollar paper bills, wish to exchange them against gold."

Some people were becoming agitated back in the crowd, as the lines grew ever longer. A man walked up to Laura and asked loudly, "Are you sure you have enough gold for all of us? I don't want to fly back to Europe with my pack of euro bills! And this crowd gives me the creeps. Are you going to be able to take care of all of us?"

Laura smiled at the man and then turned around to wave in the direction of the two hundred booths set up on the square. "Look at all these cashier desks, and you'll see that the answer is yes. Of course, you'll have to wait for a while, but we have a numbering system, and you'll each get a ticket saying at what time we'll receive you and at what desk you will open your gold account and deposit your money.

"We are geared to open fifteen thousand accounts, just today. We will keep these desks on the square as long as we need to, probably for more than a week. And to answer your question about our gold quantities, don't you worry about that. We are able to accept any amount of paper money, and we will convert it to gold for you at current market rates. So there's really no need to worry.

"I think many of you are actually confused by the fact of seeing so many people in front of a bank. When that has happened during history, it used to be during a bank run, where people feared ending up with nothing as their money had been lent out several times and came to get their deposits out. As I said, that will never happen here. This is not a bank run. Or, rather, it is an inverse one! Maybe we need a new word for it in our dictionary. I propose to call it a *bank rush*, as you come in thousands to entrust us with your deposits.

"Anyway, I thank you from the bottom of my heart for your trust, and now we have talked enough. Let's open up the bank! Sandra, Paul, all cashiers, on your marks!"

Laura stepped down from the billboard and walked back into the office building. She received a few friendly pats, and some tourists wished to have pictures taken with her. But the vast majority of the people on the square rushed directly to the cashier desks to get their waiting tickets.

Once her bank had opened, Laura went for a walk across the Reykjavik city center. She saw the other banks that were also opening their business for the first time in what a journalist had called a "brave new world." Most of the banks were Icelandic, and there were a few smaller banks from the United Kingdom. It appeared as if the large international banks had not judged necessary to be present on this market, as if their fidelity to government-controlled central banks and paper money was more important than actual business opportunities.

The one notable exception was the Zach Morgano Bank, which had opened a Reykjavik office recently and had been doing aggressive marketing before the launch of gold money. Laura stopped in front of its office, which this morning was even more crowded than those of other banks. She had to step on her toes to see above the crowd waiting in line in order to read the large billboard placed in the main window. It said, "We are so big we will never fail. On a free market for money, choose a bank that will prevail!"

✻ ✻ ✻

On January 2, Kevin Larrison had travelled for the first time in his life to Iceland. He had flown over it during hundreds of intercontinental flights, without ever caring to make a stop there or even to inquire about what was going on down there. But now he had done so and even more: Iceland was the main topic in the New Year's edition of his world-famous television show *Events that Change the World*.

The show was being shot in the now-abandoned building of the former Central Bank of Iceland, where Larrison was to interview the president of Iceland. The two men had been installed on chairs in the middle of a large marble hall, now completely empty, and their voices echoed each time they spoke. The stage was all set, and the clock approached 6:00 p.m., meaning it was around lunchtime in the United States, and the live broadcast started.

"Hello, everybody, and welcome to the New Year's first edition of *Events that Change the World*. I am Kevin Larrison, live from Reykjavik, Iceland. I'm here with the president of this small country, Mister Sigfrid Gudjohnsen. Mister President, something radical is happening in your country since last night, which I wish our viewers to learn about. You actually replaced your paper money by gold. First, tell me, what about the Central Bank of Iceland?"

The president answered: "Well, our Central Bank was useful over the last four months, in order to redeem króna paper currency against gold. But now that the redemption deadline is passed, króna bills can no longer be used as money. So we don't need the Central Bank any more, as its main task was the creation of paper money. Therefore, since midnight, it has ceased to exist."

"As you say, króna bills can no longer be used, and you have scrapped your legal tender law. Doesn't that mean that you're now the only country in the world not to have an official monetary unit?"

The president shrugged and shook his head with emphasis. "I prefer to think that we are the only country in the world to have a *real* monetary unit. We have indeed repealed the laws that forced people to accept useless paper bills as money and that forbade them from using valuable commodities such as gold as money. Iceland is, from today on, the only country in the world where people are free to use any money they want. And we already see that gold and silver are going to strongly dominate, which is not a surprise. Here, when the deadline for companies to select a legal accounting currency ran out, one hundred percent of them had selected gold instead of some foreign paper currency."

"That's amazing!" Larrison said. "Why do you think they took such a decision?"

"There are at least two obvious benefits: their cash balances will be inflation proof, and they will avoid the artificially high taxes which businesses suffer from when their accounting currency undergoes inflation. Also, it's a practical choice, as taxes also will be calculated and levied in gold from now on."

Larrison nodded. "What about banks? How will they now be regulated? In most other countries, banks are being regulated by a central bank, but as you just said, and as we can see from the emptiness of the building we're in, you don't even have one any longer."

"True," the president said. "And we now apply the simple but unusual principle of considering banks as any other business. The only specific rule we wish to enforce, and which the free market seems to apply itself in any case, is to require one hundred percent reserves on demand deposit accounts. This will put an end to the fraudulent practice of lending out the same money that someone thinks is kept safe in the bank and that he uses for doing daily payments. Of course, money on savings accounts can be lent, but then that money can't be used by the owner for making payments, as long as it's lent out."

"What about your government debt?" Larrison asked. "This stunt regarding your currency didn't wipe out the debt you owe to foreigners."

"We converted all our króna debt to U.S. dollars, which was a good thing for bond owners as the króna strengthened a lot after we announced the switch to gold. As you may understand, we didn't go all the way to convert those bonds to gold, as we believe the U.S. dollar and other main currencies will continue to be inflated by their respective central banks. And we didn't wish to let them use such inflation to get more value from Icelandic bonds they own."

"Wow, all this is impressive! But now tell me about what's happening in your country as a consequence of these changes."

"I will, with pleasure," the president said. "Our country used to be kind of a sleepy place. But since we announced this change in our monetary system, the country has literally been flooded with new business projects and capital flowing in by the day. Banks are setting up shop here since it's the only place where they can offer gold deposit banking to both Icelandic customers and to foreigners. This, in turn, is drawing companies and money from depositors who wish to benefit from such bank accounts. This whole thing has created a strong sense of pride in the people of Iceland. It is really perceived as a great success, after a financial crisis that hit the self-confidence and self-esteem of people pretty hard."

Larrison tilted his head and asked cunningly, "So, at the surface of things, it appears that you have created a perfect monetary system. But are you so sure it will work out in practice? Many people believe that a free market in money is impossible; they believe the absence of a central bank to regulate banking and control money creation would lead to widespread issues with counterfeiting and fraud. How do you propose to deal with this?"

The president for the first time during the interview stopped smiling, and he looked implacable as he answered. "We will deal with it by making sure that counterfeiters understand what high risks they would take, be they plain criminals or banks tempted to do fractional reserve lending. Judge for yourself: anybody caught with counterfeiting money will be forced to reimburse victims by providing in gold the same amount as the amount of false gold or paper bills put on the market. If they're unable to fulfill that obligation, the persons responsible will have to work in community service without pay. Their work will be valued at one gram of gold per hour, and they have to stay in the job until their debt to society has been paid back. They will not have to work in prison, but their passports will be withdrawn.

"As far as banks are concerned, they should be advised that there is no longer a central bank that can bail them out if they go bust. On top of that, bank shareholders should keep in mind that fractional reserve lending is now illegal in Iceland and that a bankruptcy filing of a bank wouldn't be accepted before the shareholders have compensated bank customers for any losses due to the fact that demand deposits had been lent out.

"This may seem harsh at first sight, but it stands to common sense. Money in demand deposits doesn't belong to the bank, and the bank has no right to lend it as it has with savings deposits earning interest. If a bank decides to dispose of demand deposits in spite of that it will have to bear the consequences. Am I making myself clear?" the president asked forcefully, looking at Larrison and then at the camera with hard determination.

Satisfied, Pete Bagnelli turned off his television set. Pete had flown in the day before to settle down in a rental apartment in Reykjavik, and to move forward with the launch of the Bagnelli Gold Mutual Fund Company. He was about to create and register it in Iceland, with the help of his main investor Cornelius Hazelton of Hazelton Growth Capital.

Pete could have stayed in the United States and managed a business registered in Iceland from there, as his friend Mark Lomack had done with the Free Men, Real Money Internet venture. But he had decided to live for some time in Reykjavik to be able to meet personally with members of the local business community. This community was rapidly expanding to include also a number of international corporations coming to set up their head offices in Iceland.

These corporations would also be target investment objects for Pete's mutual fund. So Pete and Mark were now again separated physically by a continent, as they had been for most of the years since they had graduated and stopped being roommates. But their contact had become more and more frequent and intense as their professional undertakings supported each other. Mark would earn money as a freelance consultant to help Pete with financial modeling and analysis to pick investment objects. The FMRM network would contribute by informing business leaders and the public about the attractive investment climate being established in Iceland. This would favor decisions by depositors and investors to move savings to Iceland and decisions by corporations to register subsidiaries, or even their head offices, in Iceland. Pete and Mark often used an Internet-based instant messaging and conferencing application to talk to each other. Since both had a camera on their laptops, they could see each other when talking.

During Pete's first night in his Reykjavik apartment, a few hours after dinner and the Larrison show, he switched on his computer and connected to the messaging software. As almost always, Mark's user symbol showed that he was connected and available to talk. While the clock was 10 PM in Iceland, it was in the middle of the afternoon on the US West Coast where Mark was living. Pete put his headset on, and called Mark, who answered with "Hi, man, how is Iceland treating you?"

"Fine, thank you. Not as icy as the name may suggest, but it sure is cold, and there's a little snow on the streets."

"Over here the weather is great, as always, even though I felt a bit cold when falling into the water during my lunch time surfing run," Mark said and laughed heartily.

"Drop it. You're wasting your time; you won't succeed in making me jealous for not being with you," Pete answered and laughed. "I'm so excited about being here in Iceland. Even though it's a small country with people who are pretty reserved, there's an atmosphere here these days, when you walk in the street, as if history is being written. Well, I guess history *is* being written. And everybody is so excited, starting all kinds of businesses and making plans for a bright future. It's hard to believe that this place was a financial disaster zone until just a few months ago. I guess this is what it felt like to be in San Francisco in eighteen forty-nine during the gold rush!"

"So, in the end, it's *you* who will make *me* jealous for not being in Iceland," Mark answered happily. "I guess I'll have to spend some more time over there, to check out this gold-rush atmosphere. I can tell you that it's not the kind of mood you would find in the United States these days. Even though people are starting to talk about the end of the recession, unemployment is hovering around ten percent, which is huge. I talked to Jessica recently; she's going crazy about those huge budget deficits she has to help finance in her job at the Federal Reserve. I invited her to fly over to San Diego to get some rest and chill down a bit. I don't know if she will make it though; she's so busy with her job and with taking care of her baby daughter."

Pete nodded with interest and changed the subject. "Now, dear friend, let's stop the small talk and get down to business. As the foremost consultant of my investment fund, what services do you propose to help me to get started in the mutual fund business here?"

"Well, I won't commit to sharp deadlines, since I need to spend a lot of time on developing the FMRM Web site and its contents, but I have a couple of ideas I would like to work on."

"What are these ideas, whiz kid?"

"One thing I thought of is to set up a public index of the evolution of the quantity of money of main currencies, such as dollars, euros and yen. That would introduce more transparency about monetary policy. Today, its actual contents and effects are generally concealed by the fact that observers look mostly at the evolution of consumer prices. But that's just one of many *consequences* of monetary policy. It's a much less important indicator than the increase in the quantity of money itself. The new index would serve at least two purposes. First, it would make sure market prices of gold reflect the increase in quantities of paper money, which should increase the gold price. And, second, it would provide the best possible marketing tool for you guys in Iceland who wish to convince investors and depositors from other countries to shift their money to gold denominated products, in order to inflation proof their savings."

"Interesting. Please look into that as soon as you have time and come back to me with a price quotation for designing that index and the software needed to calculate and publish it."

"Will do. Another idea I had was for something that I would provide for internal use only, in order for you to make sound investment choices. It relates to government bonds. I believe their current ratings given by the major rating institutes are quite biased, in favor of large Western countries. I guess those rating institutes are too scared and have too many conflicts of interest to be able to assess objectively the actual state of government bonds of major countries.

"I will provide a calculation model making it possible to judge which of these major countries stand a fair chance to come back to budget surpluses and to pay down their government debt and which of them are likely to end up defaulting on their bonds. The current level of bond rates can make people believe that there are no major risks involved. But my impression is that they may be as junky as those mortgage-backed securities which upset the financial world a few years ago. Only the amounts of outstanding debt we talk about here are about a hundred times larger, and so would the crash be if the governments defaulted on their bonds."

"So you'll provide me with this magic tool to enable me to bet against the government bonds that are junky. Thanks to this, I will make huge profits. Do you think that I may trigger a self-reinforcing process, which makes my profits even higher, by pushing rates of those bonds up to levels which force those governments to default on their bonds?" Pete joked.

"Pete, you know better than that. Your talk sounds like the typical caricature of a speculator. You know as well as I do that all market participants take their own decisions with their own money. Nobody will act without a reason and without consideration to contribute to some chain reaction, if there are no reasons for it. I hope and believe that a lot of people learned the lesson from the previous crisis and stopped using automatic software, instead returning to do fundamental analysis."

Mark stopped for an instant, and a look of pain and discomfort showed on his face. "I think this is true about a lot of people, not only you. In any case, I would advise you to use this new tool for yourself, without making public statements in analysis reports about your views on the government bonds. Let the return that your fund will earn speak for itself. That return should be high, if you bet on future rate increases for well selected government bonds. As evidence builds up before the eyes of the world that those public debts are indeed unsustainable and impossible to pay back without major inflation, your fund will cash in with well-deserved gains."

"Do you already have an idea of which countries that would apply to?" Pete asked, with a hint of fear in his voice.

"I have some thoughts on that, but I prefer not to share them before I have built my model. Let's talk again in a month or two. Now, I guess you're not just going to sit over there to wait for your preferred freelance consultant to provide bright ideas and tools. What are *your* immediate plans for *your* Bagnelli *Gold* Mutual Fund Company?" Mark said, with a hint of mockery regarding the length of the name but with authentic curiosity.

"As the name indicates, I will manage and sell mutual funds denominated in gold. As you guessed, I'll have a fund focusing on bonds, picking the safest corporate bonds and the least-risky governments bonds your model will point out. The fund will also bet on future rate increases for the riskier government bonds. But the first fund I'll set up is a raw material fund. I do expect to see an increase in market values of mining companies, especially regarding gold and silver. I will look closely at other metals and raw materials as well, as I think we'll soon see new shortages of other key commodities. This should happen as growth in China, India and the rest of those 'emerging markets' will pick up again.

"The second fund will be the bond fund I mentioned. The third one will be called the Iceland Gold Fund and will include only business registered here, with their accounting and tax obligations entirely in gold. As you know, that will give them an edge with respect to competitors in the same business but that have accounting and taxes in a paper currency. Obviously, I won't include any Icelandic company in that fund. But something tells me the companies that will be the first to register here will be the smartest ones.

"The fourth fund I'll create may be the most obvious, but I want to wait for a few months until the market stabilizes a little: I will call this one the Iceland Banking Fund. It will be composed of deposit and loan banks registered in Iceland, meaning that they will manage assets and accounts mostly in gold. I see an incredible growth potential in this segment.

"Just think about the fact that there are sixty trillion U.S. dollars of bank deposits in the world. This is about twenty-two thousand times more than the current deposits in Iceland. Since owners of those deposits would be crazy not to want to put them on a gold account over here, you can imagine what kind of growth that could generate! After some time, I think we will also see major investment banks emerging in Iceland. They are obviously also candidates for being part of this fund."

As Pete finished the sentence, their conversation was interrupted by a chat message to both of them. Wanting to join the conversation was Bobby Cheston, currently living in Shanghai. Pete quickly connected Bobby, and they could see him well, although there was a slight lag between the movement of his lips and the sound.

"Hey, man, we haven't heard from you for some time! How are you doing?" Pete asked impatiently and loudly, with a wide smile that showed on the Webcams of his two friends.

"Quite all right, even though it's six o'clock in the morning over here. But I've gotten used to get up early, since there are so many things to do and see over here. I feel like I would be wasting my time if I sleep too much!"

"So, what's your job like?" asked Mark, who had not talked to Bobby since he left the United States a few months ago.

"I'm travelling around the country to find the best factories to produce all kinds of consumer goods products that my employer, the U.S. market leader General Retail, wants to sell—toys, clothing, hi-tech electronics, and stuff. Basically, any nonfood products you can imagine. While this is wage-earning work, my boss, who's a U.S. expat, is a nice guy, and he allows me to work only eighty percent of my time for them. It has enabled me to have a parallel activity where I'm my own boss. There I still look for competitive manufacturing plants, though not in retail, but in industrial parts manufacturing. I help U.S.

companies in sectors such as automotive, industrial machines, construction, and public works to get in touch with suppliers. This can help them import industrial parts to be used in assembly or construction activity over in the United States."

"Why don't you hire some Chinese personnel for your private venture?" Mark asked.

"Actually, I already have, since it's impossible for me to move around in the countryside alone, or to meet the right people. More precisely, I sometimes use the translator and guide I have from General Retail also for my other work. He helped me to hire someone else who had more connections in industrial parts than in consumer products."

"So, I understand you don't have time to miss not being over here in the Western world?" Mark asked. "I hope you read the news to see that we are writing history over here, at least Professor Benson, Laura, and Pete, who are engaged in the Icelandic project of reintroducing a gold-based monetary system."

"Yes, of course I read about that every day, and I saw the press release about your FMRM network, Mark. I believe FMRM is just as important as those gold banking- and investment-fund projects. I do hope that people will come to understand the importance and value of such a monetary system. General approval is the only possible safeguard to prevent that some politicians hungry for power will destroy the new monetary system in order to reintroduce government-controlled paper money.

"By the way, I can tell you my Chinese friends are very, very interested in all this. They are feeling stronger and stronger that China has made a mistake by investing so heavily in dollar-denominated U.S. government bonds. People over here understand perfectly well the role of gold as money and as a guarantee against inflation. Mark, my advice to you is to set up a Chinese-language version of your Web site. What do you think about that?"

"Well, that's a great idea, but I don't speak a word of Chinese."

"Give me a week and I'll put you in contact with a Chinese associate who can help you create your Web site and keep it running!"

"Alright, thank you very much, but be careful who you pick. Remember, the vision that the site is based on isn't just about commodity money. It is about commodity money as a major requirement for establishing and maintaining individual freedom in society. So I'm not sure that Chinese authorities will approve of our cause, even if they may see an interest in gold money to inflation proof the proceedings they earn in international trade."

"Man, don't try to get it all at once. If you have to limit the contents of the site a bit in the beginning, then accept that. I've learned that Chinese people are quite open and intellectually honest; they are able to learn and change their mind. But it won't work if you come around explaining that their culture and way of living sucks and must be completely overhauled. In that respect, I guess they are pretty much like everybody else."

"Sure. But if you can, please find a guy who has some interest in individual rights as opposed to a thought police kind of guy."

"Don't worry; I already have someone on mind, a guy who actually was an exchange student at the Jefferson-Jackson University. He was there at the same time as us. He even took a few classes from Professor Benson. I only exchanged a few words with him back then, but I recognized his face when I met him at a party for U.S. expats here. He spent several years in the United States after graduating and worked over there for a major Internet search engine. He's now working for the same company over here, and he's leading their fight for the freedom of the Internet in China. It's a major battle. I'm sure you'll like him. His name is Chow Ka Ying, but everybody calls him just Ka Ying. He says their corporate motto is 'Don't be evil.'"

"Sounds like a good guy. Thanks a lot!" Mark said, giving a thumbs-up to Bobby over the Webcam. After a second, he added, "Then again, I hope Ka Ying will adopt *our* motto, if we manage to hire him. The one I coined for FMRM is 'Be good.'"

"That's the same as the one Ka's employer uses," Bobby remarked.

"Well, they're quite similar, and I like theirs too," Mark said. "But there's a crucial difference. Ours excludes the possibility of doing nothing, of standing in the middle of the road so to speak. I guess you remember the old and famous saying 'All that is necessary for the triumph of evil is that good men do nothing'? *That* was what I wanted in the motto of FMRM, in a shorter form, and in reverse."

"Guys, it was great talking to you," Pete said, "but it's eleven p.m. here in Iceland, and I need to get going. There's a party all night at the square in front of Laura's bank downtown. She called me not so long ago; they have already opened the champagne bottles. She was almost crying from happiness. She said they had recorded fifteen thousand new clients today! Hazelton has invited a lot of top brass to the party, including the finance minister and the president. Now, good night, guys!" Pete said.

Bobby smiled and said, "Good morning," and Mark ended the conversation, also grinning, with "Good afternoon."

CHAPTER 14:
Crime and Punishment

"Montgomery, what the hell is going on? Real estate price are going through the roof: they're up twenty percent during the first three months after we switched to gold money. And consumer prices aren't lagging far behind! In spite of the reluctance of retailers to increase prices, they're up ten percent on the same period!"

Ivar Larsen paused, realizing that he was almost panicking.

"Good day to you too, Ivar," Professor Benson said with a friendly laugh. "I'm sorry that you seem to call me only when you're upset." Benson paused and said with a grave tone, "Are you affirmative about the numbers you just told me?"

"Yes!" Larsen yelled.

"It doesn't make sense. Even if there has been an inflow of money to Iceland, I haven't heard about any significant immigration of people, nor have I heard that foreigners are buying real estate. And it's certain that people living abroad aren't bidding up consumer goods prices in Iceland. They're only using their gold accounts to make payments in their home country. The central bank has been shut down, so there's no arbitrary creation of money. Fractional reserve banking, lending out demand deposits, is forbidden by law and would be lethally dangerous for banks to practice. So what can be driving prices up? I don't see any rational explanation."

Larsen calmed down and nodded. "There must be an explanation. But what is it?"

The line remained silent for a while before Benson said, "Do you have any numbers about the volume of economic transactions? Or about the quantity of currency in circulation?"

"No we don't! That was what the Central Bank used to track. Banks are starting to publish quarterly numbers, but I haven't yet seen any consolidation for the whole country. Why?"

Benson didn't answer the question. "Do you know if retailers are all using the gold checkers and bill checkers Hazelton has developed?"

"Yes, I think most of them are using the gold-checker, and it's working well. I just heard about one or two cases where someone had tried to manipulate the gold, but thanks to the checker, they didn't get away with it and they were reported to the police. The bill checkers aren't operational yet, as Mark Lomack hasn't finished developing the software that will enable connections to the banks' central databases to check the serial number of bills. In the meantime, as each bank is offering their own paper bills, people aren't sure about whether bills are authentic or not and what they're really supposed to look like. Yesterday, we heard of the first case where a bank refused bills with its own name on it when someone came to deposit cash. It was Laura Dalaghan's bank. They said the bills were fakes."

"I see," Benson said thoughtfully. "Have you talked to Mark about this yet?"

"No, I think he's in San Diego this week. You're the first person I called when I got the frightening numbers about price inflation."

"OK. Then let me alert him. I think he needs to speed up his software development. In addition, he might want to help the Icelandic police to find out what's going on."

✧ ✧ ✧

Have you received gold-money paper bills in a large cash transaction recently? In that case, please dial this number to tell us about it. We wish to collect testimonials about how people experience our new monetary system.

The newspaper ad was full page, had vivid colors, and had the logo of the Icelandic Ministry of Finance at the bottom. However, the purpose was not the one mentioned in the newspaper ad. The actual purpose was to feed a crime investigation conducted by the Reykjavik police department, assisted by a few banking experts including Mark Lomack. Numerous testimonials were submitted, and each person was then contacted to come into the police office. Mark was assisting a police officer who was talking to a witness, Einar Jansen.

"This is what's left of the cash I got when I sold my motorbike three days ago," Jansen said and held up a pile of gold paper bills. "I've spent much of the money. But if my memory is correct, all the bills were from the Dalaghan Prudential Gold Bank and printed by the Hazelton Money Mint. Do you think they might be fakes? I was really confident since Dalaghan and Hazelton were among the people hailed as the originators of our new money and as benefactors of Iceland."

Mark tensed. "Please give me your bills. I'll be able to test our new bill-checker software on them." Mark took one of the bills and held it against a small handheld device with a bar code reader. It beeped.

"How does it work?" Jansen said, bending forward to watch with interest.

Mark answered without taking his eyes off the screen of the small device. "I just scanned the serial number on the bill, and the encrypted hologram. This information is now being checked against the database of the Dalaghan Bank using a wireless Internet connection. It can take a little while."

A moment later, the device beeped again, and a red light blinked for a few seconds. "Damn!" Mark yelled, turning to the police officer next to him. "The serial number exists, but the hologram is bogus. The bill is a fake."

Mark rapidly took a few more bills and tried them out. They all gave the same result as the first bill.

The police officer remarked severely, “Now this is unexpected. The man who was the first to launch a minting company in Iceland, hailing the free market and the absence of government regulation of money, seems to be a disguised counterfeiter!”

“What are you talking about?” Mark shouted. “That’s outrageous! It’s obvious that some criminal has made copies of the bills of the Dalaghan bank. You wouldn’t expect the criminal to print his own name on the bills, would you?” Mark replied, facing the police officer.

“I don’t know,” the policeman replied, calming down. “But I’ll ask for a search warrant on Hazelton’s printing shop. If we find any evidence whatsoever showing that the duplicate bills were made in there, then your friend Hazelton will end up behind bars for a long time.”

✲ ✲ ✲

Mark and Einar Jansen had driven up to Akureyri. The man who had bought Jansen’s motorbike had given this address. The man had shown an Icelandic passport, something Jansen had wondered about as the man had looked like a Latin American and spoke English only. He had been dressed in typical Icelandic outdoor wear, however. When Mark and Jansen rang on the doorbell, an elderly woman opened the door: “Leif Ragnarsen? There’s no Leif Ragnarsen here! I’m a widow, my husband died five years ago!”

In Icelandic, Jansen asked her, “Have you never seen a tall man with dark and wrinkled skin, looking like a Native Mexican but dressed in normal clothes?”

“No. I can assure you that I would remember if I had seen him. Here everybody is pale as volcano ash. Now will you excuse me? I’m cooking dinner for my grandchildren.”

As they walked back to their car, Mark said to Jansen, “So, the guy used a fake address, and probably a fake identity. It reinforces my suspicions. We must find him to find out who’s behind the fake bills.”

Mark called up a police officer and convinced him to launch a national search for the red motorbike that Jansen had sold.

✲ ✲ ✲

Two days later, the motorbike had been spotted outside a highway restaurant near Reykjavik. A couple of police officers wearing plain clothes immediately went there, along with Mark Lomack and Einar Jansen, who had remained on call to help the investigation. Instead of entering the restaurant, they waited outside, after Jansen had confirmed that the red motorbike in front of the diner was the one he had sold.

After twenty minutes, a man walked up to the motorbike, jumped up on it, and prepared to drive off. Jansen yelled, holding back the police officers who were bursting out of the car, "It isn't him! I don't understand. It's the right motorbike, but the wrong guy!"

The police officers nevertheless stopped the man to question him.

"Why? What have I done? What do you want from me?"

"Where did you get this motorbike from?" one of the policemen asked harshly.

"Why, I bought it yesterday. I don't think it's stolen; I paid normal market price for it."

"We didn't say it was stolen. But could you please tell us from whom you bought it?"

The man was relieved, understanding that he was not the person the police was looking for. "Oh, he was a tall man who looked like a Mexican. He spoke English with a funny accent."

"Do you know where he can be found?"

"He signed the papers of the sale stating he lives in Akureyri."

The policeman sighed. "We've already been there. It's a fake address."

"Oh," the man said thoughtfully. "I felt he was lying when he told me he lived in Akureyri. I guess it was because I didn't believe he was an Icelandic resident in the first place. He spoke English. He told me he would soon leave Iceland for a long time. He said he had finished the business he had been doing lately."

The policemen and Mark looked tensely at the man as he pursued without noticing their reaction.

"But now that I think of it, there was something else that made me feel he was lying."

"What?" Mark asked, staring at the man.

"Let me think...Oh yes! I know! It was because he held a hotel key in his hand. So I figured he didn't really live in Akureyri."

"Did you see the label on the key?" Mark said.

"Hmm...I didn't really care to look closer. But I believe it was yellow and blue. So it could have been the Viking Lodge outside Reykjavik. They use those colors."

"Thank you," the officers, Mark, and Jansen said with one voice as they left the man and dashed off.

"Let's catch this bastard and interrogate him," the policeman said.

"No, you can't do that," Mark exclaimed. "We have to tail him tomorrow morning to see where he goes to work. We need to collect evidence."

The two policemen looked at each other as if none of them wished to spend their night hiding in a car in front of a hotel. When Mark saw their faces, he yelled, "I'll do it! I'll bring Pete Bagnelli with me; we'll call you first thing if we spot the guy tomorrow morning."

☆ ☆ ☆

Pete and Mark took turns sleeping while the other kept his eyes at the entrance of the Viking Lodge hotel. Pete was in a tense mood as Cornelius Hazelton had been arrested that day at the airport, after flying in from California to spend the week in Iceland. He was arrested due to the discovery of a large quantity of false bills of the Dalaghan Prudential Gold Bank.

Pete woke up Mark at 6:00 a.m. "I can't get it out of my mind. The cops here are so damn stupid. How could they imagine Cornelius would print false bills and leave the name of his own minting company on them?"

Mark sighed as he emerged from two hours of uncomfortable sleep. "But remember the enormous quantity of false bills they have found. I heard that they estimate there's almost two tons of gold worth of false bills. That is worth sixty million dollars! And half of the false bills appear to have the label of Laura's bank. I guess she'd have been arrested too, if she were here in Iceland now. One of the investigators told me he thought Laura and Cornelius had done this in order for people to come deposit their new bills in their bank, thereby becoming their customers."

"That's just bullshit. They would never do anything like that! By the way, I'm sure that fractional reserve lending of other banks explains most of the price inflation. Even if there is sixty million dollars' worth of false bills, that's only two percent of total bank deposits. So I bet you fractional reserve banking may amount to ten times more, which would explain the price increases of twenty percent. The trouble is that it's hard to find out about it, as banks haven't yet published any statistics about their volumes of deposits versus their volume of outstanding currency bills."

Mark looked thoughtfully at Pete and was about to speak when his eyes sprung wide open. "Pete, look! I think that's our Mexican coming out of the hotel," Mark said with hushed excitement.

"I guess you're right," Pete hushed back and picked up the car key. "I'll let him just drive off; we don't want him to spot us right away."

Mark called the Reykjavik police department as they slowly started to tail the minivan driven by the Mexican. He left the city and drove north east.

After ten minutes of driving, the minivan left the main road and entered an industrial district. So as not to be spotted, Pete increased the distance between his car and the minivan slightly, but they could still see that the minivan had stopped and was parking at the entrance of a large warehouse building. Mark saw the unmarked police car approach them, and signaled them to stop. Soon, Pete, Mark, and three armed policemen sneaked up to the warehouse entrance.

Inside, they could see a group of around fifty men with Mexican looks and clothing who appeared busy with loading wooden boxes into other minivans parked inside the warehouse. Two of the men were busy dismantling a machine. One of the policemen immediately called for backup.

"That's a money printing machine!" Mark whispered. "You must go in now before they dismantle their counterfeiting machines and vanish!"

The policemen looked hesitantly at each other, but the officer in charge nodded and jumped out under a spotlight where he could be seen by all the men. He held his gun in front of him and shouted, "Police! Everybody freeze! Put your hands above your heads and line up against the wall."

The men obeyed after some hesitation; one of them reached for a machine gun but stopped as one of the policemen screamed at him. Mark and Pete ran in to open some of the boxes.

"Look! Here are three full boxes of false currency bills of the Dalaghan Prudential Gold Bank!" Mark screamed with a combined fury and triumph. "So much for putting Hazelton under arrest; you can call your colleagues to set him free right away."

Pete, who was familiar with money-printing technology, studied the printer and soon held up a metal plate. "Here is the proof that these guys have been counterfeiting currency bills of DPGB. Arrest the bastards right now!"

Mark walked up to the Mexican they had been tailing; he seemed to have the authority of a leader. "Who are you? Who sent you here?"

Pete screamed a second time, as he moved deeper into the warehouse "Guys! Come here! They have a vault in the back, and it's open. I believe they were about to empty it when we came, to get out of here for good. And you won't believe me if I tell you what's in there! Dollar and euro bills! Judging from the quantity I see, we're talking about tens of millions of dollars!"

✧ ✧ ✧

The events in Iceland made the headlines on the following day, not only in the "Golden Island" but across most of the Western world. The arrested men had all been identified as members of a known counterfeiting gang from Mexico, who had travelled to Iceland with false passports two months earlier. According to Icelandic law, they were now liable to compensate the victims of their scam for the 1.7 tons of gold that the false currency bills represented. This weight of gold corresponded to the amount of 60 million dollars, so at first, it was believed impossible for these penniless drifters to do their victims justice. However, one day later, it was announced that the dollar bills found in the warehouse amounted to 50 million dollars.

Part of the explanation was in the fact that the Mexicans had opened a foreign exchange business in central Reykjavik which over two months had collected 40 million dollars' worth in euros and dollars from tourists who all had gotten false Icelandic paper-money bills in exchange. A stock of authentic Icelandic paper-money bills had also been found, worth 10 million dollars. This money had been obtained by the resale of cars, motor-bikes, and other expensive items such as sailing boats that the Mexicans had first purchased with their false money. But many of the cars and motorbikes they had purchased had not yet been resold: a thousand cars and five hundred motorbikes had been found on a parking lot near their warehouse, and after a search of Icelandic harbors, five hundred boats had been found.

So a mystery remained about an amount of 10 million dollars of fresh dollar bills which had not come from the foreign exchange business or from resale of goods purchased with false money. Even more surprising was the fact that the Federal Reserve had confirmed that this money was not counterfeited: they were authentic brand-new dollar bills.

The obvious question was how such an amount of freshly printed dollar bills could have ended up in the possession of a counterfeiting gang in Iceland. The arrested Mexicans had claimed that they had acted on assignment from representatives of the U.S. government, and that the Federal Reserve had seen to the supply and shipment of their "fees" to Iceland. This story had been categorically denied by spokespeople from both the U.S. Department of the Treasury and the Federal Reserve. Still, no explanation was proposed as to how this giant cash reserve could have ended up in Iceland. In any case, the fact that the money was recognized as authentic enabled the Icelandic police to use it to buy gold and to refund the people in Iceland who had been fooled by the false bills. The cars, motorbikes, and boats seized were also sold and the proceeds were distributed as damages to the banks that had been victims of the counterfeiting.

On the day after the announcement of the restitution, Mark and Pete shared a beer in a bar with Cornelius Hazelton, just released from prison.

"Here's to you guys for saving my neck," Hazelton said, raising his glass.

Mark and Pete answered by raising theirs, and nodded happily. After a moment of silence, Mark looked at Pete. "What did we talk about when we discovered the Mexican in front of the Viking Lodge?"

"What?" Pete said.

"You pointed out that the amount of false bills only explains a fraction of the recent price inflation. I'm sure the bastards at Zach Morgano do fractional reserve lending. I read an article where their boss in Iceland bragged about having increased its local market share in deposits from twenty-five percent to forty percent. I haven't heard any other bank say they lost customers. This makes me think Zach Morgano has just boosted its market share by fractional reserve lending. That increase in market share corresponds to seventeen tons of gold, or six hundred million dollars! Ten times as much as the Mexican counterfeiting!

"But it's quite possible they have done it. That amount corresponds roughly to the two thousand new home loans, five thousand consumption credits, and two thousand business loans Zach Morgano boast about having made over the last two months. How can we find out what Zach Morgano is up to? The Zach Morgano management is arrogant enough to believe that the brand name of their bank relieves it of the need to declare its stocks of gold and of currency bills."

"Oh, I've got an idea!" Pete said. I'm currently dating a gorgeous girl who works as a cashier at Zach Morgano. I'll ask her to get me the needed data. I'll tell her it's just by curious jealously from one of its weaker competitors."

✵ ✵ ✵

On the following Monday morning, a large crowd waited in front of the Zach Morgano Reykjavik office way before opening hour. Many of them held in their hands the newspaper, which had reprinted an article written by Mark Lomack that had first been published on the FMRM Web site. The article was named "The Costumed Counterfeiters" and started as follows:

> *The Zach Morgano bank came to Iceland as conquerors. Its managers believed the internationally known brand of their bank would allow it unearned confidence from customers. To some extent, that's what happened, and the bank has abused that confidence. It abused it by lending out demand deposits which, by Icelandic law, a bank is obliged to keep in its vaults. This is how its market share in demand deposits moved from 25 percent to 40 percent. Zach Morgano lent out 85 percent of its ten tons of gold deposits to other people. As a result, most of the people who have deposited their gold at Zach Morgano will be unable to get it back.*
>
> *Nevertheless, we urge all customers of Zach Morgano to go and withdraw your money by Monday morning and to put it in a bank more respectful of Icelandic law and of you as customers. The good news for you is that the shareholders of Zach Morgano will have to pay up the difference when there's no more gold in its vaults! By our calculation, the missing seventeen tons of gold will be provided by Zach Morgano Iceland's five tons of bank capital and by twelve tons that the shareholders will have to pay unless the bank is able to call some of the loans it made.*

Cornelius Hazelton and Mark Lomack stood at some distance for a long while to watch as former customers of Zach Morgano walked away with their gold in briefcases or small safety deposit boxes. They knew that Zach Morgano Iceland would lose their customers and be out of business within a day or two, for having lent 85 percent of demand deposits in a country where 100 percent reserves was required.

Mark smiled. "I guess this comes as a cold shower for Zach Morgano. I mean, back home, they and most of their competitors are getting away with working with only five percent reserves. Here, three times more than that still earned them a bank run, driving them bust. Again, the truth of the statement 'One can't both have a cake and eat it' isn't a question of percentages; it's just totally true."

Hazelton chuckled. "Yes, I see a lot of justice in what's happening. Imagine that I was almost thrown into jail, accused of doing what they did. I hope everybody will realize that what Zach Morgano did had exactly the same effect as the counterfeiting done by the Mexicans. So it's right that both have had to pay back every gram of gold they pretended to have, though they didn't have it. One crime, one punishment!"

"Yep," Mark said. "Now I hope people will also understand what they should really worry about. For all the talk of private-market counterfeiting, that gang of a hundred Mexicans only managed to push sixty million dollars of false money out on the market. And now that my bill-checker software is being rolled out at all the Icelandic banks, using fake bills will be just as impossible as faking gold, thanks to the gold-checkers. But even though it was an exceptionally large scam which won't happen again, it still was ten times smaller than the Zach Morgano fractional reserve scam."

Hazelton nodded. "Yes, in the world of counterfeiting, if plain criminals are comparable to a shotgun, fractional reserve lending by large banks has the potential of being cruise missiles."

"For sure," Mark said. "But all that is just peanuts compared to the nuclear bombs of counterfeiting."

"What do you talk about?" Hazelton asked.

"I mean when the Fed creates money by signing checks in its own name. Jessica told me the people at the Treasury had them buy three hundred billion dollars' worth of government bonds late last year, which the treasury wasn't able to sell to someone else. Those newly created three hundred billion become new reserves of the bank that sold the bonds. "

"Gosh, that's five hundred times more than the Zach Morgano scandal here."

"Right, but it still is ten times *less* than the money the Fed and the Treasury created over just a few months after the subprime crisis," Mark added with a shudder. "And I wonder what they will come up with at the end of this year to finance their deficits. As capital starts to escape to Iceland, the U.S. government might have a higher-than-ever budget deficit."

"I don't mind!" Hazelton said with a laugh. "If they scare people and capital away from the United States, it will be good for business over here. I bet we may soon see a real economic boom in Iceland, if people around the world start to realize what an exciting place Iceland is to live and do business in; especially if governments keep giving them good reasons to vote with their feet!"

CHAPTER 15:
Let the Rich Pay

That winter was cold in Washington, D.C., and as the end of February approached, there was still a lot of snow on the streets and the temperature had been below freezing for more than a week. This weather situation had created traffic jams where none was normally seen. As a consequence, many people tended to be late to work.

However, the people summoned to the meeting being held that morning in the main conference room of the U.S. Department of the Treasury were not late. They had all taken necessary precautions in order to be available and on time, even though the meeting was set to start at the unusually early hour of seven. They had done so after having received an e-mail meeting invitation from the secretary of the Treasury himself, with the following label: "URGENT and CONFIDENTIAL—following recent G7 meeting".

Eight people had gathered for the meeting. In addition to the secretary of the Treasury, who had called the meeting, sitting around the oval conference table was the deputy secretary of the treasury; the director of the Department of Public Debt, James Mortimer; the assistant secretary in charge of Tax Policy, Steve Harper; and the deputy secretaries in charge of international affairs and of economic policy. The only person in the room who was not from the Department of the Treasury was Jessica Frostby, who represented the Federal Reserve in matters of public finance and of helping to finance the government debt of the United States.

The secretary of the treasury Joseph Miller was a tall, slim, and austere man approaching the age of sixty. He always wore flawless gray suits and spoke little to anyone outside the circle of his direct working environment. At 7:00 a.m., he stood and addressed the audience. He spoke with a tense but energetic tone, as this was the first time in twenty-four hours he talked about the events he had lived through during that week.

"Thank you very much for having responded to my last-minute invitation, but as you may understand, the matters I need to share with you are of utmost importance. You all know I attended a three-day G7 meeting with all the ministers of finance of Japan, France, the U.K., Germany, Italy, and Canada. Exceptionally, we had the presence of the heads of state of all the countries for the last day and evening sessions, including the president of the United States.

"You may have read or listened to the communiqué published at the end of the meeting. It contained nothing special, just a general declaration about our common determination to remain mobilized to make sure our respective countries come out of the economic crisis, which now has gone on for two and a half years, since the peak of the subprime crisis. But the communiqué was flat because the actual content of the meeting and the decisions taken were of such nature and importance that it was decided not to disclose them. Actually, it was agreed that each country, for the next couple of weeks, would keep that information restricted to less than ten people, in addition to the heads of State and the ministers of finance.

"As far as the United States is concerned, that means the information will be shared only with the people in this room, with the secretary of State, the director of National Intelligence, the chairman of the Federal Reserve, and one of its governors, Jeffery Hastings. Hastings is the superior of Jessica Frostby, here present, and he will need to know what she now will learn." The secretary of the Treasury paused as if to let his words sink into the minds of his audience, to increase their eagerness to hear more.

Before he could continue his speech, the undersecretary of international affairs raised his index finger. Looking around the room and then straight at the secretary of the treasury, he asked, with a hint of suspicion in his voice, "If you dealt with such crucial matters regarding economic policy, then how come that was discussed in a G7 meeting, and not in a G20 meeting? The G7 excludes China, India, Russia, and Brazil, just to name a few of the new economic superpowers. I do hope there's a good reason for having left them out of the loop."

"As you will soon understand," the secretary of the treasury answered dryly, "there were good reasons for discussing these matters in a smaller group. Now please, let me pursue to let you in on what we're talking about."

He paused again, drank some coffee, and put his glasses back on, as if to better see the reactions of his listeners. "As you know, we have been running very high federal budget deficits during the two years following the subprime crisis, and this third year will be no exception. Late last year, we were able to sell a major new issue of government bonds of above a trillion dollars, thanks in part to the appreciated contribution of the Federal Reserve." He paused for an instant and nodded in Jessica's direction.

"But we noticed that the usual, main foreign buyers of our bonds were becoming more and more suspicious and reluctant. The dollar is also under pressure by a flow of deposits from dollars to gold money. That flow has been accelerating ever since Iceland moved to gold money a bit more than a year ago. So I don't think we will be able to go on raising such vast amounts while simultaneously conducting a relatively loose monetary policy here. That would give people reasons to believe we are about to inflate our way toward an easier payback burden.

"Now, many of our fellow G7 countries are in similar situations, notably Japan, France, the U.K., and Italy. Other European countries such as Portugal and Greece are in even worse shape, even though their national budgets are much smaller. So what is emerging is consensus about the fact that we have unsustainably high public deficits, which we won't be able to keep financing by emitting ever larger amounts of government bonds. So we need to find a way to reduce those deficits.

"The first basic question is whether we should reduce public spending or increase public revenue. In order to reduce public spending, we would either have to reduce the stimulus efforts we've engaged in since the subprime crisis or reduce welfare and social security spending. Regarding the stimulus efforts, I, the president, and our finest economic advisors agree that the relative ineffectiveness of that program indicates that we need to *increase* those efforts, rather than to reduce them.

"Reducing welfare spending is not advisable during a period when we have the largest unemployment in a very long time. Finally, reducing social security spending is totally impossible. Just imagine if we did that, although we're just about to create a new system the very purpose of which is to spend more money in order for everybody to have social security ensured by the government!

"Our fellow G7 countries basically reach similar conclusions, especially France and Italy. In addition to having the same problems as we do with unemployment and weak growth, they also have public retirement systems and social security funds that are running enormous deficits."

Jessica wanted to interrupt to ask a question or to challenge what was being said, but she refrained after a nod from Steve that was meant to make her remain silent.

Joseph Miller continued. "So the overall conclusion is that it's impossible to reduce public spending, given the current economic situation and given the urgent efforts we need to maintain in order to fight the dreadful crisis. Now, let me come to why we wished to discuss this in the G7 circle, not in the G20.

"There is indeed an emerging consensus among the mature industrial countries. We all have extensive welfare systems and relatively high taxes that are being exposed to disloyal competition, what we call *social dumping*. The threat comes from the emerging economies such as China, India, Russia, and Brazil as well as from most of the other Asian countries that offer to produce the same products and services as we do but for much lower costs. This combines with the fact that large corporations in the Western world sell those products for much higher prices to the Western consumer. This creates a situation where large American and European companies, and their shareholders, are becoming richer and richer. At the same time, the Western consumer is bogged down in a mix of hard-to-pay-back mortgages and consumption debt. Such debts have been taken on in order to keep paying those high prices while their employment over here is threatened by blue-collar jobs moving off-shore."

At this point Jessica could not refrain from intervening and, making an effort to remain perfectly calm, said, "Sir, with all due respect, that point of view is disputed by many economists and by some hard facts. If you look at the average rate of profit on the thousand largest U.S. corporations during the subprime crisis year, it was only *one percent*. I need not remind you how much money shareholders have lost from the radical fall in asset prices. That fall is far from having been compensated by the modest rise in corporate profits and stock valuations seen over the last two years. An increase which by the way has been largely due to the loose monetary policy we have been pursuing at the Federal Reserve."

The secretary of the treasury rephrased her point in a way that fit his own reasoning. "Yes, as you point out, profits and stock valuations are picking up again, so I don't think we need to remain sleepless worrying about big business and rich people. Even if they have taken some blows, which I admit, there are only two important questions today. Who in the economic system has any margins whatsoever to pay more to cover our public deficits? And who would accept to do that without creating major social unrest, which would prevent us, the people in power, from being reelected in the next elections?

"The answer to both questions is big business and rich people! *They* are the only ones who have any safety margins left that we can squeeze, and they are few enough not to present any major risk in elections. If we talk about dollar millionaires, they represent around one percent of the population in most developed countries; a bit more here in the United States, a bit less in most European countries. But the bottom line is the same: we need not worry about the opinions of one percent of the population as far as reelection is concerned. At a time when we have dire problems, they should be expected to contribute more to saving the country than regular people, shouldn't they?"

He paused and looked around the table to see what his audience thought. Everybody gave a nod of approval except for Jessica, who looked him in the eyes. She wanted to disagree but she would not bother arguing with this man, letting him assume the responsibility for his beliefs, which he had the power to translate into action. Joseph Miller was indeed one of the four or five most powerful men in the country.

Miller was content with this silent approval from most people in the room, including all those who were under his direct command as secretary of the Treasury. "So, the G7 countries agreed to put in place concerted, significant tax increases targeting large corporations and wealthy individuals. Now, as I said, we also share the belief that we must do something about the price dumping done by the emerging countries. It's driving employment away from our countries. Therefore, the G7 also decided to do two more things: to create a tax on direct investments done by Western corporations in developing countries and to tax imports from those countries. We need to do both at the same time; otherwise, corporations will get around the problem. If we tax investments but not goods imports, they would just focus on goods imports. If we tax imports but not direct investment they would set up shell companies in those countries. They could move the goods back to the Western countries within their company and try to keep it out of our import statistics.

"When we put these new domestic taxes in place, we must be sure that the Western corporations and wealthy individuals won't be able to get away by moving their assets to off-shore tax havens. Here, the good news is the improved transparency regarding tax information that we have achieved by pressuring tax havens hard since the subprime crisis. So we're able to make sure that everybody's assets are taxed at the right place. That place is the country of residence for individuals and the country of their true activity for corporations.

"The president has asked me to create a specific enforcement agency for this purpose, which will combine some prerogatives of the police, the tax authorities, and the national and international intelligence services. That agency will be named after the law which will enact these new taxes, namely, ESBEA, as in Economic Solidarity Bill Enforcement Agency. Its staff should soon count ten thousand employees. This will also provide a welcome reduction in the unemployment rate which has been increasing, even here in Washington."

Jessica, angry and frustrated about what she was hearing, was seeing red, but she had decided to keep quiet and to remain in her role as representative of the Federal Reserve, invited as a listener to this meeting at the Department of the Treasury.

Instead, James Mortimer spoke with a hopeful and polite tone. "So, how much additional tax revenue do you expect from these additional taxes? As you know, we had about one-point-two trillion dollars of public deficit to finance this year, and it might actually, as last year, end up at one and half trillion dollars at the end of the year. While most of that is secured by the bond issue we did a few months ago, I do hope we won't have to ask the market for similar amounts for next year."

Joseph Miller answered pleasantly. "According to the first calculations I made during the night sessions at the summit, we should be able to collect an additional six hundred billion dollars a year by combining the following taxes, addressed at millionaires only: a three percent annual tax on total wealth, an additional ten percent of income tax and of capital gains tax, and a ten percent inheritance tax of the estate of all millionaires who die. We should be able to collect an additional three hundred billion dollars by increasing the corporate profits tax to fifty percent for large corporations and by making companies pay an extra twenty percent of payroll taxes for all people earning more than two hundred thousand dollars a year, and finally by a ten percent tax on direct investment in and imports from emerging countries. So, overall, we will increase government revenue by nine hundred billion dollars. Not bad, don't you think?"

James Mortimer looked with admiration at his boss, with a smile of awe. "Indeed, this is a very promising scheme. By slamming additional taxes on just one or two percent of the population, and on large corporations and foreign countries who don't have any votes at all, we collect as much money as if we would have doubled the income tax for all Americans. As we recently discussed, doubling the income tax for all Americans would be political suicide.

I also think it would be impossible to drive through, as people just wouldn't be able to pay such taxes."

"I know," Joseph Miller said calmly but triumphantly. "And that's what I mean when I say we should get the money where it is. We do want to cover our public deficits without putting public spending on a stranglehold, and without exposing ourselves to social unrest."

The undersecretary of International Affairs said, "I think we understand what will be done and why it's necessary to maintain some secrecy about it. But what is the actual plan for putting these noble ideas into practice? I assume you must have outlined a detailed calendar planning which must be respected by all countries. Because the effect of this package will probably be most powerful if the announcements and implementations are highly synchronized. That would show that we politicians are about to become as globalized and internationally collaborative as the multinational corporations we are trying to control."

Joseph Miller answered, with a smile that gradually changed from triumph to mere satisfaction and self-confidence, "Indeed, a detailed common calendar has been defined. It has been decided that all G7 countries will announce their plans on the same day, May thirty-first, which is a bit more than three months from now."

When Joseph Miller looked his way, Steve Harper, Jessica's husband and the assistant secretary for Tax Policy, remarked smoothly, "I appreciate that you leave us with three months to work out the details of what I expect to be a quite complex effort, the creation and rollout of the ESBEA. Of course, you can count on the people in this room never to speak a word about what you told us about the G7 meeting. But we still need to involve a certain number of people in order to write the new taxation law text, to prepare for the collection process, and to recruit people to the ESBEA. In order to stand a chance to conserve the secrecy of the plan, we need to postpone the main recruitment campaign to after the announcement. In order to cope with the workload for the first period, I will try to use some IRS personnel. May I ask if there is a particular reason why you wish to wait so long with the announcement and to accept the risk that it might leak out before that date?"

"Yes, there is," Joseph Miller said with a secretive smile. "As you know June thirtieth is the deadline for people who don't want to have their fiscal residence in the country for the whole year, to move abroad. The same rule applies for corporations. We should expect that some people and corporations may be tempted to leave the country when they learn that we will introduce major new taxes. So we need to wait as long as possible not to give them too much time to react. Announcing the taxes on May thirty-first, they won't have time to make the necessary arrangements for this year.

"We hope they will get over it once they have paid those taxes once. In that case, next year, they will stick around and not turn their personal world upside down by moving abroad just to avoid paying a bit more taxes. We should prepare to send them the new wealth tax amounts early July, with an immediate required first payment of most of it. Correct me if I'm wrong, Mortimer, but that should secure the cash position of the government until the end of the year."

"Affirmative," James said, nodding happily.

"Well, I hope you're right, that this won't make people leave the country," Steve said thoughtfully. "But the taxes we're talking about represent an awful lot of money to be taken from a limited number of people and corporations. It *will* hurt, for sure, even if they can afford it."

"Yes they *can*, and that's really our only consideration, isn't it?" Joseph Miller said pleasantly.

"Yes," Steve added cautiously, "they're able to pay. But they might also be able to escape. What's your view on the stunt performed by Iceland, switching to gold money last year? Don't you fear they could draw people and capital out of the United States?"

Miller looked earnestly confident when he replied. "I think that story has been blown up way beyond proportion. I know they even made it to be on the Larrison show. But the fact remains that we talk about a country representing three-hundredths of a percent of the world's economy. Instead of giving them undeserved publicity and giving the impression that we worry, I prefer to ignore it completely."

Considering there was nothing more to add, Miller stood up to signal that the meeting was ending. "I ask all of you to think hard about how you can prepare to launch this in the best manner possible, involving the fewest number of people possible with the minimum level of information given to them. I agree about Harper's remark: don't start hiring the new ESB teams right now; go as far as you can with your current teams that you can trust."

Then, for the first time, Miller showed a hard and threatening expression. "If this is leaked to the public before the announcement on May thirty-first, you can trust me to find out where the leak came from and to fire and punish those involved. So you better keep your teams under the same pressure and threat to make them keep their mouths shut."

He paused and regained his previous smooth and pleasant look. "I trust you'll all do a great job in this crucial effort. The stakes are high: to save the financial health of the country while preserving the social cohesion of the population, excluding some rich people who won't like it. I hope you're as enthusiastic about it as I am and that you feel what I and the president felt when we worked this out with our G7 colleagues. We are making history, and finally reversing the trend of the last thirty years toward ever more international market competition and dumping, by replacing it with wise international political collaboration. Go for it; I'm counting on you!"

☆ ☆ ☆

The first thing Jessica Frostby did when leaving the meeting was to make sure she was outside hearing distance from any observer. She picked up her mobile phone and placed a call.

"Mark! What I now tell you must stay between us. If anyone finds out I told you, I may be prosecuted for it. They are going nuts! They want to solve the public finance crisis by slamming giant taxes on rich people and larger corporations."

Mark remained silent for a while before saying: "Oh."

Jessica went on, "Don't you see? It will kill the economy."

Mark hummed thoughtfully and then said, "Well, maybe the economy *of the United States*. But at the same time, it might be a blessing for the rest of the world, in particular for the new gold-money system in Iceland."

"What are you talking about?"

"I mean, we're hoping for the gold-money system to grow and become important at global level. But that won't happen if the three hundred thousand souls in Iceland are the only ones to use it."

"So?"

"I mean that the tax increase program might be just what is needed for some wealthy people and large corporations to move to Iceland and convert their assets to gold."

Jessica now caught on to what Mark was saying. "Yes, of course!" She paused. "But do you really think many of them will take such a radical decision?"

"I don't know if they will see it themselves. But maybe some persuasion could do the trick!"

"Mark, that would be great, but may I remind you that you're still a computer programmer looking like a windsurfing bum, unknown to the public. How on earth will you go about to get access to leaders of large corporations?"

Mark laughed as he answered, triumphantly and full of energy: "You know that Bobby got a job at General Retail, the world's largest retail company. I heard he met the CEO when they devised the strategy for the Chinese market. So I think I'll give my old globetrotter friend a call! And our new man in China, Ka Ying, will get a chance to make himself useful!"

"What are you talking about?" Jessica frowned.

"Oh, it's just an idea I got now. But I have to check whether it's feasible. I'll tell you later!"

☆ ☆ ☆

That night, after a long day at work, Steve came home at ten. The day had started with the seven-o'clock meeting and had ended fifteen hours later by a final phone call in his car on his way home. When he arrived at home, Jessica had already had dinner and had long since tucked Lisa into bed. Lisa, who some of their friends jokingly called "Crisis Child," as she was born during the worst of the subprime crisis, was now two and a half years old. She was still taken care of during workdays by a caring babysitter living near their apartment in central Washington. Lisa was a calm and nice young girl. She took every opportunity to be with her parents, with whom she spent less time than most children of her age did.

Steve looked briefly into Lisa's room and saw that she was sleeping. He moved on into the living room and found Jessica lying on the couch, with her feet crossed and her hands behind her head. She was watching a cartoon on TV with a distant expression of boredom on her face, which did not change when she turned her head toward Steve and said, "Hi, honey, how was your day at work after that lunatic meeting this morning? My day sucked because I just wanted to cry out loud about the insanity of what I learned. But I knew I was not allowed to, since that taxation plan is supposed to be some sort of dirty secret to be sprung on the country three months from now."

"Jessica, I wish you wouldn't feel that way about it. After all, the country needs those tax revenues to get out of the crisis once and for all, and those rich people and corporations are able to pay up. So why shouldn't they?"

"Well, I'm too tired tonight to argue with you about the respect for private property rights, or about that fact that the money that will be taxed in most cases has been taxed once or twice already. But I can tell you it makes me really disappointed that you don't recognize the basic value of the right to private property. The country was built on this value."

"Honey, don't say that, you know I respect the American way of living. I just believe we're in a terrible crisis, and in order to protect and safeguard that way of living, we may need to resort to exceptional national efforts."

"Drop it. I said I don't want to hear those bogus arguments in my own living room. Save them for some public speech. But let's talk about the expediency of what is being proposed. Do you realize that it will result in worsening what the country has been suffering from for decades? That's insufficient savings and investments! And contrary to what your government economist herd keeps saying, these are the only things that can increase wealth creation in society.

"Instead of favoring saving and investment, wealth and profits will now be taxed away and will go down the drain into consumption. So in a year or two, the country will be poorer than it is today. And the people who you today claim have no financial safety margins will have even smaller margins. As long as they keep consuming more than they produce, it means that they eat up the wealth taken from richer people. In many cases, they will take advantage of the low interest rates we have today to add to it by some debt-financed consumption! In the meantime, many of the rich people and corporations, at least those who have some self-respect, will leave the country and take their businesses with them. The only people remaining in the United States will be a bunch of unemployed consumers who won't have anything to consume anymore, except the skin and fat on their own bones."

"Don't talk like that! You know I can't stand it!" Steve snapped and, with a touch of dread, said, "I agree that we run a risk of some of those people leaving the country, but what else could we do?"

"You could cut public spending. I believe it could be radically slashed without any negative consequences at all. You pay people to do work that on the free market nobody would pay for, or that would be done better and cheaper; or you just give people money to consume. The only result is to drain capital from the productive system to be consumed by nonworkers instead of being invested in new wealth creation. *That* is what you guys want to protect and maintain. If you succeed in doing it, the result will be the only thing it can be: impoverishment, unemployment, and depletion of the capital stock and productive capacity. And this once rich and proud country will be turned into a giant bunch of beggars!"

"Honey, I don't want to listen to such aggressive talk tonight. I had a hell of a day at work, trying to make up the detailed plan to implement all the new taxes and to create the Economic Solidarity Bill Enforcement Agency. By the way, that agency will be under my supervision and control," he said with pride in his voice, recapturing his usual self and his usual self-satisfaction by shutting out of his mind the words his wife just had spoken.

"Then why don't you rush into bed to get some sleep? Just to let you know, I don't feel like sharing a bed tonight with the future supervisor of the ESBEA, so I'll remain here on the couch!"

Jessica turned the TV set off. She remained stretched out on the sofa, pulled the wool blanket she had on her up above her head, and rolled over to turn her back on Steve. This was her way of saying that their conversation was ended and that he would not get any good-night kiss.

Steve hated having disputes with Jessica, but he had learned not to fight all the way, but rather to step back when it was advisable. So he turned around, walked slowly out of the living room, went to the fridge, and picked up a cold dish, which he would eat in bed.

✼ ✼ ✼

On June 1, the press room of the U.S. Presidency next to the White House was filled to the breaking point with journalists from all over the country. Joseph Miller stood at the lectern with James Mortimer and Steve Harper standing at his sides. Had it not been for their thin builds, they, with their immovable and respectful figures, might have been taken for Miller's bodyguards.

Five minutes after the scheduled time, a delay caused by the large crowd of journalists, Miller introduced the conference. "We are now in a situation of national economic emergency where we need to find additional resources to fund the public spending needed to maintain economic stimulus. We also need to ensure appropriate financing for our new social security system. Most of the American population has suffered badly from a combination of high debt, high house foreclosures, and high unemployment. Therefore, we believe it to be just that those who have been unaffected by these material concerns must now contribute to put the nation back in shape. This is why we expect them to pay new and increased taxes without complaining. This program is really aimed to reinforce the social fabric of our country, and this is why we have decided to call it the Economic Solidarity Bill."

He stopped, and his pause was interpreted by the audience as an opening to ask questions. A journalist on the front row jumped up. "Who are the people supposed to pay more to get the country back in shape?"

"The rich," Miller answered severely. "More specifically, I talk about people owning more than a million dollars of wealth. Of course, the largest corporations in the country will also have to contribute. Therefore, the top thousand corporations will, from now on, pay additional taxes."

The correspondent of a German financial newspaper asked, "Is this a concerted plan by the whole G7? I understand there are similar press conferences in all G7 countries today."

Miller answered briefly. "Well, most of our countries are facing similar problems, so it's not surprising if we come up with similar solutions."

"Never mind," said a small and skinny journalist from one of the largest Washington newspapers with an eager look on his face. "But what are the new taxes the rich people are supposed to pay?"

Miller answered pleasantly, describing the new domestic taxes and the applicable rates. The content of the ESB remained exactly as agreed within the G7 a few months before.

A correspondent of a Chinese financial magazine asked, with more skepticism than the previous speaker, "So these taxes are being introduced across much of the Western world. How come none of the Asian countries are doing the same? And do you have any new taxes which will impact international trade?"

Miller froze for an instant, but quickly hid that the question had surprised him. He wondered just who this journalist was before he gathered himself to answer with his usual smoothness. "Each country is free to decide on its own policies. As we didn't ask for the opinion of China on our current policy program, we won't try to tell them what they should do. This said, we have indeed added measures aimed at reducing imbalances in international trade."

"What imbalances are you talking about?" the Chinese journalist asked with suspicion in his voice.

"Oh, just that products from countries such as China are cheaper than those produced elsewhere, such as in the United States. In order to reduce the undesirable effect of what is the simply the result of some countries maintaining an artificially low value of their own currency, we have indeed decided on a few new taxes."

"What taxes?" the Chinese journalist said with a sudden tension.

"A ten percent tax on American direct investments in developing countries, and a ten percent tax on imports from those countries," Miller answered casually.

"Now, as there seem to be no further questions," Miller declared in spite of the fact that tens of journalists were waving their arms, "we will go back to work."

He put his arms around Steve Harper and James Mortimer, and glanced quickly and happily at each of them, before saying: "Take a good photo of me with these two men, because they represent the progress and the bright future of our country! Steve Harper, on my right, will manage the Economic Solidarity Enforcement Agency, created today. And James Mortimer, on my left, will ensure, in addition to his former role in charge of the U.S. public debt, that the additional hundreds of billions of additional taxes this plan will raise are used in the best manner possible."

✬ ✬ ✬

One week after the announcement of the ESB, Montgomery Benson called Cornelius Hazelton. They had not spoken during the past week, which had been a busy one for both of them.

"Cornelius, how are you? That tax program is a terrible blow."

"Well, to be honest, I feel like I've been run over by a truck. I mean, if I think about it, which I guess I haven't quite done yet. I just noticed that the markets don't seem to worry too much. In spite of a ten percent fall in the value of the largest stocks, a lot of indicators have actually improved. For example, the government bond rates have gone down. I guess the markets expect me and my fellow rich friends, or 'high net-worth individuals,' as the newspapers now call us, to foot the bill to erase the government deficits."

"Cornelius, don't bother about the market reactions. You need to find out exactly what it's going to do to *you*. Have you heard from the ESB Enforcement Agency yet?"

"Yes, I received a letter this morning, asking me to be present in my own office a week from now, on June fifteenth. Apparently I've been singled out as one of their top-priority targets, and they want to come here to assess my wealth for that new tax."

"The earlier that happens, the better it is for you. Then you can start to think about what you can do about it. I'll tell you a couple of things you may want to keep in mind. Because whatever the conclusion of that meeting, my guess is that you will be forced to move fast from then on."

✳ ✳ ✳

On June 15, Cornelius Hazelton showed up at his office at 8:00 a.m., as he always did when not travelling. The man from the ESB Enforcement Agency arrived at nine, and was shown into Hazelton's office by his secretary. As she opened the door of the office, she said with a mechanical voice, "Mr. Hazelton, Mr. Armstrong, Asset Inspector of the ESBEA, here to see you. Please ring me if you need any documents or other assistance."

"Thank you, Elisabeth," Hazelton said and closed the door of his office, before turning to his visitor.

"Mr. Armstrong, what can I do for you?" Hazelton asked slowly. He looked into the eyes of his visitor without showing any particular emotion in his voice, his eyes, or his expression, which all remained neutrally polite.

"As I believe you know, Mr. Hazelton, I have come here to review with you the list of all items composing your personal wealth and to have the list signed by you. The list will be your agreement to the identification and valuation of the objects listed as well as your oath as to the fact that you possess no other eligible assets than those listed. If we find out later that you do, those assets will be taxed with a tax rate of five times the normal wealth tax rate, meaning fifteen percent instead of three percent. The same will apply if you sell such nondeclared assets. You will pay twice the normal tax rates on any capital gains if we find out about it."

"How much would that be?" Hazelton asked.

"Sixty percent instead of thirty," the asset inspector said.

"So I guess I better think twice not to forget to put some item on that list," Hazelton said with a smile that revealed a mix of irony and disdain.

"Yes, that would be advisable," the Asset Inspector, ignoring the emotion in Hazelton's comment, said without emotion.

"So, please explain to me how we should proceed," Hazelton snapped.

"Very well. I have here a list of your assets which has been established by a computerized data-collection process spanning all bank, real estate, and asset broker registers in the country. It also includes information from those countries with which we have information exchange collaboration. As you may know, a certain number of tax havens have only recently accepted to participate in fiscal information exchange, and they have not yet established automatic systems for information transmission. But we will be able to check with all those countries afterward, so please make the effort not to forget anything; we *will* find out.

"Regarding your domestic assets, we requested and already obtained information from all insurance companies where you have declared assets. This helped to establish the list of your assets."

"To be sure I get it right, could you please repeat what types of assets I should include in the inventory?" Hazelton said with a sigh.

"Of course. You should include all material and immaterial assets of a resale value above a thousand dollars, excluding only furniture and other durable consumer goods for your direct and private use. You should include all financial assets such as cash, bank deposits, stocks, mutual funds, bonds, or any derivative financial securities; and also real assets, such as real estate, cars, yachts, land or marketable commodities, jewelry and works of art."

"Am I correct that you ask me to pay a three percent tax corresponding to the total value of all those assets, *yearly?*"

"Indeed, that's the main feature of the Economic Solidarity Bill and what I have come here to calculate right now. But please don't forget the additional capital gain and income taxes, which are also included in the ESB. These will be calculated at year-end to cover all transactions made during the year. As your personal contact person, I will come back to see you then," the asset inspector said, trying awkwardly and with limited success to provide a smile, such as he had learned, Hazelton thought, from customer services personnel in business enterprises.

Hazelton, who started to feel a weird form of disgust, looked out through the window to avoid the embarrassing sight of the asset inspector. The inspector was acting as if he was not there to plunder Hazelton's wealth, but for some regular business or personal appointment of mutual agreement and interest. With his back turned against the asset inspector, Hazleton said, thoughtfully, "Well, we'll see about that."

Hazelton turned back to face the asset inspector. "Would you explain to me how you will estimate the value of the items I should be taxed on? Regarding currency and bank deposits, I guess it's straightforward, but what about other assets?"

"We will estimate them at a current market price, which will appear on the list established today and which you will validate."

"What about assets that are not publicly traded? Such as for example my privately owned company, Hazelton Growth Capital. I am sole shareholder of this company, which owns majority or minority shares in around a hundred separate businesses around the world."

The asset inspector now was more and more at ease and answered pleasantly. "Much like in any of your business transactions. You and I will agree about a valuation, based on information at hand. But, of course, if I later in our verification process find out you were withholding information or making an inappropriate evaluation, then I can retroactively adjust the evaluation upward and apply the mentioned higher penalty tax rates."

"And what proof would you have to provide when doing such a retroactive reassessment?" Hazelton asked with growing disbelief.

"It's enough for me to prove that you owned the item in question. Regarding the appropriateness of the evaluation, that's up to me to judge. This may feel intimidating, but please understand that this feature is only aimed at discouraging dishonest declarations. And I'm sure you wouldn't indulge in any such thing."

Hazelton did not answer this but instead tried to speed up a meeting he was more and more impatient to finish. "Now please show me your preliminary list of my assets."

The asset inspector pulled out a pile of papers from his leather suitcase and pushed it over the table. Hazelton looked at it for a long while. The summary page of the list contained only seven items, sorted by order of increasing value: Mrs. Hazelton's jewelry, 75 thousand dollars; three cars, 150 thousand dollars; art works, 275 thousand dollars; cash and bank deposits, 1 million dollars; mutual fund pension plan, 1 million dollars; and real estate, including a house in San Francisco and a flat in Aspen, 1 million dollars. The last item was by far the largest: shares in Hazelton Growth Capital—96.5 million dollars.

After looking through the window again and shaking his head slowly as if wanting to wake up from a bad dream, Hazelton asked, simply, "So you estimate my total wealth to one hundred million dollars. Am I correct that this means I should pay three million dollars per year in wealth tax?"

"Well, yes, at least the first year. For next year, we'll see, that will depend on whether your incomes and new wealth will be larger than the tax you paid this year—whether your total wealth increases or falls."

"Of course," Hazelton said. "I think that your estimation looks all right, so I won't argue about it. I just have one question: how do you propose I provide three million dollars in cash, given that I currently own one million dollars in cash and ninety-nine million dollars of nonliquid assets?"

"Well, that's really none of my concern. It would be most intrusive of me to have opinions on such a personal matter," The asset inspector shrugged with an awkward smile.

Hazelton looked at him with an increasing but detached curiosity, as if trying to interpret the behavior of a sociopath or that of a being from another planet. After some hesitation, he managed to say, with disbelief, "So you're saying you leave me the freedom to decide, in order to pay my *first year's* due of this new wealth tax, whether I wish to keep my house, or half of my pension savings plan, or half of my bank deposits? Or if I would just keep my wife's jewelry and our cars and artworks while selling all our real estate and pension savings? Knowing I have three and a half million of sellable assets and that I need to free up three million to pay that tax."

"Yes, of course you're free to choose. But, even if that's none of my business, could you not also sell some shares of your business, bringing in a partner into HGC?"

"I don't want any partner in HGC; that business is *mine*."

"But HGC could sell some of its holdings and provide you a dividend?"

"On which I would pay an increased capital gains tax before giving away all that's left in the wealth tax?"

"Well, that would depend on the size of the dividend."

"Mr. Armstrong, I will save both of us some valuable time this morning. I'll sign this list with the valuations you have proposed. I have looked through the detailed list of the holdings of HGC. I believe it's roughly correct, even if there is no sure way to tell, given that most of those companies aren't listed on any stock exchange. And I don't think I have forgotten any other assets. You know, my life is quite focused on the items you saw on that list: my wife, HGC, our two residences, and the cars we use to move between them. I do have two wonderful grown children as well, but I appreciate the fact they are not yet counted as a taxable asset."

At this point Hazelton stopped, stood, walked over to the window, and looked again out on the green environment of the Palo Alto business campus where the HGC office was located. After a short while, he turned back to the table where the asset inspector was still sitting, and bent down and signed the wealth declaration and tax calculation form.

He then walked over and opened the door, showing Armstrong the way out. "There you are, Mr. Armstrong. I hope you're content with having obtained what you came here for, in less than one hour's time. Please allow me one last question, though."

"Of course," the asset inspector said with a relieved smile, having recognized that Hazelton seemed to feel even better than he did himself.

"Would you please remind me who has to pay the new wealth tax?"

"As specified in the text of the Economic Solidarity Bill, all private individuals with a total personal wealth of above one million dollars who are residents of the United States of America as of June thirtieth this year. As you know, most of our fellow Western countries have enacted similar legislation in order to fight the crisis." The Asset Inspector sighed, and added, "As a matter of fact, the deal with the G7 and the European Union forced us, the United States, to renounce on taxing those of our citizens who live abroad. The other countries don't have such rules, and feared they might lose out if we kept them. So from now on, the only asset class that is taxable locally, independently of the residence of the owner, is real estate."

"Thank you for your answer," Hazelton replied courteously, and showed his visitor out of the room, where his secretary took over to follow the asset inspector down to the ground-floor reception area.

CHAPTER 16:
The Salvation of the Damned

Two hours later, at noon that same day, the phone rang in the living room where Monica Hazelton was sitting on a couch, surfing the Internet on her laptop computer. She recognized the number as coming from her husband's office. She picked up the receiver. "Hi, honey, are you bored at work today? You rarely call me this early."

"Monica, I'm sorry to say this, but we have to leave the country. Now. Fast. We must have a new fiscal residence within two weeks; otherwise, government will take our house or our retirement savings or our cars, or maybe all of it unless we give them your jewelry and our artwork."

"Cornelius, what on earth are you talking about? I don't understand!"

"You've heard about the new so-called economic solidarity bill. Well, it's just a cover-up to fleece the wealthy people in the country! We are to pay sky-high taxes on our wealth in order to reduce, for some time, the government budget deficit."

"But can't we afford to pay that tax? I heard it was to be three percent."

"Yes, on total wealth. Every year. You should know that we own one hundred million dollars, according to their calculation, of which only one million is in cash and bank deposits and two and a half million is locked up in our houses, cars, artwork, and jewelry. The remaining ninety-six and half million is my stake in HGC. How on earth could I pay three million dollars, per year, without either selling all our assets or selling a share of my own company, which I would rather die than do?"

His wife was silent for a while, and then she said, "Oh, my God! What are we going to do?"

"The important thing is that we move out of the United States before July first. If we get out in time and become residents in a new country, we won't have to pay the tax for this year and obviously not for the following years either. The thing is we don't have a lot of places to go—most of Europe has introduced similar laws, just as Canada and Japan."

"So where do you want us to go?" Monica yelled, more and more worried.

"I propose that we move to Iceland. They don't have this kind of wealth tax. And, most important, this is where I now have my most promising ventures, thanks to the gold-based monetary system which Montgomery Benson helped them create."

"But, honey, they almost put you in jail last year! Are you sure we'll be safe over there?"

"Yes, don't worry. That was just a mean scheme organized by those who want to destroy gold money. But I don't think they will be able to do any harm from now on."

"I hope you're right. Do Montgomery and Angela also live in Iceland, or will they move there?" Mrs. Hazelton said with a glimpse of hope in her voice, as she would appreciate to be close to these friends.

"No, not yet, and I don't think they will in the short term. Montgomery isn't affected by that tax. But I know he spends a lot of time in Iceland, around a week per month. He works as a special advisor to the president and the finance minister on monetary affairs. He also gives advice to business leaders who come there to set up shop and who want to grasp the workings of the new gold-based monetary system."

"Iceland..." Mrs. Hazelton said thoughtfully. "Do you think we would be happy there?"

"Honey, it's the place in the world where I would most like to live, at present. You have not yet been there with me, but there's a fantastic atmosphere nowadays, as if they were rebuilding civilization, which, in a way, they're doing. Iceland is the only place in the world where people's money is now safe from inflation. The weather is kind of chilly and misty. But then again, we're used to living in San Francisco. The climate is actually quite similar, though colder."

"OK, Cornelius, let's go there, if we need to make a quick decision. But what about our children? Do you think they will stay here alone?"

"They can, if they want to. I mean, they're twenty-five and twenty-three years old now; they can manage alone when they get out of college and start to work. Or they may come with us. We'll let them decide. I have a feeling Patrick might want to come work with one of my businesses over there. Regarding Samantha, I don't know. If she wants to work in the movie industry, she sure would be better off to stay in California."

"All right, I'll call them today. But when are we leaving, and where should we stay in Iceland?"

"I just talked to Pete Bagnelli, one of my men over there. He is watching out for a flat that we can rent. I think we should plan to build our own house as soon as we can. Land prices are still low, but I don't think they will remain so for long."

"Honey?"

"Yes?"

"Are you sure we're going to be all right?"

"Yes I am. I think this will be a new start for us, and, I hope, for the whole of civilization. I think most people today don't know what a free society can be like, after last century, which was marked by wars and ever-increasing government intervention. So don't worry; just start packing your bags. I'll keep making phone calls to arrange our trip and everything else. We need not bring all our stuff directly, since we're able to keep our house. Think about it: we're able to keep it because we leave. Had we stayed, we would have had to sell it to be able to pay the tax!"

"That really is an insane policy. Don't they count on other people doing the same thing as we do?"

"Not this year, they think they have outsmarted people by leaving only a few weeks for people to get out if they want to avoid this year's tax."

"And what about next year?"

"I don't have the impression that the people who are our masters think that far. Or, as a maximum, they think about the next election. I heard it said that these taxes only impact one percent of the population. So they figure we are too few to change the course of any election."

"Cornelius, you know I'm not religious, but there's only one expression that comes to my mind: God save America."

"Yes, honey. And I think the only thing that can save America is if Americans come to understand what is about to happen. People may need to experience something terribly bad in order to understand what the good is. Look at Europe—the only countries that are not going along with the tax increases and the bureaucratization of society are the countries of Eastern Europe. I think this is because they have people still alive with an experience about what government-enforced solidarity can lead to: a dictatorship filled with citizens turned beggars and slaves."

"All right," she said, calming down. She suddenly gasped, full of worry. "How much time did you say we have before we must get out of here? And how will we make it?"

Cornelius was unable to hide that he was worried too when he answered. "We've got twelve days counting from today, before we need to have settled down in Iceland. I don't know how we'll get there. I heard commercial flights to Iceland for the rest of June are already sold out due to the large number of people that are about to leave the country. And a boat trip is way too long. I need to find a workaround." He paused for a long while, then said, "Honey! I've got it! I think I know how we'll get out of here in time."

✦ ✦ ✦

On the night of June 20, Jessica Frostby once again had had a bad fight with her husband Steve, triggered by Steve's bragging about the progress of the ESBEA activities he was supervising. As a result of their fight, she spent the night on the couch in their living room, for the third time in less than three months. However, while Steve quickly fell asleep after a long and tough day, Jessica remained awake. She was feeling more and more awkward, having to refrain from speaking out at work about her opinions on the policies being pursued. And when she came home at night, she found herself sitting at the dinner table with the supervisor of what she considered one of the most evil organizations she had ever known.

The only reason that she was still able to cope with her life was that she had found a safety valve to get rid of some steam. She was connecting to the

FMRM network Web site to catch up on news of interest to her and, above all, to talk with people who shared her ideals and worldview. She rarely met such people during her daily work at the Federal Reserve or in the G20 central bank coordination group. The hostility she aroused at work was palpable, and she had started to fear retaliation from her employer regarding her views. Therefore, Jessica had decided to use a pseudonym on the FMRM network. She called herself "Heart of Gold."

Using the pseudonym, she had extensive conversations with numerous persons, some of them using their real names, others doing as Jessica was. She would generally reveal that she's a U.S. citizen with a job giving her insight into monetary policy, but beyond that, she would provide little specifics about her own life and work.

There was one exception where her curiosity to learn more about the other person drove her to reveal a bit more about herself: in discussions with Latin Freeman. He was a very cultivated and polite person who had been to the best schools in his country. He became charming and admirable by Jessica's standards when admitting that it was only now, at thirty-five years old, that he admitted he was really starting to learn some valuable knowledge. He had told Jessica that he had gotten that from attending Professor Benson's online classes on economics. She had heard from Mark that Benson's online classes were having a great success, and she was curious and happy to talk to one of his newer students. She had not revealed that she had once been a student of Benson's back in college; that would have gone too far in revealing her identity. But she had told Latin Freeman that she was a longtime admirer and student of the teachings of Benson, and that she used that knowledge to understand world events.

It was 1:00 a.m. in Washington when she logged on, meaning it was seven in the morning in Europe. She saw a green light next to Latin Freeman's icon on her FMRM friends list. She fired away a chat to him. "Already up in early morning? How are you?"

An answer came, after a few seconds. "Not so good. Actually, I feel terrible."

"Why?"

"I'm participating in the implementation of the new policies decided by the G7. It's part of my job, so I have to do it, but I fear we're about to kill human civilization, and I hate being part in making it happen."

"I know. I feel the same. Over here, they call it the Economic Solidarity Bill. The name makes me sick, because I believe solidarity is a person-to-person feeling based on voluntary and sincere desire to help someone one cares about and considers worthy of help. The current scheme based on the idea 'pay up all you can or we'll throw you into jail' is so far from true solidarity as we could come."

"I agree. In my country, they call it 'whoever is able to pay will pay for the country, by solidarity.' That's the official slogan, but I prefer the one coined by one of the few remaining freedom-oriented Internet sites over here: 'If you're rich, either you're racketeered or you get out of here.' The public leadership doesn't like this one, since it highlights the possibility for people to leave the country, and the fact that their taxation scheme *is* a sort of racket. I guess some of these people *will* leave the country—I mean we already had a tax on wealth before, of around 1%; it now is between 3% and 4%, *per year!* A lot of people will actually have to sell their assets in order to be able to pay the tax. It will be worst for those who have most of their wealth in a family house for example, they may be forced to sell it or take a mortgage on it even though the house has been paid decades ago! I mean, when you think about this for a second, the world is really going nuts!"

"Yes," was the short but instant response that Jessica provided. Then she changed the subject of their conversation. "Can I ask you a personal question, Latin Freeman?"

"Of course, Heart of Gold. What else have we been talking about since we met? I mean, philosophical and political convictions are the most personal things you can imagine!"

"Right, but I wanted to ask you where and how you find strength to remain in a job where you participate in the forces of destruction. Where you can't inverse the course of events, even though you know better."

"Well, like you I guess, I get it from the FMRM network, and all the people I meet here, and from Professor Benson's economics classes. And there's of course my wife, with whom I can always talk, although I start to feel as if she's acting more as my psychologist than as my soul mate."

Jessica replied quickly, with heightened interest.

"Please explain."

"You see, she always cares about me and says she understands me, and gives me compliments about being so smart and having such a good job. For sure, I'm in the top political leadership clique, but so is she, as we met in a special postgraduate school which breeds political leaders. But she actually doesn't agree with me about any of my deepest convictions.

"When we met, it was not an issue, since I was just like her, a brain-washed product of that school. Just as the rest of our school system, it breeds people to hate free society and to consider public servants and bureaucrats as the only noble professions. But during my career, I have met some people, especially one woman who I remember well, who challenged my world view and made me think about fundamental issues.

"That was something I hadn't done since I was a kid, because our schooling system just teaches you that truth has no role in social affairs. They say the only thing that counts is what comes out of public opinion polls. In my postgraduate school for politicians, we focused on how to turn that into an advantage to give us more power. But this woman, and a few other people I have met more recently through FMRM, made me realize that one should never stop thinking about what is right. And that a majority of people can be terribly wrong, and quite often are. For example, in the evolution of science that was more the rule than the exception. I mean, most major discoveries have been done by someone who completely challenged current certitudes and came up with new ideas. When thinking about this, I realized we could have the same situation in current politics and monetary affairs. That woman, and now Professor Benson, have taught me more about the world and about economics than I ever learned from tens of years of so called top schools."

Jessica had not dared interrupt this long message with a question, but now she took over.

"I see. I understand. I mean, it's kind of the same thing for me. I'm married to a man who doesn't agree at all with my convictions. And that was the case even when we met. But as he's a gifted politician, he used his skill to make me believe he agreed with me, although he actually didn't. We have now been married for almost ten years, and I've started to realize it's becoming unbearable. Because I now see through the way he behaves. I have the feeling he's trying to cheat me, and to cheat reality. He seems to try to make us both believe we're a fine couple, although, objectively, we should hate each other and fight each other! I still keep the hope of changing his deepest convictions, but I'm afraid it won't work. Because I realize that he doesn't *have* any real convictions at all, except for an irresistible desire to manipulate people!" "Heart of Gold, I won't give you personal advice. I don't think either of us needs another amateur shrink. But just watch out where this leads you. There may come a point when you will have to choose between the integrity of your mind and some major things you have hooked up with during your life. Your husband or your job, for example. I don't want to tell you what to do. But don't sacrifice the integrity of your mind. I have learned that one must not. I don't think anyone can do it and still be sane."

"Well, I think that *was* some good advice! I'll have to go to sleep now, and you should be off to work. Talk to you soon, Latin Freeman."

"Sweet dreams, Heart of Gold."

✲ ✲ ✲

The evening of June 29 was hot across most of the United States, and as usual in the state of Nevada, temperatures were way above the U.S. average. However, as the sun was setting across the northern part of the state, Highway 50, for good reasons called the "Loneliest Road in America," displayed an exceptional sight. Where cars would usually drive for an hour without meeting a living soul, more than fifty trucks were now pushing east from California. They were all going to the same destination: the Battle Mountain Airport, a desolate airfield counting only ten flights per year.

The flight this night was just as exceptional as the cortege of trucks: it was a large military aircraft belonging to a retired billionaire named Kilby Rock. Rock had helped Cornelius Hazelton to get started in venture banking two decades earlier. Hazelton had now helped his former mentor by advising him how to escape the new wealth tax. Rock was very grateful, as he was in the same situation as Hazelton. Virtually all his wealth was held in businesses he owned and supervised, and he could not imagine having to sell them just to pay a tax. So he and his wife had taken the same decision as Cornelius and Monica Hazelton: to leave the country before June 30 and move to Iceland. And they had found no other means to do that except for using Rock's old but well-maintained favorite collection item: a military transportation aircraft able to carry two hundred passengers, and a hundred tons of cargo.

Three days earlier, Cornelius Hazelton had rented the truck that he and Monica were traveling in. A driver, part of the rental deal, had helped them to load their belongings and then to drive the truck. It now contained all the things they had been able to pack in a week's time. When the truck entered the airfield, one of Rock's men checked their identity.

"Hazelton? Park your truck over there on the left. A team of three people is waiting to get your stuff out of your truck and into the two containers that are set aside for you."

"Thanks," Hazelton said with a yawn. He soon brightened up when he saw the towering figure of Kilby Rock, wearing jeans, a rugged trapper's shirt, and a cowboy hat. Rock walked up to him, his arms spread out.

"Cornelius! Come here, young friend!" Rock said loudly as he squeezed Hazelton against his big stomach and held him with his both arms.

Hazelton smiled and looked hesitantly around. "If I'm correct, we are to take off within two hours. But I see tens of trucks filled to be unloaded! Let's assume we're able to load all that in one hour. But how on earth will U.S. customs have the time to clear all the stuff?"

Rock smiled happily at his former apprentice and shook his head. "Cornelius, this ain't the Los Angeles International Airport! There isn't a single U.S. customs clerk here. That was one of the things I arranged when I planned for this flight. I kept a low profile about it all. You know, it's a *private* flight. I know we're supposed to fill out loads of paperwork. But we'll have time to do that once we arrive in Iceland, and then we'll send the papers here by mail. What counts is that by tomorrow afternoon, we're all able to sign up as Icelandic residents, and go drop off our emigration sheets at the U.S. Embassy."

"I see," Hazelton said with a smile. "I just hope no one will try to try to stop our flight."

"Cornelius, don't worry!" Rock shouted. "Do you know how many people are leaving the United States this week? I heard it's almost a hundred thousand people. That means five hundred flights like ours. Sure, there are the regular commercial flights. But I can tell you, from having talked to a number of friends, that there are also hundreds of private jets like ours making the trip to Iceland, or to some other place where there aren't any ESB taxes. Before the U.S. Army starts shooting down aircrafts filled with Americans, I think there needs to be more to it than what they call tax evasion. Damn, they asked for it!"

Hazelton looked thoughtfully at Rock. "A hundred thousand people leaving the country...I hear the average wealth of these people is four million dollars. That means four hundred billion dollars are vanishing."

"Yep!" Rock added. "That money won't finance much U.S. activity in the future. I heard fifty billion will go straight into gold money. That should put the dollar and the euro in tailspin. As you know, I have labeled our flight 'The Salvation of the Damned.' I also believe our disappearance will lead to the damnation of those politicians and public figures who consider themselves as saints! Anyway, Cornelius, Monica, we need to get moving to the aircraft. Grab your hand luggage and follow me."

Most of the trucks that had crossed the Nevada desert had now arrived, and their contents were being loaded into the giant airplane. Hazelton greeted a few of the other passengers and then climbed up a ladder into the plane. He held his wife's hand and turned to kiss her. "I love you." She just smiled and kissed him in return.

Before they sat down, Hazelton turned around to look out. His last sight of the United States before leaving was a vast desert plain of Nevada, lit by feeble moonlight. He thought briefly about the fading greatness of the country where he had lived all of his life and said, in a low and sad voice, "I used to love you too, and I'd love to be able to love you again."

The July heat in Houston was suffocating. Mark Lomack, Bobby Cheston, and Ka Ying felt like prisoners in their business suits as they crossed the giant lawn in front of the General Retail corporate headquarters. The half hour of waiting in a meeting room that followed didn't bother them at all, as the room was air-conditioned, and they relaxed while drinking refreshments offered to them by the secretary. The calm suddenly ended, when Walter Samuelson, the CEO of General Retail, entered the room.

"Hi, there! I understand you're the two whiz kids whom Bobby Cheston wished me to meet. I hope you have something important to tell me and that you'll get it out fast. I've got fifteen minutes before I need to leave for the airport," the CEO said with a sharp and loud voice, shaking hands with Mark and Ka Ying, and then with Bobby.

Mark cleared his throat. "I'm the founder and leader of the Free Men, Real Money network. Ka Ying here is my man in China. I launched this network in order to promote change toward sound money, which would make it possible to improve protection of individual freedom and property rights."

Frowning, Samuelson looked at Mark. "Now that sounds like a noble goal, but what do you expect *me* to do about it? The way in which I improve people's lives is by offering them low-cost and high-quality consumer products through our retail outlets."

"Yes, I know, but we didn't come here to ask you to do something for us. We came here to offer to help *you*."

"How on earth could you do that?" Samuelson snapped skeptically.

"Mr. Samuelson," Mark said, standing and walking over to a whiteboard with a pen in his hand. "Can you remind us of your profits of last year?"

"Around twenty-four billion dollars, like the year before," Samuelson said proudly.

"With the former corporate profits tax rate of thirty-five percent, you paid eight-point-four billion dollars in tax on profits. Now, with the Economic Solidarity Bill, you will pay twelve billion dollars. If we look at it another way, your after-tax profits are down from fifteen-point-six billion to twelve billion— a decrease of twenty-three percent. If you don't do anything about it, this may soon turn into a twenty-three percent fall of your stock market value."

"So what do you propose I do?"

Mark smiled. "We have had preliminary discussions with legislators of Hong Kong and China. They are likely to accept the deal we are looking into. It consists of three features: moving the headquarters and white-collar work- ers of suffering U.S. companies to Hong Kong and increasing your presence in China. I saved the best to the end: while paying the Hong Kong corporate tax rate of sixteen and half percent, you will be allowed to have your account- ing in gold as currency, with your corporate cash reserves in a gold account in Iceland."

Samuelson froze and scrutinized Mark. "All right, I see the point in mov- ing HQ to Hong Kong. With that tax rate, we would have seventy percent more after-tax profits, twenty billion instead of twelve. But what's the point in hav- ing accounting in gold, instead of in dollars?"

Mark kept writing the numbers supporting the discussion on the white- board. "Let me take the last few minutes of your time to explain what I call 'tax on artificial profits caused by inflation.'"

Samuelson sighed, looking at his watch. "Go ahead. But you better make it short and sharp."

"Sure," Mark said. "You have sales of about four hundred fourteen billion dollars and costs of around three hundred ninety billion, yielding profits of twenty-four billion. But actually you real profits are lower, so you pay more tax than you should."

"What the hell are you talking about?" Samuelson said, offended.

"Let me explain. Over the last ten years, by the combined effect of Federal Reserve money creation and bank lending, the quantity of dollars increased by eight percent per year. Many people figure that this cancels out with respect to profits and taxes, as both costs and revenues increase. But they forget that costs are expended before corresponding revenues come in. You need to build a store before you can put goods in it to be sold. You need to buy the goods from suppliers before you can sell them.

"Let's assume that a third of the costs you need to expend in order to get the revenues of a given year have to be expended the year before. This means that if we want to compare your profits and costs without the profits being overvalued, so to speak, we would have to remove a third of eight percent from your revenues. So if we take away the inflation effect, your real profits are around thirteen billion, not twenty-four billion. And the tax you'd pay would be half of what you pay today. That would be your actual taxes if you had your accounting in gold.

"So if we combine the effect of a tax rate three times lower than the U.S. rate, with a taxable profit half of what it is today, you would pay six times less taxes than if you stay here in the United States. Mr. Samuelson, given these numbers, is there anything that might stop you from doing what we propose?"

Samuelson again sighed and looked out the window at the large, sun-drenched Texas plain. "I created this company to make profits, for sure. But I also wish to provide cheap and high-quality food to the American people. I don't want to let them down."

Looking straight into Samuelson's eyes, Mark tilted his head and said with a gentle but firm voice, "Sir, you know better than I do that you already did more than most people to help others. Your stores will remain even if you move your head office out, so you will keep doing good to the American people. You and your shareholders should not be fleeced by a law punishing the good for being good. So whatever arguments you may weigh into your decision, never *ever*, doubt your moral right to salvage the wealth of your company and of your shareholders."

Samuelson looked at the faces of the three men in the room, who were all nodding as if to help convince him. "All right, thank you for coming here. I will discuss this with our supervisory board. Now I have to leave. Is there anything I can do for you to return the courtesy of coming here to advise me?"

Ka Ying stood. "Yes, there is. We are soon going to China and Hong Kong to try to close the deal we're talking about. They are quite positive, since they're really angry about the penalty tax the Western countries introduced on Chinese exports and on Western direct investments in China. Still, they don't like piecemeal transactions, and they don't want us to waste their time."

"So what?" Samuelson said.

Ka Ying answered, with some embarrassment. "They said they would accept to cut a deal, but only if it's spectacular. They asked us to enroll at least ten of the hundred largest U.S. corporations. Since you are the first one we talk to, we need at least nine more!"

Samuelson smiled, and said as he shook the hands of his visitors before leaving the room in a hurry, "Oh, is that all? Of course, I meet with fellow CEOs several times a month. For example, this week-end I'll be at an outing with the CEOs of General Automobiles, American Electric, the American

Food & Wear Company, and General Aerospace. They are all the largest and most profitable companies in their respective businesses. Since I think they would like to remain in that position, I believe they will be very interested in your ideas!"

✵ ✵ ✵

"I wish you all welcome to our new home! I hope you like it as much as we do!"

Cornelius Hazelton smiled radiantly and raised his wine glass in a toast as he looked around the faces of the people he and his wife Monica had invited to their housewarming party to celebrate their move into their new house in a new country.

They had come to Iceland four months earlier, staying at first in a rental apartment in Reykjavik which Pete Bagnelli had helped them find. As soon as they arrived, they had bought a piece of land and launched the construction of a house. The house was now finished, and they had just been able to move in this week. The house was located southwest of Reykjavik, on a hill just a one-minute walk away from the Atlantic Ocean. The house had been built in wood, in two levels of five rooms each, with a vast terrace on the upper level accessible by large floor-to-ceiling transparent sliding doors. Inside was a large living room with a fireplace made in lava rock against the right wall, providing much-needed light and heating during the winter, which was now starting as mid-October approached.

The visitors Mr. and Mrs. Hazelton had invited for their housewarming party were seated on the corner couches in front of the fireplace. There was Montgomery Benson, who was in Iceland for the week for work. He had brought his Icelandic friend and associate Ivar Larsen, who had also been helpful to Hazelton. There were Hazelton's two young CEOs, Laura Dalaghan and Pete Bagnelli, and Mark Lomack. Mark was on a visit in order to write a story for his Web site: "Iceland's Gold-based Monetary System—History Written in Two Years." The last visitor was the one who had travelled the farthest: Bobby Cheston from China. He was spending two weeks in Iceland meeting businessmen, including Cornelius Hazelton. He was helping them to establish contacts with Chinese businesses for the many types of goods imports that Iceland now needed, given its rapidly increasing and quite affluent population.

Monica Hazelton came out of the kitchen with a plate of snacks, which she put down on the coffee table in front of the fireplace. She sat as her husband continued addressing the group.

"Even though what has happened to us still feels strange, I must say I'm satisfied with how things have turned out, and I think Monica and I will be happy in this new house and in Iceland."

She interrupted her husband. "Cornelius, everybody in this room agrees you're such a great speaker. But I think there's an even better way to share an understanding of the recent evolution of Iceland. I propose to turn on today's special television show, *How Iceland Was Transformed by Gold Money.* Is that fine for everybody?" she said, looking around the room.

She received enthusiastic nods from all the visitors, and her husband said, "Of course, Monica; that's a great idea."

Monica Hazelton turned on the TV set, just as the news anchor of the Ice TV Network, Lisa Ivarsen, introduced the show.

"Welcome everybody to this special edition providing a close look at the extraordinary evolution our country has undergone in the last two years. From being the pariah of the financial markets, we're now the most attractive place for foreign bank deposits. Previously a country of around three hundred thousand people, we now have a population more than twice as large, reinforced by investors, businessmen and workers from all parts of the world. In order to review this unbelievable development, we will have some short comments from different people who have lived through this transformation.

"Properly, I will start with the man who made it happen: our president, Sigfrid Gudjohnsen. Mister President, what do you wish to say to the people of Iceland, and to the rest of the world, two years after we started to use gold as money?"

The president, who was sitting in front of a camera in the presidential office, said, "I wish to say I'm very happy we took this decision, and my only regret is that we didn't do it earlier. Then again, the severe crisis we had in our economy was decisive to make it happen. In this situation, we accepted to study and eventually decide on something we might have considered preposterous, had it been presented to us in a context without a financial crisis. But we had everything to win, and we got advice from a number of excellent experts, above all from Professor Benson of San Francisco.

"So we took this crucial step. We went through a tough period in the beginning, when counterfeiters tried to abuse our new system. But we fought them back, and our gold-money system came out of that crisis even stronger than it was before. The results are available for everybody to see. But nevertheless, the minister of Finance will spell out to you the economic numbers behind what should be called what it is: a revolution of our economy and of our society!"

The camera moved to show a smiling finance minister. "Indeed, as the president said, we have seen a remarkable evolution of our economy. While our population has doubled, our national product has almost tripled! This is due to the large number of wealthy individuals and of head offices of large Western companies that have moved here over the last months. These people wanted to escape from the recent so called ESB taxes introduced across most of the Western world. Our GDP per person will this year be close to one-point-seven kilos of gold, or, for any foreign viewers who still insist on speaking in paper-money reference: sixty thousand U.S. dollars.

"Regarding our government debt, it has been significantly reduced over these two years, and it is now only a few percents of our GDP. Since our government budget has shown a major surplus for two years, we have paid back most of the debt, and the remainder will be liquidated before the end of the first quarter next year. From then on, Iceland will not have public debt anymore. At least as long as I'm Finance Minister."

"Could you explain this last point?" Lisa Ivarsen asked. "Our viewers, especially people abroad who may want to minimize our success, might think that it's due only to wealthy immigrants providing a lot of tax revenue. One may wonder how moving to gold, as such, would lead to a reduction of public deficits?"

The finance minister answered with the same confident smile. "That's a good question, and I'll be happy to answer it. Indeed, changing from paper money to gold doesn't, in itself, change the situation of public finance. What changes is our decision that government will never again dilute the value of people's money in order to finance public spending or to be able to more easily pay back old debt. Moving to gold, we first recognized the idea that the only money government can spend is money raised in taxes. Second, we also recognized that taxes should be as low as possible, as growth can and will emerge only based on private investment. That is made possible when people and businesses are able to keep as much as possible of their wealth.

"The numbers from our two first years with gold money illustrate my point: the taxation level in Iceland is now below twenty percent of GDP, and we still have a major budget surplus. Obviously, those who claimed that government 'stimulus spending' would be necessary to generate growth have also been proven wrong. Every economic indicator is growing: production, consumption, investment, productivity, you name it; *except* government spending!"

Lisa Ivarsen looked straight into the TV camera. "Thank you very much; that was our president and our finance minister. Let's turn to our guests in the TV studio. The first is Malcolm Perkins. He emigrated from the United Kingdom to Iceland a few months ago. He will answer this question: 'What are the rich people doing who come to Iceland? Are they just sitting around with their gold hidden away, living off the interest of their financial placements?' Malcolm, please tell us your story."

"Right, thank you. I can assure you that the stereotype of the unproductive capitalist is as false in my case as it has been through history. I left the U.K. because I was no longer able to work and invest freely. How come? Well, I was subject to the new wealth tax for so-called rich people. But if I had paid it, my ability to keep investing in new business ventures would have disappeared, which is my main activity as a business angel. Since I have come here, I have already invested in four new ventures, all quite different. I helped the founder of a spectacular spa to install it in the middle of real geysers out in the countryside. I have helped the software company which creates new technology for the gold-coin automatic teller machines. My third project was to launch a large Japanese restaurant. Such food is becoming highly demanded as the population of Iceland becomes more international. My fourth project is the most capital intensive one, and here I'm only a minority owner: it's a geothermal energy production project, where I signed up as investor for a project started by a large, private energy company."

"Thank you, Malcolm, for your testimonial," Lisa Ivarsen said. "I believe you have shown us what great contribution people like yourself have given the economic development of Iceland. Some people may still find your situation, as a wealthy investor, quite far from their own daily life. In order to complete the picture of what we call 'the new faces of Iceland,' I have also invited Martin Rowling, an American who left his hometown in Illinois in order to come to live in Iceland with his family. Martin, please tell us your story."

Martin Rowling cleared his throat and looked a bit intimidated about being on live television. "Right. I was just a regular manufacturing worker back in Illinois. I had worked for twenty years in the same plant, building parts for the automotive industry. Two years ago, I heard about Iceland's move to gold, and a friend told me about the Free Men, Real Money network. I went to the Web site and started reading, and I read a lot in the next days and weeks, following links to many locations. Among all the things I learned, a few of them are key to me. The first is how central banks, like the Fed in the United States, are reducing the value of people's savings by creating ever more paper money. I can tell you about this since I've been saving for fifteen years in order to be able to send my two kids to college. I have always put my money in treasury bills and the like. But when I learned that the dollar quantity in the USA had increased by eight percent per year over ten years, I understood what was going on and that most of the savings I put away was just going down some evil drain. With a return of three percent on my bonds, my money actually lost five percent of its value—every year!—while the cost of the education I was going to pay with that money kept increasing, in proportion to the increase in the U.S. money supply.

"That was almost two years ago, just after Iceland moved to gold. The week after, I transferred all my savings to a gold deposit account in Iceland, and from then on, I have had all my paychecks sent directly to that account. I paid my U.S. bills with a bank card backed by gold. I felt good about this, because from then on I was no longer being robbed; I was the most inflation proofed consumer and worker you could imagine."

"But you still remained living in the United States for one more year," Lisa Ivarsen pointed out. "What made you take the additional step of moving to Iceland with your family?"

"It happened half a year ago. The plant I worked in was a small business, with around three hundred employees. Our boss was a nice guy who had kept us on for a long time. He had earned quite a lot of money, but all of it was held in stock in his business; over time, he had got a lot of stock options from the founder and initial owner. So he ran into trouble with the new ESB wealth taxes—he was forced to sell a large chunk of the company shares he owned, to be able to pay that tax. But he wanted to stay in the USA in spite of all that. He once told us, 'I'll manage; I'll just have to work a little harder.' Then it turned out that our major customers in the automotive industry were hurt by another new tax, the one that increased the tax on profits of large companies. All of them decided therefore to squeeze their subcontractors, and that's how the plant I had worked in went bust four months ago. And *that* is when I decided to move to Iceland with my wife and my two kids."

"But did you not consider getting a job in some other plant? I mean, the United States is a large country, and I believe there are still a lot of companies doing automotive manufacturing in Illinois?" Ivarsen asked.

Rowling looked thoughtfully into the camera, before answering. "Well, you're right, I guess I could have gotten another job. But what really made me leave was another thing I learned on the Free Men, Real Money network, from a lecture of Professor Benson which I attended."

"What was that?" Ivarsen said with authentic curiosity.

"You know I told you the main goal of my life savings was to be able to pay college for my kids. Benson explained something which now is obvious to me, but which I had never heard before. I realized from his lessons that even though my savings had been proofed by my gold account, I would still not be able to pay for college for my kids. I realized what could be possible if education came under the same competitive pressure as the automotive industry, what cost savings and innovation *that* could produce.

"I heard Iceland would accompany the move to gold with a thorough privatization of education and health care activities, and I believed we would have a chance of reaching our goals over here. So I talked it through with my family for a few days, and they all bought it. We moved here two months ago, as I found a job as a worker on a geothermal heating plant. My wife works as a waitress at one of the larger hotels in Reykjavik, and we were able to rent an apartment in the outskirts of the city. Our kids? They are in high school, and they're both looking forward to pursuing their interests in university."

"Thank you, Martin; it was great to hear your story. One last question though. Please tell us how you now use money, gold, in your daily life."

"Sure. Actually, the difference isn't that big, as I didn't even have to change my bank account when moving here. As when I lived in the USA, I mostly use my bank card for larger payments, and I mostly use silver coins for smaller transactions. Sometimes I use gold paper bills. Those bills look pretty much like old-fashioned paper money, but they are instead warehouse receipts to the gold I hold in my bank. So I don't use physical gold that often, except when someone requests it. For example, last week I bought a used car from a guy. The price was two hundred grams of gold, and the guy would not take my gold bills. He said that he had been so badly fooled by banks in the subprime crisis and that he had been fooled by fake gold paper bills in last year's counterfeiting scandal. So he preferred to have the real thing before his eyes. So I took out two hundred grams of gold from my bank and brought it to close the deal, and it all went fine."

As the show approached its end, Monica Hazelton lifted the remote control to turn off the television. She glanced over the smiling faces of their guests and finally looked at her husband. "I believe that was an interesting show to watch! It looks like the horrible financial crisis of the world has a real silver lining to it, at least for Iceland and for us!"

"Monica, I guess you mean a *golden* lining!" Hazelton said with a gentle laugh and rose to kiss his wife.

A second later she returned his kiss and said with a smile: "Now, Cornelius, won't you go on to tell *our* story?"

Hazelton smiled back. "Sure! You may know that when we left, we kept our house in San Francisco; it's one of the paradoxes, or I should say absurdities of our story, that in order to keep our house in the United States, we had to leave the United States. Put differently, if we had stayed and paid the wealth tax, we would have had to sell the house to get the money to pay the tax.

"Now, thanks to the quick arrangements you all helped us to put in place, we got out of there in time. Our daughter Samantha will move into our house with her boyfriend, as they're still based in San Francisco. So we will know the house is being taken care of. While we have been able to keep all our real estate and physical assets over there, there's one thing that I now have turned into one hundred percent Icelandic: my company Hazelton Growth Capital. I did this for several reasons. The first and simplest is that it makes sense that the company is registered wherever *I* am. Second, Iceland is now by far the strongest growth market we have in HGC. The two ventures run by Laura, the gold-money Internet bank, and by Pete, the gold-based mutual fund company, are on their way to becoming my fastest-growing and most successful ventures.

"By the way, it's likely that my son Patrick will come here to run the Hazelton Money Mint, which also has had staggering growth. Patrick will graduate from college next year and might move here after that."

Benson remarked, "All right, Cornelius, but that's nine months from now. Since the minting company has got your own name, I guess you will step in yourself to run it before your son comes here?"

"I will, but I won't be able to do it full-time, since I have so many other things to do. Apart from overseeing Laura's and Pete's businesses, along with the rest of HGC's portfolio companies, I'll look into other business sectors which are booming or will do so shortly. I'll look at goods imports, which is why I have started to talk to Bobby. With his help, I'll try to expand the number of consumer products available for the quickly growing and highly demanding population. I'll also look into energy and heating, although I don't yet have enough capital for such investments. The entry ticket is typically around a billion dollars."

"You mean thirty tons of gold?" Benson said, with an even larger grin.

"Yes, I'm sorry; I still haven't quite got used to stop talking about dollars. But I soon will, especially since I grant that you're right to repeat that gold and silver, and possibly some other valuable commodity, are the only things which deserve to be called 'money' at all. Government-controlled paper currencies are being used as if they *were* money, but they actually aren't, since they didn't emerge on a free market as something people accepted in order to trade."

"Cornelius, you don't have to explain to show that you know all that. You know you have always been my best student, at least if I count people of my own age and if I limit myself to businessmen," Benson winked with his left eye toward the four former students of his who were present in the room. "Apart from you, many businessmen appear to have a hard time to learn what is actually in their own best interest."

"Sure, I don't need to tell you what you all know, but I should admit I spend a lot of time thinking about economics, and about what's happening to the world. It still gives me the creeps that people back home actually believe they are saving the economy by slamming taxes on the rich. For sure, their private property is taken away, and this type of taxes drops the entire pretense about taxation being different from theft.

"Beyond that, just look at the impact on the economy. If I had stayed there, I would have paid three million dollars in extra tax, on top of the hundreds of thousands of dollars of taxes I already pay each year. I would have paid those three million after being forced to sell my house, clear out my pension plan, and liquidate all my cash holdings. The money would just go down the drain as one drop in the ocean of public debt, being used up for consumption by the government itself or by some people they handed the money to. So, basically, I would have liquidated savings and investments in order to finance someone else's consumption.

"My point is that, even if a lot of rich people stay in the United States, the economy will still go down the drain. When they have taxed away the last wealth of the rich, there will be no one in the country able to save and invest, just a bunch of indebted consumers and a government in an even worse financial situation. It drives me crazy that this just goes on. Montgomery, thank you for having convinced Iceland to create this haven I could escape to. I hope you'll be able to convince more people to follow my tracks, and more countries to follow Iceland's example."

Benson said, mysteriously, "You should know that we're working quite hard on that. Forgive me that I can't tell you anymore about it today. The people I'm dealing with have requested that it remains totally confidential."

Hazelton looked at Benson for a second, smiled, then frowned before turning to Bobby and changing the subject. "Now you have come a long way to meet with us here, and I much appreciate it. Why don't you tell us a little about how things are over in China these days? I guess they must have gone mad as the Western countries slammed taxes on imports from and direct investment into China?"

"Yes, the last few months have been quite hard for us Americans. At the same time, I get a lot of sympathy from Chinese people who now know me well enough so they don't mix me up with politicians back in the United States. They are interested in working with Iceland, not only because Iceland has no tax on imports from China but also because they are becoming worried about the future of the dollar. Several of my contacts for medium-sized or large Chinese industrial companies have placed their cash holdings in gold accounts in Laura's bank instead of owning dollars. So you'll see when you start doing import business that a lot of people will be happy receiving payment directly in gold, and you'll be able to pay them in an Icelandic account."

"Good and interesting news," Hazelton said. "I guess when our gold money becomes the standard currency for international trade, we will have won a major victory!"

Benson intervened, shaking his head gently. "Cornelius, not so fast; you know we're still far from that point. Iceland is still a country of less than one million people, so all the trade we're able to do won't count for much, currently. And regarding what you said before, about changing people's minds, that won't be fast either. Actually, I think we're up for a period when the politicians in the United States and in Europe will think they finally got it right."

Hazelton frowned. "What do you mean?"

"Just wait until they start counting the tax receipts of this year," Benson explained. "I bet we will hear a lot of triumphal talk about the new tax plan which generates a lot of revenue, to be used for 'stimulus consumption,' which they believe will put the economy back into growth. If you want my guess, we're up for at least two more years of expanding government and taxes in the Western countries.

"At the same time, you should not expect that they underestimate the importance of the role Iceland is playing as a new financial center that proposes an alternative to the paper-money currencies of the main countries. Don't fool yourself into thinking that by coming here you're just engaging in some private tax evasion. The meaning and importance of your act is much stronger than that. You're actually taking sides in a philosophical and ideological war where the Big Government side is being struck in a spot which was its invincible strength for more than a century: its monopoly on creating money."

CHAPTER 17:
Business-bashing Backlash

"It works!" James Mortimer shouted, clenching his right fist in a gesture of victory. "Thanks to ESB, we managed to collect nine hundred billion dollars more in tax revenue than the year before!"

It was February, eight months after the announcement of the Economic Solidarity Bill and two months after the end of the first fiscal year with the new and increased taxes. Statistics were now available in order to assess the results. In the Washington, D.C., office of the Department of the Treasury, Steve Harper, in charge of Tax Policy, and James Mortimer, in charge of Public Debt and of public spending allocation, were meeting in a small conference room, where they planned to spend a few hours together analyzing the new data and taking any appropriate decisions to go forward.

Not trying to hide his satisfaction, Steve replied happily, "You mean thanks to *my* ESB *Enforcement Agency*. May I remind you we had to get the money from the rich people one by one, making them sign asset declaration forms, digging out all their treasures hidden across the world? That was a lot of work. I do hope the secretary of the treasury, and the president himself, will recognize the crucial role we have played to put the country back on its feet."

"Sure, go right ahead and try to get all the credit for it," James said, slightly annoyed. But he went on, smiling as widely as Steve. "The best in all this is that the budget deficit for this year will be ridiculously small, just about a hundred billion dollars, or below sixth-tenths of a percent of GDP. I bet that the government bond rates will fall when we announce that this year's bond issue will be ten times smaller than that of last year. Who said large government spending isn't sustainable, or that it doesn't deliver results?"

"I didn't, for sure," Steve answered happily. "I certainly believe we're on the right track to win the fight against the economic crisis. At the same time, we confirm the credibility and the power of the government of the United States."

"We do. My only concern is not to lose my job as Director of Public Debt. If deficits disappear, so might the need to issue government bonds. Can you imagine a world without government bonds? Where would people put their cash in order to have a safe fixed-income placement?"

"Well, I'm afraid I can, and that makes me think of something we might worry about now," Steve said thoughtfully and with less enthusiasm. "The number of rich people who actually left the country to escape from the ESB taxes was quite limited last year, around eighty thousand, or just about two percent of them. But I'm more worried about what big business is doing. A lot of corporations are setting up shell subsidiaries in Iceland, to manage their cash over there. They not only hope to inflation proof their cash reserves, but also to pay less tax back home."

James's face darkened. "Those bastards! They always counter whatever noble policies we devise." He paused. "Let's show them who'll have the last word. I have an idea!"

"What?" Steve asked with interest.

"Let's forbid U.S. companies from having subsidiaries in Iceland. Let's suggest to our friends in the G7 and the European Union to do the same. That should calm down large corporations who engage in tax and cash optimization at our expense."Steve smiled at James. "James, that's a very good idea. You're quite useful and creative for someone who is just supposed to care about public debt financing and spending allocation."

James returned the courtesy, smiling back. "Oh, I'm happy to be of use. It *is* also my job to make sure that financial and human resources stay in the country. Or, as we call them, less romantically, taxation resources."

✿ ✿ ✿

Laura Dalaghan had lived in Colorado for almost ten years, since she had founded the Dalaghan Prudential Internet Bank. It still had its headquarters in the same Denver office building where she had started out with just two employees. DPIB had survived the subprime crisis and had grown steadily during the three and a half years since then. But it grew much slower than its Icelandic subsidiary DPGB, where *G* stood for *gold*.

One of the explanations was that many clients of DPIB had chosen to transfer their deposits to the Icelandic subsidiary, giving them protection against the inflation in the dollar-money supply. The Icelandic subsidiary already had more than a hundred thousand customers. It was forecasted to outgrow its mother company, which had a hundred fifty thousand customers, well before the end of the year.

Laura was the CEO of both the mother company and the subsidiary, thanks to several factors. The first and most important was the total confidence the shareholder Cornelius Hazelton had in her competence and in her management ability. The character of their bank, which was Internet oriented and virtual, also helped. She had been able to serve the whole of the United States from Denver, so adding Iceland hadn't changed much. Still, the gold-based monetary system of Iceland was something radically new, and that had forced Laura to spend a lot of time in Reykjavik during the first months of launch in Iceland. Since then, she had the habit to spend around a week every month there, to meet with her Icelandic management and to meet potential and strategic partners in the rapidly growing and dynamic Icelandic economy.

Her desire to remain in Denver was linked to her family life. Her husband Kevin was still running the same hunting-and-fishing business as when they had met and fallen in love nine years earlier. Kevin's livelihood was dependent on closeness to the Rocky Mountains, as was the whole family's leisure habits. Andrew, seven years old, and Janet, five years old, both loved spending their weekends in the mountains and the family spent their vacations there. They did alpine and cross-country skiing in the winter and hiking or river rafting in the summer. Andrew had begun participating in downhill ski competitions for kids, and this April weekend, he had achieved his first victory. As they were driving home on the Sunday afternoon from the resort where he had competed, the mood in the car was understandably exalted.

"Andrew, stop hanging out of the window when Daddy is driving!" Laura said, turning back and pointing a finger at their son, who would not sit still in the backseat of their car.

"Oh, I want to hang out! The air is so warm and nice here in the valley." her son replied.

"Honey, I know spring is coming and that's nice. But what you're doing is dangerous. We'll stop in a while to have a break along the road. You'll be able to play a little in the grass, with Janet."

"All right, it better be soon," Andrew, sulky, said while sitting back in his seat.

"Sure, ski champion, just close your eyes for a few minutes and go over your perfect race once again," Laura said to her son with a smile, then turned back to look at the road ahead of them.

She turned on the radio to listen to the news. She tuned in one of their favorite channels. A news report that sounded important was on. The speaker was saying: "Starting July first this year, a new regulation called Patriotic Finance for Growth will be in effect. It may raise some eyebrows at U.S. banks and corporations, as they will have to refrain from having subsidiaries in so-called tax havens. The ban will also cover countries considered to have normal tax systems but which attract an excessive amount of foreign capital. These countries are now more and more frequently called capital havens. Examples are Switzerland, Luxembourg, and the newcomer in the world of international finance, Iceland, with its unique gold-based monetary system. In sum, according to the official statement from the U.S. government, 'The purpose of the Patriotic Finance for Growth regulation is to encourage business in the United States. With this new regulation, we will no longer see American corporations contributing to the outflows of capital which do harm to our country.'"

Laura turned to her husband. "Listen to this! What the hell is happening?"

The speaker on the radio continued. "American companies will no longer be allowed to have subsidiaries nor be majority shareholders of companies in these countries. The regulation goes even further: shareholders should be advised there is no use to try to dismantle the link between their U.S. Company and its foreign subsidiary to escape the ruling. Even if they do, a U.S. company having the same majority shareholders as a company in a tax or capital haven won't be allowed to operate in the United States. So shareholders will have the choice between selling or shutting down their off-shore business, or else to do one of those things to their U.S. business. An additional benefit expected from this regulation is that it will increase the attention paid by American companies to their American customers. It should also improve their loyalty and spirit of collaboration with the government and the Federal Reserve in ensuring the smooth functioning of our monetary and banking systems."

Laura turned pale, in spite of the tan she had at this time of the year after weeks spent on sunny mountains. "Kevin, do you understand what this means? Hazelton will have to sell DPIB. Or DPGB. Or shut the first one down in order to focus on the second! He can't do that. He won't do that. He would never accept to!" she yelled, more as if to convince herself that such would be the case, than actually believing it.

"Laura, calm down, and don't frighten the kids," Kevin said with his usual reassuring voice. "I'm sure there will be a way to work this out."

She remained upset, but spoke more quietly, to avoid the children over-hearing their discussion. "I don't know. What was said is pretty clear cut. I can see why they are putting it through. It's quite smart, granted their purpose is to stop American companies from avoiding U.S. taxes, and from sending capital abroad by setting up subsidiaries in capital havens. They are betting companies will consider their U.S. activity much more important, so they will accept to give up having subsidiaries in places like Iceland. Now, larger companies who are paying huge corporate profits taxes after the ESB may, of course, be tempted to move their headquarters out of the United States to escape all this."

"So, what do you worry about, if that's how you think companies should react?" said Kevin, revealing that he had never understood much about Laura's work, nor made efforts to do so.

"Honey, come on," she said with some irritation. "Forget about the large corporations. Look at *my* situation. Cornelius Hazelton is strongly involved in both our U.S. bank and our Icelandic bank. We will not accept to give up either of them. And today, they are of similar size and profitability. So the choice would be hard for him. But if he had to make a choice, which I hope he would never do—"

Kevin picked up on what she was saying. "He would do what?"

"Sell or, worse, shut down our U.S. Denver-based Internet bank," she said quietly, as if fearing that her words had the power to translate into reality, once they were spoken.

"You don't think he would do that?" Kevin said, a bit more anxious.

"I said I don't think so. But I don't know. I have to talk to him about it. I better do that fast. Last time he was squeezed by a new law, he made the decision within a few days to move out of the country. That was less than a year ago, and I expect him to move fast this time too, whatever he does."

"So, what could save us?" Kevin asked with fear in his voice.

"Well, something would have to happen to make them repeal this regulation. I guess they would, if they understood it will hurt the U.S. economy.

Maybe if the drain of capital and people leaving the United States keeps increasing, the people in power might hear reason."

"Do you think that will happen?" Kevin said with renewed hope.

"There's a chance. I hear Mark, Bobby, and their friends in the Free Men, Real Money network have some top-secret stunt underway that's supposed to prove to the U.S. government that it's have gone too far. Well, I hope they will succeed."

☼ ☼ ☼

The sun was shining on one of Hong Kong's most prestigious golf courses in a beautiful day of mid-May. As usual, it was filled with businessmen and politicians who came to combine business and pleasure. Ka Ying knew some key decision makers both in China and in Hong Kong from his time at the Beijing University, and he knew that this place was one of the most appropriate places for a meeting of the highest importance. Mark Lomack and Bobby Cheston had been surprised by Ka's insistence, but they had accepted the setup. They had flown in two days earlier to prepare for this day, and they had even bought Chinese golfers' clothes, under Ka's attentive supervision. Their partners for this round of golf were distinguished. They were Hong Kong's finance minister and a powerful deputy of the Chinese Finance Ministry.

Mark had heard Ka's advice not to talk shop until their counterparts showed that they would accept to. But he had a hard time to apply the advice, as he had crossed the world with the purpose of having an important discussion, not to play a round of golf. So both Mark and Bobby were relieved when, at hole sixteen, the Chinese deputy minister said, "That was a nice shot, Mr. Lomack. Have you also been successful in your effort to enroll U.S. corporations for our common project? Remember, I told you we will have a deal only if you enroll at least ten of the hundred largest firms and only if they all accept to create at least ten thousand jobs in China while setting up their head office in Hong Kong."

Mark's attention instantly increased, as he tucked away the putter. "Oh, right. Well, I trust that you will be satisfied with what we achieved." He faked indifference and dug in his golf bag for the club to use for his next shot.

The Hong Kong minister, who was standing next to Mark, asked, "What? Tell us."

Mark was content to continue with some fake indifference. "Oh, maybe we shouldn't take all the credit for it. The Patriotic Finance Regulation that was recently introduced actually helped several corporations to make up their minds, as it strongly reduced their possibility to optimize cash and taxes as long as their head offices are in the U.S."

"So?" the Hong Kong minister said.

"Well," Mark said casually, "in this favorable context, we actually managed to surpass the objective: we enrolled twenty of the hundred largest American corporations, including seven of the top ten."

"Is that true?" they said with one voice, and in Chinese.

After Ka Ying had translated, Mark said, "Why, yes. The twenty companies actually make up almost twenty percent of the stock market value in the United States. They have more than nine million employees, half of them in the United States. Even if they keep some activity over there, by moving their headquarters and of part of their operations abroad, they will not only make the headlines; they will create a virtual earthquake in the U.S. politics.

"I have estimated that the move of their combined cash balances into gold will mean a shift of around three hundred billion dollars from the U.S. to Iceland. It will increase the quantity of gold money by a factor of six; it was around fifty billion before this move. And it was less than *five billion* when Iceland first started to use gold money."

"And how many jobs will be created in Hong Kong and in China?" the Hong Kong minister asked eagerly.

Mark shrugged and said pleasantly, spinning a golf club in his hand as he used to do with pencils, "Oh, I believe it will be a lot more than your minimum requirement. I would say that each of them will create at least fifty thousand jobs, so that would mean around one million altogether. I guess one-third will be in Hong Kong, and two-thirds in China."

"This sounds good," the Chinese deputy minister said, displaying a false seriousness as he struggled to hide his excitement. "Please remind me what you ask from the People's Republic of China?"

"It's quite simple," Mark said. "You will allow the Chinese subsidiaries of these companies to do all their accounting in gold and to hold their cash in Iceland, just like their Hong Kong–based mother companies. It will be a favor you have never before granted to foreign companies. But then again, I believe the stakes are high for you. It's a historical opportunity for you to teach a lesson to the United States and the European Union not to mess with China. But, of course, we're talking about giant American corporations. They have firmly told us they won't move until they have a written guarantee that you will play along with the agreed setup."

Ka Ying, who must have sensed that the right time had come as they reached the green of hole seventeen, pulled up a paper from his golf bag. He spoke slowly in Chinese for what seemed to Mark and Bobby a very long time, before handling a pen to the Chinese and Hong Kong politicians. They both burst out in wide smiles and took turns grabbing the pen and signing the protocol, sealing the largest deal of corporate exodus the world had ever seen.

✲ ✲ ✲

On June 20, Cornelius Hazelton stood at a viewpoint on Ellis Island, outside of New York. One year had passed since he'd emigrated from the United States to Iceland, and he felt a strong emotion standing on this small island that once was the entry point to the United States for twelve million immigrants.

This day, and ever since the ESB taxes had been enacted, the flow of migration had been going in the other direction. Hazelton thought about his own escape the year before, and picked up his phone to place a call to the man who had helped him leave the country.

"Kilby? Cornelius here. How are you doing?"

"Fine, and you?" Kilby Rock answered with his powerful voice. "Where are you?"

"I'm in New York, overseeing the passenger ships preparing to leave. I thought about you, since one year ago, you were the travel agency and I was the traveler. Now I'm in the travel business myself, helping people escape before this year's deadline for the ESB wealth tax, ten days from now."

Kilby Rock chuckled. "Cornelius, don't try to fool me, or yourself for that matter. We both know you do it in order to increase the number of customers for your Icelandic bank and mutual fund businesses. I even heard that you pitched your bank's savings services along with the boat tickets."

"Sure, and I don't have any problem with that," Hazelton said more solemnly. "It's in my interest, and in theirs. Anyway, the passenger-ship business I started really fulfills a crucial demand. Just imagine; this month, an estimated five hundred thousand people are leaving the United States, for good. Almost half of them are millionaires subject to ESB taxes. There was no way that all these people could have gotten out of the country unless the supply of ship transportation increased significantly. This is what I made happen."

"True," Rock said. "That which last year could be dealt with by a number of private jets, now requires tens of the world's largest passenger ships making several roundtrips between the East Coast and Iceland. I just wonder: how far will this go? At this pace, there won't be many people left in the United States. And those who leave are the wealthiest and most industrious."

"Yes," Hazelton said thoughtfully. "That is what I read at a board here on Ellis Island. I mean, it said that the people who left Europe a century ago to try their luck in the United States were the most industrious people in their countries. It makes me shudder that the flow now is going in the other direction. To answer your question, I don't have any idea where or when it will end."

"Maybe not," Rock replied, "but we shouldn't count the U.S. government out just yet. Even if their ruling forbidding American companies from having subsidiaries in capital havens seems to backfire, I'm sure they won't give up like that."

Hazelton remained absorbed in his thoughts. "Maybe. I need to go over to the harbor to talk to my crews. See you soon Kilby," he said and hung up.

Hazelton stepped into a small speedboat and quickly crossed the Upper Bay over to the Brooklyn side, where passengers were loading onto two giant ocean liners he had leased.

He got off his motorboat and elbowed his way through the crowd waiting to board, most of people dragging more luggage behind them than they could carry. A man had climbed onto a wooden box and started waving his arms.

"Tickets to Iceland! Tickets to Iceland! The last tickets available that will take you to Iceland before June thirty! Two thousand dollars only! That's a lot of money, but much less than what you'll save if you emigrate before June thirty! Tickets! Tickets!"

After some time, Hazelton managed to find his local manager in the crowd. They went through the lists of passengers for the two ships and checked the schedules which would take them to Iceland in four days' time. Similar ships were leaving from many places along the East Coast. The longest travel time was six days, from Florida to Reykjavik. After half an hour, Hazelton left the manager who embarked the ship. Hazelton himself had a flight back to Iceland the following day.

The crowd on the quay diminished; the only people remaining were relatives waving good-bye to their emigrating family members or friends. Hazelton sat down on a bench to rest from the day's effort, and from the emotion he felt when he saw the two ships depart from the New York harbor under cheers and screams, interrupted by a couple of loud blows from the ships' whistles. To escape emotionally, he placed a call to Pete Bagnelli, who was in Iceland helping the teams of his mutual fund company handle the flow of new customers expected for midyear.

"Pete? You all right?"

"Yes, fine. I'm having dinner with Laura. I'll put you on speakerphone. How are you, boss?"

"You know I don't like whining, but I was almost sobbing a minute ago. I should really be in a great mood; we have ten thousand customers who are just leaving New York on our leased ships. About half of them signed up to put money either in Laura's bank or in your mutual funds. But it's the sight of Ellis Island and of the Statue of Liberty that breaks my heart. Those two places were meant to greet people coming here to try their luck in a free world. They now wave good-bye to people who leave the United States to search happiness elsewhere."

The line remained silent for a while; then Laura said with emotion, "I understand how you feel, boss. I guess it would have been even worse for me, had I been there. My great-grandparents came from Ireland to New York a century ago. They would be horrified to know that people now emigrate in the other direction, especially since the calamities they wanted to escape were related to nature, fertility of the soil and such. These days, people leave the United States because of man-made evil, which feels a lot worse. So I've got the same mixed feelings as you about those new customers on their way here. I guess this is what it feels like to earn one's living in the funeral business."

☆ ☆ ☆

The American national day on July 4 had a bitter flavor for most Americans. After the announcement that five hundred thousand people had emigrated from the country before June 30, another news item announced on July 3 created severe shock: the coordinated announcement on behalf of twenty-four of the country's largest corporations that they were moving their headquarters out of the United States. Twenty-two of the companies were relocating their headquarters to Hong Kong, and two to Singapore. All claimed they were moving significant amounts of blue- and white-collar jobs to Hong Kong, and even more jobs to mainland China. All the companies further declared that with approval from Hong Kong authorities, their corporate accounting currency was to be gold, with their cash reserves held in Iceland. To make things worse, similar announcements had been made by eighteen of the largest European corporations. Corporations denied that their actions were concerted, and there was not yet any mention of who was behind this move.

Jessica Frostby spent the evening of July 4 alone, as Steve had flown over to visit his parents on the West Coast. Lisa had since long gone to sleep, so Jessica was relaxing alone in front of the television, as always, with her laptop computer at hand. As the clock approached midnight, she had read most of the reports about the corporate exodus and about the unending wave of emigration. The emotional sum of all this reading felt so dark and negative that she grappled for something to make her feel better. As more and more often, in such situations, she decided to hook up to the FMRM Web-conferencing software. She was happy to see that Latin Freeman was connected, although it was 6:00 a.m. in Europe.

"Hi there, where are you? Can you talk a little?" Jessica started.

"Why, yes, I'm actually in a hotel in Frankfurt; I'm here on business."

"Really, I'm more and more curious about what business you would have in Frankfurt. Why don't you tell me a bit more?"

"You know we agreed to remain confidential about who we are and what we do. I don't want to have to worry about where such information would circulate."

"Sure, I know. But sometimes I feel I want to know who you are. And to let you know who /am! We might like each other, you know."

"We already do. I think. Even though we don't know everything about each other. I guess I can tell you my current trip is related to the exodus of large corporations and of a lot of individuals. It's the top issue on the mind of politicians across the whole Western world, I guess."

"Yes, certainly. I'll have a meeting tomorrow at my job on that topic. I can tell you I feel strongly about it. You know my ancestors were from Sweden. They left it to search for better conditions of life in the United States. Now the flow is in the other direction, away from the United States. And I'm scared, since I fear it can become much worse that it already is."

"What do you mean?"

"I mean that over just a few decades, almost 25% of the Swedish population left the country. 25%! Now I hear politicians say that we shouldn't worry about the current exodus. They say it's just a few rich and mean individuals and corporations that are leaving, and that the flow will soon stop. But I don't think that's true! I mean, the number of people who left the United States is just above 600 thousand people, or 0.25% of the population. That's a hundred times less than how many left Sweden one century ago!

"Of course, the risks and costs involved were much higher back then. I believe that the reasons for leaving now are just as compelling, at least for the rich people who are subject to the ESB. Why should they accept to carry the burden from a mess created by politicians who have driven public spending and public debt up to unreasonable levels, just to win elections? When they are just a six-hour flight away from freedom! I guess most of them like their country and wouldn't want to leave it. But with what they're now made to endure...Let's not talk anymore about public affairs, or about our work. I wanted to ask you a question, or at least get your advice."

"Go ahead."

"You know, I'm starting to think about quitting my job. I can't stand it anymore. I have the impression of committing treason to all my beliefs and to everything FMRM stands for. In my current job, I'm really on the other side. They should not even let me be a member!"

"Have you always been?"

"Been what?"

"On the other side."

"Spiritually, never. But ever since I started working, yes. There was not much of a choice in the area I wanted to work in. I had the choice between working at a place I didn't like or accepting to abandon what interested me most."

"For how long have you been working?"

"About ten years, ever since I graduated from college."

"Ten years is a long time. How could you put up with it for so long?"

"Because I expected to get the opportunity, one day, to defend the values I want to uphold."

"Do you realize that if you quit now, you might never get that chance again? You know, I've been thinking about the same issue, but my conclusion is not to quit, not now."

"Why? Explain," Jessica typed, almost before having finished reading his previous sentence.

"You know I'm in a quite powerful position in my country. Just like you I'm not really able to influence things as I would want to. I have convictions about individual freedom which are unusual here in Europe. Still, I think we're coming to a point when people like you and I must stick around."

"Why?" she wrote, not in defiance but in eagerness to know more about an answer she expected to be convincing, as most things said by Latin Freeman.

"Because I think we will soon come to a point when the whole system will break down. Public debt and the number of people living on the back of others keep increasing. Businesses and rich people are leaving the Western countries at an ever faster pace. If other countries follow Iceland's example, things may go fast."

"Do you think that will happen? That other countries will do as Iceland? The idea of it makes me excited!"

"Yes, I hope so and I think so. I mean, it stands to reason that they are creating a much better monetary system. Just look at how Iceland has been transformed in the span of only a few years! At the same time, we should also expect Western governments to increase repression back home to try to stop the drain of people and capital. In that case, the productive people who remain in the Western countries will be the major victims. I think we also should expect the Western governments to try to destroy the gold-money system. If they don't, I think they will run a losing battle against the drain!"

"So, maybe we should stick around to help our friends. I have friends both here in the U.S., and in Iceland, who will be in trouble if what you say happens."

"Yes! I bet you would be the best double agent they could ever dream of, inside those structures of power that may hurt your friends!"

"Maybe you're right. Thank you anyway for telling me this. I guess I don't have a lot of people who can counsel me, and maybe I don't really see as clearly as you do where the world is going."

"You know what you should do, if you want to catch up on all that?"

"No?"

"FMRM has launched a monthly international sharing meeting. They call it the Human Rights Alert Session. People from different countries speak up about how they are suffering from crazy new laws and regulations. They started it after the ESB laws were enacted last year, and it just becomes more and more interesting—and horrifying—to listen in to those sessions. They are mostly on videoconference though, but I listen in, as a bunch of other anonymous users. You should too."

"I guess I will. But you can bet I'll remain anonymous in there. You know, one of the leaders of the FMRM is an old friend of mine, and even he doesn't know I'm Heart of Gold, or that I hang out on the network at all. I guess I'll tell him one day, but not yet."

"No, you must not because what we just talked about. As things will get uglier and uglier both in the United States and here in Europe, you'll get more and more opportunities to be valuable to your friends in your role as a double agent. But the risks you take will increase in the same proportion. You don't want to be prosecuted for treason or something! Even if what you do is good, you must understand that something like that can happen."

"Yes, you're right. I'll keep the lowest possible profile. And I'll look into the Alerts Session; it sure sounds interesting. But if you see me in there, you act as if you didn't know me, right?"

"But I *don't* know you, even if I want to, more and more!" Latin Freeman wrote and sent a smiley over the communication screen.

"Right, you don't. But in some ways, you know me more than anyone in the whole world. This is getting complicated. But now, as usual when we have spoken for too long, I need to go to bed, and you need to go to work. Have a good day, Latin Freeman."

"Good night, Heart of Gold."

CHAPTER 18:
Speculation and Strangulation

"We are about to make history, taking Social Security out of the mean world of selfishness and profits, where people pay to themselves and don't care about others," said Joseph Miller with a loud and vibrant voice. It made him sound like a gospel preacher rather than a secretary of the treasury.

"We won't let some unpatriotic bastards escaping abroad with their wealth prevent us from reaching this noble vision. They think they outsmarted us by leaving the country before June thirty to avoid the ESB taxes. But we'll show those traitors they made the wrong decision. You have my word on it: I will make anything in my power to destroy their gold-based monetary system."

The meeting's aim was to decide on domestic policy regarding public spending, and to decide on a policy to counter the drain of capital and people out of the United States. For this reason, the secretary of state was also present. In the room were a few direct reports of Joseph Miller: James Mortimer, in charge of Public Debt and public spending allocation, and the head of the Department of Health and Human Services, handling social security, assisted by his economic advisor, the recent economics Nobel Laureate Samuel Kruglitz. Most of the leaders of the U.S. government, including Joseph Miller, appreciated Kruglitz's advice. His popularity among politicians came from his ability to invent new ideas about where politicians could make themselves useful by increasing government intervention in society. Kruglitz had been one of the main advocates of the new Social Security system which the United States was putting in place. Sitting next to Kruglitz was Jessica Frostby and her boss, Jeffery Hastings.

After his dramatic introduction, Joseph Miller reverted to his usual formal, monotone way of speaking. "Today we have domestic issues to discuss, and then a foreign policy issue with respect to the drain of people and capital. We will start with the domestic issue. As you remember, a year and a half ago, we launched a daring but crucial program along with other leading developed countries. It aimed to maintain our policy of uncompromising economic stimulus, in spite of all the criticism we have received from some observers. Our strongest critics were the business community, and what I like to call the 'inflation hawk faction' of the Federal Reserve." He looked coldly at Jessica, but not at Hastings.

"Today, I think we can claim the results are promising. In spite of a few traitorous individuals and corporations having left the country, consumption spending is up this year, just as is gross domestic product. Samuel, why don't you, as our expert, explain what has happened over the last year," Miller said, looking with admiration and recognition at Kruglitz.

The professor took his glasses off, stood, and started pacing the room as he began speaking. "What has happened is quite simple: we have taken money out of the hands of rich people and large corporations, who wouldn't have spent that money or who would have just invested it in their business. We have given it to consumers and government agencies, which have spent it on consumption. As you all know, consumption is the motor of the economy, as witnessed by that fact that it constitutes around eighty percent of GDP.

"As you also know, consumption spending has a multiplier effect on economic growth. When someone spends money on consumption, that money comes into the hand of someone else, who in his turn will spend it, and so on and on. Unfortunately, people don't consume all of the money they get, but will typically save some part of it, say ten percent. That's what we call a 'leakage' out of the consumption multiplier effect. It means that a given consumption will only generate a limited additional activity. If the leakage was zero, the economic stimulus would be unlimited, and GDP would grow at an enormous speed. We can conclude from the current evolution of economic indicators, that the leakage has been limited and, thus, that our stimulus policy has been a success."

Jessica raised her hand and smiled courteously, actually much too courteously, which Kruglitz would have understood had he known her better. But he didn't, and he appeared flattered and seduced by her smile and nodded for her to speak. She asked a simple question, "Am I correct that you claim a situation where people consume all their money will generate unlimited growth, while a situation of major saving and investment would generate an economic depression?"

Kruglitz was still flattered by what he interpreted as a way of complimenting his thinking. "Yes, you have perfectly well understood my reasoning, Mrs. Frostby!"

Jessica still smiled broadly. "So should I conclude this country was built by a bunch of people who crossed the Atlantic Ocean, put up tents, and then just sat down and started consuming all they could? Should I consider that the idea according to which this country was built by people who saved to build or buy their own homes by putting away as much capital as they could to start businesses, is just a nineteenth-century superstition? Even though that's exactly how my great-grandparents, who emigrated from Sweden to the United States, have told their story to their descendants?"

There was a moment of silence in the room, which Jessica broke while maintaining her seductive smile. "I'm sorry, Professor; that was certainly a stupid question. Please proceed to explain about the success of the current policies and, I'm sure, of those to come."

Kruglitz frowned, and after a moment of hesitation, he went on. "The recent tax increases have reduced the government budget deficit to very little, and we have seen proof of the success of the stimulus policies. Therefore, I have advised the president and Mr. Miller to accelerate the new welfare programs and the development of government-backed social security. This will put still more money in the hands of consumers and will further accelerate the process of economic growth and wealth creation."

Jessica once again could not resist asking a question. "Just to be sure everybody in the room understands: you're saying wealth creation will be boosted by consuming existing wealth?"

Kruglitz again frowned, but this time, he answered. "Well yes, of course. If people don't consume what they have, then they won't need to replace it. That's what's wrong with saving, and this also explains why war creates such rapid economic growth."

"Thank you for going all the way to your conclusion: you do claim that destruction of wealth generates prosperity. So why don't you advise the president, who seems to pay great attention to your advice, to drop a few nuclear bombs on our largest cities? I can tell you *that* would create a gigantic need for replacement of goods, which should generate a fantastic growth, by your reasoning. If by any chance you're concerned by the loss of human lives, you can suggest evacuating those cities before dropping the bombs. That way, only capital and material wealth would be destroyed."

Once again, everybody was silent, and Jessica felt obliged to put Kruglitz back in his previous comfortable mood. "Sorry again, Professor, for this digression. Please go back to your economic outlook, which we are all eager to hear."

Kruglitz frowned thoughtfully and shook his head as he looked around the room to check the faces of his audience. They all seemed to urge him to continue his speech, which he promptly did. "As I said, we will reinforce further the economic stimulus we have been doing for four years now since the last crisis. I'm not sure we will need to increase taxes even more. We should be able to pump up those budget deficits a bit more again, now that the financial markets have come out of their irrational suspicion about government bonds.

"If, by any chance, we would have problems with the coming bond issues, you guys at the Fed will just have to do your job by creating some fresh money and buy the unsold bonds." This time he looked harshly at both Hastings and Jessica, as if to obtain their commitment to play along in this political con game.

Jessica again replied, now without hiding some defiance behind her smile. "Have you ever thought about the fact that this perpetual deficit spending is just like the investment scams you love to put private investors into jail for? Only your setup is about a thousand times bigger, counting money in trillions instead of billions. And if I understand you correctly, you aim to extend that principle to this new Social Security system? We would copy the feats of France, Italy, and others, who are running staggering deficits in their systems? Deficits that keep growing every year!"

Miller was fed up with what he considered as intellectual games, and stood. "Enough of this talk! We aren't in a social sciences campus coffee shop here. We are talking about the economic policy of the United States! Now, Mr. Hastings, you have heard the outlook described by Professor Kruglitz, regarding our future policies. Can you confirm that the Federal Reserve will take its responsibility and will play its role regarding future bond emissions? And in guaranteeing the continued access to cheap and abundant credit? This may be well needed to compensate for money flowing out of the country due to unpatriotic egoists who move abroad, or send their money abroad!"

Looking at her boss, Jessica wished he wouldn't say what he would say, but knew that he would. She closed her eyes and gnashed her teeth, when she heard Hastings respond.

"Yes, Mr. Miller, you can of course count on the Federal Reserve to support the crucial policies needed to get our country back in shape. I mean to keep moving in the promising direction Professor Kruglitz just described. You have my word and our chairman's word. He's in perfect agreement with me on matters of monetary policy."

"Very well!" Miller exclaimed. "I think we now can move on to the foreign policy issues. While I share the optimism of Samuel about what we're trying to achieve within the United States, I shall admit that I'm worried about the consequences if the drain continues. It seems the Patriotic Finance Regulation has backfired: instead of refraining from having subsidiaries abroad, a lot of corporations are ready to leave the country instead. So I have decided to repeal the regulation.

"I believe we must change tactics, if we want to reach our goal. I mean, our goal is not to destroy business in the United States. It is to destroy the gold-money system which is pulling our resources out of the country and is challenging the supremacy of the dollar as the world's reserve currency. I now would like to hear some fresh ideas on how we could achieve this goal, without hurting our economy anymore than we already have with the ESB!"

"Then *I* have a suggestion to make," Samuel Kruglitz said triumphantly. He stood up and started to walk around the meeting table. "You know the pitch the people in Iceland use to attract people's savings. They say that gold money is inflation proof, emphasizing that no one can create gold in the way our central banks create paper money. That may be true. But what they don't say is that the market value of gold in terms of other goods and monies can vary, both upward and downward. I guess they're so sure that the value of gold can't fall significantly, that they even forget about this possibility! I can offer you a quite easy way to destroy the value of gold, which would of course, as a consequence, destroy the whole system of gold money."

"Samuel, how could that be done?" Miller whispered with a trembling voice, bending over the table looking at Kruglitz.

Kruglitz stopped pacing and stood at the far end of the oval table, facing Miller who sat at the opposite end. "I won't bore you with a lengthy explanation about the basic workings of the market economy. But you're all used to hear talk about prices reflecting the balance between supply and demand. If demand for a good increases, then its price will also increase. But if supply increases, then the price will fall.

"So what we need to do to destroy gold money is to reduce demand for gold, and increase supply. What I propose is a way to radically increase the supply of gold, which would make its value fall dramatically. That, in turn, will destroy the credibility of gold as a safe way to store one's money for the future without losing purchasing power. Then people will start to sell their gold to get dollars back. The demand for gold will eventually dwindle, and the gold price will plummet. From then on, no one will ever again question the supremacy of paper money!"

Miller, both eager and impatient to hear the conclusion, barked, "Damn it, Samuel! Get to the point! How can we achieve a radical increase in supply of gold? As you said just before, governments can't create gold in the way we print paper money."

Kruglitz displayed a radiant and confident smile. "Oh, it's quite simple. I have always defended the idea that gold is a 'barbarian relic.' Consequently, I find it ludicrous that people care to dig up gold from mines to use it as money, when we can just print paper bills. I always found it unnecessary for central banks to hold gold reserves. Today the United States, through the Federal Reserve, owns eight thousand tons of gold. And the European countries own even more, around eleven thousand tons. Since this gold is just collecting dust in vaults, why don't we just put it up for sale on the open market? *That* would make the gold price dwindle, and we would achieve your goal, Joseph, of killing the gold-money system. In two words, our plan would be to use *speculation* as a means to *strangulation*."

Content with his demonstration, Kruglitz sat down. Miller turned to Jeffery Hastings. "What does the Federal Reserve think about the proposal from Kruglitz?"

Jessica was about to respond in the place of her boss, but she abstained, biting her lower lip.

Hastings said, "Well, I wouldn't agree that the gold reserves are useless. But, of course, I agree that flooding the market with gold would deliver a serious blow to Iceland. And I agree about the importance of destroying their monetary system, which has been devised and promoted as the opposite of ours." His face revealed a sting of hatred. "They even had the nerve to shut down their central bank, claiming it was useless or even harmful. So we better show them they were wrong. We must make sure that gold money will disappear and that government-backed central banking will have the last word!"

Miller nodded enthusiastically. "I'm pleased to hear that we all agree on what needs to be done. I don't mind selling off much of our gold reserves, especially as it's for the good cause of safeguarding government's control over money. And, of course, the dollars we retrieve by making the sale will be put to use in our public spending and stimulus efforts."

✵ ✵ ✵

As Jessica left the meeting, she did what she had done after learning about the ESB: she called Mark Lomack, in the hope that he, as usual, would see a way to respond to what she considered a desperate situation. She rapidly explained to Mark what she had learned during the meeting.

When she had finished, she said, "What do you make of it?"

"It should be considered as a declaration of war from big government. They are terrified about what would happen if they lost the power over the lifeblood of human civilization: money. I guess we must prepare to react as is proper in a war: to defend ourselves with all available means."

"What do you think we could do?" Jessica asked.

"I'll warn Hazelton, Laura, and Pete. They need to prepare their banks and fund businesses to survive the fall in the gold price, which will be hard to counter in the short term. Then we need to counterattack."

"How?"

"I can think of several things we can do. On FMRM, I will focus our next thematic Web conference on the issue of the gold price, to explain why people should be comfortable with the long-term value of gold, whatever speculative attacks it may suffer. Pete, as an investment manager, may need to find even more clients who want to invest in gold. They may have a unique opportunity to buy it cheaply. And last but not least, I must talk to Professor Benson."

"What do you think the Professor could do?" Jessica said with hope and curiosity.

"I can't know for sure. But, I mean, he was the one who made all this possible, by convincing Iceland to move to gold. I guess the time has come for him to find other larger and more powerful countries to do the same!"

✵ ✵ ✵

Late that night, Jessica awoke from a nightmare. It involved the breakdown of the gold-money system in Iceland, and she had seen in her dream newspaper headlines about triumphant U.S. political leaders, with a statement from Samuel Kruglitz, saying, "As the lighthouse of human civilization, the United States again has fought back the appearance of barbarism in the world. Let's hope that a monetary system without government control will never ever again be seriously considered, anywhere."

She bounced up from her bed and realized she was soaking wet. She slipped out of the bedroom without waking Steve, and went to wipe her body dry and to sit down in the living room sofa with her laptop computer. It was three on a Saturday morning, and she hoped that Latin Libery Lover would be connected on the FMRM. He was.

"Hello, how are you?" she typed.

"I'm fine, just had breakfast. But what are you doing up at this hour?"

"I had a nightmare. The conflict in my job is getting worse and worse. Now it seems that the organization I work for will actively destroy that which I cherish most! If they succeed, several of my friends will perish! And all the efforts of the FMRM will fail! There won't be any gold money any more, and governments will be able to keep on inflating the money supply, destroying what remains of people's savings, to pay for a few more years of budget deficits!"

"Heart of Gold, calm down! One must never panic. Often, the worst attacks can be turned into counter-attacks!"

"What?"

"You know, as in martial arts, when a fighter manages to use the force of his opponent, and send it back to him. The aggressor is beaten by his own blow!"

"I see your point, but how could that apply to my work?"

"Tell your boss you want to be in charge of the plan they have devised to destroy gold money. If you're in charge of it, you'll be able to collaborate with the people you're supposed to destroy, and let them get away, or counterattack!"

"But I already feel terrible by contributing to their destruction! How could I live with it, if I had to be the one holding the sword that delivers the final blow?"

"Well, if you hold the sword, you can choose to withhold that last blow. Or discreetly hand the sword to those who you're supposed to destroy!"

The chat screen remained blank for a long while, then Jessica typed: "That's a fantastic advice, Latin Freeman! I'll do it! And before then, I'll go back to sleep, and this time, I'm sure I'll dream a beautiful dream, not a nightmare!"

✲ ✲ ✲

"Jeffery, I would like to be in charge of Operation Destroy Gold."

It was eight o'clock Monday morning, and Jessica displayed her most seductive smile as she bent over the desk of her boss, offering him a glimpse inside her light white summer shirt.

Jeffery Hastings yawned, put his coffee mug down, and looked at her with a strange look in his eyes. "But I thought you didn't like when we engage in activist policies at the Fed. I even had come to think you were a friend of the gold-money system. Don't think I've forgotten the fights we had during the subprime crisis. You gave me hell for creating a few trillion dollars to turn the economy around!"

Jessica hesitated for a moment, but maintained her enthusiastic smile. "Oh, yes. But back then, you were destroying the purchasing power of the dollar. I'm really a defender of hard money, because I think that people should not be abused for having trusted the signature on the dollar bills. So what you're doing now is great. You're acting to protect the stature of the dollar, thereby protecting the savings of the American people."

Hastings mulled over Jessica's words and bit his lower lip. "All right, why not? You sure did a good job with the subprime crisis plan, once we had agreed on what to do. So I'll let you run the operation, if you're that highly motivated. I'll talk to the chairman to make sure he's OK with it."

"Great! Thank you, Jeffery," Jessica said, softly patting her boss on the shoulder with a sensitive touch.

Hastings stood up and, with a hard look on his face, looked her in the eyes. "Just one thing. Don't ever get soft on those bastards. Remember that the objective is to kill the gold-money system. Whatever it takes! And be damn sure to play along with the European and Japanese central banks. Use your network from your previous job at the IMF. But make sure this remains a secret operation. Don't stage any spectacular meetings. And, of course, keep it among friends. Only the people who are in on the ESB are our friends. So not a word to the Chinese, Indians, or Russians."

"Of course, Jeffery. I won't let you down!" Jessica walked out of the room smiling to herself.

✲ ✲ ✲

The day after, Jessica picked up her phone and called someone she had not talked to for a couple of years, as she no longer was a permanent member of the G20 central bank coordination group.

"François? Jessica here. How are you?"

"Oh hello, Jessica! I'm fine, thank you very much," François Leclerc said with the manners of the top politician he was, but he let a touch of friendliness through in his voice.

"François, I believe you have heard that our superiors, the central bank leaders of the G7, have agreed on a secret plan to sell gold on the market, in the purpose of pushing the gold price down, to destroy the credibility of Iceland's gold money system."

"Yes", François said neutrally.

"Well, I'm in charge of the operation inside the Federal Reserve. So I wanted to check with you who can be my contact inside the European Central Bank. Since it needs to remain totally secret, I would be happy to work with people I know. Like you."

"Oh," François said with a touch of disappointment. "I wouldn't have expected you to lead such an operation. If you succeed, you will destroy what you always told me you considered as good."

"François, wasn't it you who taught me that in society one must be ready to meet people halfway and accept differences of opinion? I guess I have come to accept that my views are not shared by a majority of Americans. So I try to represent them as best I can."

"All right, whatever. Now, if you're the one to do it, I'll try to be on the project too. I'll talk to the president of the ECB. But as we can't have any official meetings, we need to coordinate by phone, or by Internet."

"Sure. And I hope you get the go ahead to work with me on this. Let me know once it's confirmed. In the meantime, I'll contact the Japanese. Take care, François."

"You too, Jessica. And I hope you're not selling your soul here."

"Don't worry, François. Something tells me I'm actually about to redeem it."

Cornelius Hazelton was sweating, even though the July weather in Reykjavik was chilly. He had called a meeting with Laura Dalaghan and Pete Bagnelli to see how they could fight the crisis that their gold bank and gold mutual fund businesses were suffering with the speculative attack on gold. To get advice in this situation from the man whose judgment he trusted more than anything in the world, Hazelton had asked Montgomery Benson to be present by videoconference from California.

"Montgomery! Good to see your face. It doesn't look as bad as mine did in the mirror this morning," Hazelton said as Benson came on the videoconference.

"Hi, Cornelius! And hi, Laura and Pete!" Benson said merrily. "How are things over in Iceland?"

"As you may guess, not so well. I'm worried about the fall in the gold price. If people come to believe what Western governments are telling them, that gold is a useless and dangerous savings option, then we might see a run on our banks, killing the whole gold-money system."

"Calm down, Cornelius. We're not quite there yet. Don't you know that Mark Lomack is planning an FMRM conference a week from now where he will line up the arguments for an *increase* in the gold price?"

"Sure, I heard about that, but I don't dare to hope it will turn things around. We now have a gold price at forty percent below what it was before the speculative attack started. We are trying to set up a response to fight against the fall. My two young stars here have come up with good ideas, but I'm not sure what results we'll be able to reach." Hazelton looked with affection at Pete and Laura.

"What are your plans?" Benson asked.

"We have started to look for people who accept to buy the gold that is being put on the market by central banks. We are using both our Icelandic and Hong Kong branches to find customers, and Laura and Pete are doing a great job promoting gold accounts and gold-denominated mutual funds. But as you can imagine, we aren't able to convince enough customers to buy gold currently, as they see the market price fall."

"Oh," Benson said with an anxious frown.

"Luckily, we've got some other ways of fighting back. Pete has hooked up with Bobby Cheston and Ka Ying who are in China and Hong Kong. They are trying to persuade the large Western companies who moved their headquarters there to keep selling dollars and buying gold. They are also lobbying the Chinese government, which had very small gold reserves, for them to buy gold. We are telling all these people they will never ever be able to buy gold that cheaply. I really hope we will end up being right, because I'm putting both my own and my friends' necks on the line."

"What are you talking about, Cornelius?"

"As I'm quite sure the efforts I mentioned won't be enough, me, Pete and Laura are making a private bond issue that we are selling to people in Iceland who still own dollars or euros. Some of my rich friends, like Kilby Rock, will hopefully buy large chunks. We're even approaching all regular citizens of Iceland. Most of them don't have that much savings except for gold, but I hope they will be able to buy some of our bonds. The bonds are sold in U.S. dollars, and we'll use the proceeds to buy gold."

"Wow, that's a risky bet," Benson remarked. "If the Western governments reach their goal, you'll be hard pressed to pay people back on the bonds, won't you?"

Hazelton nodded anxiously. "You're right. We will be able to pay back the bond money if the gold price remains above twelve hundred dollars an ounce. But I hear people from the Federal Reserve saying that the target price they consider reasonable is five hundred dollars an ounce. If that becomes reality, we'll go bust. We'll go to history not as the heroes of a new monetary system based on gold but as the brains behind one of the larger junk-bond scams of our time!"

"I see," Benson said.

He surprised the three people watching his face by displaying a serene smile. Pete Bagnelli took over. "Professor, I don't understand. How can you look so sanguine? Don't you see we're approaching disaster? If the central banks continue unloading gold, we won't be able to resist. They have sold two thousand tons, and I hear they still sit on an additional eighteen thousand tons! There's just no way we will be able to absorb that."

Benson's expression suddenly switched to a much harder one. It resembled that of an army general starting a war. "Cornelius. Pete. Laura. I ask you to trust me, even though I can't state the reason why you should. If I did, I would break my word. But don't give up. Keep on fighting. You're not as alone as you may believe!"

CHAPTER 19:
White Knights Enter the Fight

Professor Benson looked carefully to the left and to the right before crossing the Boulevard Saint-Germain, as he was slightly intimidated by the speed and impatience of car drivers.

He had travelled from California to Paris. Now, in late July, Paris was very busy with a strong increase in the number of tourists, and the weather was hot. Benson sweated a bit in his beige linen suit, and he regularly wiped his forehead with a paper napkin.

He looked around him, as if expecting to be followed. He wanted to make sure that the meeting he was going to would remain what it was meant to be: a well-preserved secret known only by himself and the person he would meet. He saw no one who paid any attention to him whatsoever.

At three in the afternoon, he confidently walked up to the outdoor terrace of a well-known café in the heart of the Paris's Latin District. He looked around for a few seconds and spotted a tall man standing at the bar, wearing sunglasses and a summer hat. He looked like an affluent summer tourist, wearing a casual but exclusive summer suit and a white summer shirt with two buttons opened and without a tie.

Benson walked up to the man and said, as he had been instructed to, "This is a beautiful day with a golden sun in the sky."

The man answered as Benson now expected him to. "Indeed, it is, and seeing it makes me want to bring it down and give it to my love."

They both smiled secretly, and stretched out their hands to greet each other.

"Nice to meet you, sir," Benson said.

"The pleasure is all mine, Professor. Let's sit down at the table at the far end of the terrace."

They walked across the café and sat down at an isolated table. They both ordered coffee and stretched out in their chairs, which were positioned against the sidewalk, as most Paris café chairs were, in order to let guests observe passersby and the street life. For the two of them, it had the additional advantage of letting them speak without showing that they were together, because they did not face each other.

The man started talking, without turning his head toward Benson, and he kept his hat and sunglasses on. "I much appreciate you could make it here to meet me. I did want us to meet in a place where neither you nor I could be recognized by people in the streets. Paris also brings the additional advantage that few will understand what we say to each other, as we speak English."

He stopped speaking and looked around at the tables next to them. People were talking loudly in French at one of them and in what sounded like Italian at the next one. The noise from the car and bus traffic, running by at a short distance from them, was loud. This noise added to the sounds from people passing by on the sidewalk and drenched all café conversation into a humming background noise. This rendered intimacy to every conversation, even though café tables were quite close to each other.

Benson saw that his acquaintance was comfortable to pursue their discussion. "You're welcome, sir. As I said, I'll do anything I can to help you. And, without false modesty, I think I may be one of the best advisors you may find on this topic. I do believe I'm the only person in the world who combines a longtime theoretical knowledge with practical experience about the topic we are to discuss."

"I agree, and this is why I was so keen to meet you. Let me just briefly explain, in some more detail, my view of the current situation. Our country has for a long time been a haven for capital and for savings. We have prospered by being a place known for its steady institutions, based on the respect for and the defense of private property and individual freedom. Our country uniquely combines two key things. The first is affluent immigrants and foreign businesses that register and work in our country. The second is a native population with a very mature view on individual responsibility and therefore a high expectation about individual freedom.

"Populations in some European countries have sometimes been described, even by their own political leaders, as cattle. But *our* population understands and recognizes the value of private saving and investment as the key means both to long-term prosperity and to individual autonomy and financial security. Those ideas about deficit spending on consumption or about government-backed retirement or social security systems piling up deficits have *never* been accepted in our country. And we're today happier than ever about that, seeing how countries like France and Italy are going down the drain with ever-increasing public debt. And the United States seems to follow the same path."

The man paused and looked around again to check that they were not being listened to, before continuing. "In the current economic context, we're more eager than ever to preserve the lifestyle and fundamental values which made our country what it was and still is. I will summarize those values as the Three Ps: peace, production, and prosperity.

"But as you know, over the last years, we have been the target of attacks from larger countries. They wish to discourage investments and savings from foreigners in our country in order to better use and tax those savings in their home countries. We have accepted to provide information to foreign tax authorities when violation of law has been suspected, and this has started to scare some investors away from our country. But I think it's a marginal phenomenon since a lot of people have already declared the assets they hold with us. As long as they don't sell these assets, they don't pay that much tax anyway, except for the rich people and large companies who are subject to the new ESB wealth taxes in the Unites States and in the other large Western countries.

"As you know, many of them are leaving their country, or will do so. But what we have started to see recently is a much more significant phenomenon. For the first time ever, our currency is no longer seen as a 'hard money,' when compared to the gold currency of Iceland! So we have seen a faster and faster outflow of savings to Iceland, above all bank deposits. We have also seen a lot of people wanting to hold equity and mutual funds in gold denomination, which today is only possible in Iceland. I should add that this happened before the current wave of speculation against gold. The speculation has slowed down the drain from our country too.

"But I don't consider the speculation against gold as an argument against gold money. I rather see it as an opportunity for us to get the gold we need cheaper that we otherwise would. And since I believe the gold price will increase strongly in the future, buying it cheaply will give a nice boost to the purchasing power of our people who will exchange their paper money against gold, at the current rates when gold is relatively cheap.

"So our president and I have come to the conclusion that we should do what Iceland have done: replace our currency with gold, and do it now, as fast as possible. The only question is *how* to do it, after confirming that it's actually feasible in our country. And this is where your experience will be valuable."

Professor Benson had been listening with full focus, not even hearing the noise from the street and the café. "I see. I think you're perfectly right in your analysis. If you want to preserve the values you mentioned, you have to do what Iceland did.

"Your 'three Ps' are not compatible with a paper money. You have gotten away with it for a few decades only for two reasons: because you didn't inflate your paper currency too much and because there was nothing else than paper money anywhere in the world. Well, if the first criteria still holds true, the second no longer does. So my advice to you would be to go through with this as fast as possible, in order to avoid that capital leaves your country in the meantime.

"Even though I appreciate your positive outlook on the future of gold money, you should realize that Iceland's new gold-money system is currently under severe attack from large Western governments which wish to destroy it. You may actually *save* the system, if your purchase of gold can cushion the effect of massive selling from Western central banks.

"If your move goes through, then the gold-money system would be too large and too strong for attacks such as the current wave of speculation to have any chance to succeed. So yes, *please*, move as fast as you can. Once you join Iceland, you will from then on form a new international community of gold-based money and trade. That community should hopefully grow further, as other countries come to understand that they would benefit from joining it."

"All right, I agree that we need to move as fast as possible. But you know that we will have to hold a referendum—our constitution makes that unavoidable."

"Well, I understand. That is something Iceland didn't. On the other hand, I'm confident your population will see the benefits from this project, and my guess is that they will vote massively in favor of it."

"Yes, I think so too. We will of course carefully explain the consequences of both possible outcomes of that referendum. Assuming the referendum goes through, we will then do what Iceland did: redeem our paper money against gold, and shut down our central bank once it has helped to buy the gold we need. By the way, did you look at our numbers? Do you think we will be able to get all the gold we need, if we use up our foreign exchange reserves and our gold reserves?"

"Yes, I *have* looked at those numbers. Unfortunately, it won't be as easy for you as it was for Iceland. They had a very small economy, with many fewer bank deposits to redeem, and they had relatively high foreign currency reserves, so their foreign currency reserves were enough for them to buy all the gold needed to redeem all the bank deposits. However, in your case, the total amount of bank deposits to redeem is worth about three hundred fifty billion U.S. dollars. The sum of your gold reserves and foreign currency reserves will cover only a third of that. So basically you need to find two hundred forty billion dollars to go through with the operation."

"Oh, God, that's a lot of money. That would be almost fifty percent of our GDP. Do you think we will be able to do it, and how?"

"Yes, I do, you just need to find the right mix between several possible sources of raising the money. You will be helped by the current context. Once your move to gold becomes known, a large share of the money leaving Western countries these days due to new taxes will go your way. According to my calculation, the net inflow of people to your country during this year and next, if you move to gold, will be over one million people, over half of whom would be dollar millionaires. In that population you will also see a few hundreds of the world's dollar billionaires."

"All right. I guess that would be great news to our economy, but how could that help us raise the needed money?"

"Your government owns significant equity holdings worth seventy-six billion dollars. I don't think you need to keep all that, especially now that there won't be any role for government to back the monetary system. So sell at least half of that, raising forty billion dollars. This leaves you with the need to finance two hundred billion dollars. Here I suggest you to be bold and creative."

"How?" the man said with heightened attention.

"By issuing government bonds of that amount, promising a payback within three years. You could offer a variable coupon rate pegged to the GDP growth your country would show over this three-year period. Investors will compare this to what happened in Iceland after the move to gold, where GDP has grown by fifty percent a year. You could propose a minimum rate of ten percent, able to increase up to twenty percent, depending on GDP growth. That would be a *very* attractive bond offering, considering that the currency behind it would be gold, which is inflation proof."

"Wow. That *is* a bold, but interesting, idea. But how would we be able to pay back such a large amount of debt in such a short time?"

"Think about the incoming population of hundreds of thousand people, many being wealthy. They will want to settle down in a nice residence. You won't be able to free up enough real estate that fast, so there will have to be a lot of new construction.

"As your government still owns quite some land in the country, you could sell, say, five hundred thousand land lots of two thousand square meters at two hundred dollars a square meter. That would bring in two hundred billion dollars! At the same time, you would solve the problem of providing housing for all the new residents without creating a speculative price bubble on the real estate market. My guess is that you would raise that money in less than a year, so you could pay back the loan, with less interest, before the three-year period is over. Now, there are a couple of problems I haven't yet mentioned."

"What?" the man said, revealing worry for the first time.

"If you want to be able to buy the gold you need at a good price, you need to keep your plans secret from the Western central banks. I don't think they would accept selling their gold to you. You will need to pitch and sell the bond issue without explaining what the money will go to. I guess you can say that you will finance a transition period to lower taxes and that the debt will be paid back by privatization of public property, which is perfectly true."

The man sighed, thinking hard about the implication of Benson's words. "Wow, that's a challenge. And you said there's a second catch?"

"Yes, I don't think you will be able to sell these bonds to your own citizens only. That would require each of them to put up thirty thousand U.S. dollars. So you will have to address the international financial markets in order to be able to raise the two hundred billion dollars you need. Then again, don't be pessimistic. The United States has raised ten times that amount, with much less attractive interest, just to finance an annual budget deficit, so I'm confident you can make it."

"Professor Benson, you don't know how happy I am to have contacted you for advice. I feel much better now, as I now *know* we will be able to make it."

"The pleasure is all mine, being able to help you. If you wish, I may act as your consultant on these matters. I also recommend you ask members of your team to attend courses in sound economics which I hold on the Internet-based Free Men, Real Money network."

"Very well. I'll now go back to talk to our president, and I think it's time to let the rest of our government into the secret. My plan is to do all the preparations of the referendum and then announce it quite a short time before we will hold it. For sure, this will limit our possibility to convince people to vote for it. But it will also give less reaction time, which I see as more important, for what I expect to be very negative if not hostile reactions from the world's large economic powers. Do you agree with my analysis?"

"I certainly do. Start buying gold, and silver, on the markets right now. And launch your bond issue as soon as humanly possible, to buy all the gold you need. You will have to take a bet on the result of the referendum. Try to set the date of the referendum to end of August. I know it may seem too close, but I fear a renewed speculative attack on gold before the end of the summer. And if that happens, you need to be ready to step in, as the white knight of the gold-money system, to save it from destruction! After your referendum, and provided you have the necessary gold, you will be able to operate the switch on December thirty-first."

"Very well," the man said again and stood, signaling he had gotten what he wanted from the meeting and was ready to leave. Switching back to the more mechanical voice which he had used for their first exchange of code word sentences, he said, "I'm now confident I'll be able to bring down the golden sun and give it to my love. I'm very grateful for your help, Professor, and I shall contact you again shortly for further discussions of this topic."

The man stretched his right hand out to shake Benson's, and with his left hand, he slipped a business card directly into Benson's left shirt breast pocket. Benson shook his hand and nodded with a smile, but did not find any words to say before the man turned around and walked away.

Benson, who had some time to kill before catching his flight back to Iceland, sat down again at the café table and ordered a soft drink to cool down from the hot summer sun and from the excitement the meeting had aroused in him. While he was waiting for the soft drink, he pulled out the business card from his pocket. It was slightly larger than usual business cards, which made it possible to have the name and title of his acquaintance in no less than six languages, three on each face of the card.

Benson smiled to himself as he put the card back into his pocket, looking around to make sure nobody had seen it. Then he looked up again at the deep blue sky where the golden sun was still high this early in the afternoon. He emptied his glass and congratulated himself on his contribution to what he thought would be the next milestone of the monetary revolution the world was undergoing.

✲ ✲ ✲

Two weeks after the call he had received from Jessica Frostby, Mark Lomack had come in early to the office of FMRM. At 6:00 a.m., he was to facilitate a Web conference uniting over a hundred interested listeners. Many of them were chief financial officers of the large Western companies that had moved their head offices to Hong Kong while holding their cash and accounting in Iceland. Other participants were investors who had put a lot of money in gold recently, including representatives of the Chinese government. All participants were there to understand the development of the gold price, which now played a major role for the value of their investments. Most of them were highly concerned by the recent fall in the gold price.

Mark waited until 6:05, finished his coffee-and-donut breakfast, and started. "Welcome, everybody, to today's conference. The topic was selected for its importance with respect to current events. Let me dive directly into my introduction. As you have learned from frequent blog posts on the FMRM over the last two weeks, governments of the G7 countries, led by the United States, have decided on a joint plan to destroy the gold-money system of Iceland. Their plan is to flood the market with gold in hopes of making the price of gold plummet. As the gold price starts to fall, they expect people to begin withdrawing gold to exchange it for dollars. Today, we will look at the gold price as such, what determines it and how it's likely to develop."

One of the Chinese participants remarked, "But I read an interview with the president of the ECB, he said the rumor about a giant sale of gold is false. He said that if the gold price is falling, then maybe people just had come to realize that gold is an outdated savings product."

"Yes," Mark answered, "of course they will deny any deliberate action on their part, in order to make people believe that we see an actual fall in the market price of gold, and not just a giant market manipulation staged by governments. Now, let me remind you of some key figures.

"Before Iceland moved to use gold as money, the gold price hovered between one thousand and eleven hundred dollars an ounce. It then increased to twelve hundred dollars. After that, when many large corporations moved their headquarters out of Western countries to have their cash reserves in gold in Iceland, the price climbed up to around fifteen hundred dollars. This was the logical consequence of an increased demand for gold, to be used as money, and of continued monetary inflation in dollars and euros.

"As you may know, the price of gold has now fallen, in less than a week, almost forty percent, down to below one thousand dollars per ounce. While it's hard to obtain precise statistics, we estimate central banks in the Western world have placed around three thousand tons of gold on the market for sale. As the market doesn't easily absorb such a quantity in such a short time, we see the price falling. By the way, thank you to those of you who bought some of that gold. I think you made a good deal given the low price you paid, and you helped slow down the fall of the gold price."

The chief financial officer of General Retail said, "Yes, we all know that the stakes are high for us now that we have most of our cash reserves in gold. But could you remind us how the gold price influences other aspects of the world economy?"

"Yes, sure, good point. Since gold is now used as money in Iceland, the purchasing power of the people who hold their money in gold will depend on the gold price. Their purchasing power depends on how gold is valued compared to all other goods. Let's look outside Iceland's borders.

"The key thing to watch is the price of gold, expressed in other kinds of money, such as dollars or euros. This gold price will influence the cost of imports to Iceland and how much money Icelandic exporters get for the goods they sell abroad. It will also be very important for people living outside Iceland who have a gold deposit account there and spend their money somewhere else.

"For example, a person living in the United States doing purchases there using a credit card backed against his Icelandic gold account will get fewer and fewer goods for his money if the gold price falls. Today, we see governments and central banks sell gold to make the gold price fall. They hope that everybody who has decided to hold savings in gold will get the impression that they have made a bad decision. If many people who hold gold money today get nervous, sell their gold, and revert to dollars for their savings, then the gold-money system may disappear. *This*, of course, is the purpose of the current market manipulation by governments."

The asset manager of a large mutual savings fund asked with a tense voice, "What should determine the gold price in the long run and what arguments do we have to claim that gold won't just lose its value overnight?"

"Right, this brings us to the core of today's conference. The price of all goods is determined by demand and supply. For our purpose, we can consider the demand for money to be roughly constant. That holds true except for unusual events such as hyperinflation, when people get rid of their money quickly, or a debt crisis, when people may want to increase their money holdings to be able to pay back debt. If demand is constant, then supply can still influence prices. For more than a century, the policy of central banks across the world has been to steadily increase the quantity of paper money, more or less quickly. That increase has been much faster than the increase in gold quantities. Need I remind you that up until forty years ago, the price of gold was set to thirty-five dollars an ounce? The change in the dollar–gold price between then and now is of a factor around forty."

A few *wows* were heard from participants who were not aware of this radical evolution of the gold price, seldom mentioned in news media or in mainstream education.

Mark continued. "As mentioned, the gold price was fifteen hundred dollars an ounce before market manipulation started. If that price was too high, as governments now pretend, then it would require that from today on, the quantity of gold in the world would increase faster than the quantity of paper money. That has never happened in history, and I don't think it ever will, because the very purpose of creating paper money in the first place was to enable government and banks to create money as fast as they wished."

"What do you think the gold price should be two or three years from now?" a Hong Kong politician asked.

"I believe the target price in three years should be around two thousand dollars an ounce. That might sound huge, but my assumption is that the quantity of gold only increases by a few percents per year while quantity of paper money will increase by ten to fifteen percent per year. That would give a compound increase of around forty percent over three years.

"Let's consider that the price of gold before speculation started was a good reference price. A forty percent increase on the price of fifteen hundred dollars an ounce would bring the price up above two thousand dollars an ounce. As markets try to anticipate future changes, the target price of two thousand dollars an ounce might actually come true much earlier, as soon as the market understands the risk for paper-money inflation."

The Hong Kong politician asked, "What makes you think the money quantity could increase by forty percent in three years? That sounds crazy!"

"Well, as I just mentioned, the average increase during the last forty years was only slightly less than that. Today in Western countries, we see an unprecedented situation of very high government debt and yearly government deficits amounting to more than thirty percent of the tax revenues. As this goes on and on, year after year, the mountain of debt just keeps getting bigger and more and more impossible to pay back."

"Alright Lomack," the CFO of General Retail said, "we've got your point. I agree that your forecast for the long term makes sense. But what is your advice to us today? If it's true that all the governments of the Western world are colluding to kill the gold price, we may go down with it."

Mark took a deep breath, and then answered, raising his clenched fist. "My main advice is don't panic. Keep the long term view in mind. Don't start selling your gold even if the price keeps falling. Instead, you should consider it as an opportunity to buy gold at a discount you may never ever see again.

"The governments and central banks want to provoke the end of gold money. Don't let them succeed. Money developed on the free market as a tool between traders. We recently put it back into that role after a century of government hijacking of money. So now is the time to stand up for the right to trade and save freely in a monetary unit that no government can destroy for its own purposes!"

☆ ☆ ☆

"Frostby! The time has come to finish the job. You have my authorization, indeed my formal order, to sell *all* the gold holdings of the Federal Reserve, if needed, to make the gold price go through the floor!"

The chairman of the Federal Reserve, Clarence Clearwater, sat down and thoughtfully lit a cigar. Jeffery Hastings nodded approvingly.

The fourth person in the room, Joseph Miller, added, "Yes, we really want the gold price to fall down to as close to zero as possible. It must happen in two steps. The first step is a massive sale of gold from us and from our European and Japanese friends. That should drive the price down to a range between five hundred and seven hundred dollars an ounce. This level would be an important psychological barrier to go through. We could issue a statement to emphasize that the price is less than half what it was just a few weeks ago.

"At that point, the second step will kick in, which is the chain reaction of panic we hope will spread among all the businesses and individuals who have put their cash reserves in gold. They thought they would escape the erosion of purchasing power caused by dollar inflation. If we succeed, they should lose more purchasing power in less than a month than they would have lost in ten years of holding dollars on a cash account!"

"Jessica," Jeffery said, "is this all clear? Are you ready to launch this last phase of our operation in the coming week?"

She looked at the three men with the insensitive expression of a hit man, hired to commit murder and not to think about the moral rightness of his actions. "Of course. Just one thing. In order to sell such huge quantities of gold, you need to give me full freedom about to whom I can sell it. There appears to be buyers in the Asian markets. I need to push as much gold as I can to them."

"Yes, by any means," Clearwater replied. "Just make sure none of it goes to those Icelanders. The purpose of this operation is to strangle their monetary system, not to boost it with a large inflow of gold savings purchased at below-market prices."

"Good point, Clarence," Miller added pleasantly. "While selling the gold of course is a Federal Reserve operation, the Department of the Treasury will also take its responsibility. In order to get the best possible effect in the second step of the plan, I plan for a propaganda campaign that should even top the draft campaigns for World War Two. Uncle Sam will again stare at citizens from millions of posters. This time, he'll say, 'Be a patriot! Sell your gold! Use dollars! Save the American Way!'"

☆ ☆ ☆

Jessica emerged alone from the meeting. Her heart was beating much faster than usual, and she was sweating terribly in the summer heat of Washington, D.C. She looked around, checking that no one was close to her. Then she rapidly dialed a number on her mobile phone.

"Jessica? It's been a while!"

"Professor, you have to help me. You know I accepted to take charge of the Fed's gold-selling operation. I thought I'd be able to influence things in the right way. But now I'm asked to sell all the remaining gold of the Federal

Reserve, in order to sink the gold price once and for all. The Treasury is preparing some giant propaganda campaign to provoke a panic among people owning gold!"

She heard Professor Benson breathing during a moment of silence, before he said, "Jessica. Now is the time not to be afraid. You remember when I told you I'd rather have you inside the Fed in charge of its dirty deeds than anyone else in the world? That never was more true than today. Don't worry. Go on selling the gold. It should fall into good hands."

"But...I'm afraid the price will dwindle! Don't you see; we're talking about eight thousand tons of gold. Seventeen thousand tons if we add in the European and Japanese reserves!"

"Jessica, I now will ask you something I never did as your teacher. But I believe you trust me enough by now to accept this, because I can't tell you more at this point. Trust me when I tell you to go on selling all the gold you can. Just one question. What's your timeline?"

"I'm asked to keep selling gold piecemeal during August. Then they want a radical increase in the selling and in the propaganda by end of August, when people return from summer vacations."

"All right. So, please, do what I now tell you. Sell the gold during August, but not more than a third. Save two-thirds for the end of the month. The price will keep falling, but I hope it won't be too bad. Now I need to talk to Mark. We at the FMRM will now step into the propaganda war, the war of the minds!"

CHAPTER 20:
War of Money, War of Worlds

"Will the Gold Price Go through the Floor?" said the headline of New York's major financial newspaper.

By the middle of August, the gold price had fallen to eight hundred dollars an ounce, after a continuous selling from central banks of the Western world. News reports from major television shows and newspapers accounted for the fall by quoting political and central bank decision makers, who claimed that this evolution was "a healthy move back to the best and most modern currencies, the dollar and the euro, away from that outdated pipe dream of using gold as money."

As rare voices of a different opinion, Mark Lomack and Montgomery Benson had drafted a short letter, which was to be sent by e-mail to the 150,000 subscribers of the FMRM. By using fee-based commercial e-mailing, the letter would be sent to an additional ten million people, half of them in China and India, using translated versions prepared by Ka Ying and an Indian FMRM member. For both mailings, it was estimated that each recipient would forward the letter to ten people. The letter read:

These days, an intense propaganda from Western governments claims that gold money is not only outdated and preposterous but also dangerous and loss-generating as an investment object. Governments urge all citizens of the world to sell their gold and to keep their savings in paper currencies. Efforts to sink the gold price, and thereby create an uncontrolled panic of gold sales, are becoming stronger and stronger. We wish to present this situation for what it is: a war between paper money and gold money, actually a war between government control and individual freedom! The outcome of this war will be decided by the verdict and vote of the world through the financial market of buying and selling gold.

At the FMRM, we believe that today's political democracy in Western countries is harmful. As constitutional safeguards of individual rights and property have been removed, elections are decided in a game of interest group warfare where groups try to rob each other with taxes, regulations, and bans. However, we consider the voting process of the market where people take buying and selling decisions to be perfectly legitimate. Why? Because people are disposing with their own, and not other people's, property. In this way, a voter has to bear the full consequences of his vote. That's the meaning of accountability, which comes with freedom.

In the coming weeks, the financial market will propose an informal, but quite real, referendum about money. Every citizen of planet Earth who owns money can participate in this vote. The choice you will have to make is to buy gold, to sell gold, or to do nothing. The result of the process will be either the survival of the gold-money system created in Iceland or its destruction and disappearance.

You must understand that the stakes in this vote are much higher than the return on investment you may make on your current cash holdings. This is why governments of the Western world are deploying a level of propaganda we haven't seen since World War II. The issue you vote on is whether money should be allowed to be a free-market commodity such as gold, with a monetary system without government intervention. In such a world, you will have the possibility to save money for your future while knowing its value cannot be destroyed by the government.

In the world of paper money, you will have to worry about waking up someday to find out that government has doubled the quantity of paper money and has effectively stolen half of your wealth by destroying the purchasing power of money. That is the extraordinary power they want to defend! That is how governments financed both World Wars, and how they now are financing their accelerating budget deficits. That is their only way out to be able to pay back the mountains of government debt that decades of annual deficits have piled up!

So, don't take this lightly! Vote! Buy gold! You will not regret this act of heroic defense of your individual freedom. We are not suggesting that you make any form of financial sacrifice. The gold price today is around $700 an ounce. It went down from an initial market price of $1500, due to massive market manipulations by central banks. At the FMRM, we believe the gold price should soon be not $1500 but above $2000 dollars an ounce, as the quantity of paper money should increase by around 40% in the coming three years, while the quantity of gold will remain quite stable. Come to our Web site to find some suggestions on how you could cast your vote in this historical battle. Also, most important, please send this letter on to ten friends who care about individual freedom and sound money!

The Free Men, Real Money network

✲ ✲ ✲

One week after the FMRM chain letter was sent out, Joseph Miller and Clarence Clearwater met for lunch on the outdoor terrace of a prestigious Washington restaurant. They were sitting at a table out of hearing distance of others and were enjoying a glass of white wine with their appetizers.

"Here's to the next century of central banking controlled by the Federal Reserve!" Clearwater said triumphantly, raising his glass in a toast. "It's funny that this situation, which I guess we can call an existential crisis of our monetary system, happens almost exactly one century after the creation of the Federal Reserve. So if we now succeed in killing the gold-money free-market alternative, I hope our government-controlled system will be safe for at least one more century."

"Oh yes, I believe it will," Miller said with conviction. "When people lose a lot of money, the memory of that remains through generations. Just look at the German hyperinflation after World War One. The descendants of the people who lived through that are still having nightmares about losing all their savings through inflation!"

"Yes, and that's why they're so stingy about the 'price stability' they absolutely want the European Central Bank to defend. But I must say they have become easier to deal with in the last few years, with the debt crisis of several European countries, and since the Germans themselves have a giant debt that needs financing by creative means!"

"Indeed!" Miller replied gaily, and this time he raised his glass to Clearwater. "I don't know who among your forefathers invented the genial system combining a government-backed central bank controlling dollar printing with legalization of fractional reserve banking, but *that* is what our current power as a government is based on, and *that* is the only monetary system that will remain once we have finished the job with Iceland."

Clearwater raised his glass in response, and said thoughtfully, "Yes, talking about the people who created the Federal Reserve System. I met with some of their descendants over at Wall Street a few days ago: the leadership team of the Zach Morgano bank.

"On my request, Zach Morgano is reopening its retail bank subsidiary in Iceland. They weren't so keen to do it, as they went bust two years ago over there. But I explained to them that this may be the revenge they have been waiting for. So they reopen next Monday, and it will be the first bank in Iceland these days that does *not* accept gold deposits—only dollars and euros!

Miller frowned, worried. "Are you sure Zach Morgano will be allowed to reopen in Iceland after the counterfeiting scandal they provoked?"

Clearwater chuckled. "Joseph, don't forget Iceland takes pride in having no bank regulation whatsoever! Anybody can open a bank over there, and Zach Morgano will do fine as long as they don't revert to fractional reserve lending. Even the monetary unit isn't imposed by law; gold is just the current choice established on the free market in Iceland. I am confident markets will now switch back to dollars and euros.

"If next Monday becomes another one of those 'Black Mondays' of financial history, then the Zach Morgano people and the other Wall Street banks will be on the winning side—a sweet revenge for the blows they took during the subprime crisis."

"That's very good news," Miller exclaimed. He closed his eyes. When he opened them again, he said, "I just saw in my mind how we must play this out. I envision a giant bank run in Iceland next Monday, where people panic to get their gold out of their bank in order to sell it and put it in dollars in the Zach Morgano bank. If we set it up well, that should kill the gold banks, after just a day or two."

"Wow, now you get me dreaming too," Clearwater said. "But how will you make that happen?"

"Two things: I will now push the button regarding our propaganda campaign to U.S. citizens. The European Union is in the loop and will launch a similar campaign. Second, you should personally give a call to the Frostby woman. You need to ask her to push the button too, to step up the speed of gold sales.

"This weekend I want so much gold up for sale on the market that no one will buy it. I am confident that the gold price will fall below five hundred dollars an ounce. *Then* we'll be able to make an offer to the owners of gold bank accounts that they can't refuse. We'll give them an offer limited to forty-eight hours, where we propose to buy their gold way above the market price, provided they put their money back into a dollar account. Even though I think it isn't really useful, we would build up again a small U.S. government gold reserve, after having sold it all just a week before. I don't care about paying more for the gold than we sold it for earlier. Even with a financial loss, destroying the gold-money system would be our best investment ever in the service of government control over society!"

☆ ☆ ☆

Saturday morning was misty in Reykjavik, a typical day in the fall, but a hesitant sun added some warmth to the chilly scenery. At an hour when most people had not yet had breakfast, Cornelius Hazelton was already pacing the main meeting room of his office, in front of Laura Dalaghan, Pete Bagnelli, and Mark Lomack. Bobby Cheston and Ka Ying were participating across a video connection from Hong Kong.

"I'll be damned! We are trying all we can, but I fear we're running a losing race against those evil bastards in the U.S. and European governments. For those of you who missed the GNN show of last night, let me just summarize the key points.

"The secretary of the treasury and the chairman of the Fed were on the *Manuel Jones Economic and Political Outlook* show. They made an outright appeal to people from all over the world to sell their gold, 'while it's still time,' as they put it. They announced that the Federal Reserve and the European Central Bank have agreed on a deal with the Zach Morgano bank in Iceland to repurchase gold from corporations and private individuals at fifty percent above the market price. They are committed to this, provided people sell their entire gold holding and provided they do it between Monday morning and Tuesday evening next week. Those hypocritical bastards said this was a 'gesture of responsibility from the governments of the developed world to help people get out of their foolish and overly risky investments in gold.' That is how they justified the contradiction of offering to purchase gold from people while flooding the market with gold by selling out the reserves of the Fed!

"We all know that the only purpose they're aiming for is to destroy our free-market monetary system! So unless things change, I fear we're up for a run on Laura's bank and on Pete's gold mutual fund on Monday morning. Please, each of you, give me a status report on our latest efforts. Pete, Laura, start with the situation here in Iceland."

"Well," Pete said looking hesitant and feeble, "over the last week we have hit the roof about finding people in Iceland who can and want to put more money into gold. All the richest people who came here last year with you Cornelius have already taken heavy positions. Hell, Kilby Rock sold his military aircraft to an American in order to get ten million more to put into gold, even though it was one of his most precious belongings! So most of the people who moved here have bought all the additional gold they can buy. In the last few days, we've gotten more and more calls from people who want to *sell* their gold to get dollars. Just like you, Cornelius, I fear that last night's GNN show will make hell break loose on Monday morning."

Laura took over. "At my bank, we also managed for some time to make people increase their gold holdings, to absorb some of the gold that was put on the market by the Fed and the ECB. As you know, that effort soon flattened out, and we had to leverage all the assets of Hazelton Growth Capital to be able to borrow some more money. When that couldn't go any further, Cornelius, Pete and I made this bond issue where the honor behind our three names was the only guarantee the buyers could get. Our issue raised thirty billion dollars, for which we bought a thousand tons of gold. Ninety percent of the money came from rich people such as Kilby Rock. But we still have around ten percent, or three billion dollars' worth of bonds, that have been sold to the public in Iceland. Do you understand? Each Icelander has put on average three thousand dollars in our bonds!

"It makes me sleepless when I think about that we will be unable to honor our obligations unless the gold price remains above twelve hundred dollars on ounce. On Friday, it was at seven hundred dollars, and it should keep falling after the U.S. government's statement.

"So the situation is quite disastrous. In order to slow down the fall in the gold price, we need to be able to purchase a lot more gold. But our own positions are leveraged to the limit, and we can't find any more external investors here in Iceland. Basically, adding up the efforts of Pete's funds, of my bank, and the private bond offering, we have managed to absorb sixty billion dollars of investments, which allowed us to buy about two thousand tons of gold. But we can't get any further."

Hazelton wiped sweat from his forehead. "OK, that's not good news. Mark, please go next; the FMRM's current work may be our last hope."

"I hate to say it Cornelius, but I'm not so sure about that," Mark said with a low voice. "Let me summarize the results since we made our e-mailing. Objectively, the result is a fabulous success. Of the one and half million people who are FMRM subscribers or who got the letter from one of them, fifty percent signed up for an average purchase worth ten thousand U.S. dollars. And for the e-mailing to ten million non-FMRM members across Asia, which is estimated to have reached a hundred million people in total, we saw two million people buy, on average, ten thousand dollars' worth of gold. Altogether, this resulted in collecting almost twenty-eight billion dollars. But that only purchases around one thousand tons of gold.

"Bobby, Ka, why don't you give the latest update from Asia?" Mark turned from the screen back to Hazelton. "While we were sleeping, they were making additional efforts this morning to find institutional investors to purchase gold."

Bobby cleared his throat. "Well, you guys together were able to obtain the purchase of three thousand tons of gold. That's the same as Ka and I have achieved over here. We have been lobbying eighteen hours a day in the last weeks, focusing on two types of potential buyers: the large Western corporations that moved here on our advice not so long ago and the governments of the larger Asian countries. I hate to say it, but I'm afraid we too won't be able to get any more people on board from now on, after the statement on the GNN last night which everyone over here watched.

"While we've been telling them that the gold price should never go below fifteen hundred dollars, and should soon be at two thousand, they now heard the two most powerful people of the banking world talk about a target price at or below five hundred dollars an ounce. So I expect that we won't get any new purchase orders now. But I'm sure we'll get a lot of angry calls from people wondering how and why we convinced them to buy as much gold as they already have."

Hazelton stood up and paced the room furiously, smacking a flower pot with his hand. It crashed to the floor and broke to pieces. "Damn! Damn! Damn! We're trapped!" he yelled, his face all red. "And they're now preparing to unload even more gold during the weekend and early next week to make the price plummet. Mark, do you have any idea how much gold they may still put on the market, knowing that we won't be able to buy any more of it anyway?"

"I've got an idea about the numbers," Mark replied. "But I suggest we call Jessica Frostby. You know she's in charge of the Fed's gold selling."

"Right, call that traitor up!" Hazelton yelled. "I hope she'll explain to us why the hell *she*, another of Montgomery's students, is leading the charge against gold money."

"Cornelius, please don't talk like that about Jessica," Mark said shaking his head reproachfully. "I'd rather it be her than anyone else in that job today. Let's call her. Even though it's two in the morning in the United States I'm sure she will answer."

Mark was right. Her sleepy voice came through the loudspeaker in their office. "Hello? Mark, is that you?" Jessica said, yawning.

"Yes, we're gathered in Reykjavik, with Bobby and Ka on the line too. We are coming to the conclusion that our shared efforts over the last weeks have enabled gold purchases of six thousand tons. I believe that two thousand tons have also been purchased by other investors. So while all of the eight thousand tons sold by the Fed and the ECB so far have been absorbed, the gold price has kept falling. And, worse, we aren't able to find any more buyers. After the GNN show last night, we even fear the people we have convinced to buy will turn into sellers by Monday morning. Our second worry, which gave me a nightmare last night, was the idea that the Fed and the ECB could keep unloading the rest of their reserves. What can you tell us about that?"

"Hold on. Let me head to the living room and join you on the Web conference." As she got connected, her face appeared with a tired smile and was partly covered by her uncombed blonde hair. "Hi guys!" she said, waving into the Webcam. Her face turned dark as she went on. "I'm afraid I don't have any good news for you. I was given a formal order yesterday to put all of our remaining gold reserves for sale during the weekend, to make sure the market is flooded by Monday morning. If we add the reserves of the Fed, and those of the ECB and the Japanese central bank, we're talking about twelve thousand tons of gold.

"The only thing that has limited my panic was the words of Professor Benson last time I spoke to him. He told me not to be afraid, and to keep selling the gold, that there would be buyers for it. That was more than a week ago, and things have changed since then. I got the order yesterday, and since then I've been trying to reach Benson on the phone. Impossible! He doesn't pick up my calls, and his phone seems to be off. I don't know where he is, or why he doesn't answer."

Mark frowned and added, thoughtfully, "Me too. I haven't been able to get hold of the professor for the last few days. Since he and I started to work together within the FMRM, he always told me when he would go away."

Ka Ying stepped up in front of the Hong Kong Webcam and screamed with a panic he could not hold back: "I just got a text message from my contact in the Chinese central bank. He said he has received orders to sell the one thousand tons of gold they have purchased if the gold price goes under five hundred dollars on Monday morning! What are we going to do?"

A heavy silence filled the room and the Web conference, as none of them knew what to say. Mark was the only one to speak. "We are going to do something which we have always done, but which is now harder than ever. We will trust the professor's words. But as long as we can't get in touch with him, we have to act on our own. I will send out a call for help within the FMRM, to have our European and American supporters come to Reykjavik to help us.

"Laura, Pete, I suggest you bring in a few hundred temp workers for Monday morning. We are facing a run on your banks, and you need as many people as possible to convince your clients not to take their gold out and sell it for dollars. Laura, as an exceptional measure, I suggest you take down your Internet bank until further notice. Let those who want to close their account wait or come to Reykjavik to the branch office on Monday. That should slow down withdrawals somewhat. We'll have to hope that the gold price doesn't fall further on Monday morning, even though I have to say that all the data at our hands indicates it will!"

✧ ✧ ✧

Banks and other businesses usually opened at 10:00 a.m. in Reykjavik, but this Monday the streets were already crowded with people at seven, and banks had committed to open at 9:00 a.m., or before, on this particular Monday. The atmosphere was electrified, not only due to the light that reflected from streetlamps down through the thick fog but also from the tension of the people elbowing their way through the streets of the city.

The Zach Morgano bank, one of the largest Wall Street banks, had already opened their dollar-only retail bank at seven that morning. They had tens of employees pacing the nearby streets, trying to bring in new customers. Flyers had been dropped over the city during the night by an American military aircraft, and hundreds of thousands of these sheets were blowing around on the ground. The sheets read, in large bold letters:

> You now have 48 hours left to close your gold deposit account, if you still have one. By courtesy of the Federal Reserve and the European Central Bank, the Zach Morgano Bank will purchase your gold at 50% above the market price during this limited period. Before the weekend, the gold price was $700 an ounce. We can't promise you it will stay at that level. In fact, it is quite possible it falls much, much lower! It is our responsibility as statesmen to strongly recommend that you sell your gold now, early Monday morning, to minimize your losses.

At the bottom of the page were the handwritten signatures, and the titles and names, of the president of the United States, the president of the European Commission, and the Japanese prime minister.

Laura Dalaghan had followed Mark's advice and had hired extra personnel to stand in front of the Dalaghan Prudential Gold Bank's main office, to try to dissuade the people who were lining up to get their money out of the bank. By eight, one hour before opening, more than five hundred people were in front of the closed office doors. The situation was similar at all other Reykjavik bank offices. Crowds also grew at the Zach Morgano office, although for an opposite reason. Its first customers of the day were people who had stored gold in their own home, and now came to sell it to open a dollar deposit account with Zach Morgano.

Mark Lomack stood on a square outside the city center of Reyjkavik to which he had been forced to retreat. He had gathered a crowd of ten thousand people. Some of them where Icelanders and many others had come to Iceland by plane and by boat during the last two days, following a desperate call Mark had launched on the FMRM Web site. Mark now addressed the crowd using a loudspeaker, standing on a pile of ten wooden pallets that trembled dangerously from the morning breeze.

"Friends and lovers of individual freedom and sound money! It may seem to all of you that we're running a losing race. But we must not give up, as long as there is the slightest hope to avoid what we all fear will happen today. I thank you from the bottom of my heart for coming here today! Please, let's all spread out to go talk to the people. We have to dissuade them from closing their gold-money accounts. Tell them they're making the worst mistake of their lives if they accept the idea to sell their gold, and thereby their financial independence and freedom.

"I won't bother you with a long speech. You know all the rest. Now go out and help save the gold-money system. Be good! But remember, whatever situation you come into: no fighting! The word is our only weapon. It's the most powerful weapon there is, and I'm confident it will prevail and that people will hear reason!"

The silence after Mark stopped speaking was soon filled by a warm but short applause, after which the FMRM representatives spread out over the city. Mark himself walked into the city center, where he had planned to meet with Ivar Larsen at a street corner near the main square, Laekjartorg.

"Hi, Ivar," Mark said to the giant man with a long beard, who gave him a forceful pat on the back.

"Hi, Mark," Larsen said. "Always happy to see you, even though this is quite a sad day for me, and for my country, at least that's what I fear it will be."

"We shouldn't give up without a fight," Mark said loudly. "Everybody is already counting the gold-money system out. They forget that today, the quantity of gold used as money is higher than it ever was. It was ten thousand tons a few months ago, for a gold price of fifteen hundred dollars an ounce. Now the quantity of gold used as money is eighteen thousand tons, with a price that has decreased to seven hundred dollars. How can people be so blind they don't see the fall in the price is just a giant market manipulation?"

"Well, I guess they may see that. At least the financial markets. But at the end of the day, people will look at their own purchasing power if they have their bank deposits in gold and at the return over time if they hold gold as an investment. So I fear that the repurchase offering the Western governments are making today will be an offer people won't dare to refuse. Just imagine: they're getting fifty percent above the market price!"

Mark was seeing red with anger, not because of Ivar Larsen but because of the Western governments. "But today, the market price may fall to five hundred dollars, or less. So people will get no more than seven hundred fifty dollars an ounce. Those governments who pretend to do people a favor forget to tell that the market price, before they started manipulating it, was fifteen hundred dollars. And I showed in a recent conference that it should climb to two thousand dollars not long from now!"

Larsen shrugged and sighed heavily. "Well, you're certainly right. But I fear that even your crowd of ten thousand FMRM people won't be enough to dissuade people from selling their gold. Just look!" Larsen waved his arm in the direction of a nearby bank office where a long line of people were impatiently waiting to be let into their bank to draw their gold out. The clock was now 8:30 a.m., half an hour before opening time.

"And let's assume," Larsen continued, "that just half of the people who hold gold today for monetary use will want to sell it. That would put nine thousand tons on the market. Rumor has it that the Fed and the ECB are about to unload their remaining twelve thousand tons. It's obvious the gold price will fall below any reasonable limit, which would only increase the panic selling."

"Damn it!" Mark said. "By the way, what's your president doing today?"

Larsen looked sad. "Oh, he's locked into his office, and doesn't want to speak to anyone. Ice TV asked him to come for an interview this morning, but he refused. The only person he wished to talk to is Montgomery Benson, but we have been trying to call him, without success, for several days. I admit I'm disappointed too. Hell, Montgomery helped us get all this started, and now that we're facing disaster, he isn't here to help us out!"

Mark looked intensely at Larsen. "Don't be so sure about that. I can't reach him either, but I hope he is working for the same cause as we are. He has never let me down before, and this is the fight of his life. I'm just impatient to hear from him, and to know what he's doing!"

The two of them had been walking while speaking and had now reached Laekjartorg, where a giant television screen was installed. Two famous reporters were standing there delivering live broadcasts: Lisa Ivarsen of Ice TV and Kevin Larrison of the GNN.

Lisa Ivarsen had just started her broadcast. "Once again Iceland is at the center of the world's attention. However, this time our local population is not so happy and proud about it. There's a widespread revulsion because people believe we are being punished by a hostile operation launched by the Western superpowers, who apparently wish to destroy our unique monetary system. When we launched it almost three years ago, we couldn't imagine it would arouse such resentment, not to say hatred, from the United States and the European Union."

Kevin Larrison, who was just coming on the air, said, "Hello to all our viewers across the world. At this hour, only Asians and Europeans are likely to be up. But we're an around-the-clock news channel, and this, ladies and gentlemen, is likely to be the scene of breaking news.

"I came here three years ago to observe the triumphal launch of the Icelandic free-market monetary system. I don't wish to sound like a vulture, and I should say in all honesty that this doesn't make me feel happy. But today I believe I will witness the *end* of this unusual social experiment. U.S. government spokespersons have stated at several occasions that gold money is an anachronism in our modern big-government era. Probably, today will be the day when they will be proved right. Even though their opponents, such as the Free Men, Real Money network, claim that the fall of the gold price is only due to the largest market manipulation in history.

"Well, it may be so, but it sure seems to be turning into a self-reinforcing spiral of gold selling and price fall. Now, your guess is as good as mine about what will really happen, but in any case we will know shortly. Banks here are to open in 10 minutes."

Mark sighed as he had listened to these two statements. "I'll leave you here, Ivar. I'll make a tour around the banks, but first I'll go talk to Laura Dalaghan. Let's meet here in front of the television screen in a little while, when the markets have opened. And tell the president to get out of his office. Does he consider himself a leader? Does he want to defend what we have built together? In that case, today is the day when he should be out in the streets."

"All right, I'll talk to him," Larsen said without energy as Mark Lomack ran in the direction of the Dalaghan Prudential Gold Bank.

When Mark arrived to Laura's bank, the clock had just turned 9 a.m., and there was a riot in front of the office doors where people were pushing each other to be able to get in.

"Let me through, goddamn it! Bugger off!" a tall and fat Englishman screamed. "I have travelled all the way here to get my gold back and to sell it. So you better make sure I get it right away. I need to run over to the Zach Morgano bank to sell it. I heard the market price of gold might fall from seven hundred to less than two hundred dollars before the day is over!"

The security guard of Laura's bank tried to control the man, but hundreds of other people were no less upset. Laura was also there and tried to get the situation under control.

"Shut up and stand still all of you!" she screamed loudly and with the kind of unyielding authority that compels obedience. The people in front of her office doors froze to listen. "Anybody who disturbs the order is going to be locked up by our security forces and handed over to the police! Then you would likely spend the day in arrest, and you can forget about selling your gold today.

We will of course allow those of you who wish to close your gold accounts to do so. But I won't tell you this again: be respectful and wait in line, or else!"

She turned away from the crowd and smiled at Mark, whom she had seen approaching.

"How are you?" he said with a dull smile.

"As you see I've got some adrenaline in my body right now, but I'm afraid that tonight will be the worst night in my life. If we see mass withdrawals, not only will the gold money system be destroyed but, in addition, Pete, Cornelius, and I will suffer a personal financial disaster. We'll be broke, and we'll be hung out as criminals of any filthy investment scam."

"Laura, we're not there yet. Let's not give up quite yet. Why don't we look at the market price this morning?"

She smiled thankfully at Mark for reassuring her and nodded. "Yes, sure. Let's go into Pete's trading room next door. He's there already."

"Hey, man," Pete said with a tense smile when Mark entered the trading room followed by Laura. "You remember when I went bust using your software during the subprime crisis? This time, according to my calculations, the debt I might end up with could be a thousand times higher, if it all goes as the vultures of Big Government are hoping."

Pete laughed in a strained manner, and Mark looked severely at him. "Stop joking about your own ruin, damn it. For the time being, you're still alive and well, so let's look at the numbers."

They bent over a screen where the gold trading prices of Asian and European markets were displayed.

"Hell," Pete exclaimed when he was able to interpret the grid of numbers faster than Mark and Laura. "Jessica wasn't kidding. There are indeed twelve thousand tons of gold out for sale. So the Fed and the ECB are trying to unload *all* their gold. And there is also a forecasted sale this afternoon of a thousand tons on behalf of the Zach Morgano bank! They are consolidating sales by private retail banks that have signed the deal with the Fed to buy gold from depositors and then they unload it on the market for nonmonetary use."

"Alright, but what does this do to the gold spot price?" Mark said tensely.

Pete switched across a few screens. "Hell again! It's creeping down towards five hundred dollars an ounce. Remember what Ka Ying said. That's the lower limit the Chinese government had set beyond which they too will sell the a thousand tons of gold they recently purchased. And Bobby called me yesterday to say he had got a message from the CEO of General Retail, Walter Samuelson, saying that they too would sell if that price was reached. Incidentally, Bobby will then be fired for having dragged the company into one of their worst financial deals ever!"

Pete was starting to sweat despite the damp, cold air in the room. "What the hell are we going to do? I might be hung by a wild mob before the day is over! And Laura and Cornelius too! And you, Mark, you'll not be in a sweet position either, having convinced millions of people to purchase gold recently, at much higher prices!"

Laura, who now had understood how to read the trading screen screamed as from physical agony. "Aaagh! Damn! Damn! Damn! The price just went down to four hundred ninety dollars! And there are still twelve thousand tons of gold for sale, and no buyers seem to be coming in!"

Laura picked up a telephone and hysterically dialed Jessica's mobile number. "Jess? Sorry to wake you up in the middle of the night!"

"You're not waking me up," Jessica answered with pain in her voice. "Do you think I could sleep on a night like this?"

"No, I guess not. Now, can't you do anything to stop the gold sales? It is killing the gold money system, and it's killing me, Pete, and Cornelius personally!"

Jessica was sobbing as she answered: "You know I would, if I could! But I can't. Hell, the Chairman of the Fed himself, along with Jeffery and the other governors, are probably sitting in the office watching the same screens as you do. They have been gloating in triumph about this for the last few days. They won't let anything stop them now."

As Laura was starting to sob to, both from her own distress and from hearing her best friend cry on the phone, Mark and Pete screamed with one voice, "Look at the gold price!"

"It has climbed to six hundred dollars. And two thousand tons were just purchased!"

"Wow! What's happening?" Laura yelled, wiping some tears from her eyes. Jess, do you see the same thing as we do?"

"Yes I do," Jessica screamed, her voice trembling with delight as it came over the telephone loudspeaker.

"I beg your pardon?" Pete said, trying without success to look casual and sanguine. "While you said those words, four thousand more tons of gold went off the market. And the price is now eight hundred dollars an ounce!"

They all froze as a loud beep was heard. It was Mark's mobile phone; he had received a text message.

"It's from Benson," Mark screamed with excitement. "Listen!" he said and then read the message aloud:

> "So sorry for having been out of reach. Regret couldn't tell you what I was up to, would've broken an oath. Hope you will forgive if my actions help turn around the terrible situation. Mark, I'm sure you are in Reykjavik. Rush over to Laekjartorg and keep an eye on the giant television screen. Breaking news should soon appear./ Benson."

Laura screamed, "Jess, turn your TV on; talk to you later!"

The three of them ran out of Pete's trading room onto the streets of Reykjavik in the direction of Laekjartorg. Mark had the presence to fire away a brief blog posting that would instantly reach 150,000 subscribers of FMRM:

"Turn your TV on! Watch! I think our time has come!"

☆ ☆ ☆

As they arrived at the Laekjartorg square, they saw that Kevin Larrison had stepped up on a small scene with cameras on for a live broadcast of the GNN that was being displayed on the giant screen at the end of the square. Larrison said with a vibrant voice, "Breaking news, breaking news! The continuous fall of the gold price stopped a while ago, as enormous amounts of gold have been purchased on the international markets." He paused and listened to something he was being told in his earpiece. "It's truly unbelievable. This morning, twelve thousand tons of gold were up for sale, and the gold price went down to four hundred ninety dollars an ounce at its lowest. But now, only half an hour later, the price has jumped up to fifteen hundred dollars, and those twelve thousand tons of gold have now been purchased and are no longer on the market!"

Larrison's voice rung vibrantly from the loudspeakers and was heard over most of Reykjavik's city center. As a consequence, many people who had been waiting at banks to withdraw their gold abandoned their places in the lines and ran off in the direction of Laekjartorg to hear what was going on.

Larrison continued. "Now, if all this may seem like black magic, be assured it surely isn't." He again paused to listen to instructions. "I believe we're about to learn the explanation to what's happening. A press conference is about to start in Bern, the capital of Switzerland. We'll tune in to it to listen to the Swiss finance minister, Klaus Hopfman."

As the camera showed the Swiss finance minister, Mark screamed loudly so that most of the people on Laekjartorg heard him. "Look who's sitting there next to the minister. It's Professor Benson! Professor Benson!"

Ivar Larsen, who was in the crowd, ran up to Mark, Laura and Pete. "Wow, what the hell is going on here, friends?"

They all hushed as the Swiss finance minister started to speak. "Ladies and gentlemen, I'm happy to announce the intention of the Swiss Confederation to follow Iceland's lead. We will abandon the Swiss franc and introduce gold money. The decision has been taken by our government and will be confirmed in a referendum next week.

"We have already purchased all the gold we need to redeem all the demand deposits in Switzerland, which amounts to the equivalent of three hundred fifty billion U.S. dollars. We have done so by purchasing twelve thousand tons of gold under the favorable conditions that have prevailed recently on the gold spot market. We realize the price of gold will never ever again reach such low values as it had up to this morning, and *that* is good news for everybody who intends to keep their gold money. May I remind you it's the only inflation-proof monetary investment the world has to offer?

"You may wonder how we managed to buy all this gold. We already had gold, dollar, or other currency reserves amounting to one hundred ten billion. And we have sold public stakes in business enterprises for forty billion. The remaining two hundred billion we financed by very attractive three-year government bonds we started issuing two weeks ago. These bonds will provide holders with an interest between ten and twenty percent, depending on our GDP growth. The high interest rate enabled us to complete the subscription last week. And now the good news I can announce to the subscribers is that their interest and principal will be paid *in gold*!"

Larrison was shocked by what he was hearing, but after again having received instructions from his earpiece, he said, "We will now switch to Washington, D.C., where the country's leadership apparently has stayed awake to follow these dramatic events. It appears the president has something to say to us."

The screen switched to an image of the American president standing at a speaker's booth with the Homeland Security Officer on one side and the secretary of the treasury, Joseph Miller, on the other side. The president said, "Ladies and gentlemen, you have probably heard today's breaking news about Switzerland following Iceland's lead and scrapping its central bank and paper money to move to a free-market gold-based monetary system.

"Some people claim that these countries are reinventing money and are creating a freer and better world. What you all should realize is that whatever the evolution in Iceland and in Switzerland, what they are doing is harming the United States. It represents a clear and present danger to our national interest. Why is that? Their purpose is to attract people and capital out of the United States, thereby intending to reduce our taxation base and the resources of our government. They intend to make the dollar, the world's most prestigious monetary unit, appear as an unsafe placement subject to accelerating inflation.

"Therefore, in order to account for the fact that Iceland and the United States from now on have diverging national interests, I will submit on the next NATO conference a request to expel Iceland from the NATO. We are not threatening Iceland with war. The United States remains a peaceful country, and our military intentions are limited to defensive action. But it *does* mean that we will not save Iceland if a foreign power attacks. Iceland's current course of action may antagonize many countries, and they have exposed themselves to such risks. Indeed, it's a blatant provocation to most of the developed world.

"Regarding Switzerland, its status with respect to the United States will change from that of a neutral country to a country considered as a potential enemy. Its relation to the United States will thereby, from today on, be the same as for Iceland."

The president stopped speaking, and the homeland security officer took over. "We should all keep in mind that the Icelandic and Swiss leaderships didn't come up with these stunts on their own: they have been given advice by people who are in fact American citizens. These men represent the so-called Free Men, Real Money network, or FMRM for short, which is advocating gold money. They are advising people to send their savings to Iceland and to sell off their dollars or euros on the gold market. Of course, this is an action contrary to the national interest. Therefore, the American subsidiary of the FMRM, which is a limited liability company, or LLC, will be dissolved without further notice. Its leaders may be prosecuted for treason against our national interest."

The screen went back to displaying Kevin Larrison, who still was standing on a scene at the other side of the square. "Those were the words from our president and homeland security officer. Regarding the American citizens who have advised Iceland and Switzerland, one of them is about to speak, from Bern. Let's switch to listen to Professor Montgomery Benson."

Mark and his friends cheered, and as they looked around, they saw that Laekjartorg was now crowded with tens of thousands of people flowing in from the surrounding streets. Many were waving Icelandic flags or flags in the color of gold.

The image on the giant television screen switched back to Bern just as Montgomery Benson started to speak. "My first words will be to those of my friends who along with me are the target of the cowardly and evil words we just heard from the U.S. leadership. Mark, Pete, Laura, Bobby, it's no good to get upset by all this, even though I understand that you might. These reactions were expected. Don't worry; the Free Men, Real Money network is alive and well with or without a U.S. physical office.

"Regarding the talk about prosecuting us for treason; I dare them to try. A prosecutor will discover that we are not defying American law and the country's constitution—we are actually some of its last defenders. But as I have said before, it's true that this war of money *is* a kind of war of worlds. It is a philosophical war against the defenders of Big Government. Ours is the side of individual freedom, and they will certainly soon find out that we are much more dangerous to their kind of world than they ever imagined.

"We have won the first battle in this war. They tried to destroy gold money by pushing the price of gold down by selling their gold reserves. They won't be able to try that stunt again, since they have sold all the gold they owned. By our standards, where only valuable commodities can be money, the American and European governments are now *penniless*!

"So, to hell with their threats; they will have to get used to the existence of the gold-money system of Iceland and Switzerland. It is the frontier of a new world based on the values of peace and production. May it spread fast to replace that old world which is about to crumble under the weight of giant government-backed schemes of debt that can't be paid back, which I call the Pyramids of Destruction!" Benson sat down and remained silent.

The sound of his voice was replaced by a tremendous noise on the Laekjartorg square in Reykjavik, where a giant crowd now was jumping, screaming, and waving flags in the air. Ivar Larsen lifted Mark above his head and carried him through the crowd to the scene on the other side, where Kevin Larrison had stepped down and left room for the president of Iceland, who was climbing up, provoking an even louder cheer from the crowd. The image on the giant television screen switched to Ice TV, where Lisa Ivarsen was speaking with tears in her eyes.

"The press conference in Bern is now over, but Montgomery Benson and Klaus Hopfman have accepted to stay with us for an exclusive duplex. I guess there aren't so many more words to be said, but we're happy to just have them with us during this moment of intense national pride and relief here in Iceland."

The crowd again cheered, as Benson's face came back on the screen. He apparently had tuned in to Ice TV and could see the crowd on Laekjartorg. He was moved, too, and waved happily. As Larsen put Mark down in front of the president of Iceland, Laura, Pete and Cornelius Hazelton also came up on the scene.

"Here's to the health of our monetary system, and here's to our heroes!" the president shouted into a microphone as he opened a champagne bottle, and some in the crowd did the same.

Laura had tears running down her face from happiness and relief. She fired away a brief text message to Jessica.

"Thank you! Now you can go to sleep! We'll party for you!"

The others were just laughing wildly, and raised the glasses handed to them to toast to their triumph.

✲ ✲ ✲

For the second time in his life, Bobby Cheston sat waiting in the anteroom to the office of Walter Samuelson. This time, he had not himself made the appointment with the CEO of the world's largest retail firm. His boss had requested him to fly from China to Houston, without further explanations.

This time, too, Samuelson was late, and Bobby had time to become nervous as he waited. Even though he was hoping for a good outcome, he was unsure of what to expect. He just said to himself, as if to stop worrying, "If he had wanted to fire me, he wouldn't have made me fly over here."

"Cheston!" someone with a dark voice suddenly screamed from behind his back. Walter Samuelson startled Bobby and took him into a large, empty meeting room filled with blinding light from the strong sun.

"Hello, sir, what can I do for you?" Bobby said hesitantly as they sat down next to each other by the large table of the conference room.

"First of all, stop calling me sir. I'm Walter to you!" Samuelson said loudly, patting Bobby brusquely on his shoulder. "Second, I would like you to take full responsibility of our Asian markets. You are hereby named CEO of General Retail Asia."

Bobby smiled from surprise and needed a few seconds to find the right words. "Thank you for having such confidence in me," he finally said. "Even though I almost made the company lose billions of dollars over the last months."

"As you said, *almost*." Samuelson laughed. "What counts is the result. The result is that the ten billion dollars of cash we have put into gold over the last year and a half are now worth almost twice that! Not to mention the tens of billions we saved in reduced taxes thanks to the move of our headquarters. I recognize that the danger we were in was not so much your fault anyway. Hell, the most powerful governments of the world wanted to kill the gold-money system you and your friends helped to create—and they failed! So let me tell you how much I admire what you guys have done. The job and the salary I am offering you are just a drop in the ocean compared to your achievements. Congratulations, Bobby. I hope you'll keep surprising me in the future in the same pleasant way!"

☆ ☆ ☆

Jessica Frostby was typing frantically on her keyboard.

"I did what you told me, and it ended well! We saved the gold-money system. I don't think I ever felt this good in my entire life."

Latin Freeman answered with the same speed. "I knew it would!"

He stopped, thinking about the next words to type. "What are you going to do now? Will you quit your job?"

"No, I don't think so. I'll stick around. As they weren't able to kill the gold-money system, I now hope that the U.S. government will accept to apply more reasonable policies. If they continue their reckless deficit spending in spite of the existence of gold money, now also in Switzerland, the situation in the United States will just go out of control. Since they won't allow that to happen, I now hope they will stop running budget deficits!"

Latin Freeman sent a smiley that was shaking its head. "I'm happy you're optimistic. It shows that you feel happy, or at least benevolent. But I'm not sure you're right. But never mind. I'd like to ask you something else."

"What?"

"Don't you think we could meet for real? I would like to."

"Me too! More than anything else in the world! But I don't dare. I have sworn to myself that all my actions on the FMRM must remain confidential. And this isn't a good time for me to let the country's leadership discover my links to the organization that outsmarted them so badly recently."

"I understand. So we'll just have to wait some more. I'll wait as long as I have to, even if I hate it."

"So will I, Latin Freeman! Now I need to go to bed. Have a good day!"

"Sweet dreams, Heart of Gold!"

✲ ✲ ✲

Cornelius Hazelton was serving beer in pint glasses to the guests sitting in the sofas of his living room: Mark, Pete, Laura, and Professor Benson. Bobby Cheston had just entered the room, arriving directly from the airport, as he had arranged to make a stop in Iceland during his flight back from the United States to China.

"Congratulations, big boss," Benson said to Bobby with a friendly smile.

"Thanks for those words, Professor. And thank you for saving our necks last week. I prefer not to think about what situation we would have been in today unless you had arranged the deal with Switzerland."

"No need to think about it; it's a no-brainer!" Hazelton said. "Laura, Pete, and I would have been bust, and likely prosecuted by furious investors who would have lost all their money in the gold funds we set up to cushion the price fall."

"Thank you for thanking me," Benson said. "But all that is history now. I prefer to look forward into what the future might bring. The governments of the United States and of Europe have failed in their witch hunt against gold money. They will now have to live with the coexistence of sound money and their own government-backed paper currencies. Let's hope that pressure will make them hold back on their deficit spending a little. The large Wall Street banks that have been colluding with the Fed and the government for more than a century will have to watch out for the three of you. You can beat the hell out of them in the battle for the sixty trillion dollars of bank deposits in the world!" Benson shouted, raising his beer mug to Hazelton, Laura, and Pete.

"Yes, that's our goal!" Pete said with enthusiasm and chuckled. "It was really cool yesterday to see the Zach Morgano bank close down its Reykjavik branch." A wild laughter exploded from him. "I even heard the branch manager had asked for permission from headquarters to go into gold banking, as no one here wanted their dollars any more. He was fired as soon as his request reached the ears of the CEO of Zach Morgano, who is rumored to be a close friend of the Fed chairman!"

"I sure hope you keep beating those gangsters," Mark said. "They have been parading for decades as the foremost representatives of private enterprise and of the market economy. It has dragged shame on both these key features of human society. But even if their ability to wreak economic havoc by fractional reserve lending will be constrained by the emergence of one hundred percent reserve gold banking, I'm still worried for the future."

"Why?" Hazelton asked.

"For two reasons," Mark answered. "The first is that the people in power in the United States and in Europe still believe that big-government, deficit spending, and monetary inflation is what will get the world out of economic trouble. We all know how dangerously wrong that is."

"What's the second?" Hazelton urged.

Mark grimaced. "The fact that our democratic system and its pork-barrel logic will keep pushing the politicians into continuing their mad race of deficit spending and inflation. I fear large countries may vote their way into slavery, which will become necessary to pay the huge taxes needed to pay back deficits."

"You're too pessimistic," Hazelton said. "Look at what happened last week. People went back to gold money and helped our system survive."

Mark's eyes were dark as he answered. "Yes, they did, after *we* had made sure they wouldn't lose a penny in doing so. But before that, a vast majority of the citizens and investors of the world were ready to sell out their freedom and future, just to make sure they wouldn't lose a few thousand dollars from fluctuations in the gold price. Most of them certainly didn't even bother to think for a minute or read the one page message we sent out explaining that the target gold price should be two thousand dollars an ounce. That's the price now, *today*, only one week later!

"But because the Fed and the government said, without any rational argument, that it should be below five hundred dollars, most people believed that without thinking. A world of unthinking people can only run toward disaster. So if we want our success to be lasting, the challenge for FMRM to spread knowledge and understanding about money and freedom is as important and daunting as ever!" With a worried frown, Mark put his beer mug down on the table.

✡ ✡ ✡

At the same time, key people of the American political leadership had come together for a top secret meeting that was held off site, outside Washington. The room was dark, and the people settling uneasily around the table could barely see the face of the President as he started speaking. "Welcome gentlemen. I am glad you could all come to this important meeting despite the short notice. As you know, we have a situation which we need to address. The FMRM movement needs to be brought under control. They think their gold money can curtail government power, and compel us to reduce public spending. We recently failed in an attempt to kill gold money. So now I want you to take care of the people who invented it instead! We will reconvene here in one hour. Then I want each of you to come up with a game plan."